PRAISE FOR JUDITH MOFFETT

AND THE FIRST ~~~
THE HOLY Gi

THE RAGGED

"Everyone who plays a role in th. ......cated narrative is a stubbornly self-possessed individual . . . You will be engaged and moved."
—*The New York Times Book Review*

"*The Ragged World: A Novel of the Hefn on Earth* is based on her well-received tales of the gnome-like Hefn. . . Moffett has done a marvelous job integrating them into a book the publisher refers to most accurately as a stunning mosaic. Each story is a tile, part of a larger pattern which, viewed as a whole, reveals the intelligence and the skill of the maker." —*Locus*

"Moffett has yet to write anything I don't like, and this book works well either as a novel or a series of related stories."
—*Science Fiction Chronicle*

"A small, moving, personal novel spliced together from previously published and new material (including the widely admired "Tiny Tango"), about the effect on a few intertwined lives when aliens assume control of our planet. —*Kirkus Review*

"Moffett handles her story and its characters with marvelous warmth and empathy. You, like me, will find her imagination a wondrous place to visit." —*Analog*

TIME, LIKE AN EVER-ROLLING STREAM (Vol. II)

"Moffett's combination of harsh realism with visionary zeal addresses contemporary issues and personal struggles with compassion and insight." —*Library Journal*

". . . an exceptional sequel to *The Ragged World*. . . Fine insights on alien/human understanding permeate a compelling, dramatic and realistic story."—*Bookwatch (San Francisco)*

"Thanks to some adroitly handled introductory matter, the new book stands on is own as a narrative. More to the point, it breaks new ground in the successful integration of science fiction and the mainstream novel."
—*The New York Times Book Review*

"Pam Pruitt is a real person. Her problems are real ones. Moffett's picture of the Ohio Valley is so lovingly realized that it leaps off the page, dense, pungent, textured. The Hefn are real, and strange."
—*Fantasy & Science Fiction*

"Keenly and lovingly observed reality, in place, event, and character, to a degree rarely found in fantasy or SF . . . This is good work."
—Suzy McKee Charnas

For Shayne Bell and the Xenobians

Bascom Hill Publishing Group
212 3rd Avenue North, Suite 570
Minneapolis, MN 55401
612.455.2293
www.bascomhillpublishing.com

ISBN - 978-0-9802455-4-7
ISBN - 0-9802455-4-0
LCCN - 2008930975

Book sales for North America and international:
Itasca Books, 3501 Highway 100 South, Suite 220
Minneapolis, MN 55416
Phone: 952.345.4488 (toll free 1.800.901.3480)
Fax: 952.920.0541; email to orders@itascabooks.com

Cover Illustration by Shawn McCann
Typeset by James Arneson

Printed in the United States of America

The Bird Shaman

HOLY GROUND TRILOGY VOLUME III

The Bird Shaman

HOLY GROUND TRILOGY VOLUME III

By

Judith Moffett

Acknowledgments

Thanks for help with this book must go first to the group named in the dedication. Xenobia began many years ago at Brigham Young University, when students of a charismatic professor named Marion Smith decided to start a writing group focusing on science fiction and fantasy. Orson Scott Card, Dave Wolverton, and William Shunn had all been members; Shayne Bell was still attending regularly, and it was he who brought me in, in 1995. At that time the group was composed of some of those same former BYU students—practicing Mormons many of them, though not all—but by this point it also included outsiders like myself: writers in the field, living in Salt Lake City, with no connection to the Church of Jesus Christ of Latter-day Saints. The first three chapters of this novel were critiqued by Xenobia. I wish they could all have been. Ginny Smith, a Xenobian who moved back to Kentucky shortly after I did, vetted several later chapters, and Shayne himself did yeoman duty as a critic while I revised and re-revised the chapters that became my story "The Bradshaw." (He also loaned me his Ape-English Dictionary, my own having disappeared decades before.)

Xenobia did more than critique early drafts of part of this novel. The group was my window into Mormon culture, and without some such window I would not have dared take on the task of describing the LDS Church with the intimacy I do here. My views—based on more than three years of living in Salt Lake, and a lot of discussing, reading, and thinking—are my own; but it was membership in Xenobia that allowed me see the culture from the inside.

The tutelary spirits behind all my novels are the late Anna and Harlan Hubbard and their homestead in Payne Hollow, Kentucky. Anna and Harlan are the real people "represented" by Hannah and Orrin Hubbell in this book and its predecessor. They have, literally, my eternal thanks and praise.

A novel of this kind requires a lot of research, and I owe a huge debt to more books and monographs about rock art and shamanism than I can possibly cite here. Outstanding among these are Polly Schaafsma's work on the Barrier Canyon Style of Utah, and that of Solveig A. Turpin and the late Jim Zintgraff on the Pecos River culture of West Texas. I've quoted extensively from the Zintgraff/Turpin book *Pecos River Rock Art* on the subjects of dart-headed figures and bird shamans. Wallace Stegner's *The Gathering of Zion* and Susan Arrington Madsen's *I Walked to Zion* were invaluable sources for the story of the Mormon Trail. I learned about shamanism from texts as different as Mircea Eliade's essential *Shamanism* and Robert Moss's several books, fictional and non-, that vividly describe lucid (he prefers "conscious") and precognitive dreaming. Stephen Karcher, distinguished translator and interpreter of the *I Ching*, was my primary source for bird divination. The best aid to imagining the impact of rock art in the landscape is *Sacred Images: A Vision of Native American Rock Art,* text and photographs by a number of gifted artists, Foreword by N. Scott Momaday; but best of all is to go and see it for yourself.

For help with the fieldwork part of my research I'm grateful to a number of people. In 1995, Shayne Bell led a small group of friends on a tour of the Moab area, during which I first laid eyes on the rock art of several prehistoric cultures and was changed for life by the experience. Ten years later, Dorde Woodruff and Jim Olive drove many hours and miles to show me a number of hard-to-find Barrier Canyon Style (BCS) pictographs, including those described in this story. Among other kindnesses, Dorde compiled for me a loose-leaf binder crammed with information about the rock art we were heading out to see, including many printout pages of discussion and interpretation then available on Jim Blazik's illuminating website. (It was Jim who made the remark, loosely paraphrased on p. 333, that "some would say [a certain image] indicates shamanic transformations, others that rock art can't be objectively understood.")

John Remakel guided me to several sites near Moab (and saved me from falling off a cliff while climbing up to one of them). It was John whose directions finally helped me find the site I'm calling Dead Mule Canyon here, with its ethereal pictograph panel. David Sucec shared his expertise on BCS art and the culture that produced it. Before his death in 1998, my husband, Ted Irving, cheerfully agreed to spend vacation time looking at rock art. His company made what was fascinating, fun.

For existing to study and preserve prehistoric rock art, and for providing much helpful information, I'm grateful to the Utah Rock Art Research Association (URARA) (www.utahrockart.org) and the Rock Art Foundation (RAF) of Texas (www.rockart.org). Many of the helpful friends and writers mentioned here are members of one or the other, and I have belonged to both for years. Interested readers can learn more about the art referred to in this book by checking out the websites of these organizations, and by Googling "barrier canyon style" and "pecos river style."

My agent, Amy Stout, formerly an acquisitions editor at Bantam, applied her editorial skills to the manuscript and made me do an extensive rewrite before she started sending it around. This is a better book because of her.

The pictograph on the cover, showing two Pecos River Style bird shamans and their escorts, is after Forrest Kirkland's watercolor of the original in Kirkland and Newcomb, *The Rock Art of Texas Indians*.

The four BCS pictographs and one Pecos River pictograph reproduced in these pages appear courtesy of Jim Blazik, who took the photographs, produced the files, and was extraordinarily generous both with them and with his time.

The drawing by Harlan Hubbard from *Payne Hollow*, on p. 91, is reprinted by permission of Gnomon Press. Passages in quotations that purport to be the writings of Orrin Hubbell are drawn from the same source.

My sources on child sexual abuse within and without the Mormon Church are manifold. Of particular interest is a special report entitled "Latter-day Sinners," published in the December 22-28, 1994 issue of the *Phoenix New Times*, which gives a cogent overview of the roots of the problem in the LDS community.

Versions of parts of this novel previously appeared in *The Magazine of Fantasy and Science Fiction* as novellas entitled "The

THE BIRD SHAMAN

Bradshaw" (1998), "The Bear's Baby" (2003) and "The Bird Shaman's Girl" (2007).

Special thanks to Michael Ward, for technical assistance and help with the cover illustration, and to Vicki Mahaffey, for making time to proofread the manuscript on her Roman holiday.

PART ONE

Revelations
2037

Into my heart an air that kills
   From yon far country blows:
What are those blue remembered hills,
   What spires, what farms are those?

That is the land of lost content,
   I see it shining plain,
The happy highways where I went
   And cannot come again.

—A. E. Housman, *A Shropshire Lad,* "XL"

CHAPTER 1

The Truce of the Bear

15 FEBRUARY 2037

At the Friends Meeting in College Park, Maryland—the town where Carrie Sharpless had lived the second, or post-meltdown, half of her very long life—a memorial service was in progress. According to Quaker custom, no one was actually running the service. People would stand in place and say something about Carrie. Then they would sit down, and there would be silence for a time while the assembly reflected upon what had been said, and then someone else would get up to speak.

It was all very informal and unrehearsed—very genuine. The only sour note, but it was a good loud one, came from the dozens of spectators crammed into the back benches and along the walls—local people, not friends of Carrie's or members of the Meeting, who had crashed the service in hopes of getting a look at the Hefn, Humphrey, who'd been Carrie's good friend. No public announcement had been made that Humphrey would attend, but the connection was known, and the possibility of hearing a Hefn deliver a eulogy for a human being had brought the gawkers out in force.

Whenever a Hefn appeared in public there were bound to be gawkers. Pam knew that and was used to it, but these annoyed her. Like the media, which had been prevented from entering, they were out of place at a private funeral. Scrunched into the second row between Humphrey and her ex-lover, Liam O'Hara, she tried to focus on what white-haired Frank Flintoft, a widower now, come alone all the way from his sheep farm in Yorkshire for this, had to say about his old, old friend.

Yorkshire farmers are men of few words. Pam could feel Liam tense up beside her as the gruff, brief speech came to its end; and almost as soon as Frank had sat down, Liam—a short, athletically built man in his late thirties, face soft and boyish under thinning brown hair—was on his feet .

On Pam's other side, Humphrey shifted his weight to peer intently up at his brightest pupil. The bench and the Hefn's oddly jointed body hadn't been meant for each other, and the cushion Pam had remembered to bring for him didn't seem to be helping much; he must be fairly miserable. But given Humphrey's fascination with human bonding, and his closeness to the people most affected by Carrie's death, Pam knew that wild horses couldn't have kept him away from this service, let alone mere acute physical discomfort. In fact, when the news of Carrie's stroke and prognosis had reached him, he'd decided at once to postpone hibernation in order not to miss out on her final rite of passage. This was passion, not ghoulishness; Humphrey had his own things to say about Carrie, and he wanted, with an avidity that was almost comical, to say those things—to truly include himself in the occasion.

Liam's hands gripped the back of the bench in front of him. "I knew Carrie all my life," he began. "She was my dad's cousin. Carrie and Matt didn't have kids of their own, and we all lived pretty close to each other in Philadelphia, so Carrie used to take my friend Jeff and me hiking in the park when we were little, with a bag of doughnuts and a thermos of hot tea . . . "

He spoke steadily enough, but Pam, who could read every slightest nuance in Liam's voice and face and general demeanor, knew how upset he was—how drawn and exhausted. His shapely hands, tight on the bench, were bone-white; and the parallel scars, which ran across the backs of his white hands and vanished up his jacket sleeves, stood up in ropy welts.

Abruptly, without willing or wishing it, Pam found herself remembering the time, just after their apprenticeship at the Bureau of Temporal Physics had ended, when the two of them had encountered the bear.

~

THE BIRD SHAMAN

June in the Poconos. Shiny new leaves everywhere, from oak canopy to blueberry undergrowth; mountain laurel in delicate, fading white bloom; blue sky, bright sunshine spangling the river, green violently overwhelming the winter brown all across the long low mountains. Pam and Liam, a matched set of newly-minted temporal technicians, going-on-eighteen and going-on-nineteen, on holiday together as Terry Carpenter's guests at his cabin on Lake Winnepaupack.

Day after day the warm, sunny weather holds. At Port Jervis they launch the canoe that had belonged to Jeff Carpenter, Liam's friend, and paddle it down the Delaware to the Water Gap—45 miles of mostly whitewater rapids—camping two nights on islands in the river. The shad have spawned and are dying; their floating multitudes of smellily unraveling corpses are all that qualify the delight of being on the river. The journey is highlighted by happier sightings: five bald eagles, dozens of great blue herons, mergansers and goldeneyes and geese, does and spring fawns coming down to drink, a porcupine or two, a trillion songbirds. Even before the alien Broadcast accelerated the process a decade ago, by putting human fertility on hold, wildlife of every sort had been increasing all through the protected upper Delaware valley. Pam identifies the birds by song, and calls out their names happily to tolerant Liam: summer tanager! song sparrow! Baltimore oriole! yellow warbler! towhee! chat! cardinal! She knows these eastern songbirds like the back of her hand, and will miss them out in California.

They reminisce a lot about their other canoe trip three years before, in the spring of '14—The Canoe Trip That Changed History, says Liam, with a bow of acknowledgment to Pam. In the spirit of that earlier trip they harmonize on many, many stanzas of "Peace! Be Still!" (and compose several wicked new ones of their own). As before, their paddling together is another sort of expert harmony; and their relationship, which can be fractious, glides along day after day in perfect harmony as well. A magical journey, one to treasure for a lifetime.

On the last day Liam borrows the car—a perk of Terry's position as Chair of the Senate Committee on Alien Affairs—and they cross the river at the Delaware Water Gap and drive up the derelict Old Mine Road to a trailhead Liam knows about. The Appalachian Trail runs along the ridgetop above them, parallel to the river; this shorter trail ascends more or less straight up from the road to the ridge to connect with the AT. The climb up is stiff, and they get sweaty and winded (and a little bit fractious, nothing serious), but the high long view of tiny, shiny Walpack Bend, the S-curve in the Delaware through whose boiling rapids they'd gone whooping and paddling like blazes just a couple of days before, takes Pam's breath away, what's left of it. Terry's chicken sandwiches are fabulous.

For variety they descend by a different route, the Kaiser Trail, a rough jeep track that will deliver them onto the Old Mine Road about a mile below the car. Unlike the gorges and stony cliffs through which their upward track led them, the mountainside here is park-like, a mixture of large trees and spindly saplings doomed to be shaded out before they can mature. This trail is wide enough for two to walk side by side, and Pam and Liam tromp along in their boots, making no attempt to be quiet, tired now and less inclined to sing than to argue. They are in fact quarreling fairly loudly about some damn thing or other—afterwards neither of them remembers what—when Pam happens to glance to her right, through the open area below the high canopy, and sees the large, dark, motionless object shaped like a barrel on end, some fifty meters away.

Her mind tries several times to reject the obvious in favor of something less problematic, but finally "Omigosh," she blurts, interrupting Liam's tirade, "it's a bear."

"Yeah, right," says Liam irritably; he hates being interrupted. But then he looks where she's pointing. "Yikes, it *is* a bear! Jesus Christ Almighty! How come it's just standing there? When I see bears up here they always take off." He slows almost to a stop and grins nervously at Pam. "Okay, you're the Girl Scout, what do we do?"

Pam, casting about frantically to call up anything she's ever read or heard about bears, says, "Just keep on going, don't make any sudden moves. Black bears are supposed to be more scared of us than we are of them, unless it's a sow with cubs."

They resume walking. "I didn't see any cubs, did you?" Liam glances over his shoulder. "It's all right, he's leaving," he reports with relief.

Pam looks too. What she sees she will remember for the rest of her life: the instant when the bear appears to change its mind, swings back around and charges toward them, swift and straight as a bullet. "No he's not," she says, scarcely able to take this in, "he's coming!"

You're not supposed to run, and Pam's brain is still debating whether to stand tight, call the bear's bluff, but her feet have taken off. She and

Liam tear up the shallow slope to the left of the trail, leap over a little creek in a gully, dart between the skinny trees. Away from the trail the footing is bad, the ground littered with branches invisible under thickly matted clumps of last year's leaves. Pam glances back just in time to see the bear bound across the gully, closing fast.

"I don't believe this! What the hell are we supposed to *do*?" Liam asks again, half laughing. No more than Pam does he seem able to accept the moment as a real one, continuous with the reality of graduating from the BTP and shooting the Walpack rapids.

"Climb a tree?" Pam pants, remembering as she suggests this that tree climbing is grizzly-attack strategy; black bears are skillful climbers. All the same she starts looking around for a climbable tree, because what else can they do? It's that or be caught on the ground.

But no luck: every tree in sight is either a smooth-boled giant, its lowest branches twenty feet out of reach, or a sapling too slender and weak to be of any use. "Maybe we should split up," she gasps, and strikes off down the slope, running as if in a nightmare, just as Liam swings one leg over a middle-sized log fallen at an angle against a living tree. The log's trunk is mossy and slippery but . . . frantically Pam scans the slope as she sprints, looking for a thicket of young trees growing in a tangle that she can maybe keep between herself and the bear.

The whole time she's aware, in a detached way, of her mind—superbly trained problem-solving mechanism that it is—continuing to search swiftly, methodically, for an answer to the present problem. But school problems set by Humphrey, however difficult, always had solutions. What if this particular pop quiz doesn't have one? She thinks again and again that the bear's bound to break off the chase, but what if it doesn't?

And then Liam shrieks, and Pam, skidding and twisting in mid-stride, sees the bear bowl him under the angled log with a swipe of its right paw, and plunge after him. Liam huddles on his stomach, arms wrapped around his head and neck. The bear swipes again, powerfully, too fast to follow; Pam sees a bursting bloom of red and then she's *there*, whacking at the bear's snout with her backpack, which she doesn't remember taking off, yelling, whaling the tar out of the bear to beat him off of Liam's huddled, bleeding form. For a timeless interval everything's a loud whirling blur with Pam at the center. And then, miraculously, the bear is lumbering away.

Pam, unhurt, drops her pack and helps Liam sit up. The backs of his hands and arms are scored with deep claw-marks and bleeding profusely; there's blood all over his shirt. But none of his wounds are spurting, the bear didn't hit an artery, and his own daypack, ripped to pieces now, has protected his back. Pam pulls the shreds of the pack off him. He's dazed. If he goes into shock they're in big trouble, and he doesn't have the luxury of being wrapped up in the emergency blanket with his feet elevated. They have to get off the mountain.

But he probably won't go into shock if the bleeding can be stopped. There's nothing absorbent bigger than a gauze pad in Pam's first-aid kit, but there is an Ace bandage. This she unrolls, cuts in two with the little scissors on her Swiss Army knife, and wraps one piece, not too tight, around each of Liam's forearms, to apply pressure. She does this coolly and efficiently; then she hauls him to his feet. They have to get going. The bear might come back.

Their panicked flight has carried them into deeper woods. No sign of the Kaiser Trail. Stumbling over the uneven slope in their haste, angling downhill, they cast about for it, or rather Pam does—Liam's gone from being dazed to being hyper. They aren't really lost—if they keep heading down they'll eventually hit the river and the road—but if they have to bushwhack it'll mean a tough, slow, scratchy descent through the bear-fraught wilderness.

When they do finally strike the trail—much farther away than expected; the amount of ground they've covered astonishes them both—they light out, Pam more or less steering Liam, toward the road, the river, the car, and safety. High as two kites on adrenaline, they jabber and babble and talk on top of each other all through the downhill scramble. "They aren't supposed to charge you! They're supposed to back off if you don't threaten them—" "Except if they've got cubs! Maybe she had some cubs up a tree, and the trail went between her and the tree—" "No, I think it was the chocolate and trash in your pack, I think that's why she went for you instead of me, I didn't have anything but the first-aid kit—"

Down and down the wooded mountainside they rush, casting anxious looks behind them, peering between the tree trunks; but finally they sight the trailhead barrier, and the road beyond, without another glimpse of the bear.

In her frantic haste to get away, Pam's pack has been left behind. At the road they stop while she cuts Liam's tee shirt off him, tears it into strips, unwinds the blood-soaked elastic bandages, and wraps the strips of shirt around his arms and hands. The tube of antiseptic is still on the mountain. So is the bottle of Numbutol, and this process is making Liam's wounds hurt in earnest. "All the miles and *miles* I've carried that first-aid kit, and the only time I ever really *needed* it, I haven't got it!" Pam gripes, mostly to distract her patient, who is gasping and grimacing. She wants him to sit down and wait while she goes for the car, but he refuses so absolutely that she doesn't waste energy arguing. He's not bleeding too badly now anyway; the emergency measures seem to be doing the trick.

The adrenaline starts to wear off while they toil up the Old Mine Road together. Pam feels sick; Liam's in pain and his teeth are chattering. The road hasn't been repaired in twenty years, Pam has to watch where she's walking for both of them. "All the t-t-times I've been up here hiking and c-c-camping in these m-m-mountains," Liam complains, "all the bears I've b-b-bumped into, and n-not one of 'em was ever the least bit ag-g-gressive, not w-w-one!"

"Maybe your number just came up."

"Yeah, m-maybe s-s-so." Now that the acute peril is past, Liam's shuddering all over in reaction to the trauma.

A poem has been running through Pam's head all the way down the trail, and now for lack of a better distraction she starts to recite it, panting, in time with their double-quick pace:

"Up from his stony playground—down from his well-
    digged lair—
Out on the naked ridges ran Adam-zad the Bear;
Groaning, grunting, and roaring, heavy with stolen meals,
Two long marches to northward, and I was at his heels!"

Liam's face smoothes out; he loves Kipling, they both do. "'*I* was at *his* heels!' A guy with a d-d-death wish! Is that the one about R-Russia?"

She nods, puffing. "The Truce of the Bear."

"'Eyeless, noseless, and l-l-lipless, something, something of b-b-blank . . .'"

Pam picks up the thread where she dropped it:

"Two long marches to northward, at the fall of the second night,
I came on mine enemy Adam-zad all panting from his flight.

21

There was a charge in the musket—pricked and primed was the
  pan—
My finger crooked on the trigger—when he reared up like a
  man.'

Then, realizing where the poem's leading, Pam breaks off. "Oops,
sorry, bad idea, I'm creeping *myself* out!"

"D-d-don't s-s-stop! Keep g-g-going!"

"No, it's gruesome! It's the worst thing I can think of to be quoting
right now, I shouldn't've started."

"Come on, I w-w-want to hear it!"

Pam argues some more, but finally she does continue, the rhythm
is irresistible:

"Horrible, hairy, human, with paws like hands in prayer,
Making his supplication rose Adam-zad the Bear!
I looked at the swaying shoulders, at the paunch's sag and swing,
And my heart was touched with pity for the monstrous, pleading
  thing.
Touched with pity and wonder, I did not fire then . . .
I have looked no more on women—I have walked no more with
  men.
Nearer he tottered and nearer, with paws like hands that pray—
From brow to jaw that steel-shod paw, it ripped my face away!"

Pam stops. "Listen—" she starts to demur; but Liam shakes his
head. He's not shivering quite so badly. "Keep going, I'm fine. Go
on. Finish it."

So she goes on:

"Sudden, silent, and savage, searing as flame the blow—
Faceless I fell before his feet, fifty summers ago.
I heard him grunt and chuckle—I heard him pass to his den.
He left me blind to the darkened years and the little mercy of
  men."

Then she breaks off again in relief. "I see the car!"

~

Tightly packed as they were in the row, Liam jostled Pam out of her reverie by sitting down. She'd heard nothing of his speech beyond the first sentences. Startled at the sheer vividness of what she'd been remembering, Pam made an effort to fix herself in the present—did a breathing exercise, rubbed her face, discreetly tightened several muscle groups in sequence. Being able to get such deep trances was an excellent meditation tool, but you wanted to pick your time and place. It was spooky when it happened by itself—not to mention (in the present instance) painful.

The silence lasted a good while. Pam had time to get herself in hand, and then to wonder, as she had on the plane, whether she wanted to say anything herself about Carrie. Now would be the time, but her mind was a blank. Carrie had been kind to Pam when Pam was a fourteen-year-old first-year Apprentice at the BTP, when the Bureau was based in Washington and Liam would sometimes bring Pam out to College Park for dinner with his extended family. They had liked each other. She could say, "When Liam and I were just starting to be friends, poetry was almost the first way we connected, and Carrie taught Liam everything he knows about poetry"—but this, though true, put the emphasis in the wrong place. This service wasn't about Liam or herself.

Would Carrie have spoken at a memorial service for Pam? Pam didn't think so. What could *she* have said? "I hoped for both their sakes that the kids could make a go of it, but I knew Liam awfully well, and there was something about the fit that didn't feel quite right." (Not even Carrie would've said *that* in a public setting!)

By the time Terry Carpenter rose to take his turn, Pam had decided to hold her peace.

Terry made a lot of speeches; you wouldn't need to recognize him as a famous face to figure that much out. "On the day when the time window opened," he began, in a damped-down version of what Carrie used to call his "stentorian" voice, "I was a student at the University of Pennsylvania—a junior. I'd been working on a take-home exam, an exam for Professor Sharpless's class in American poetry. The year was 1990. Now, when the window opened, and I saw Liam O'Hara and the Hefn Humphrey standing on the other side of it"—he gestured across the room—"Liam over there hadn't even been born yet in real time—but in the time window, he was a good deal older than I was."

At the reference to himself, Liam smiled faintly and nodded in acknowledgment. Humphrey did whatever it was the Hefn did to convey the impression of a smile. Having lived so much among humans, he did it better than most of them; today, delighted at being included, he did it especially well.

Terry bent toward the Hefn in a half-bow. "Now, of course, those two could only look through and talk through, they couldn't step through and neither could I. Naturally Humphrey wiped every trace of our meeting from my mind, and he made a good job of it. Had Carrie given the class a different exam, my memory of the event wouldn't have been triggered by her questions; had she not been concerned for my state of mind, and come back to the park with me, there would have been no witness to vouch for any part of my experience on that fateful day . . . "

It was what Pam had expected Terry to talk about, the story his political career had been founded on, the one that had linked his life to Carrie's for keeps. There could hardly have been a soul present not familiar with it; but Senator Carpenter was chief mourner here and they all gave him their attention, even the crowd in back.

As he talked on, embellishing the tale, Pam smiled to herself to think how Carrie, an English professor all her working life, and a canny, tough old bird of 85 the last time Pam had been to see her, had despised cheap rhetorical flourishes like "that fateful day." She'd have been cross as two sticks with Terry for making her the occasion of a phrase like that. She'd be spinning in her grave.

Not that Carrie actually had a grave, or ever would. At the moment, in fact, she was attending her own memorial service, on the bench next to Terry, in a cardboard box from the crematorium. The arrangement would have made her grin like a wolf and fire off some piece of tomsawyeresque self-parody—"She warn't *bad*," Pam could imagine Carrie's rough old voice saying, "only misch*ee*vous like"—while snorting and tossing her head like an elderly horse at her old student's politico-babble.

It was true, as he'd so often said, that in the park that day—all of 47 years ago; Pam, the ex math prodigy, did the calculation in a flash—Terry had been a twenty-year-old undergraduate with lots of dark, curly hair, and Liam had been years older than that. Observing the trim, bald Senator from Pennsylvania as he picked up steam, Pam thought that despite the erect posture and confident manner he looked older today than anyone, impossibly old, a ruin of grief. "For many terrible years," he was saying now, "Carrie was the only person—the *only* person!—who believed I had seen what I'd seen and heard what I'd heard. Her faith in me, in my experience, helped me hang on to my sanity. It supported my decision to enter the law, and politics—to prepare to respond when the calamity, the nuclear disaster foretold by Liam out of the future, finally occurred." His voice suddenly shook, and he touched his eyes with a folded handkerchief.

Pam wriggled in her seat, uneasy with Terry's emotion, uneasy also because of having heard so often, from Carrie herself, how wobbly her faith had been, throughout those "many terrible years," in her student's wacko experience. And how guilty she'd felt, knowing he depended on her belief, yet plagued by an unbelief she couldn't banish. Beside her, Humphrey also wriggled and adjusted his small, powerful body, trying to get more comfortable.

Terry went on and on, as if not quite knowing how to stop, his voice alternating between senatorial habit and a kind of stricken bewilderment. Pam had arrived in Washington bound and determined not to get suckered into feeling anything, but by the time Terry finally sat down her throat was aching. Knowledge undid her. Terry had lost his only child in the Peach Bottom meltdown "foretold" by Liam in 1990 from thirty years in Terry's future, had watched his first marriage fall apart and then, not long after, buried his much-loved second wife. In the end, only Carrie had remained to bear witness to everything in his life that had mattered most.

Carrie, and of course Liam, who had been his dead son Jeff's best friend. It was Carrie, not Liam, who'd first told her about Jeff.

Acutely aware of Liam's left ear, about a foot from her nose, she tried not to sniff too audibly. When Liam's sister Brett, sitting in front of them between her husband and old Frank Flintoft, stood up next, she managed a couple of more effective sniffs under cover of Brett's first words; but at once, despite her care, Eddie Ward glanced over knowingly from his place on Liam's right.

He smiled, with a sympathy that was probably real, if momentary. Pam looked away. She stared at Humphrey's hands as he propped them on either side of his cushion to hitch himself back.

While Brett was making the assembly chuckle, telling how Carrie was famous in the family for liking her party food served in four courses—first dessert, crackers-cheese-and-veggies, little sandwiches, second dessert—Liam shot his sleeve and glanced at his watch, clenched over the long diagonal white scars on his left wrist.

~

June in the Poconos, new leaves glittering down the slope of the long, low mountain, blue river glittering to the left of the ruined road they struggle along, Pam's own voice forcing the words of a suddenly terrifying poem through a fog of anxiety—and then the wave of pure relief: "I see the car! We're almost there!"

Liam smiles too, safety and painkillers now in immediate prospect. "So we are. Well, you have to put these things in perspective. I got off p-pretty light."

Pam doesn't say what she's thinking, which is how easily it might have been a very different story. That's when she realizes, for the first time, that by beating at the bear, presumably driving it away, she probably saved Liam's life. It makes her feel strange. She doesn't remember turning back, doesn't recall making a conscious decision to go back; the whole point of splitting up was so that one of them might have a chance to get away.

And that's when she understands—it shouldn't be a surprise, though it comes as one—that she will never ever be able to run away from Liam in deadly danger. Even if fleeing might make better sense, even if staying and fighting would only mean both of them getting killed. In the same flash of insight she perceives something else: that Liam *could* leave *her* in such a fix. He might not, but he could choose to—he has that choice. She doesn't.

Not that Liam is a coward, not at all. Three years earlier Pam has seen him risk his life for Humphrey, and knows that despite getting liberally peppered with buckshot he'd do the same thing again every morning before breakfast if necessary. Humphrey saved Liam's life once too, or at least talked him out of committing suicide, and that's how things are with Liam and Humphrey. And she also knows that Liam would have risked anything—*anything*—to try to save Jeff.

Liam would have died to save Jeff. But not, she entirely understands, to save Pam.

~

Snap out of it! she told herself, now truly alarmed. *Stop this!* It wasn't like dissociation—ghastly feelings and the world turning plastic—but even so, this interior time window was one she wished to look through strictly by choice and in private. What could be making her slip into trance involuntarily? What was going on?

Well, for one thing, being here with Liam, his left shoulder pressed against her right—*that* was going on. Pam thought suddenly of that story Terry had been telling for umpteen years, of how an exam question about a deer poem had triggered his memory of the deer he had seen in the park. Had something triggered her own detailed memory of the bear attack? Something about Liam? Maybe.

After Brett's message the silence drifted on. Pam closed her eyes and thought about Liam and herself.

Through all the wrenching shifts and alterations time had brought about since the bear-attack spring of 2017, that home truth—that she would always rush helplessly to Liam's rescue, that he might or might not rush to hers—held fast. Pam would be grateful to Liam forever for taking the initiative in the valuable and, for her, self-defining, relationship they'd had for a while. But all through the time in Hurt Hollow and Santa Barbara, when they'd been lovers whenever they could manage to get together, which wasn't all that often, the fundamental, unspoken, mutually recognized inequality persisted.

And it persisted even after Pam left the Hollow, to live with Liam in California and go back to work for the BTP. But not till Liam had met Eddie out there, and become so besotted with him (and so entangled in a web of clumsy deceptions in consequence) that Pam had faced him down, then gone to Humphrey and requested reassignment—not till then had it finally pushed them apart.

"Maybe we better split up," she whispered, too softly for Liam or Humphrey—or Eddie—to hear. Yes, very well. Correct and necessary to go away and leave Liam behind with Eddie in California, thence to wash up eventually on the shores of the Great Salt Lake. But even now—nearly two and a half years after leaving Santa Barbara and twenty years since the bear's heart-stopping charge across the Kaiser Trail—Pam knew she would still be powerless to abandon Liam in a state of mortal danger.

She didn't need to look in order to visualize Eddie in excruciating detail. Curly black hair, receding. Swarthy, mustache-punctuated handsomeness, losing focus as it beef-ified. Dark eyes, long black lashes. Dark loafers. Custom-tailored dark suit, doing what could be done to minimize the wearer's one-way journey from huskiness into forthright corpulence.

Without intending to she suddenly pictured Eddie in his expensive funeral outfit, thrashing and squealing beneath the avid teeth and claws of the bear—a fantasy so real and delectable that it revealed to Pam more than she really cared to admit about the depth of her dislike. She opened her eyes, frowning. But then, perhaps only a saint could feel sorrow at the conviction that, in a fix like the one she and Liam had coped with fairly well, Eddie would go all to pieces. Or the absolute certainty that Liam could clear right out of there *too* if he felt like it—wouldn't have to put his life on the line for Eddie's life, any more than for Pam's. *That's something anyway*, she thought, and smiled kindly at Liam when he glanced past her at Humphrey, for having that much sense at least.

The Hefn was slipping down off the bench; he was ready to speak now. As his hairy horny feet found the floor, as he reached up to clasp the back of the bench in front of him with his hairy, gray, four-pronged hands, a greedy murmur stirred the gaggle of curious strangers at the rear of the room.

Most of humanity had hated the Hefn from the day of their arrival, and many who hadn't, who had seen in them the Earth's one hope of avoiding ecological ruin, were beginning to question the point of a cleaned-up planet that lacked a signifcant human presence. The youngest human beings alive—the very last of the Last Generation—would soon turn 23, and the Hefn still had nothing to say about when their bosses, the Gafr, intended to lift the fertility ban. By now the whole world was wondering if the aliens were ever going to let people start making babies again—whether, in fact, they'd ever intended to let them.

But however they felt about the alien takeover of the world, the hope of seeing a Hefn in the flesh could still turn people out in droves. It was a celebrity thing. The Gafr continued to run the world from their ship parked on the moon. In twenty years of long-range occupation, no human being had ever laid eyes on a Gafr. Few could claim to have seen a live Hefn either, though one or another of the eighteen Hefn Observers addressed the world's people, via the media, almost every day. Wary of another mass-hypnosis episode, most taped the broadcasts and watched the tapes, but everybody watched. Often enough it would be Humphrey's own stumpy figure they saw on the screen, and that, added to his role as Founder and Director of the Bureau of Temporal Physics, would be enough to make him a kind of celebrity; but he'd also starred in a Hollywood movie a couple of years before, and that made him a real one. People *might* come out on a February afternoon for a glimpse of an important Senator, or of Liam, the math whiz who'd discovered the Hot Spot equations and made the cover of *Time*. A Hefn movie star, though, was a sure draw.

Humphrey threw back his shaggy head and uttered a piercing, desolate sound, something between a bellow and a howl.

People half-rose. Even Pam was startled, but Humphrey called out at once, very pleasantly, "Do not be alarmed. Among my people, this is the noise of grief." He let out another lowing bellow, and one more for good measure, then looked brightly from side to side until the rattled audience had recovered its composure.

"We have no tears, you see," he continued when they were still. "But when one of us dies his friends feel grief, as you do, and they must let the grief come out, as you must, or be ill. And so I make this loud and sorry sound for Carrie Sharpless, who was my friend.

"Working among you so long, I learned a great lesson. A bond of friendship between humans is not the same as a bond between Hefn and Hefn, or Hefn and Gafr. Our bonds exist from necessity, there is no choosing. And yet. From my time with Terry Carpenter, and Liam O'Hara, and Pam Pruitt, I have learned that a Hefn can bond with a human *in the human way*. For a Hefn, too, there can be choice. I chose Terry. I chose Liam and Pam. And they chose me." Whereupon Humphrey executed one of his pirouettes and clutched Pam against his hard, hairy body, with its patchy places where the hair had fallen out from the anti-hibernation drug Sleepynot. His beard, coarse as a broom, scraped the skin of her neck. She hugged him back, throat cramping. Liam sobbed once. Everyone peered and craned, trying to see what was going on.

Humphrey straightened up. "Ahhhhhhh but also! I learned the hard corollary. Where bonds are chosen, they can be unchosen. Among you, disconnection is common. It is very common." His flat eyes turned upon Liam's haggard face. "A friend damages an old bond in forging a new one. No help for this. Friends quarrel, their bond is destroyed. Neither may be to blame, yet there is much pain."

Pam felt a rush of grateful warmth; she knew, and knew Liam knew, that Humphrey was alluding to them, that he regretted their breakup and Pam's departure from Santa Barbara and had little use for Eddie. It was old news, but being even slightly on the outs with Humphrey made Liam miserable and Pam could feel his tension increase as their old teacher ground this familiar ax in front of everyone.

"Also," said Humphrey, "bonds are broken by death, which no one chooses." He glanced at Liam, who smiled briefly. "And so, now I will speak of Carrie Sharpless.

"I will say two things.

"One thing. Terry Carpenter became my friend. He brought me to the house on Calvert Street, where Carrie lived. And Carrie made a blackberry cobbler for me.

"Every day, in that time, I felt how the people of Earth hate the Hefn. I feel it every day in this time also. Now I am accustomed to this hatred. Then, I was not.

"The second thing. Carrie was bonded to Terry and to Liam. My own bonds to Terry and Liam formed and strengthened. But the bond between Carrie and myself appeared spontaneously, a product of these other bonds, like a chemical reaction. Catalyzed, yes, it may be, by a very fine cobbler! It so surprised me to discover that such a thing could happen. And now that knot has come undone. And I am very, very, very sorry."

The Hefn sat down—that is, he hoisted himself back onto the cushion and pushed himself straight. Pam put her arm around him. He patted her knee, satisfaction streaming from his whole body. Pam was touched, tickled also; Humphrey's determination to honor the obligations of friendship was so hilarious in a way. Carrie, who'd been extremely fond of Humphrey, had been known to laugh helplessly while repeating to intimates his earnest explanations of how attached to her he was. She would have loved his eulogy, though it would have made her grin her wolfish grin. "Carrie would have loved it," Pam whispered, and Humphrey beamed harder; it was like hugging a potbellied stove.

"Bonding!" A man's ragged, angry voice shouted from the back of the Meeting. "What the hell do you know about it? Bonding to some old lady that never had any kids of her own—how about *us* getting bonded to our own kids and grandkids? Hunh? When are the Gafr gonna let us have some kids again, that's what I'd like to know!"

Twisting around like everybody else, Pam could see an agitated form and a red face against the back wall. Being in church may have restrained most of the other gatecrasher types, but there were growls of agreement and a woman shouted, "Family is the only thing that matters! The *only* thing! You don't know beans about human bonding if you don't know that!"

Humphrey had scrambled up now and was standing on the bench, facing the back of the room. When he held up his arms, several people bolted for the door. Humans had been mindwiped back to early childhood for threatening a Hefn; the Ban itself had been effected by mass hypnosis, in the time before humanity had fully grasped what the aliens could do.

This alien waved his upraised arms in a wholly alien gesture. His hair stood out from his body, giving him the look partly of an alarmed cat, partly of a defensive porcupine. "This is the memorial service of Carrie Sharpless, and y*ou will be silent*," he said, not loudly, but in a weird, metallic, inhuman voice, a voice to freeze the blood. Pam had heard him use it only once before: to state his intention of murdering a man who had tried to murder him.

Nothing about the small gray figure, in fact, seemed human now, and everything seemed dangerous. The room sensed the difference and went very still. The Hefn pranced on the bench, gestured some more, made as if to speak again; but Brett O'Hara was suddenly kneeling, leaning over, clutching at him from behind. "Humphrey! Don't!"

When he whipped round at the unexpected interference, she grabbed his arm. "Don't. Carrie wouldn't want you to. And anyway, you know they're right."

Humphrey did the Hefn equivalent of staring, then breathing deeply several times, getting his outrage under control. His aura of gray hair partially deflated. When finally he disengaged himself and turned back to the electrified room, his voice had resumed its human semblance, but had not lost its steely authority. "You. You. You have attended this service, not to honor the dead, but to shout and remonstrate. You demand permission to reproduce your . . . *disreputable* kind. Brett O'Hara claims also that you are in the right." He glared round the Meeting. "To me," he said, "it seems otherwise. I have been a better friend to you than you know or deserve, I have pleaded your case with my lords the Gafr, but I say now that if this decision were mine to make, I myself could not encourage you to hope."

~

Anybody can say anything at a Quaker Meeting, including hecklers and Hefn; but the Clerk of the Meeting had obviously decided that they'd all had enough excitement for one funeral, and stood to make her announcements the instant Humphrey stopped lecturing and got down. They were now (she said) to hear an old recording of the Philadelphia Boys' Choir singing Mozart's "Alma Dei Creatoris." Carrie had requested this in her will. The recording had been made at the choir's final concert, just before all the boys, together with their conductor and bus driver, had been killed in the Peach Bottom Power Plant meltdown. The soloist was Senator Carpenter's son Jeff, then twelve years old. The music would conclude the service, which would be followed by a reception featuring the four party-food courses Carrie had loved. Everyone was welcome to stay, but all (she said, rather severely) were reminded of the nature of the occasion and requested to respect it.

Briefly, then, music immobilized the room. But as soon as the sound of singing had been replaced by the sounds of people rising and beginning to talk, Pam turned to Humphrey, who'd gone into the contracted posture of extreme Hefn agitation, arms and legs clamped so tight against his torso he looked like a large, dirty, rather lumpy tennis ball. "I don't think they came to heckle, Humphrey, I really don't. They came to get a look at you and got carried away by what you said."

"I will not talk of this now." As he spoke Humphrey uncoiled smoothly, placed his hands of the back of the bench before them and vaulted over, agile as a monkey. He jumped down hands first and trotted stiff-legged across to Terry on all fours—a mode the Hefn virtually never assumed in public.

Pam sank back and widened her eyes at Liam. "Godamighty."

"Godamighty indeed. What did he say?"

"That he wouldn't talk about it right now. I told him I didn't think those people came here planning to make a disturbance, I thought they just got carried away. That's what I *do* think. How could they know he was going to talk about bonding?"

"Well," said Liam, standing up slowly, "whether it was planned or not, they violated Humphrey's sense of fitness but good. I've never seen him this upset, have you?"

"Only once. After the tornado, when he was going to kill Otie Bemis."

"Till you talked him out of it." He darted a glance at the Hefn, on his feet again with Terry bent over him, speaking urgently. "Listen, we're skipping the reception. Terry and Humphrey and I are taking Carrie's ashes out to the Ragged Rock to scatter them. That's what she wanted. Maybe you better come too, Pam—calm him down, smooth his ruffled feathers." He started to shrug into his topcoat.

"*I'm* not going," Eddie put in quickly. *So don't say no on my account*, he meant.

Pam pictured the bear ripping Eddie's face off, smiled and shook her head. "No point. He doesn't want to talk about it yet—and anyway, I'd rather not crash the party."

Liam didn't try to persuade her; it really was something for just the three of them to do. The Ragged Rock, in a park deep inside the radioactive zone created by the power plant meltdown, had been holy ground for Jeff and Carrie and himself. It was holy ground for Terry, too, because that was where Terry had seen Liam and Humphrey through the time window, back in 1990. When Liam, age fourteen, had set off on his solarcycle to die of radiation poisoning like Jeff, the Ragged Rock had been his destination. Pam had never seen the place. Anyway, she had her own 61-acre parcel of holy ground.

The Meeting was emptying out, most of the strangers leaving, family and friends drifting toward the rec hall where tables had been set up, everybody murmuring in a subdued, uncertain way. It occurred to Pam that Carrie wouldn't have minded the disturbing turn the occasion had taken. Carrie had relished a good commotion. She and Eddie got up too, and they all sidled out of the row and started up the aisle. "Will we see you again before you go back?" Liam asked her. Again he glanced worriedly at Humphrey.

"I guess not. There's a Gaian delegation flying back to California tonight and I'm hitching a ride."

"They're stopping in Salt Lake?"

"Just to let me off. There won't be another flight for two weeks. Will you guys be taking the train back?"

"I probably am," said Liam, "It'll take a week or so for Terry and me to get Carrie's affairs sorted out. But maybe Eddie could catch that plane."

He stopped. Across the way, Humphrey and Terry now had their heads bowed over the box of ashes. "Not the perfect moment to ask a favor, but—" Liam cleared his throat. "Humphrey," he called quietly, "will it be okay if Eddie flies home with Pam and the Gaians tonight? It'll save him having to cancel three more days of sessions."

Humphrey was still for so long that Pam had time to wonder whether he intended to answer at all. But when he spoke, it was to her: "Is this acceptable to you, my dear?"

Oh Humphrey, Pam thought, weak with relief, *God, I love you, you mangy old furball!* His voice sounded almost normal; maybe he was all right. Aloud she said, "Sure, it's fine."

"Then Eddie may fly home with Pam Pruitt and the missionaries."

Except for the five of them, the room was empty now. Terry gave the box of ashes to Humphrey to hold while he draped his coat over his shoulders, then took it back and followed the others up the aisle, with Humphrey following him.

At the door Eddie gave Liam a long, showy hug and a kiss while Terry pecked Pam on the cheek and Humphrey put her mind further to rest by laying his hand on her shoulder and saying, "I will be in touch, Pam Pruitt." As the three ash-scatterers went out into the winter mildness, and the door swung shut behind them, Eddie touched Pam's arm. "I'm sorry you feel so much hostility toward me," he said in his warm, sincere, psychologist's voice that could linger so sweetly on the high notes of a tenor solo. "I understand, of course, but I just wish things could be different. For Liam's sake if nothing else. He's very attached to you, you know."

"Hey," said Pam lightly, "we got you on the plane, didn't we? Can't have everything."

She walked away from Eddie's sorry, fleshy face, into the rec hall and the reception in progress, and stood in the doorway, getting her bearings, trying to shake off the effects of the scare they'd all just had. A minute later Brett's husband, Eric Meredith, appeared at her elbow with a plate of petit-fours. "Talking to yourself already, huh?"

She grinned, pleased to see him; Eric was a nice guy. Nicer than his wife in Pam's opinion, though just at the moment she was disposed to think rather well of Brett. "Just remembering a poem." She chose a little chocolate cube and popped it into her mouth.

"Is Humphrey okay? Wow, wasn't that something? For a minute there I thought those wiseacres were dead meat."

"I was thinking before, though, Carrie would probably have enjoyed the fuss." They both grinned, but Pam's expression turned serious. "I think he's okay, he was talking pretty normally when they left, but if Brett hadn't intervened I'm actually not sure what would have happened." She hesitated, then admitted to Eric what she'd been reluctant to admit to herself: "Please tell Brett thanks from me for saving the day today, if I don't get a chance to tell her myself. But I've got a feeling there's going to be some major fallout from this."

"The media, you mean?"

"The media on one side, and the Hefn and Gafr on the other. *Humphrey's* probably okay," she repeated, "but I think this incident's really serious, in a symbolic sort of way. The truth is, Brett was right, and the hecklers were right, even if they picked a bad moment to make their point. If something's not done soon about the Ban . . . " She shrugged and helped herself to another of the little cakes Carrie had loved, a pink one.

Eric looked her soberly in the eye. "You guys, the ones the Hefn listen to, the ones they trust—you've got a lot of responsibility." That said, he changed the subject. "So, what poem were you 'remembering'? Something you learned from Carrie?"

"Unh-unh, not me, but Liam did. Or sort of semi-learned—not as well as 'The Ballad of East and West' or the Mowgli songs."

"Yeah, Brett learned all those Kipling poems from Carrie too. Those kids were so lucky to have somebody like Carrie practically living right in the house with them. Nobody in my family knew poetry from pig swill."

"I was just quoting a little piece of one to myself. It won't make sense out of context but—

"When he shows as seeking quarter, with paws like hands in
     prayer,
That is the time of peril, the time of the Truce of the Bear!"

CHAPTER 2

The Truth About the World

15-16 FEBRUARY 2037

Only distantly aware of where she was and why, Lexi Allred, eleven years old and small for her age, lay on her back on the couch and thought about Jason. Or not thought exactly. It was more like living inside a fantastic story, one long saga made up of different episodes, that unfolded in such a real-seeming way that coming out of it every time was like being dropped back into the ordinary world with a bone-cracking jolt. Lexi thought fairly often about Neil Reeder, the actor who played Jason on their TV series *A Thousand Miles*; but this VR-type phenomenon bloomed into being only here, in her grandfather's dark, familiar living room, with her dead Granma's picture on the piano and her grandfather doing something to Lexi a million miles away.

The weird thing was that she never remembered anything at all about this magical place she could go to, except when she went there—when she was whisked there without wishing or trying to be. Then, presto! the entire saga in all its shining clarity and detail, starring Neil and herself, would explode, possess her mind and start to roll forward, better than the best actual episode of *A Thousand Miles* the two of them had ever acted in together.

The fantasy was like a spinoff of the series. In the real show, a father called Henry McPherson and his wife, Margaret, were pulling a handcart loaded with all their possessions for a thousand miles and then some, over the plains to the Rocky Mountains and the

Great Salt Lake Valley beyond. The family had emigrated to America from Scotland. Lexi played Kate, Henry's daughter by his first wife, Ellen, who was dead. Soon after Ellen died, Henry joined the Scottish Church of Jesus Christ of Latter-day Saints, and there met and married a widow called Margaret Scott with a son, Jason, played by Neil. Within a few years there were three more children: Harry, Mary Ann, and Sadie.

In 1856 Henry and Margaret decided to emigrate with their family to Zion, which is how the Mormons thought of Utah and especially Salt Lake City. They crossed the Atlantic on a sailing ship, the *Thornton*. Tragically, there was a cholera epidemic in New York when they landed, and Harry and Mary Ann both caught it and died. Margaret had also been very sick, but she recovered, and when she was stronger the five survivors traveled by train to Iowa City and joined the Edward Martin Handcart Company—576 Mormon men, women and children, hauling or riding on handcarts.

They set off from Iowa City on July 26. Right at the start of the trip, just a couple of days out of camp, there was another tragedy: little Sadie was run over by a provision wagon and killed. With such a tiny pool of child actors to draw upon, the producers had needed to eliminate all the children except Jason and Kate; but exactly such disasters as these really had befallen plenty of the children immigrating to Zion.

The handcart pioneers were menaced by Sioux and Pawnee raiders, rattlesnakes, wolves, herds of stampeding buffalo, heat, cold, rain, and the limitations of the flesh. They were always worn out and hungry, their feet swelled and bled and their shoes fell apart, people got sick and fell in love, and quarreled with each other over who would stand watch and herd the oxen, and how to divide up a buffalo if one was shot or an ox if one died of exhaustion. Sometimes people died too, like little Sadie, and toward the end of the journey the suffering from cold and starvation—for the Martin company had started much too late in the year—was going to be terrible. It was an exciting show to watch, and filming it week after week was the best thing in Lexi's life. Not just because she was a star, though that was fun. Because of Neil-being-Jason.

Neil was terribly nice to Lexi when he was being Jason and she was being Kate, in a long raggedy dress and bonnet and shoes that buttoned up over her ankles. He would let Kate sneak a ride on the handcart when she was too tired to walk another step (tired or not, if you weren't sick you were supposed to walk), and carry her piggyback across the Platte River, which the company had to ford again and again (it was a very crooked river). Jason would tell her stories when she was frightened or sad, and sing funny songs to make her laugh.

He'd also saved her life about a dozen times—fighting a Pawnee warrior that tried to steal her, climbing down a steep bluff she'd fallen over and bringing her back up. Stuff like that. Lexi had spent a whole afternoon halfway down that bluff, hanging on to a willow tree, while Neil came down a rope time after time, till their director was satisfied. All afternoon Lexi had watched the seat of Neil's pants descend toward the little ledge where she was supposedly stuck, and heard him yell to her over and over, "Don't be scared, Katy! Hang on tight now! I'm comin' to get you!" And at the end she got to hug her arms around his shoulders, while he hauled them both up out of danger.

Neil-being-Neil though, between takes, wouldn't give Lexi the time of day. She didn't know why he was so mean. It made her sad.

But that didn't matter now. Now, in the movie in her head, Jason had crawled under the cart where she was sleeping and was gently shaking her shoulder. "Wake up, honey," he whispered into her ear.

Kate turned on her side and burrowed under her coat, but Jason shook her again. "C'mon, Katy, wake up!"

She rubbed her eyes, suddenly alert, sensing danger. "What the matter? What's wrong?"

"Shhhh! Nothing's wrong, we're just leaving. I'm taking you away from here."

"Why? Where we going?" Wide awake now, Kate peered past Jason. The buffalo-chip campfire in the middle of the circle of carts flickered its red light across the face of the man on watch, Brother Prentiss, who'd fallen asleep. All around them, humps of exhausted people and blocky handcarts lay silent. The silence was so intense it rang in Kate's ears. Somewhere in the darkness a coyote ki-yi'ed and was answered. "Where are we going?" she whispered again.

"Somewhere safe," said Jason in a serious, grown-up way. "I'll tell you after we get started. But now we have to go. Come on, get your shoes on." He pulled Kate's coat off her and helped her sit up. "Hurry up now. I took some bread."

Shivering, Kate fumbled with her shoes, tying them on with strips of rag because most of the buttons had come off. When she was done he pulled her up and helped her put on her coat and bonnet. "Quiet as a mouse now. Keep close to me."

Jason took her hand and they slipped away like shadows. Away from the firelight the stars leapt out, stippling the whole sky. The ground was rough and stony, sagebrush snatched at Kate's dress with its stiff, twiggy little hands. "What about Papa and Mama?" she worried. "Do they know we're going away? Will they know how to find us?"

Jason tightened his grip on her hand, looked down, and had just opened his mouth and drawn breath to answer Kate when something seemed to rip Lexi's body in two. The star-speckled night on the plains vanished; she was back in her grandfather's dark living room, shocked and scared, struggling to scramble away from the source of the pain. She heard herself cry out, "*Ow!* Don't! Don't, Granpa, it hurts!"

"I'm so sorry, honey, I can't help it, I just can't help it." Granpa's voice came from up above her head. "I love you so much, I don't mean to hurt you, I'm being just as careful as I can." He was breathing hard, pressing her down, and then the ripping came again, so terrible that Lexi couldn't believe it.

The searing pain, and realizing she couldn't get free, ripped an actual shriek out of Lexi. Claustrophobia stopped her breath; she thrashed and flailed. "Shhh, shhh, please, hush now, hush honey," she heard Granpa say. Abruptly the burning agony ended and the sofa cushions bounced up as her grandfather slid off onto the floor. Then at once a weight across her chest pinned her to the couch again while something hard and smooth, like a club, rammed into her mouth. The sound of panting and groaning surrounded them as Lexi, fighting frantically for air, choked and gagged on a sudden salty wetness like glue in her throat.

Then the light was on. Her grandfather, barefoot in jeans and sweatshirt, was on his knees swabbing at the floor where somebody had thrown up. He had a bucket of water and a rag. Lexi's face felt stiff. "Jump in the shower now, honey," said Granpa, not looking at her. "We'll go get us a pizza, how'd you like that? Before I take you on back."

~

Pam woke up with a crick in her neck as the plane was landing. Through the window she could see a few lights and a blurry expanse of white and not much else; it was nearly nine and the city had already rolled up most of its streets.

They taxied toward what had been the terminal when commercial flights were still operating, but was now a vast storage facility, a black hulk with square corners. As soon as the brakes screeched, Pam got up stiffly and hauled her bag down from the overhead compartment. Eddie and the five weary missionaries, bundled in blankets, appeared to be sleeping through the stopover; but as she moved up the aisle, trundling her luggage like a pull toy behind her, one of the missionaries opened his eyes and said "You going to Hurt Hollow for the conference?"

"I'm not sure. It's on the calendar, but it won't be up to me."

"They all want to see you. Tell Humphrey you need to rejuvenate your roots," said the missionary around a yawn.

"Humphrey's going to be dead to the world, it's Alfrey we need to work on."

The man groaned and made a face, and Pam turned to exit the plane. The pilot had maneuvered into place with such precision that she only had to step from the open door onto the platform extension of the TRAX station, jumping her trundle across the gap with a little jerk on the handle.

The single car that had been dispatched to meet her was waiting on the track. She crossed the platform, waved to the driver, hauled herself and the bag aboard, and slumped into a molded plastic window seat as the door closed and the car began to move.

It wasn't much warmer inside than out. An employee of the Bureau might rate a seat on an official plane, and even a special TRAX car, but the Hefn deeply disapproved of energy-consuming comforts like adequate heat and air conditioning. Easy for them to be sniffy about heating; they had hair.

Light rail had come to Utah just in time for the 2002 Winter Olympics, a controversial afterthought at a time when the freeways were crammed with smog-spewing private cars, and a thousand commercial flights landed and took off from the airport every day. During an inversion the air had been so full of particulate crap you couldn't see across the street.

This little airport spur had hardly been used since 2011, when the Hefn Directive ended air travel for ordinary citizens. The rest of the system was used hard. At the turn of the twenty-first century, people had tried their best to make the politicians spend the light-rail money on more and wider freeways. Ten years later, when the Hefn said no more private cars, those same people had been very glad to have the TRAX system in place. And now the tracks stretched from Logan in the north clear to Cedar City, and the Salt Lake Valley authorities had stopped imposing no-burn days during temperature inversions.

The car slid out of the terminal building. Pam flipped up her hood, tugged on her gloves, and looked out the window.

The right-of-way described two sides of a triangle, running south alongside the canal before swooping east toward the center of town. The moon was high and full, lighting up the snow; and the little cluster of office buildings at the city's heart, faintly outlined in lights, appeared trivial and tiny set against the massive, glistening ridges and deep folds of the Wasatch Range behind them. Pam's window put a momentary frame around this spectacular picture. What might the title be? As the car swerved eastward, and thus broadside to the long flat trough stretching south between the Wasatch and Oquirrh Ranges, she thought of some:

Proper Perspective
Q.E.D.
Snowscape with Temple
Hefn Go Home
The Truth About the World

~

For the past hour Lexi had existed in a daze with a red burning at the center, like a damaged robot. Take a shower. Get dressed. Get in the car. But when Granpa opened the door of the pizza place, and the smell poured over her in a thick humid wave, her stomach lurched and she thought she was going to be sick again. "Here we are, here we are," said Granpa cheerfully as they went inside. "What do you want on your pizza, sweetheart? Pepperoni, that's your favorite, right?"

She couldn't look at him but, staring past him at the door, her mind suddenly stopped slipping around and became crafty. She nodded. "Pepperoni. And m-mushrooms."

"And some pop? A Coke?" She nodded again, fixing her gaze on the door behind him. "A large Coke, okay then," he said. "I'll see if they've got the caffeine-free. You go find us a table, and I'll be quick as I can."

Lexi felt him move away toward the counter, and almost that fast she was out on the sidewalk, running like a deer.

For the first desperate minutes she simply ran, ignoring the burning, her one goal to put as much distance as possible between herself and her grandfather before he'd discovered she was gone. The sidewalks had been shoveled and she went fast despite her bulky boots, but there seemed to be two or three dogs behind every fence, barking their heads off as she pounded past, giving her away.

To avoid the dogs she did something she would never have done ordinarily: cut across Seventh East and through an alley of enormous junipers into Liberty Park. She'd been told a hundred times that the park wasn't a safe place after dark for anybody, let alone a little girl in an almost childless world. But the park seemed empty of people now, and finally Lexi stopped, sweaty and completely winded, in the shadow of one of the huge cottonwood trees planted by Brigham Young himself, gasping so hard she had to bend over.

She couldn't just keep running, she'd have to think of someplace to go. Her parents were in a meeting of the ward, she could go there, but what could she tell them? *Granpa's been doing stuff to me since I was six, only today for the first time he hurt me so now I'm telling?* They would ask why she hadn't told a long time ago, and Lexi wouldn't know how to answer that. They would say she was telling a wicked lie. They would say it was her fault. One way or another, she knew, they would back Granpa up. Especially Mom would. Granpa was Dad's stepfather and First Counselor to the stake President. Mom always backed up the Church authorities, always, no matter what.

She could find a phone and call Marcee, her producer, and ask somebody to bring a sledcar down and pick her up. But the thought of trying to explain why they should burn that many fuel credits on her account, when Granpa was already slated to be bringing her back from her day off, made Lexi feel suffocated with embarrassment and shame. Nobody on the show would believe her either. Marcee was nice, and would be upset and worried about her, but they were all like her mother in that way, backing the Church against everything else. The Church was *paying* for *A Thousand Miles*! She pictured Marcee's distressed frown and Neil's sneer. The thought of Neil knowing anything at all about it was unbearable.

By now Granpa might have contacted them already, they might know she'd run away. The police might be after her by now. Lexi was no crybaby, but she sobbed a couple of times at this thought. Should she maybe call the bishop? The bishop was one of Granpa's best friends, always telling her how wonderful it was that their ward had a real family in it, three generations, with real testimonies.

It was cold and scary, there in the dark by herself. Lexi's sweat had turned icy; now she started to shudder, in a kind of paralysis of cold, fear, and indecision.

Then, exactly as it had in the pizza shop, her head cleared. Like a forgotten dream popping back into her mind, she saw Jason holding her hand, stealthily drawing her away from the camp, leaning toward her to say . . . and just like that, his words popped into her mind too, and she knew! She knew the secret of the fantasy, and she knew what Jason had been about to tell her, even if it didn't make any sense. The safe place they were going to was the Gaian Mission on Fourth South. Father and Mother would never look for them there. They weren't going to be Mormon handcart pioneers anymore. They were going to be Gaian missionaries, in a different story.

At the central station under Crossroads Mall, opposite Temple Square, Pam got out—calling "Night!" to the driver—and climbed the stairs to the street. As people could hardly help doing, she glanced upward at the dramatically pointed stone spires of the Temple, its golden angel gleaming under the moon, before looking around for a taxi. One more leg to this journey, then bed. TRAX stopped running at ten and there were no pedestrians on the street, but a few horse cabs always hung around until midnight or so, and Pam hailed one.

The cab of the taxi was even colder than the rail car, but there was an old blanket on the seat and Pam wrapped herself up in it. Block after block of brick bungalows, nearly identical under their thick cappings of snow, flowed past her grimy window as the horse clopped south. Third South, Fourth South, Fifth, Sixth, the streets measuring their distance from Temple Square as if it were the center, not just of the city, but of the universe. The white mountains of the Wasatch bulked up behind the houses, not so overwhelmingly as when seen from the airport, miles farther away, but impressively visible at intersections.

At Thirteenth South the taxi turned due east. On the north side of the street, the cleared solar panels on the roofs reminded Pam that she'd made no arrangements to have her own roof panels brushed off while she was away. Her plane to Washington had taken off through a breaking storm. The panels would've been blind for three days now; the house would be freezing. Wonderful. Something else to squeeze in tomorrow morning.

But as the taxi skirted the southern edge of Liberty Park, Pam caught a glimpse of the Aviary's flamingos, asleep on one foot in the deep snow of their enclosure, and smiled. Heads tucked under pink wings, they looked miserable and ridiculous, like lawn ornaments that should have been brought inside at summer's end. But the flock had come through other Utah winters well enough, and this would likely be no different. Neither for them, nor for her.

~

The sign on the lawn said WASATCH GAIAN MISSION. Lexi could read it even without any streetlights, the moon was so bright. Anyway, she already knew what it said. She'd been aware of the sign, and of the house, for a couple of years at least; once she'd read a whole library book about the Gaians, an off-limits book for an LDS kid. Her parents would have told Bishop Erickson if they'd known about it, and he would have told her that the Gaians were servants of the Hefn, and the Hefn were servants of Satan.

Lexi was afraid of the Hefn, but she didn't really see how they could be servants of Satan *and* train the Gaian missionaries too. What the Gaians believed sounded nice. The book said their religion was about healing the world. They wanted every single person to connect to the Earth (which they called by an old name for Earth, Gaia, to make it easier for people to think of it, or her, as one huge organism) by having a personal piece of Ground to cultivate and watch and learn from. They believed that if people did that, if they really paid attention, they wouldn't be able to treat the Earth like something to be used.

Bishop Erickson said the Earth's natural resources had been put there by God *for* people to use, and conservation wasn't that important because pretty soon the world was coming to an end anyway; the reason Mormons called themselves Latter-day Saints was that these *were* the latter days. A lot of people thought that the Hefn being here, making everybody do what they said, just proved the Church was right.

Lexi was a Mormon born and bred; she loved having ancestors who'd been Mormon pioneers; she loved singing "Come, Come, Ye Saints" and "Abide with Me, 'Tis Eventide" and the other hymns; the people in her ward were pleasant and kind; but some part of her had stored away an impression of Gaian goodness like an emergency kit. Some part of her—the part that remembered the splendid secret story of Kate and Jason when the other parts had forgotten about it completely—had known there might be an emergency someday, and had made its provisions.

There were lights in the windows. Heart thumping, Lexi walked up the steps to the porch and rang the doorbell.

~

Pam stomped on the doormat before letting herself into the cold and dark of her house, bumping the trundle over the threshold. The ride home had taken forever, the cabby's horse had thrown one of his rubber shoes—the modern version of having a blowout. She was chilled clear through and dog-tired.

The message center was chiming softly. Pam switched on a lamp, saw her breath swirl out—a frosty ghost—and vanish. Welcome home. The chiming set her teeth on edge. "Play messages," she instructed it crossly. Tossing her gloves and scarf on the table, she sat down to pull off her boots with stiff fingers as the little screen obligingly lit up.

At the sight of Jaime Rivera's broad, pleasant face, Pam's own face relaxed. Jaime was a very nice guy. As "gafr" of the Wasatch Gaian Mission, he was one of two people with whom Pam was required to liaise on behalf of the Bureau of Temporal Physics and the aliens, and Jaime made that part of her job a pleasure.

Usually. Now there was anxiety in his expression and voice, and as soon as he started talking, Pam's almost-smile died away. "Hi, Boss. Glad you're back. Hope the funeral wasn't too rough. Listen, not to beat about the bush, we got us another child sexual abuse case tonight." He imitated the hand-flapping gesture of an unhappy Hefn. "If you could come in as early as possible tomorrow I'd appreciate it. Some unusual angles to this one. We've got the kid here and we'll keep her overnight, assuming you've got no problem with that. Sabrina's been in and that's what she recommends. Give me a quick buzz when you get this, okay? Just so I know you're back in town. The perp's a Mo, by the way, and so's the kid—his granddaughter."

Jaime waved and cut the connection. "Shit!" said Pam. "Goddammit." She flung her coat, inside out, over the back of the chair and stood up. "Reply," she ordered the machine; but instead of a green light and beeping prompt, it redisplayed a glum Jaime. "Hi, Boss. Glad you're back. Hope—"

"Not 'replay,' gearhead! 'RePLY! RePLY!'"

Rebuked, the screen blanked, flickered, bleeped. The green light came on. "Jaime, I just walked in the door. There's some stuff I've *got* to do in the morning, but I'll try to be in around eleven, okay? No problem about keeping the kid at the Mission overnight. Not our lucky winter, is it? The trip went all right, thanks for asking. Send. Erase. Next message."

The screen displayed an elderly man seated behind a massive desk. He had on a suit, a string tie, and—something rarely seen nowadays—a pair of spectacles in wire frames. Pam groaned. This was her other chief responsibility, a person as implacably her adversary as Jaime was entirely her friend. The old fart glowered into his message camera. "Ms. Pruitt. Brigham Parker here. I need to speak with you about a matter of considerable urgency. Please get in touch with this office at your earliest convenience."

Parker was an Apostle of the Church of Jesus Christ of Latter-day Saints, one of the Quorum of Twelve, who were next in authority after the President and his two Counselors. Whenever there was trouble with the Hefn, the Church sicced Brother Parker on Pam; and since friction between the Hefn and the LDS Church was intense and chronic, the two saw a lot of each other, a necessity disagreeable to both.

Officially and unofficially, the Mormon Church was as opposed to the Hefn Takeover as it was possible to be. Not even the Ku Klux Klan or the Reproductive Rights extremists despised the aliens more. And in fact the Mormons had good reason to hate the Hefn, for no community had been more devastated by the Broadcast and the Ban. Equally, between aggressive fertility and environmental arrogance, no community in the developed world better represented everything the Hefn saw as destructive to the Earth than the LDS Church. Church and Hefn were natural enemies in an unequal power struggle; and Pam, as BTP emissary to the hostiles, had her work cut out for her. Her job was partly to listen politely and nod while the church leaders expressed their righteous outrage, but mostly to report to Humphrey any sign that the Mormons were about to foment an inconvenient rebellion.

"Reply," said Pam. "Camera off. Brother Parker, this is Pam Pruitt. I've just come back from Maryland, from the funeral of an old friend. I have a busy day tomorrow, but I'll be in touch as soon as I possibly can. Send. Erase. Next message."

"There are no additional messages," the machine said humbly.

"Good," said Pam. "Let's try and keep it that way."

As expected, the solar batteries were almost dead; there was just enough juice to keep the pipes from freezing, work the TV and a light or two, and supply the message center with its pittance of power. Wind-generated city electricity, expensive but plentiful, would have to be switched on tomorrow. For tonight the Bureau Emissary to the Church of Jesus Christ of Latter-day Saints turned the gas fireplace insert on low, shut the door to the hallway, brought two comforters from her freezing bedroom, and bunked down on the couch.

She awoke to snappy chiming, maddening and insistent. It wasn't even light outside. She stumbled up, wrapping a comforter around herself, and padded in her socks to answer the phone. "Camera off. Hello."

It was Liam, looking better than he had at the service, but as if he had slept in his clothes, poorly. "Hi. Aren't you decent yet? I didn't wake you up, did I?"

Pam closed her eyes. He knew perfectly well which time zones they each were in. "What's up? It's the crack of dawn out here."

"I thought you might like to know how it went yesterday, scattering the ashes. Want me to call back later?"

Pam squinted at the clock: 7:12. "No, never mind, I need to get up soon anyway. How'd it go?"

"Pretty well, considering that Humphrey had totally unhinged the occasion beforehand." Liam smiled wanly. "He'd commandeered the shielded chopper they use for trips into the Zone. We landed in the parking lot, already suited up, and walked up the road. The road's in pretty bad shape and the White Trail had almost disappeared, but we made it. To the Ragged Rock. And we had some silence, and then Terry quoted 'Traveling Through the Dark,' that poem on Carrie's exam, the one that triggered his memory of the time window. That part was *so* eerie. Then we shook the ashes out of the bag, all around the base of the Rock and some up on top, up where Carrie and Jeff and I used to sit and eat doughnuts. We took turns. And we left the bag and box there, on the ground, and just walked back out and flew back to College Park. The chopper has a decon unit."

"What sort of shape was Humphrey in?"

Liam rolled his eyes. "He didn't say much, but he seemed very engrossed in shaking the ashes around. You know how he gets. It may have mollified him some, participating in that little ritual—but you were right, he didn't want to talk about what happened, and he took off in a plane as soon as we landed, without saying where he was going."

"It's serious," Pam said.

"I know. Will you be in touch with him before he goes to sleep?"

"He said he'd be in touch with me. You know what sticks with me the most? His dropping down on all fours. The only other time I ever saw him do that was in Hurt Hollow, remember? When he decided to revert to his heritage as a predator, and went dashing out the door?"

"And got stung by the bumblebee," said Liam. Both grinned at the memory, which nevertheless had its sobering side.

"How's Terry holding up?"

"He's awfully broken up. I'm kind of worried about him. I tried to sound him out about Humphrey last night, but he couldn't seem to focus."

"Will he put the house on the market?"

"I'm trying to persuade him to. It's way too big for him to live in alone, but he doesn't want to sell it yet—you know, and admit that that whole part of his life is over and done with. Listen, could you put on the visual? I hate talking to a blank screen."

"Camera," said Pam to the machine. "So what's really on your mind? I have to get cracking pretty quick here." The room was very cold; she wrapped the comforter tighter around herself.

Liam smiled, and various unspoken messages passed between them. Liam to Pam: *You know I had another reason for calling, that I'm upset and need to talk to you.* Pam to Liam: *You know I'll give you whatever you need, even though we're both aware that I couldn't count on you to return the favor, and that my self-respect suffers from accepting this unequal and unfair arrangement, and I resent you for it.*

"I dreamed about Jeff last night," he said.

Pam paused. "You know, in all these years I'd never heard that tape. How come you never played it for me?"

Liam shook his head, shrugging. "It was the tape, and going out to the Ragged Rock too, I guess. You know, Carrie and Matt were *at the concert* when they made that recording. We all sat together. It was right to play it yesterday, but it felt so strange, being there between you and Eddie, listening to Jeff's soprano voice singing that solo . . . kind of dizzy-making."

"Like time running backwards," Pam mused. "Eddie and I are thesis and antithesis. We should precede the synthesis, not follow it."

"Well." Liam grimaced. "Maybe. More like, maybe I still haven't got it straight. And maybe I never will, maybe some things in life . . . you just never do get over, and never do get right. You just keep turning one way and then the other, bumbling back and forth, and every time you turn too far and miss it."

An alarm went off inside Pam. "Sounds like grist for Julie's mill to me," she said. Julie was Liam's on-again-off-again therapist, as well as being Pam's regular therapist, with whom she was currently working. "Look, I really can't talk very long right now. A child-abuse case turned up at the Mission last night. *Another* one. And I've had a call from Brother Parker, almost certainly about the same business—Jaime says the perpetrator is a Mormon."

"Sexual abuse? You've got what, three dozen kids in the whole state of Utah, and somebody's abusing one of them?"

"There are actually several hundred kids in Utah, because it's Utah, and somebody's abusing several of them that we know about. Plus God knows how many more."

Liam looked genuinely shocked. "Jesus, that must be just terrible for you. Couldn't Humphrey assign somebody else?"

"Humphrey doesn't know from child abuse, and anyway, it's a

whole lot more terrible for the kids. I'm okay with it. Really."

Pam was now more than ready to break the connection, but Liam stalled. "I thought Mormons were a lot like Baptists. Isn't that why Humphrey sent you out there—because you'd understand where they're coming from, as a former fellow religious fanatic?"

Humphrey sent me out here because I asked him to get me away from you, as you very well know, Pam said to herself; to Liam she said, "Oh, partly, I guess—not that Humphrey knows from Baptists, really, either."

Again, they both smiled. There was a lot Humphrey didn't know. "Well," Liam persisted, "but what about your dad? *He* never went beyond talking and looking. I'd have thought the last person to be caught dead actually *molesting* a child would be that kind of gung-ho religious type, Baptist, Mormon, whatever."

"No, it's more complicated than that," Pam said. "Dad wasn't a pedophile. He didn't start looking or talking till I hit puberty, and he only did that much because he didn't know he wasn't supposed to. But since when does being a Baptist, or a—a *voodoo* practitioner, for chrissake, have the least little bit to do with what turns somebody on?"

Liam looked embarrassed, as well he might. "It doesn't. I'm a moron."

"You *are* a moron," Pam agreed. "Twenty or thirty years ago, remember, there was that huge scandal in the Catholic Church, parish priests abusing boys. Not girls, boys. Actually, I've been thinking a lot about this lately. Back in the old days, the LDS faithful were expected to forego sexual outlets completely until marriage. Then after marriage they were supposed to have as many children as they could possibly provide for—and it wasn't just that it was expected of them, either; everybody *wanted* lots of kids. Before the Ban, they were both the most sexually repressed *and* the most kid-and-family-centered people I every heard of, with more organized youth activities than you could shake a stick at."

"Aha. And all those Scout troops needed leaders."

"They did," said Pam. "If you were a good God-fearing Mormon pedophile, you had no problem finding victims, in or out of your own family, and nothing much to stop you, or help you stop if you wanted to. Have I mentioned what a tremendously patriarchal society this is? Child sexual abuse was a special problem for the Mormons long before the Hefn came." She jiggled from one foot to the other, looking at the clock. "If you're interested in this I could send you some stuff to read. Listen, it's *freezing* in here."

Liam ignored this hint. "The Church must have done *something* about it, they'd have had to!"

"Encouraged repentance and forgiveness. Told wives the kids needed their father at home."

"That's it?"

"Pretty much. I mean, it would be some nice guy everybody liked, good helpful neighbor, paid his tithing, played Santa Claus at the ward Christmas party every year. His bishop would explain, and really believe, that it was basically a moral problem that could be cured with prayer and counsel. They were all morons, just like you. Listen, I *have* to clear my roof panels off and get over to the office, and there's two feet of snow outside. Want me to call you tonight about that dream?"

Liam gave her a look that said, *I got what I needed, you may go.* "Can't. I'm having dinner with Terry tonight, to decide about the house and all."

"Oh, right."

"I'll send you a transcript of the dream, okay? Good luck with today."

He cut the connection. Pam said loudly to the blank screen, "Goddammit, why don't you call *Eddie* up and get *him* to hold your hand? It's even earlier where he is!" But she knew the answer to that one. It was herself, not Eddie, who most reminded Liam of Jeff.

Mormon history fascinated Pam. Founded by a visionary and led for decades by a genius-level businessman, the LDS Church was a purely American product. Early on, persecution, climaxing in martyrdom, had united and empowered the Mormons as a people set apart. They established a kingdom in a desert, and the kingdom thrived. Deprivations? Plagues of locusts? Military occupation? Mass arrests and jailings of polygamous husbands? They rose above it all, and the more they suffered, the more indomitable they grew. A mulish determination to triumph over adversity seemed hardwired into the collective Mormon psyche. As a people they were tough as nails. The more Pam knew about them, the more she admired them for it. She wondered seriously whether—had she grown up LDS in Utah, the scion of pioneers—she could have managed to separate herself from her religious community, as she had from her own Baptist origins, solely because she didn't believe in its doctrines anymore.

Twenty-seven years of Hefn occupation had begun at a time when the Mormon Church had been under heavy attack for environmental arrogance and repressive policies toward homosexuals and women, and when oddball issues like the use of firing squads, husbands who hadn't realized their wives of several years were actually men, and bizarre political scandals, kept making the sober citizens of Utah look like a tribe of Hottentots. Once again adversity had united the Latter-day Saints. Morale might well have been running higher than ever right now—except for one thing.

Traumatic as it was for all Earth's people, the Baby Ban had utterly demoralized the Mormons. As Pam had explained to Liam, what was a biological imperative among people everywhere was a theological imperative as well for the LDS faithful. She had heard one psychologist hypothesize that after two dozen years without children, the gulf between expectation and possibility had given the Mormon community a collective psychosis. She had also seen a report stating that some of the Mormon kids sacrificed to abuse, grown up now and struggling with the consequences, believed the Ban had been brought upon humanity by God, so that no more innocent children would have to be victimized twice in order to keep the Church from looking bad in the eyes of the world. In the effective theocracy that was Utah, opinions about the Ban, obviously, ran to extremes.

Because a small number of people worldwide had missed the Broadcast, and thus the Ban, somewhere on Earth a few children were always being born, mostly via artificial implantation from the limited supply of viable ova and sperm. Pam, remembering her own arboreal childhood, felt sorry for these kids. What could be normal about a childhood spent under a microscope, in a world top-heavy with angry adults? In places where technology still didn't reach everybody, and in communities like the Amish ones, where people didn't hold with the telly and had mostly missed the Broadcast, children had formerly been at such high risk of being stolen and sold that the U.N. now required each infant to be marked at birth with a serial number, an implanted chip, plus a laser tattoo on the upper thigh. Pregnant women, surrogates as well as naturals, were registered at the end of the first trimester. They were keeping track of every single child.

Normally the aliens allowed people to commit and punish crimes however they pleased, except for environmental crimes and threats against themselves. But after ten years and several dozen incidents of abuse—and after Humphrey, knowing what he knew about Pam, had finally carried his point—they had assigned child welfare to the

Gaian network to oversee. Worldwide, a large force of psychologists was also under contract to the Hefn for the purpose of helping the Gaians cope with kid problems of all kinds, and most kids did have problems. The larger Amish settlements, over their own protests, had special teams assigned to them. In Utah and Idaho, where the need was also somewhat special, child welfare oversight was included in the job description of the Bureau Emissary to the Church of Jesus Christ of Latter-day Saints—i.e., Pam. The Hefn wanted somebody in Salt Lake full-time, keeping an eye on things.

If it turned out that the Ban was lifted someday, it wouldn't matter to the Gafr how badly damaged this small generation might be; but if it never was—and always assuming that humanity would not then be exterminated outright—these same young humans would have to repopulate the world and coexist with the aliens. In that case, the less damaged they were the better for all concerned.

~

From her position on the roof Pam could hear the phone chiming faintly through an upstairs window. She finished brushing off her solar panels, refusing to hurry, then dropped the modified broom and descended the ladder, which she folded and locked. She retrieved the panel broom and propped it handle down in a corner of the porch. Inside again, she glared at the phone. "Chime off. Telly on."

The TV screen lit up in the middle of the morning news—and Pam's scalp slowly prickled at what she saw there: Humphrey with his pelt all puffed out, prancing on the meeting-house bench, lambasting the people who had crashed Carrie's service. She heard again the chilling mechanical voice, and saw Brett O'Hara reach over the back of her pew and grab Humphrey's arm. She saw her own back and Liam's, twisted toward him in postures of alarm. The incident hadn't just been reported; somebody had managed to record the service on a phone.

The picture and sound quality weren't great, but anybody could see perfectly well what was going on. "I have been a better friend to you than you know or deserve," Humphrey's utterly alien voice now declared again, "I have pleaded your case with my lords the Gafr, but I say now that if this decision were mine to make, I myself could not encourage you to hope."

It sounded terrible. Pam hadn't fully appreciated what an uproar Humphrey's demonstration would cause in the present atmosphere of deepening anxiety about the fertility ban. Chilled by her lack of foresight, she stood with a snowy boot in one hand, waiting for what would follow.

A woman's earnest face replaced the scene of agitation. "That was the Hefn Humphrey, filmed while attending a memorial service yesterday at the Friends Meeting in College Park, Maryland," she said. "I have here with me several guests who we've invited to comment on the import of Humphrey's statement." The camera drew back to reveal three figures seated at a table: Junior Bemis, son of the late televangelist; Cleo D'Andrea, Vice-Chair of Terry's Senate Committee on Alien Affairs—and Brett O'Hara. "Humphrey himself was unavailable for comment, as were the other Hefn Observers, or so they claim. On my immediate right is the Reverend Otie Bemis, Jr. . . . . "

"Sound off," said Pam. She dropped the wet boot and hurried half-shod, *clump* slap *clump* slap, across to the phone, shrilling "Play messages!"

But instead of Liam, or Humphrey himself, it was Jaime on the screen. "Can you get over here pronto? Our little guest has disappeared. Fill you in when I see you, I'm starting a search."

Pam struck the wall with her palm, hard enough to make it sting. What next? There were no more messages, but while she was considering whether to call Santa Barbara, the phone signaled an incoming call—and there was Humphrey's own dear hairy gray face on visual, saying "Hello, my dear, hello."

"Hello yourself," said Pam with profound relief. "I've just been finding out what a ruckus you've raised. Where are you, anyway?"

"In a phone booth, some distance east of Del Rio, Texas." His voice sounded perfectly normal, i.e. "human." "Tomorrow I will be on the moon; but first I am coming to see you. You can tell me what it means to 'raise a ruckus,' though I can guess this time perhaps."

"You're in Texas? You're coming here, to Salt Lake?"

"There are things to be told. I would tell them to Terry and Liam also, but they are involved with Carrie's business and this cannot wait. And I must sleep. And it must be told personally. So I will come to Salt Lake and tell you, and later you will tell the things to them for me."

"Why didn't you talk to me in College Park, and save yourself a trip? What are you doing in Texas, by the way?"

"Since College Park," Humphrey said placidly, "everything is different."

Pam glanced at the furious pantomime on the TV screen. Junior was leaning forward and speaking emphatically to Brett, punching the air with his forefinger as if struggling to keep from poking it into her eye. *Of course everything's different*, she thought. *Now who's the moron?* "Humphrey, we're having a local crisis here today. I'm not sure how long I'll be tied up. When will you get here?"

"I will land in Salt Lake this afternoon."

Liam's sister was waving both arms now and appeared to be shouting at a furious-faced Cleo D'Andrea, while the newscaster leaned toward them, ineffectually trying to break it up. "I might not be able to meet your plane, unless you absolutely need me to," Pam said distractedly. "Are you coming to the house, or what do you want to do?"

"I do not wish to be observed." (*Good thinking*, Pam almost said.) I will come to your house after dark."

"Okay. There's a cobbler in the freezer. I have to run. See you tonight, then."

"A cobbler?"

"I've been saving it for you."

"Blackberry?"

"Serviceberry. You'll like it, don't worry."

"I am not worried, Pam Pruitt," the Hefn said. "I am thinking, you have never failed me. You are a person who keeps faith."

He cut the connection. "I'm not that great a baker, though," said Pam to the blank screen. She was touched, but she knew that something disturbing had just been said, or implied.

But first things first. Abandoning all thought of calling Bureau Headquarters, Pam headed for the mud room and her ski boots, yelling "Telly off!" over her shoulder. The fastest way to the Mission, or anyhow the most direct, least maddening way, would be the cross-country ski track.

In the kitchen she paused just long enough to remove the cobbler, made last summer with wild berries picked in the mountains, from the freezer and set it on the counter.

CHAPTER 3

Runaway

16 FEBRUARY 2037

"It was almost ten o'clock, I was just about to lock up and go home, when the doorbell rang." Jaime couldn't sit still. He waved his arms around as he paced, crossing and recrossing the beautiful Navajo rug whose red-black-and-white pattern covered most of the Mission's plank floor. "At that hour I figured it was probably some goddam Danite in a white sheet, so I switched on the watchdog—and there was this little girl standing there, all by herself. *Well,* I thought, somebody could be using a kid for a decoy, so instead of opening the door I just slid back the chink and asked her what she wanted.

"So she goes, 'Could I please come in?' and I go, 'I'm sorry, the Mission's closed. Can you come back tomorrow morning?' And I can see through the camera, I mean, she just kind of jerks like I beaned her with a baseball. And she goes, 'I have to come in *now,*' in this voice like she's trying not to cry, and I have to decide, and I decide she's what she looks like, a kid all by herself. So I open the door and in she walks—and it's Alexis Allred!"

The name rang no bell with Pam, slouched back on the couch so she could watch Jaime pace without getting a crick in her neck. "Should I know who Alexis Allred is?"

Jaime ran his hands through his tousled hair, already standing up in a thick black brush. "Boss, don't you ever do anything at home but sit around writing poetry? Don't you ever turn on the telly? Alexis Allred is one of the kid actors on that big hit Mormon series,

A Thousand Miles." Pam shook her head and Jaime lifted his arms and let them drop. "They're filming most of it right here in Utah! It's about those LDS immigrants that walked from Iowa all the way to the Salt Lake Valley, the ones that crossed the Rockies pulling handcarts. I know what you're going to say," he said, holding up his hand, palm outward. "Put kids in a show, you pretty well guarantee great ratings. Well, maybe so, but this show is interesting as hell even *apart* from the kids, especially if you live out here—it's fantastic LDS propaganda, by the way—and this girl, Alexis Allred, she can act like nobody's business! There's an older boy that's not half bad either. Actually, the whole cast—"

"Okay, Jaime, you've made your point, I promise to watch it sometime," said Pam. "But getting back to last night."

Jaime had perched on a chair during his discourse about *A Thousand Miles*; now he jumped up, shoved his hands in his pockets, and started pacing again. "Sorry, sorry, I'm just so goddam . . . well, she came in and I recognized her right off the bat—she's a beautiful child, just beautiful—but disheveled, you know, hair all mussed up—she's got this long blond hair—and I said something like, 'You're Alexis Allred, aren't you? What in the world are you doing here this time of night?' And she says, 'I just turned eleven. I want to take the test to be a missionary.'"

"Hunh," said Pam. "*That's* a poser."

"Damn straight. So I go, you know, 'Why would a terrific little actor like you want to be a missionary instead? Kidding around, like. But then I see from her face that she's dead serious, so I explain that we don't take people by age-group any more, not since the Ban caught up with us, we screen everybody over eleven at three-year intervals, and so forth and so on, and if she still wants to be a missionary in 2039 she should come back then and we'd test her, and she says, 'But that's *two whole years*.'

"So then I go, like, 'Do your parents know you're here? Can I take you home in a taxi?' And bingo, she plops down in the floor and starts to cry, and she cries and cries and *cries*. She can't stop. It's like she's waited this long and she just can't wait any longer. I keep asking her what's the matter, is she hurt, is she scared, why does she want to be a missionary so bad? But nothing doing.

"Well, so after a couple of minutes of this I try to get her up off the floor, but when I go to lift her up, she screams. She won't let me touch her. She crawls away from me and climbs up on the couch, and huddles at one end with her arms wrapped around herself, and by now she's just about hysterical. So finally I switch on the inside camera, which I should've done before I opened the door, don't remind me, and then I call Sabrina and ask her to get down here pronto, and Sabrina talks to her and examines her." Sabrina Glassman, a local gerontologist, was a Gaian steward who worked pro bono for the Mission.

Pam's heart had sunk. "Had she been raped?"

"She had a small vaginal tear and some bruising. She told Sabrina her grandfather did it. Sabrina stitched her up and said keep her here overnight, and that she'd call the police and Bro Peckerwood, in that order, herself. Then she went on home, and I called you."

"Bro Peckerwood left me a message, right after you did. He'd put his black suit back on and gone back down to his office to send it, too, so I guess the Church is taking this one seriously."

"The grandfather is some big muckamuck in his stake," Jaime said gruffly. "Parker contacted the studio, too—Alexis is supposed to be on location tonight. I got a call from her producer or director or whatever, Martha or Marcia Something, wanting to know if the kid was all right, and when she'd be able to go back to work. No, that sounds too cold-blooded; she was obviously concerned, but she put my dander up anyway. You know. The Church sponsors the show, so the show must go on."

"To be fair," Pam reminded him, "it's not just the Church." Their last case had been a boy whose stepbrother had been raping him since he was tiny, and who had finally tried to kill himself by jumping off a ski lift. The stepbrother was a Gaian, an early convert from Catholicism, but not, thank God, a missionary. It should have been next to impossible for a really bent person, such as a nascent pedophile, to slip undetected through the minefield of psychological tests devised for missionary applicants. (The Gaians would never have taken Pam herself, though she had passed without difficulty though the screening process for BTP Apprentices.) But with people constantly trying to wreck the credibility of their mission, even a single child-abusing missionary was more than the Gaians could afford.

Pam pulled her thoughts away from Billy Freeman's horrible brother. "So you took the call from the producer or whatever she is," she prompted.

"Right." Jaime sat, elbows on knees, hands dangling, looking up at Pam. "After that I called Claudia and told her I'd have to stay here overnight. She wasn't real thrilled about that, it's the third time this week I didn't make it home till after midnight, so we talked for a while. Then I went to check on the kid. I was going to fix her some soup or something, but she was asleep on the cot in the records room, dead to the world. Sabrina gave her a pain pill, but also I think she was just plain tuckered out. *I* was, I can tell you, I was totally beat. I closed the door, and came in here and switched off the camera, worse luck, and I must've been asleep before I hit the couch. Didn't even take my shoes off. Next thing I knew, it was morning."

"And no Alexis."

Jaime jumped up again, walked over to the window, walked back to the chair and sat in it. He scrubbed his hair with both sets of fingernails. "I didn't realize she was gone right away. Her door was closed. I took a shower and made some coffee, and then I guess I was just waiting around for you to show up so I could go home. I don't know what made me check on her—just something to do, you know? But anyway, I opened her door just a little crack, and she wasn't in her bed, so I went in. She wasn't anywhere in the room. Or the bathroom. I searched the whole house, top to bottom. She wasn't anywhere."

"And that's when you called me this morning."

"Right. I wanted instructions. I was thinking, maybe we should notify the cops about a runaway."

"Hmm." When they themselves had a stake in the outcome, the Hefn preferred not to compromise their image—of omnipotence— by involving the local police. Who would of course be following up Sabrina's report sometime that day, but maybe she and Jaime could retrieve Alexis first. "It could come to that, but they'll be on the case anyway, we'll wait till they get here. You said you were starting a search?"

"Hard to find out anything without calling her parents or the cops. She didn't leave any tracks, the walkway's cleared and sanded, so's the sidewalk in both directions. I asked a few people if they'd seen a girl, but the trouble with being gafr of this outfit is, my face is too well known. If somebody took her in, they sure weren't telling me about it." He rubbed his face with both hands, vigorously. "In short, no. And I don't know *why* she left, either. That's been bothering me."

"How'd she get out of the house?"

Jaime shook his head ruefully. "Looks like she walked right out the front door. The key was in the lock this morning, and I *know* when I locked up after Sabrina I hung the keys back on the hook, I remember doing it. No tracks under any of the windows, nobody got in or out that way."

"You didn't hear her leave, obviously."

"Boss, if a herd of buffalo had stampeded through this room last night I wouldn't have heard 'em."

So Alexis had slipped out of the house the same way she came in. Pam had a sudden thought. "You said you turned off the inside camera. What about the porch camera?"

Jaime shot up before she was finished and strode into the hallway. "No! Yes! Hooray! Still taping! Thank God I was so tired! Wait, I'll patch it through to the monitor in there." He rushed back in and threw himself on the couch next to Pam. "Rewind to, lemme see, twenty-two thirty hours. Scan for images. Playback, normal speed."

It was policy for every Mission to operate security cameras inside and out during open hours, mostly as a deterrent to anyone who might take it upon himself to teach them Hefn-lovin' Gaians a lesson. Also— to obviate suspicions about their own conduct—all Mission gafrs, not just those in Utah, ran their indoor cameras at any hour when an abused child was to be interviewed, and some Missions ran their outdoor watchdog cameras round the clock. Till recently, though, the Salt Lakers hadn't worried much about damage to their building. Besides, the unretracted lenses were fairly easy to find and disable.

But nobody had disabled this one, trained on the front door. "Time: Oh one thirteen hours," said the speaker, and Pam watched the door open a little bit and the small figure slip through. Moving carefully, she turned to pull the door to behind her, and Pam saw by the light of the porch lamp that Jaime hadn't exaggerated; Alexis was a truly beautiful child.

Then Alexis turned back toward the street—and stopped in surprise. "What're *you* doing here?" she called softly to someone out of camera range; and a male voice replied, "I got it out of Marcee where you were. I liberated a sledcar. How come you're leaving?"

~

"Want a sandwich?" Neil said, and all of a sudden Lexi was starving. She nodded. "Here. Cheese and pickles. I grabbed some of these to eat on the way down. There's nothing to drink but water."

"Water's fine," Lexi said. She pulled a plastic cup out of the holder and filled it from the little tank on the dash. It was warm in the sledcar. The sandwich was delicious. Why Neil was being like Jason was a mystery, but Lexi didn't care why, she was just glad.

He had parked on a quiet street a few blocks from the Mission, saying "Don't want to run the battery down any more than I have to. It's supposed to snow tomorrow." He waited while Lexi finished wolfing her first sandwich and started on a second. "Listen," he finally said, "I know about what happened."

Lexi stopped chewing. She swallowed the bite and laid the sandwich in her lap.

"When you were late, Marcee got fidgety," said Neil. "Then she got a call from your grandfather, saying you decided not to come back up tonight, and he'd bring you up in the morning."

"He told her that?" For the first time, Lexi thought about what Granpa had done when he carried their pizza to the table she was supposed to be saving and she wasn't there.

"Yeah. Marcee thought there was something fishy about it. I mean we had a six-o'clock call, or at least we did till she found out there's supposed to be a storm. And then, just about the time she was thinking of contacting your parents, Brother Parker called and said you were at the Gaian Mission, because they were accusing your grandfather of . . . "

"Don't say it!" said Lexi quickly. "I don't want you to say it. Marcee shouldn't have told anybody." Anger at this betrayal—or at something—swelled inside her like a red balloon. Tears started to her eyes. She wrapped the rest of the sandwich back up in its waxed paper and put it on the floor.

"She was just kind of babbling in shock. It's true, isn't it," Neil said soberly, watching her. "Isn't it? If it is, then there's something I have to tell you. That's why I came down here, to tell you this."

The pills were wearing off; the seat, though padded, hurt. Lexi was still exhausted. She squirmed, wishing Neil would stop.

"You don't have to say anything, I don't want to discuss it or whatever, but—" Neil looked away. "But I just needed to tell you—I know I haven't been very nice to you. I'm sorry. See, I was jealous. I was really jealous of you right from the start. I know that's not much of an excuse, but I was."

Taken aback, Lexi stared at him. "What for?"

"Because your family is really your family." Neil swallowed, blinked, gripped the joystick with both hands. "I mean, you're really related to your parents genetically. I'm not, I'm not related to my mom and dad. They both heard the Broadcast as kids. They paid a surrogate a small fortune to have me, and they paid a *big* fortune for the plasm."

"What's so bad about that?" Most kids had biologicals and surrogates, even natural parents used a surrogate sometimes. Lexi knew Neil's mom from the *Thousand Miles* set. She seemed very nice.

"Well sure, right, you wouldn't want your mom to go to any *trouble* or anything, having a baby," Neil said, and to Lexi's amazement his voice was suddenly high-pitched and shaking with fury. "I would never, never, never do that to a kid. Okay, just try to imagine for a minute what it feels like to have parents—I mean *biological* parents— who sold their sperm and eggs for megabucks to some fertility clinic, so some walking uterus could be implanted with an embryo made in a test tube, and carry it for nine months, and have *you*! I mean, what kind of people would *do* that? Think about it. What if *your* real parents were a couple of sleazes who would sell the parts of themselves that were going to turn into you, and then—just—walk away! Just get rid of you! But the worst thing about it is, the surrogate."

Neil's voice rose even higher. "Say your mom's a good Mormon and she wants a son, and she believes she *should* have a son. So say she can't have one naturally, but she could be implanted if she wanted to. But that's nine months of inconvenience, so instead she pays some anonymous woman a lot of money, and the woman does the dirty work, and then you're born—out of *her* body—and then *she* gets rid of you!" Neil's voice shook with his outrage. "I can't even find out who they all are till I'm twenty-one."

Lexi tried, but still couldn't see why Neil was so furious. She hazarded a guess: "You mean, find out so you can do Temple work and get sealed to them?"

He looked more outraged than ever. "Are you kidding? Didn't you hear what I said? They *dumped* me!"

Then how come he wanted to find out who they were? It was too much for Lexi. She had no idea why he'd swiped a sledcar and come looking for her in the middle of the night to tell her this. "Well, I'm sorry, but I guess I don't see what it's got to do with me."

"Oh—" Neil sighed gustily and leaned back in his seat. "I just realized tonight, when I heard about, you know, what happened, that maybe having your family be your real family might not always be all that perfect either. I always thought it would be so wonderful, having a grandfather that really was your own actual grandfather. See, the idea that your *own grandfather* might do something to hurt you, that was a whole new idea. I mean, it was a big shock. And then I thought about how mad I always was at you, and I felt bad about that. I just wanted to say, from now on I'll try to do better, that's all."

Lexi felt like bursting into tears. What Neil was saying was impossible to take in. That Granpa was Dad's stepfather, not her actual grandfather, seemed beside the point, a technicality. She could think of nothing to say back, except "Well, okay then."

"Okay then. Good. So now I think you should put the seat back and go to sleep for a while. There's a blanket and a pillow in the trunk. And then in the morning we can figure something out."

Abruptly, then it *was* morning. Lexi woke up to find Neil parking the sledcar in front of the public toilets in Liberty Park. "Comfort stop," he said, "before it starts getting too lively around here. They just unlocked the gates. Hurry up, and try not to let anybody see you."

Children attracted attention wherever they went, all children, whether or not they were TV stars. Lexi slipped into the building, locked herself into a stall, and peed. The pee burned her stitches and she gasped and gritted her teeth. There was nobody else in the Ladies' Room and nobody coming in; she splashed cold water on her face before bolting back to where the sledcar waited, poised like an opaque soap bubble at the curb. Neil was back already and they glided away the instant she was inside. "Breakfast is going to be a problem," he said. "We better stop and think a minute." He angled the car into the curb in front of the entrance to the Aviary, which wouldn't open for a couple of hours, and dialed the battery down to Low Heat. "Why'd you leave the Gaian Mission in the middle of the night, by the way? You never said."

"Oh." Lexi had been feeling better; now she had to think about why she'd felt so bad. "I had a nightmare. It woke me up. It was *horrible*." The ghastly image flashed again behind her eyes, and she shrank into herself. "It was my—my granpa really, but he looked just like Brigham Young, with the beard and all? He was yelling at me, shouting over and over, 'You WEREN'T supPOSED to TELL! You WEREN'T supPOSED to TELL!' And every time he said TELL he'd hit me with this thing, kind of a leather stick, and every time he hit me I'd stop breathing. I was struggling and struggling to breathe. And then he just started roaring, no words, just this noise like a . . . roaring siren or something, and then he turned into a mountain lion. Not his head, but the rest of him, and he sort of pounced into the air and landed on top of me and I woke up."

Neil whistled. "So then you got dressed and sneaked out?" She nodded. "Why? I'd've burrowed down and pulled the covers over my head."

"I felt awful," Lexi said in a little voice. "About telling. Granpa's the First Counselor to our stake President. I probably got him in trouble."

Neil frowned. "Listen, Lexi, that's not right. He got *himself* in trouble."

Lexi said nothing, because what was the point? She felt how she felt.

Neil let it drop. "So—where were you off to, if I hadn't turned up?"

"I was gonna find a pay phone and call my mom."

"Well, is that what you want to do now?"

Again Lexi looked at her lap. She pictured Granpa in the dream, disguised in Brigham's absolute authority, whacking at her with the stick. She thought of her mother, refusing to hear a word against Granpa. "I'm not sure."

"Well," said Neil, "I'm starving, and there's no way we can buy breakfast around here without getting noticed. I should get this sledcar back anyway, before they report me too. So, I could take you home first, or you could ride back up with me if you want. But what I *think* is," he said, "is I should probably drop you back at the Mission. You're gonna end up back there anyway, till things get worked out."

"Unh-unh," Lexi protested, "they were only keeping me overnight, I can't stay there. They won't let me become a missionary till 2039."

Neil turned to stare at her. "No, no. Look. The Gaians handle *all* the child-abuse cases"—Lexi flinched—"ever since the Hefn assigned it to them. Haven't you seen those telly ads? But you don't have to become a *missionary*, for hell's sake. Where'd you get that idea?"

It was news to Lexi that the Gaians handled all the child-abuse cases. Did that mean there were lots of cases? "I don't remember seeing any ads. I went there because I *want* to be a missionary."

Neil's jaw dropped. "You want to be a *Gaian missionary*? Since when?"

"Since a while. They won't let me take the test now though. Not for two more years."

"My heck, this is crazy! A Gaian missionary! Oh man, I can see the headlines now: 'Handcart Girl Joins Alien Sect.'" This second new idea seemed to have thrown Neil as hard as the first one, only in the opposite direction. "What about the Church? What about acting? What about the show? Were you just going to *quit* the Church? Your parents would for sure have something to say about that!"

Lexi shrugged. "If I can't be a missionary I was figuring I might as well keep on with the show."

Neil sprawled back against the door of the sledcar in his amazement. "What about the *Church* though? Did you lose your testimony or what? I mean, how could you just quit?"

"I guess I might get excommunicated now anyway," she said bleakly, not looking at Neil. Her throat ached. Where was the Jason-like person who, only a minute before, had been telling her it was Granpa that had gotten them both in trouble? You'd think he could see how that kind of trouble might mess up your testimony a little bit.

The truth was that whatever he felt about her family situation and his own, Neil-as-Neil was a standard-issue Mormon boy, inducted into the Priesthood at twelve, expecting to go on an LDS mission in a few years before being matched up with—"called" to marry—a fertile Mormon girl whose parents, biological or natural, had been out-of-earshot children in 2013 when the Broadcast happened. It was Neil-being-Jason, not this boy, who had clasped the hand of Lexi-being-Kate and led her away from the camp, to safety.

They sat for several moments in silence. "Well," Neil said finally, "okay, let's everybody calm down. Number one, I don't think you should be deciding stuff like this for yourself right now. But, number two, if you don't feel like going home then I reckon the Mission is probably the best place for you. Like I said before, you're gonna end up back there anyway, one way or another, and somebody needs to be looking after you. Might as well be them."

~

"Hear that whine? Sledcar. Viddy off. It's somebody she knows, in a sledcar." Jaime got up and started pacing again, not quite so aggressively. "She didn't sneak out to meet him, by the sound of things."

"Think he just turned up? That's quite a coincidence."

"Too true. A teenage boy, is that what he sounds like to you? She seems way young for it—and in the circumstances—no, wait a second, he said he got it out of Marcee? That producer's name was something like that—it's the other kid, Reeder, the kid from the show!"

"I guess," Pam said reluctantly, "that we'd better bring in the folks in blue."

"Phone on," said Jaime promptly, with obvious relief. "They could be anywhere by now." He strode across the Navajo rug, confronted the camera. "Salt Lake Police." The screen resolved into the image of a uniformed female officer, who began to recite, 'If you are calling about an emergency, say the word *Emergency* . . .'" and at that instant the doorbell rang.

Pam sprang off the couch and opened the front door. Side by side on the porch stood the grubby girl they had just seen on the security tape, and a redheaded boy who looked to be fifteen or sixteen.

"If you wish to report a crime, say the word *Crime*," instructed the digitalized policewoman. "Oh my heck," Jaime exploded. "Cancel call!" He charged toward the door. "Get yourself in here, young lady! We were just about to call out the cops on you."

"Jaime, never mind," Pam said, lightheaded with relief. "Alexis, am I glad to see you. I'm Pam Pruitt. Please come in, both of you, and tell us what the Sam Hill you've been up to."

"Uh, I have to go," the boy said, taking a step back. "I was just walking Lexi to the door."

"This *is* the other kid from *A Thousand Miles*, Reeder, Neil Reeder," Jaime said in a quick aside to Pam. "You're the guy with the sledcar, right? You picked Alexis up in the middle of the night?" Peering past the young people, Pam could see it, a blue bubble on skis drawn up to the curb.

"Uh, yeah," Neil said. He looked above the door. "Oh. I get it. You guys have a watchdog camera."

Pam nodded. "We saw Alexis leave. You were out of visual range, but we could hear the car, and the two of you talking."

Jaime said, "Come in for a minute anyway, Neil, okay? Are you kids hungry? Have you had breakfast?"

"No," said the girl suddenly. "And Neil's starving. And so am I. Come on, Neil, we can call Marcee and tell her where we are. Come *on*." She grabbed the boy's arm with both hands and pulled him inside.

~

Two hours, two large breakfasts, and many phone calls later, Pam and Lexi were alone in Pam's office at the Mission. Jaime and Neil had left for their separate destinations. Pam was placing a call to Brigham Parker, the last call she hoped to make that day. Over her desk were pinned a big, bumpy map of Utah, a relief map, and a colorful poster.

Lexi, told to stay out of camera range, was examining the poster. "Grow Into Your Ground Together," it said in cursive writing that was like twining vines, with mint-green leaves and little white flowers. Under these words was a sepia-toned photo of some people working on a farm. They were all dressed in overalls and clodhoppers and broad-brimmed straw hats. One overalled man was plowing behind a team of mules, and the rest, men and women, were following along behind, sowing some crop or other, Lexi thought maybe corn? Big bags of seed were slung around their necks and shoulders. They were all wearing dazzling smiles and looking as if there was no place they'd rather be and nothing they'd rather be doing.

Lexi frowned. Did Gaians have to work on farms? The book said they cultivated a personal piece of ground, but she'd gotten the impression that they meant something like the garden in *The Secret Garden*: a place more wild than tame, with lots of roses and a fountain, and a snug stone wall around the whole thing.

"Good morning, Brother Parker," Pam said, and Lexi looked. There was Pam at her desk, lean and plain, dressed like a man in wool pants and a thick brown sweater pulled over her large chest, and there on the screen was Brother Brigham Parker at *his* desk, an Apostle of the Church and a member of the Twelve, wearing his dark suit and looking as if he'd just eaten a pickle. "I'm sorry it's taken me so long to get back to you," Pam was saying.

"Yes, Ms. Pruitt. Yes . . . after speaking with Dr. Glassman last night, I had called to discuss the situation concerning Brother Edgar Young. As I suppose you realize."

Lexi closed her eyes. Brother Edgar Young was Granpa. If the doctor had told Brother Parker about him, because Lexi had let the doctor see what Granpa did, the jig was up—she'd be excommunicated for sure. That was okay in a way, but in another way it was terrible. She would *have* to join the Gaians now. But she didn't want to be a farmer and drag a sack of seed around a field.

"I assumed that was probably it, but there's nothing much to discuss, as I suppose *you* must realize. The case will proceed as is customary when such allegations are brought. As soon as possible Alexis will be interviewed by a Hefn." Lexi's mouth fell open. Interviewed by a Hefn! Oh—because a Hefn could read her thoughts and know if she was telling the truth! But what if the Hefn really were the spawn of Satan! "If her story is confirmed," Pam was saying, "and there's little doubt on that score, her grandfather will also be interviewed, and then assigned to a therapist. Beginning now, and unless or until the therapist signs a release, Mr. Young is forbidden to leave town or to have any contact whatever with his granddaughter, alone, or in the presence of others, or by phone or letter. Lexi will get counseling too, of course."

I will? thought Lexi. *I don't want counseling. I just want it to stop, I don't want to think about it anymore.*

"She'll continue working if she likes, but if she doesn't want to live at home when the show is shooting at the studio, she won't have to. We'll place her in appropriate custody till she changes her mind about that, if she does. Her parents can see her whenever they like, assuming they don't impede her therapy, so on location and on the set her mother can continue to serve as the responsible adult."

Brother Parker looked ready to explode. "Alexis Allred is an LDS child. I protest your forcing her to submit to an interview with a Hefn, and I protest your assuming jurisdiction over her."

Pam's voice got louder and firmer. "If the LDS Church had acted to protect her, the Gaians would not have been obliged to intervene, and you and I wouldn't be having this conversation." Lexi saw Pam lock eyes with her adversary. "I've advised you before, Mr. Parker, that it would be in everyone's best interests for the Church to report cases of this nature to the Gaian Mission as soon as they become known. The bishops could be making a much more vigorous effort to find out whether abuse is going on in their wards, and I suggest again that you demonstrate some leadership to that end. It's not as if there were very many kids for them to keep track of."

"I don't need you to lecture me on my duties, Ms. Pruitt," said Brother Parker in a tight voice.

"And I don't enjoy lecturing you," Pam replied (not quite truthfully, Lexi could tell), "but as long as the Church puts its image above the welfare of its children, the leadership exposes itself to reprimand."

"I do not accept that Hefn authority over the Church is legitimate," he replied. "Most particularly, I do not accept it in light of the performance I witnessed on this morning's newscast." He smiled thinly as Pam acknowledged this thrust by failing to parry it, and pressed his advantage: "Another time, perhaps, you might care to explain why I should defer to their authority on *any* moral issue. The fact that I'm forced to submit to their power has no bearing whatever on their morality—or on our own. Phone off."

Pam blinked at the blanked screen. "Nice shooting, you old mud turtle," she murmured. "I should have anticipated that."

"What was he talking about?" Lexi asked anxiously.

Pam swiveled her chair around to look at her charge. "The Hefn Humphrey was on the TV news this morning. He got upset yesterday at what some people said to him and kind of blew his stack." She smiled as she said this, as if it wasn't very important. "Nobody looks too good having a tantrum, do they?"

Lexi smiled back, but anxiously. "Is Humphrey the one that's going to interview me?"

Pam's eyebrows went up. "As a matter of fact, I guess he is. Don't worry," she added quickly, seeing Lexi's frightened face, "he's a friend of mine, you won't mind talking to him. Actually, he's coming here to Salt Lake today—I forgot all about it in the general uproar."

Lexi said quickly, "I don't want any counseling. I don't want to talk anymore about what happened." At this Pam looked thoughtful; but before she could reply Lexi said, "Can I ask some questions about the Gaians?"

Pam hesitated—Lexi could almost *see* her wondering whether to push the counseling question—then sighed and stretched. "Sure. I'm going to make myself a sandwich—want one?"

"I'm still too stuffed from breakfast."

"Come on in the kitchen with me anyway. We can talk in there."

When Lexi perched herself on the hard kitchen chair, she winced. Without saying anything, Pam shook two pills out of a bottle and brought her a glass of water to take them with; and then, briefly, she squeezed the back of Lexi's neck. While Lexi swallowed the pills, making a face, Pam opened a cupboard and took out an end of bread and some odd-looking brown stuff in a bowl ("soy butter," she explained) and a glass canning jar of jelly ("red currant") and started putting it all together. "What do you want to know?"

"That poster in there." Lexi pointed at the ecstatic seed-bag carriers and the mule driver. "Do all the Gaians have to be farmers?"

"No, though quite a few of them are. Or heavy-duty gardeners. Do you know the story of how the Gaian movement got started?"

If the book had said, Lexi didn't remember. She shook her head.

"Let's see if I can give you the nutshell version. Okay: before the Hefn came, human activity was destroying the Earth. When the Hefn got here they were outraged, and started in right away to make us clean up our act. The main problem was too many people, so they ordered us to slow down the birthrate, and when we didn't, that's when they made the Broadcast that imposed the Baby Ban."

Lexi nodded; she knew the LDS version of that story.

"Afterwards Humphrey formed the Bureau of Temporal Physics, to train human Apprentices to use the time transceivers—I was an Apprentice, that's how I got to know him. The idea was that we could use the transceivers to look back through our prehistory and try to locate a time when people were living in harmony with the Earth. Then we could observe them and copy what they did. Well, turns out the magic moment, at different times but everywhere, was just when hunting and gathering was being supplemented in important ways by agriculture. We call that moment the Crux. A crux is a crisis, a turning point." Pam sliced her sandwich in half, put it on a plate, put the plate on the table. She poured herself a glass of cider from a ceramic whisky jug.

"So then the Hefn recruited and trained a group of missionaries, to go around the world converting people to responsible stewardship on the Crux model. Not that many of them could actually be hunters and gathers now, obviously. What the missionaries did was help each convert to develop a relationship with one special piece of Ground, with a capital G. But you know about that part, right? Jaime told me *you* wanted to be a missionary." She sat down across from the girl and smiled at her before picking up a sandwich half and biting into it.

Lexi wasn't quite so sure anymore. "Well. I might. I read a book about it once."

"*A Bit of Earth*, by Beatrice Trace? A book for kids?"

"Yeah. 'Might I have a bit of earth'—that's what Mary Lennox says in *The Secret Garden*."

Pam glanced up at Lexi with respect; the girl had effortlessly assumed a British accent and another sad child's wistfulness. "Wow, you *are* a good actor! That's right. *A Bit of Earth* is a pretty old book, but it's a good one." She took another bite.

Lexi felt confused. "So—does that mean missionaries *do* have to be farmers?"

Mouth full, Pam shook her head. She made the bite go down with a swig of cider. "Not necessarily, but they do have to be Elementals, and Elementals tend to end up being farmers, or hunters, or herbalists, or something of the sort." Seeing Lexi's bewilderment, Pam put her sandwich down and leaned her forearms on the table. "Here's how it works. For the past ten years or so, Gaian stewards have been divided into five groups of specialists: Mentals, Elementals, Temperamentals, Sentimentals, and Sacramentals, corresponding loosely to the intellectual, physical, psychological, emotional, and spiritual aspects of experience. Any of those can be good Gaians, but if you're going to *convert* people to connect intensely with the Earth—and that's the job our missionaries do—you need to be passionate about growing food, and be able to stir that passion up in people who've never felt it before."

Lexi pictured the white-capped red sandstone formations in the Needles district of Canyonlands. She pictured various dramatic spots along the Mormon Trail, where episodes of *A Thousand Miles* had been filmed, and felt rebellious. "What if you just, like, love being out in nature? Isn't nature Gaia?"

"A passion for nature's important, all right, but by itself it isn't practical enough. Same with a passion for growing orchids, say, or training guide dogs. People have to eat, and they have to learn how to provide themselves with food and raw materials in such a way that the Earth isn't damaged in the process. More than that, they have to *want* food and goods to be produced that way, what we call 'sustainably,' so much that they're willing to pay the extra cost in money and work. The Hefn will lift the Baby Ban when that happens and not before."

"Oh!" So *that* was the connection between the Gaians and the Ban.

"If you decide you want to be a missionary after all, and if you pass the test, permaculture farming will be a big part of your training. You'll also learn to use a bow and a blowgun, and to fish and set snares. Those are missionaries being trained, on that poster out there."

"Oh," said Lexi again, disappointed and rather dismayed. "I didn't know that. The book didn't say that."

"It's an old book," Pam repeated. "But there are Elementals who are neither missionaries *nor* farmers, and four other types of Gaians to be. And they're all excellent stewards. Steward is our word for member. Tell you what. There's a recruitment disk in the library, made back when we used to sign missionaries up as sixth-graders. I saw it in there just the other day. If you watch that, it'll answer your questions a lot better than I can." She started to get up.

Lexi could tell Pam wanted her to go and play the disk now. To keep her talking a little bit longer she cast about—like Liam, had she known it—for another question to ask. "Um, that book said every Gaian has a special piece of Ground, like Mary's was the Secret Garden? What's yours?"

The ploy worked; Pam settled back in her chair. "A place in Kentucky. A long way from here."

"What's it like?"

"Big. Hilly and woodsy, right on the Ohio River bank. When I lived there I used to keep goats and bees."

"Why don't you live there now?"

"Oh—lots of reasons." Pam sighed, then smiled at Lexi. "I'll probably be going back to visit in about six weeks, though. It'll be nice—the very start of spring. Not much like Utah. Lots of rain."

"Don't you miss it?"

"Mm-hm, I do. It's hard on Gaians, being away from their Ground for months at a time. Mine is a Hot Spot, too—you know about Hot

Spots, don't you? There's enough of those down in southern Utah, in the big parks. Midwestern Hot Spots are great training sites for farm-challenged missionary wannabes. Nothing like a Hot Spot to help bring out the dormant farmer in people."

"What's 'dormant' mean?"

"It means a quality that's inside a person, but is still asleep. Being in a Hot Spot can wake it up."

"Oh." Lexi had gone on vacation trips to some of the big Utah parks—Canyonlands, Escalante, Zion, San Rafael—but she'd never heard of a hot spot. They were all pretty hot spots except in winter, but Pam wasn't talking about weather. She shook her head. "I don't know what they are."

"I think the disk goes into that. Let's go find it, okay? Then, whatever you don't understand, I'll try to explain later." Pam drained her glass and stood up.

Seeing the conversation was really over for now, Lexi said "Okay," slid carefully off her chair, and followed Pam into the library.

~

The disk began with a shot of a group of kids in overalls standing in a small field (*Another cornfield!* thought Lexi; but it turned out to be a big midsummer garden interplanted with corn, bush beans, and pumpkins, very lush and pretty), singing a spirited song called "Gaia Is Our Ground." They ran through a couple of verses and then started humming, all together now, in time to the music, slowly raising and lowering both arms straight out from their sides like bird or angel wings, in some kind of salute, with thumbs holding both middle fingers down and indexes and pinkies spread wide like horns. Lexi was thinking what a bunch of dweebs they looked like, doing that, when a Hefn walked out on his strange stumpy legs to stand between the choir and the camera. "My name is Humphrey," he said. "These young people are Gaian missionaries in training. And this . . . is Gaia." His arms waved out in a wide gesture; the camera swooped rapidly back from Humphrey, garden, river valley, forest and continent, until a blue-and-white Planet Earth filled the whole screen.

Humphrey, who was going to interview her! "Stop! Rewind!" Lexi commanded; and then, where the camera had zoomed in for a clasp,

"Okay, pause." Leaning close, she studied the strange face, bearded below and covered everywhere else with short gray hair, the eyes large, opaque, and flat, without pupils. Humphrey.

"Play," she said presently, and again the alien made his sweeping, two-armed gesture and the picture zoomed back to show the globe of the world. Lexi nodded, a terse, professional nod. The production values seemed pretty good to her, but seeing so many kids the same age together in one place felt weird. That alone told you the disk hadn't been made very recently.

The first part of the program was all clever, colorful graphics, illustrating how every part of the field she had seen was connected to every other part at the microscopic level. You could follow a bacterium named Rod as it bustled around breaking down some goat manure dug into the soil, another named Eeco inside the small intestine of a deer mouse, a molecule of methane (Pugh) in the same mouse's intestine, a water molecule (Hoh), the egg of a honeybee (Bea), a grain of zucchini pollen, (Polly), or two dozen other molecules.

The disk was interactive, you were supposed to tell it what to show you. Lexi said "Hoh" and watched the water molecule, in mad career, evaporate from the surface of the broad river flowing beside the field, condense in a cloud, fall among the cornstalks as rain, percolate up through the soil (right past busy Rod and lots of munching earthworms) into the root hair of a pokeweed, lose its hydrogen atom to a starch molecule and exit through a pore on the underside of a leaf to be inhaled by a red-tailed hawk, and on and on. Then she tried Bea, and got a lesson on pollination, bumping into Eeco, Hoh, and Pugh in the course of that story.

Whatever you chose, in fact, you encountered the other characters and finished up with a view of the whole field, where the tangled-up trajectories of Hoh, Eeco, Rod and the rest appeared as swirling trails of light, each a different color, the chosen character of the moment brighter than the rest. Different kids did the voiceovers—way too brightly—but the script was interesting and clear. She realized she was enjoying the program and was glad Pam had persuaded her to play it.

The next part showed what happened to all these characters when unnatural things—air pollution, chemical fertilizers, pesticides and herbicides, and the sweet corn whose genes had been tweaked to withstand them—took over the field. Again you had a choice of whose fate to follow, but the stories were a lot shorter. An insecticide, brought back to the hive on a corn-pollen grain, poisoned Bea while she was just a little comma-shaped white larva. Rod starved because no organic material had been added to the soil. The deer mouse got sick from eating some corn full of pesticide molecules; being sick slowed him down and the hawk caught and ate him— and the following spring laid eggs with shells so thin they broke. A robin ate some poisoned worms and died having seizures. Rainwater full of chemicals ran off the field, whose soil had too little organic material to soak it up, and polluted the river. One way or another, everything died.

The conclusion displayed the chemicals too as lines of light; but instead of swirling and returning, in the jolly "sustainable" way of the cast of living characters, the chemicals moved in only one direction. More always had to be brought to the field over the polluted river, and the soil became more and more sterile apart from its monocrop of gigantic, unnatural corn.

Production values in this part of the program were also good. The villainous chemicals came across as gross, really hideous, not cute little Frankenstein's monsters or Draculas but very well drawn all the same. It was hard to do that—make something ugly yet interesting. The program obviously wasn't a balanced presentation of anything; the people who made it didn't want you to think carefully about what they were saying, they wanted you to feel upset and angry. They wanted you to stop resenting the Hefn for not letting food be grown that way anymore, and be grateful. It was a hard sell, just like the Church's, and just as good a job. But nothing she saw in the program moved Lexi like the idea of a secret garden had moved her in *A Bit of Earth*.

The next part, on genetic engineering, was shorter but scarier. The Hefn had stopped gene modification too, of course, but they couldn't undo what had already happened before they arrived. There was a pesticide called Bee tee, for instance—a noble-looking medieval foot soldier in green chain mail on Lexi's screen—that farmers had sprayed on their crops for years. Bt was a soil bacterium, acceptable to organic farmers as well as to agribiz types. The program showed armies of green-mailed soldiers with broadswords being launched into a cornfield from a mechanical sprayer. It zoomed in on one group of them crouched in the forest of silks sprouting from the top of an ear of corn, while a gigantic striped dragon-caterpillar rippled up the husk toward them on its many stumpy feet. Another zoom, and Lexi could watch the caterpillar's mouth parts chomp and swallow chunks of corn silk along with dozens of Bt soldiers, rather like the whale swallowing a bunch of green Jonahs. Once inside, the soldiers energetically poked their swords again and again into the caterpillar's stomach walls. The poking paralyzed its gut, it stopped eating and soon died, as did those who had killed it. The program showed caterpillar, soldiers, and all decomposing harmlessly into the soil at the foot of the cornstalk.

But for twenty years before the Hefn came, more and more farmers had stopped spraying Bt. Instead they bought seed potatoes, and corn, soybean, and canola seed, from a chemical company that had spliced bewildered-looking Bt soldiers—these not so much grass-green as neon chartreuse—right into the genomes of the seed. This meant that clouds of corn pollen, and insect-borne pollen from the bean and rapeseed fields, even from the little lavender flowers potatoes make, every grain of it containing Bt in its genes, was abundantly loose in the world already, with results nobody could foresee. "Because," said Humphrey in voiceover, "it is impossible to be certain, from experiments done under controlled conditions, how a substance will behave when released into Gaia's indescribable and unimaginable complexity, where everything affects everything."

The Bt bacterium for instance, instead of breaking down quickly as it had done when farmers sprayed it on their crops, began building up in the soil; you could see the neon armies reassembling, alive and well and looking for something to do. Nobody had foreseen that, nobody knew why it was happening or what it would mean. (Lexi knew, from her longer perspective, that it hadn't meant anything much, but also that if the Hefn hadn't come and put Monsanto out of business, things might have been different. Not even the Church tried to deny that. Pollen drift from Chinese poplars engineered for rapid growth had produced sterile, brittle, commercially useless lumber in Church-owned forests far from China.) The segment ended with a group of white-coated scientists, peering through microscopes and fooling with lab equipment, slowly dissolving into a group of children playing with guns and grenades.

Now Humphrey, still surrounded by organic cornstalks, was back onscreen. "Once upon a time," he said, "there was a girl who loved a piece of ground." The camera shifted, keeping Humphrey in view to one side, but focusing on someone else, a girl older than Lexi, climbing up a path above the garden toward a house. The river rolled at her back, an enormous expanse of water, dwarfing Utah's Jordan River and the creeks in the mountains east of Salt Lake. Lexi leaned forward, caught by the beauty of the scene and pierced with momentary envy for the girl. Who was she—an actor, or just one of the missionary recruits, walking through the part? "The girl's name was Pam," said Humphrey's voice (he was outside the picture now) "and the place was called Hurt Hollow.

"There was no Gaian Movement when Pam was a child, but there have always been people who thought and felt the way the Gaians think and feel, and Hurt Hollow had been lived into by such people for fifty years. Pam's home was nearby, and she visited Hurt Hollow as often as she could."

Lived *into*? Lexi ran the disk back a bit, to be sure she'd heard that right, and Humphrey said it again. A special Gaian term, then. Lived in a place so long you were connected really deeply with it—something like that?

The distant climber onscreen had turned away toward a smaller building not quite so high up the hill as the house, and now the camera angle shifted to the little building, so the viewers could watch the girl approach. From the front, and close-up, Lexi saw that this Pam was older than she'd thought, and was startled to see large breasts under Pam's enormous sweatshirt. The girl wasn't even a little bit pretty, her shoulder-length hair was mousy and straight and she had a big nose; but beautiful, blond, neatly built Lexi was somehow not put off by any of this.

"It was at Hurt Hollow," said Humphrey's voice, "that Pam learned the ideas and mastered the skills that help a person live into a piece of ground." Lexi registered that, unlike the missionary kids, the Hefn was actually a very good actor. (She decided she had guessed right about the peculiar term.) "The kind man who lived there kept goats, and taught Pam to care for them . . . feed and milk them . . . make butter and cottage cheese and yogurt from their milk . . . and compost their manure to fertilize the garden."

Onscreen, Pam had fastened a nanny goat's head in a kind of clamp, given her a pan of something to eat, and was washing her heavy udder with a cloth she slopped several times in a bowl of water. Murmuring to the animal, Pam crouched on a stool and grasped two of the teats. Her hands moved; thin white jets of milk clattered into a pail . . . Lexi sat bolt upright. Goats! *Pam!* This was Ms. Pruitt, a long time ago, and this place by the big river, with Pugh and Eeco and the rest, was her Ground!

"He kept bees, and taught Pam how to care for them and how to take the surplus honey off the hive," Humphrey's voice declared. And there was Pam (presumably) in a white coverall and helmet and veil, moving within a cloud of bees. A moment later there was Pam, straining milk through a cloth. Then, in rapid succession: picking blackberries; laying tomatoes into a bucket; stirring a big kettle and pouring red sauce through a funnel into glass jars; turning a pile of garbage with a pitchfork; pulling a string of fish into a long squared-off rowboat; pouring honey onto a big slab of cornbread.

"From this kind man, Jesse Kellum—from his instruction, but most of all from his example—Pam learned that everything at Hurt Hollow was connected to everything else, that every least part of Gaia is essential to the whole."

And there was Pam herself—not an actor or missionary, just an older girl, a plain person—hunkered on a low chair in the wooden house, one hand holding the other wrist, speaking directly to the camera for the first time. "Everything here at Hurt Hollow is connected to everything else," she stated, repeating Humphrey's words in a voice Lexi recognized. "The garden and the goats are watered by rain, or the creek or river. Turnips and corn from the garden feed the goats, manure from the goats fertilizes the garden, the crops and goat milk, and what we make from it, feed us . . . and, eventually, the goats feed us too. The bees drink creek and river water, gather nectar and pollen from the garden and the trees and wild plants, and raise more bees and make enough extra honey for us to have plenty too. They pollinate the garden and the orchard so we get beans, pumpkins, melons, berries, apples, cucumbers—everything that makes a flower in order to develop a seed-bearing fruit. The corn is wind-pollinated but the bees love corn pollen and gather that too.

"Every year we save enough seed for the next year's crop. All the weeds and husks and skins, everything we don't eat, gets composted and goes back into the garden. We compost our own wastes too—very carefully—along with the parts of the fish and groundhogs and deer that we don't eat. *Everything's connected*, you can see it and feel it, just on this one small piece of land. Hurt Hollow is exactly like the world, just as complicated and just as simple. It's a lot of work to live like this, but if you love doing this kind of work—being part of the cycle of sustainability—then you don't mind. Farming can be pure drudgery, I guess, if you try to grow the wrong things for where you live, or grow too much of just one thing, or don't rotate your crops or take more out of the soil than you put back in. But for me it's always been a joy." At the word *joy* her earnest expression was broken by a look that was, indeed, so joyous it was impossible to doubt her.

Lexi sat in a tumble of emotions. This wasn't just acting, reading a script. This was a person talking straight from the heart about something she cared about passionately. The only other place Lexi had ever seen that look and felt that passion was at church sometimes, when people were bearing their testimonies; and she saw for the first time that being a Gaian was a religious thing, like being LDS, and that Gaian missionaries were real missionaries, no more and no less than Mormon ones, doing the same kind of job.

The disk played on, Humphrey pulling the cartoon lesson about Gaia's tiny, interconnected building blocks together with Pam's "testimony," while Lexi thought furiously. She still didn't want to be a farmer (though the goats were great). But she wanted terribly to care about *something* as much as Pam cared about Hurt Hollow, with a heart that open and a joy that real.

When the disk ran out she reported back to Pam. "There wasn't anything about Hot Spots."

"No?" Pam glanced up at the clock. "I've got a couple hours' more work to do here. Tell you what. How about stretching out in the records room and taking a nap? And then I think you'd better come home with me for tonight. There's plenty of room, and we can talk about Hot Spots over dinner if you like." She flashed a grin. "You can give me pointers on my acting."

Right in the middle of this speech Lexi had felt her face being distorted by an enormous yawn. The thought of going home with this lean person, Pam, with the chopped-off hair and big bosom, who could milk a goat, and had enjoyed bawling out Brother Parker on the phone, appealed to her so much, and made her feel so much relief, that falling asleep on the cot a minute later was as easy as floating to the bottom of a well.

~

Pam was tired, Lexi must surely be exhausted despite her nap, both were deeply disturbed, but life goes on. At five o'clock Pam, followed by Lexi, got off the Ninth East streetcar at the end of her street and retrieved her skis and poles from the clamps attached to the side. The long, narrow skis were clipped together with rubber ski bones; she put them on her shoulder and gave Lexi the poles to carry. "It's just a block from here. Are you hungry again yet? I wonder what I've got in the house that we can heat up for dinner."

"I'm starving," Lexi admitted. "*Now* I'm starving. I could eat a horse."

"Do you like spaghetti?" Lexi nodded. "Good. I canned a zillion quarts of spaghetti sauce last summer. It's not fancy but there's lots of it. Oh, and my duck started laying last week. Eggs and pancakes for breakfast."

"You have a *duck*?"

"Mm-hm. Two ducks. I raised a few last spring to keep the snails down, and then I thought I'd bring a pair through the winter so they could breed me a new batch for this year."

"What happened to the other ones from last year?"

"I gave one pair to Jaime. He's got more room than I do. The others, well, I butchered and ate them. They weren't pets, Lexi," Pam said at her guest's horrified look. "I realize people do have pet ducks nowadays, people keep just about every animal smaller than a woolly mammoth as a pet, but my ducks were livestock."

Lexi walked a few paces. "But . . . what was it like to kill them?"

"Awful," said Pam promptly. "It was awful. It was so awful I decided to stick to things like eggs and honey from now on, where you don't have to kill anything in order to reap the harvest. Somebody has to do it, though. I butchered a goat once, a long time ago when I was tougher. Here we are." She turned in at the house and mounted the front steps, Lexi in tow. "Let's just put this stuff here in the rack for now."

There were lights on inside. "Do your ducks have names?" Lexi was asking when the door opened and she made a startled squeak. Pam turned and found herself looking into Humphrey's shaggy face.

He pushed open the storm door with one hand; in the other he held a bowl and spoon, and the beard around his mouth was purple. "I see you found the cobbler," she said. "Humphrey, this is Alexis Allred. Lexi, this is the Hefn Humphrey. I expect you two have seen each other on the telly."

~

It turned out that Humphrey had been following *A Thousand Miles* quite faithfully, and knew all about Kate and Jason and their adventures. Lexi, on the other hand, had never been allowed to watch Humphrey's reports or news conferences or to see his movie, *The Hob*—or anything at all except the missionary training disk, today—and was as nervous about being this close to him as if he were a ferocious uncaged zoo animal that somebody had said wouldn't hurt her.

At first. By the time dinner was over, and both Pam's guests had red circles of spaghetti sauce around their mouths, Lexi had forgotten her fear. Humphrey hadn't asked Pam what the girl was doing in her house. He merely chatted about the show and the weather, and finally remarked, "It is fine to sit at a table beside a child again, don't you agree, my dear? It puts me in mind of the time when you and Liam and the others first came to Washington, when the Bureau of Temporal Physics was only beginning. And of the first classes of missionaries, such very young children they were, do you remember? Those were hopeful times."

Pam remembered. "Lexi thinks she might like to take the test in 2039 and become a missionary, but she's not too crazy about farming so she's not sure just how that'll all work out."

Humphrey dropped his fork, which clanged on his plate, and made the jerky flapping gesture Jaime had imitated on Pam's message tape. "*No,*" he said; and the metallic "alien" voice stopped Pam's heart. He repeated at once in his "human" one, as if translating: "No. No. *I* am not sure just how it will all work out, but it will not work out like that. Lexi will not become a missionary in 2039. No more missionaries are to be recruited. There is no more time. The Gaian solution has failed. My dear," he said, and gripped Pam's hand in his own forked hairy hands, "that is what I have come to tell you, that we have *failed.*"

Pam's Journal

17 February 2037, Tuesday, SLC. Something happened today that brought back the events of April '14 with gut-grinding force. I was attacked by a mob—I and Jaime and a dozen or so other Gaians, in Temple Square. Jaime had four teeth knocked out; I've got two black eyes and a broken nose. Eight hours later my hands are still shaking so bad it's hard to hit the right keys.

All day yesterday, while Jaime and I were absorbed in Alexis Allred's abuse case, that recording of Humphrey's freakout was playing on the telly over and over, all around the world. I'd seen a little bit of it in the morning but then I was at work all day, and brought Lexi home with me, and Humphrey was here when we got here. So I didn't realize till Jaime woke me this morning what had been happening.

The only thing on the telly was live coverage of mass demonstrations: London, Chicago, Beijing, Tokyo, Moscow, Rome, DC, Tel Aviv, Rio, Dar es Salaam, the capital cities of Burundi and Malawi, all over Central and South America. People yelling, marching, brandishing signs: EARTH FOR HUMANITY! NO MORE THREATS! WE DEMAND OUR RIGHTS! HEFN GO TO HELL! Lots of blown-up pictures of babies. Here and there an actual child carrying a sign: MORE KIDS LIKE ME! An entire globeful of frightened, angry, frustrated hecklers.

Jaime had decided to organize a counter-demonstration and had phoned to clear it with me, but that was just a courtesy, anything of that nature is his call. I would probably have done the same in his place, like hundreds of other mission gafrs licking their wounds tonight and wondering what in God's name they were thinking of. Certainly it never occurred to me to try to talk him out of it, in fact I rushed around and got dressed, and went down there to help Maddie make some signs, while he rallied the troops.

Whoever could get there gathered in the Mission office around noon and headed downtown, a colorful little cohort all wearing teal and tan—Jaime had decided we should be in uniform, or in sashes and straw hats at least, to enhance the visibility of what was a pretty small bunch compared to the crowds of anti-Hefn demonstrators. I wore my BTP uniform with a Gaian sash. We'd made these signs: GAIA IS OUR GROUND, pictures of Earth from space, things like that. There were cops all over the place, and I started to feel a tad bit nervous when I realized what a lot of people had turned out, but we represented the authority of the Hefn, after all, and it didn't occur to me for quite a while that we might be in danger.

The closer we got to Temple Square, though, the denser the crowd and the more people cursing and shouting hateful things, and I was shocked to realize that the mere sight of us infuriated people so much that, had the police not been there to hold them back, we might have been assaulted. Along about then I started to wonder if the counter-demonstration had been a mistake, and so did Jaime, but we couldn't very well slink away, we'd been too successful at being visible.

It happened just after we'd passed through the gates on South Temple. There was a big crowd of people in Temple Square, listening to a speaker and all holding baby-picture signs overprinted with LET THE WAITING SPIRITS COME! and BE FRUITFUL AND MULTIPLY AND REPLENISH THE EARTH. A forest of defiant babies. They were blocking our way, and as we started to pass through the middle of the group, several men threw their signs down and went for us.

We were dumbfounded. Like with the bear, I just could not believe they were actually charging toward us and actually intended to hurt us. Attacking a Gaian is the next worst thing to attacking a Hefn, but something just snapped in those people, the way something just snapped in Humphrey, and suddenly we were in an actual fistfight, and way, way outnumbered. More and more of the baby-picture gang joined the fracas. The speaker shouted and shouted for them to stop, but things got out of control very fast. Before the police broke it up—and I bet the cameras confirm that they looked the other way for a bit before wading in—our people had gotten absolutely beaten to a pulp. Split lips, torn ears, fractures, bruises and contusions, blood all over the place. Josh and Simon are still in the hospital, concussed. They knocked us down and pummeled and stomped on every single one of us. If the cops hadn't finally broken it up, I really believe they would have killed us all.

It was the same almost everywhere Gaians came out to oppose the demonstrations: the crowds would not tolerate any sign of support for the Hefn. It's amazing that nobody anywhere got shot or stabbed.

From here it couldn't possibly be plainer that we should all have kept out of sight today, and let the crowds vent some of their frustration just massing and yelling. By showing up—in uniform!— what did we do but offer them a tempting target? Why, oh why didn't somebody foresee that? Liam and I were in the meeting house at Carrie's funeral, we if anyone should have understood the depth of fury those hecklers represented. But Liam was grieving and had Eddie with him, and all *my* attention, then and later, was on Humphrey.

We were warned and ignored the warning. It's inexcusable. What did we think we were doing, marching *right into Temple Square* like a smug little troop of Junior Woodchucks?

We've all fallen into the habit of assuming nobody would dare to risk challenging the Hefn, meaning us, in the clear light of day. Today we were challenged by thousands. How can a handful of Hefn locate and punish all those people? And if they can't, will the implications be lost on anybody? A lot of arrests were made, in the interest of crowd control, but local law enforcement won't turn those people over for mindwipe, they just won't, and who can blame them.

We Salt Lake Gaians made the local, national, and world news, our casualties being especially impressive and Mormons vs. Gaians always being worth a sound bite or two. They interviewed the guy who threw the first punch, at the police station; *he* wasn't hurt at all, and sure enough he was LDS. *They were taunting us,* he said, *they were just begging for it!* The Hefn could make an example of *him,* but what earthly good would that do?

Our side fought back, pretty well in fact—the wounded from both sides were in the ER together, glowering across the waiting room at each other—but not me, I just stood there in sheer disbelief till somebody punched me out, which they did almost right away.

A nurse packed my nose to stop the bleeding. The damn thing is the color and size of a rubber clown's nose; I'm supposed to put an icepack on it for 20 minutes every couple of hours. At least my eyes aren't swollen shut, like Ariel's.

When I shut *my* eyes I'm 14, I'm hiving a swarm at Hurt Hollow, and Otie's mob is sweeping past the bee yard wearing that same frenzied look, to capture Humphrey and torture him, and Liam and I can't do a thing to make them stop. A tornado ex machina and Hefn thought control resolved that situation. What's going to resolve this one?

Humphrey was right. The Gafr are right. The Mission has failed.

18 February 2037, Wednesday, SLC. He must have known already, at Carrie's service, that the Gafr in their wisdom had declared the Gaian effort a failure. Which helps explain why he threw the fit that caused this global uproar.

When he suddenly announced the decision over dinner, to me and Lexi Allred, I was full of protests: Whaddya mean "failed"? What the hell are they talking about?

Jaime is sick about what happened as a result of our pathetic counter-demonstration. His jaws are wired shut over his four reimplanted teeth, but he's been sending messages of apology to everybody, even the guys arrested for beating us up, even the police.

How the Hefn are responding to it is, they've published a list, with photos and full ID, of exactly one hundred people known beyond any doubt to have assaulted and beaten Gaians last Monday somewhere in the world. At least one Gaian-beater from every riot site except Tehran and Kabul (too many people willing to commit suicide) will be scapegoated. Systematically hunted down, no matter how long it takes. Anyone caught obstructing the process will be swept up in the net with the others. Minds will be probed as deemed necessary, no exceptions. They've already got thirteen of them. In the end I expect they'll catch them all, and it won't surprise me if they all get wiped. It probably wouldn't be any different even if Humphrey were awake.

Our fault, our fault, our fault. We incited them to riot, out of sheer stupidity. No: our *failure*—and not just of judgment on Monday, or failure to keep in touch with how regular people feel. What we've been doing *has not worked*! Not nearly well enough. If we can't figure out how to become more effective we are sunk, the Baby Ban will never be lifted.

For that matter, should the Gafr entirely lose patience they could still exterminate us all.

3 March 2037, Tuesday, SLC. The First Presidency of the Church has denounced the rioting and officially apologized to the Gaians, but has also expressed outrage about the arrest of the two LDS attackers who made the scapegoat list. The church's position is that local law enforcement should handle the case. As it would, had anybody but us Hefn stooges been the victims. Bro. Parker called to deliver the apology personally, a pretty galling business for me, since we both knew our going out there on 2/17 was foolish and he didn't bother to conceal his satisfaction about our error, and also because it's impossible to be dignified and imposing when you look the way I do right now.

They're holding 39 men and 3 women at Thingvellir, names on the hit list plus a few accomplices. Amazing how quickly they collared that many. People are starting to turn themselves in, to spare their friends and relatives from being probed. Globally the mood's swinging away from frenzy toward fear, and the uproar has died down to an upmutter.

In other words, by acting swiftly and ruthlessly the Hefn have regained the upper hand, for now. I purely hate what they're doing, but it's been much more effective than I would have believed.

Unlike the Gaian Mission. I'm obsessed with the Gaian Mission's fatal lack of broader appeal.

Humphrey stirred up this hornets' nest, then went straight to the moon to hibernate; he doesn't even know what an upheaval he caused. (He'll say it was the hecklers that caused it when he finds out.) Palfrey and Jeffrey have been running the manhunt, along with their army of hired goons. Alfrey isn't talking to anybody just yet, but I had a voice-only message from him a week ago: "You must come to Hurt Hollow. Humphrey wished it before the disturbance; now he would insist." So I'm going for certain, hopefully with something useful to say. I'm glad, I guess.

The Apprentices on active duty turned out to demonstrate with the Santa Barbara Gaians, but people out there are used to seeing the uniforms, and the Hefn presence is a heavy reality in SB, ergo nobody got assaulted. I'm the only one who'll arrive at the conference with two purplish-yellow eyes and a tender nose.

Obviously our conference can now be about one thing only. Somehow in the next few weeks we have to come up with a plan. We *have* to. Liam tells me several Apprentices are very resistant to abandoning the old Mission, Artie especially. They've been arguing. Artie's such a pure mathematician, the notion that something perfect in concept has to *work* to be valid is hard for him to wrap his mind around.

13 March 2037, Friday SLC. Something Lexi Allred's counselor said when we met yesterday started me thinking. We were discussing the Mormons, why they'd been so wildly successful when so many startup religions of the 19th century eventually petered out. Amy thinks the history—Joseph Smith's martyrdom, Brigham Young's genius, the incredible hardships the pioneers endured—are the stuff of legend, extremely attractive to certain types of people. I think it's more than that, but their history is mighty compelling. At Amy's suggestion, I ordered up half a dozen episodes of that series Lexi acts in, *A Thousand Miles*, and spent the last two evenings viewing them.

It's very impressive, Jaime was right. Story, writing, acting, all first-rate. Lexi's really wonderful in her part. It ought to be a family show, that's how it would have been billed when I was a kid in a family. Watching it, I gradually became aware, in a way I hadn't before, that the problem's not just that there aren't any children now, it's also that there aren't any young *families*. I'm no more immune to the myth of the happy family than anybody else, I found myself guiltily pining for what I was watching on the screen: two devoted parents and their son and daughter, forming a warm center within this larger community on the move.

Humphrey and I took eleven-year-old kids, kids Lexi's age, out of their homes and families to train them for mission work at powerful Hot Spots like Hurt Hollow. There were good reasons for it, but now I'm wondering for the first time whether that policy mightn't have hurt the movement somehow.

Traditionally, Mormon missionaries leave home at 18, to do mission work for two years and then go back home, get married, and settle into normal life. It's not a lifetime commitment. Our kids went into the mystico-agricultural equivalent of a monastery. Think about this.

19 March 2037, Thursday, SLC. Everybody on the hit list is now in custody. They're holding 112 rioters and accessories at Thingvellir. Yesterday the Hefn pronounced the sentence we all feared: mindwipe to the age of three.

We—Apprentices, gafrs, stewards—immediately threw ourselves into arguing that the Gaian counter-demonstrators are to blame for what happened, not their attackers, and that in the circumstances mindwipe is cruel and unusual. Messages urging clemency have been pouring in to Godfrey as the next best mediator—what irony that Humphrey should be sleeping now!—but the Gafr see the Gaians as being mere stand-ins for themselves and the Hefn that day. Which in fact is how the rioters saw us—creatures as close to the aliens as they were able to get at.

The Gafr are adamant that examples must be made. All we've accomplished is to persuade them to make fewer of them. They've agreed to set up a lottery, 112 balls in a tumbling cage, each with a name on it. 25 will be wiped, the rest go free. The victims will appear afterwards in the usual telly display.

Jaime can't stop crying, everybody's sick about it. No matter what happens now, the Gaian Movement will have to live with guilt over this. The way the LDS Church has had to live with the Mountain Meadows Massacre, and still push on.

There is such a thing as being criminally stupid.

CHAPTER 4

Thicker Than Water

27 MARCH 2037

At Hurt Hollow the Ohio River is half a mile wide. Delivered upon its southern bank from the beaches of California, Liam O'Hara drew humid air deep into his lungs and regarded the view before him.

It was one of those mild, pale-blue days of earliest spring in northern Kentucky. From bend to bend in either direction, and all across its great width, the river reflected the color of the sky. So that a person standing on the metal dock at Hurt's Landing beheld a wholly blue world—a blue disturbed only slightly by streaks of thin cloud above, and streaks of a deeper blue in the flat, calm water.

Last year's faded weeds and brambles, and the still-leafless trees, made little impact on this wide world of blue. To Liam, fresh from Santa Barbara, the huge benignity of the prospect felt both deeply appealing and a little unreal. He stood at the end of the dock, remembering the first time he'd ever stepped onto it in his life, almost a quarter of a century before. He and Pam had climbed out of Pam's father's canoe and stood looking, not back at the water, but up the bluff, to the gate in the hurricane fence dividing Jesse Kellum's beautiful, handmade house from the river. And Pam had said, "Hunh, that's weird. The gate's still locked."

Then she had produced a key and unlocked the gate. And they'd passed through together, into the transformed life Liam had been living ever since.

As if summoned by these memories, the living Pam now broke into them. "Alfrey's ready to get started. He sent me to round people up."

Liam turned. Pam stood leaning against one of the posts in the open gateway, hands jammed into the pockets of her parka. "I didn't hear you coming," he said. "I was a million miles away. Wow, your face is an interesting palette of colors, all right. They don't show up nearly as well onscreen." As he spoke he was already mounting toward her, and she was backing away up the hill as he approached. "Close the gate or leave it open?"

"You can lock it. Everybody's here."

In another week the volunteer curators would start arriving to ready the Hollow for summer visitors, but for now they had it to themselves. Obediently he wrapped the chain around gate and post and clicked the padlock shut. "Artie make it?"

"Artie and Will hitched a ride on the chopper with Alfrey, from Louisville. Samantha walked in. Marshall got posted to Washington last night, he'll be here tomorrow, and everybody else came over on the boat with us."

"Samantha *walked* in? Why?"

"Says she never had and always wanted to. The trail's in bad shape; she stuck to the road the whole way down."

"Isn't the road in bad shape too?"

"Not *as* bad." Pam strode steadily up the steep bluff ahead of Liam, head down, voice neutral. They climbed in silence now toward the small, elegantly formed wooden house set well up the bluffside. Smoke billowed from the chimney; somebody had lit a fire. Liam hadn't visited Hurt Hollow in years, but this footpath had once been so familiar under his feet that he felt he could climb it in total darkness if he had to. More slowly though. Pam set a stiff pace; by the time they stepped onto the flagstone patio, Liam was puffing. He turned for a last long look at the blueness and paleness before following her into the house.

The fire, crackling smartly under the beaten copper hood of the fireplace, had taken the chill off the room, and eleven chairs had been arranged to face the hearth, but no one was sitting in them yet. A dozen people and a Hefn were clustered at the tall window, made of many smaller windows, like a honeybee's eye facets, under the high peak of the roof. This composite window faced the river;

they had all been watching Pam and Liam hike up the bluff, and "Now our company is complete," said the Hefn, Alfrey, when the latch clicked behind them. "Let us be seated, and let us begin."

Pam headed for the chair farthest from the fireplace, but Liam took a cozier seat himself, exchanging greetings sotto voce with the newly arrived Artie, Will, and Samantha as everyone sat down. Alfrey let them get settled, not actually tapping his foot but conveying an impression of foot-tapping forbearance in the uncanny way the Hefn were able to do that sort of thing.

Alfrey was, of course, standing in at this gathering for Humphrey, deep in hibernation. There was not a soul in attendance who did not regret this fact; but Humphrey had stayed awake so long, and taken so much Sleepynot, that his body hair had been falling out in clumps and hanks. He had looked like a case of terminal mange before he'd left for the moon. It was possible that his lapse of control at Carrie's memorial service was at least partly a result of his physical condition; and so, desperate times or not, they had to make do with earnest, charmless, humorless Alfrey, fresh and sleek from his own long sleep, in working out how to respond to the worst crisis the Gaian movement had had to face since its inception.

The mood was sober, even queasy. Two days before, the twenty-five rioters selected by lottery had been wiped and displayed, and the images of grown men and women stumbling about, crying in bewilderment like three-year-olds, haunted them all. The sight of wiped humans convicted of crimes against the Hefn had never been easy to deal with, but there hadn't been a public displaying for a long time, and the experience had left the conferees in a funk. They were professionals, determined to do their job to the best of their ability, but at the moment that job was not a source of pride.

Behind Liam, Pam slid low but still felt conspicuous. She'd worked with most of the people in the room and liked them. At one time or another they'd all been Apprentices at the Bureau of Temporal Physics and been trained by Humphrey to operate the time transceivers. And they were all committed Gaians; Apprentices who had not later embraced the Gaian Mission no longer worked for the BTP. But Pam alone, of all the Apprentices ever trained, had lost the math intuition for which they had been selected and by means of which they set the coordinates in placetime so that a window could open into the past.

Hurt Hollow was Pam's Ground. As she'd admitted to Lexi, she missed it more or less constantly. This very house had been her property and even her home for a while. She'd been keen to revisit the place, and wanted desperately to help save the Mission and get the Ban lifted. But being back here in company with the other Apprentices rubbed salt into the wound of her missing gift, and she hadn't anticipated that. The rest were much too preoccupied with the question of how to appease both the fed-up Gafr and fed-up humanity, and too frightened about what would happen if they couldn't, to waste energy pitying her, that was obvious; but she glared at Alfrey anyway, willing him to get the show on the road.

"I am here with you today," said Alfrey obligingly, "because our friend and colleague Humphrey cannot be. Our task is delicate and difficult. The original purpose of our conference, planned long before the riots, is necessarily altered. We are not to discuss missionary recruitment and training, but to 'throw out our agenda.' We are to 'brainstorm.'" The quotation marks around these terms were audible. "All of you are aware that the Gaian Mission as we have known it has been judged a failure by our lords the Gafr, that this judgment was forcefully confirmed by the events of February 17, and that if we cannot find a way to make it more effective the future is uncertain. I will go further. The future is grim. Artie."

Artie Moskowitz had been a dazzling prodigy and was now a deeply committed Gaian, a Mental like all the former Apprentices except for Elemental Pam. She had known him in Santa Barbara before being assigned to Salt Lake, and thought him bristly but brilliant. A lot of the theoretical work on finding the Cruxes, placetimes in prehistory where humans had interacted with their environments in ways that were healthy for both, was his. Now he said, "Look, before we get into the riots I need to be clear about something." Alfrey nodded. "The Gafr declared the Mission a flop even *before* Humphrey freaked out at that funeral, and before all hell broke loose. I want to know why."

"Yes," said Alfrey. "Some weeks preceding the memorial service of Carrie Sharpless. Yet they have doubted for much, much longer. Artie, consider. Consider, all of you, how Humphrey and Godfrey persuaded our lords to be lenient with the people of Earth. Consider that the first generation of missionaries began their work more than twenty years ago. Consider what has been accomplished in those twenty years."

"We found the models," said Artie hotly. "We located Hot Spots galore. We trained missionaries, set up missions worldwide, taught thousands upon thousands of people how to choose and bond with a piece of Ground and support all cultivated ground being worked sustainably. We started a *religion*, for chrissake, or at least revived an ancient one! We made converts all over the world, and we helped enforce the Directive while we were at it. Starting with nothing but an idea, we got all that up and running. So what exactly do the Gafr mean by 'failed'?"

"In numbers," Alfrey replied instantly. "The thousands upon thousands count for too little in a world still populated by some billions, as you, Artie, a fine mathematician, understand very well. How many demonstrators took to the streets on February 17? How many Gaians?" He paused to let that sink in. Artie's face went red and tight. "Also, you know I think the expression 'preaching to the choir'? Not many Gaian converts have truly experienced conversion. Not many minds have truly been changed. Not nearly enough minds. The Gaian mission has been seeking to persuade biological beings to overturn a nature formed through eons of evolution for exploiting, competing, and passing on its genes. Your failure was thus inevitable, and this the Gafr had already come to understand *before* the riots demonstrated their correctness past any possible doubt. The question we are charged to ponder is: What now?"

Artie said tightly, "I get it about preaching to the choir, Alfrey, but it's not like every single person who joined the Gaians was already a card-carrying member of the Nature Conservancy or the Sierra Club! Some people did a one-eighty on this. Not enough people, okay, I admit that, but it's crazy to scrap the whole approach without even trying to improve it!" He laughed bitterly. "The riots have you guys running so scared you're ready to just dump twenty years of good healthy baby out with the bath water."

Several people made faces at the "baby" metaphor. We *are* running scared, Pam thought, and well we should be. Twenty-five people were mindwiped yesterday because of us. Judging by their expressions the others apparently agreed with this; and nobody spoke in support of what Artie had said.

Alfrey stirred. "This baby of twenty years," he said evenly, "is drowned. We must begin anew. Who will speak to this."

Artie snorted, pushed back in his chair, folded his arms. Liam held up his hand, and Pam steeled herself, guessing what was about to happen; Liam knew she'd arrived with a proposal, but not what the proposal involved. "I think we should hear from Pam," he said when Alfrey recognized him. "She's the former Baptist, she's the one that sold Humphrey on the conversion experience concept in the first place."

"Yeah, Pam," put in their old schoolmate Raghu Kanal, "if it works so great for the Christian evangelicals, how come it hasn't worked better for us?"

They had all turned in their chairs to look at her, and Pam was suddenly conscious of her battered appearance. "Well, that's the question," she agreed. "I'd been wondering about that even before the Gafr's verdict, and since the riots I've been thinking about it pretty much nonstop. I've come to some kind of radical conclusions, actually." She glanced at Alfrey. "Should I start now? This will take a while."

A bland gaze. "Yes."

"Okay, here's my analysis." Mentally she squared her shoulders. "Religions and cults typically start with a founder, a charismatic figure who's believed to have had a revelation. Everybody can think of examples: Moses, Jesus, the Buddha, Mohammed, Emmanuel Swedenborg, Mary Baker Eddy, Mother Anne Lee, and, my personal favorite, Joseph Smith." (There were smiles.)

Samantha sat forward. "So James Lovelock would be ours, right? For having the revelation of Gaia?"

Raghu was shaking his head. "Lovelock's actually not a very good example of what Pam's talking about though. His 'revelation' was a eureka moment of scientific insight. He was always saying how surprised he was that so many religious people approached him, while so few scientists took the Gaia hypothesis seriously at all when he first presented it."

"Right," Ellis volunteered. "We derive from his idea, but the religious possibilities were developed by other people, like that woman, what's her name? The one that wrote *Sacred Gaia*."

Liam spoke up. "Anne Primavesi, but *she* was really just a Christian theologian, I mean she understood Gaia, but not as a direction to go instead of Christianity. She just kind of tacked Gaia onto a belief system she already had."

"I mean she did see Gaia as religiously relevant," Ellis said, "whereas Lovelock himself was a lifelong atheist, he didn't care at all about spiritual questions."

Lest the discussion wander any further down this interesting byway, Pam stepped into the pause. "He was also the total opposite of charismatic, from what I've gathered. I doubt that anybody would have followed him anywhere because he'd inspired them personally. So no, I don't see Lovelock as founding the Gaian *movement*, for the reasons Raghu and Ellis mentioned, even if we do celebrate his birthday every year. What I was getting at is, that instead of a human founder, we had the Hefn." She gave them a moment to take that in. "Think about it: space-faring, time-bending, mind-reading, world-saving superbeings, come down to Earth to preach the gospel of environmental responsibility. Or, more specifically," she said, "we had Humphrey."

"Well—and Otie Bemis I guess, if you want to count him," Samantha added.

Several people snorted and rolled their eyes. "I do and I don't," said Pam. "In his own cockamamie way, Otie did us some good for a while. I make no such claims for Junior, mind."

"Jooonior," Samantha moaned, and other people moaned along with her. They'd all seen clips of the news show, the morning after Carrie's funeral.

"Right now, though, just focus on Humphrey in the role of religious leader. Forget about Carrie's service for now and think about how Humphrey seemed to us at the BTP, when we were in training. Remember back then? He brings the transceiver technology to humanity and teaches us to use it. He intercedes with the Gafr on our behalf. He likes humans, he likes *us*, he's charming as hell, he cares about Earth profoundly, and of course after the tornado he's involved in conceiving the Gaian Mission. Humphrey inspired tremendous faith in some of us, maybe in Liam and me more than the rest of you, but we did have faith as a group in what he and we were doing, as Apprentices and then as Gaians." She paused. "Isn't that right? Didn't we all feel that?"

There were nods all around the room. Pam nodded too. "I actually think Humphrey's pretty plausible as the founder of a religion," she said, "if that were all. But now, here's the kicker. The context he, and we, have always had to work in, is the Directive and the Ban. Meaning that while Humphrey and the missionaries are out there trying to inspire people to assume stewardship of the Earth voluntarily, the other Hefn are busily mindwiping whoever violates the Directive."

She waited for somebody to respond. After a while, "Bite the carrot or get whacked with the stick, you mean," Samantha said. She looked worried.

"Right. Plus, the Baby Ban. Making it a crime to farm with petrochemicals is one thing. Mass sterilization is another, and think how long the Ban's been in effect now! People started leaving us ten years ago over that, and now, obviously, they've reached the boiling point."

"My God, sterilization, mindwipe—you make us sound like Nazis!" Karla Finnigan flounced in her seat.

"No, " said Will in a tight voice. "She's making the Gafr sound like Nazis. We sound like collaborators, which is what we are." He shot a sharp look at Alfrey, who stared back impassively.

"So what if we are? It's in a good cause!" Raghu objected. "Healing the world, working to get the Baby Ban lifted—"

"—while the guys we work for eliminate the egregious dissenters," said Liam curtly. "Will's right. The cause is good, everybody here believes in the Takeover, no need to squabble amongst ourselves. But the mission is hopelessly compromised by the carrot-or-stick thing. As soon as you say it, it's obvious. How come nobody realized that till now?"

There was a brief pause, during which Pam answered Liam's question to herself. Then "Humphrey," said Roger Dworkin flatly. "I don't mean he swayed us on purpose. Just that it's so natural for Apprentices and Gaians in general to see him as a world-saver, we forget how many other people always picture the Hefn with a tail and a pitchfork, till something like that funeral reminds us."

"They see collaborators like that too," Pam said, remembering Temple Square.

"Sure it's natural for us, we're the blue-eyed Aryans!" said coffee-eyed, black-haired Raghu crisply. "We're Apprentices, we'll never be at risk of mindwipe. But Will, *Gaian principles are good*! You believe in them as much as I do. Being forced to comply doesn't change that. They're *good*."

After a moment, "A stick is a stick," Will said grimly.

"And hindsight's 20/20," Samantha added. "We seem to be hopelessly bad at foresight, right across the board."

Silence fell again, while each Apprentice tried to grapple separately with the confoundments of their situation. It occurred to Pam that the missionary training camps, besides being cloister-like, had amounted to a sort of Gaian Jugend for indoctrinating kids, back when there were any kids.

They discussed the subject uneasily for a while longer; then Alfrey stirred and stood. "So. Let us now take a break, and then we shall ponder the question further."

Raghu said, "Is this it on the radical conclusions, Pam? Or have you got something to propose?"

She nodded. "I think I have. Don't know if you guys will agree."

~

"What *is* it that makes people so balky about doing what they're told, even if their life depends on it?" Liam wondered to Pam. "Like, 'Where do you get off, telling me not to eat that apple? I'll eat it if I damn please.'"

The two of them had climbed up a creek bed to the top of the bluff, high above the house, and had reached the place where the 2014 tornado had knocked down all the trees. Brush and vines, and then saplings, had grown up all between the dead hickories and oaks, so the going was tough. A lot of the undergrowth had thorns. In high summer the area would be impenetrable; now it was possible to progress by balancing along the tops of the felled trunks and jumping the gaps, helped by whatever offered itself as a handhold.

"Oh, they never really think their life depends on it," Pam said. "The serpent says 'Hey, buddy, thou shalt not surely die,' and Adam and Eve say, 'Way cool!'"

"But they won't listen to reason either! *Ow*. Goddammit." Liam teetered atop a log examining his knuckle, then stuck it in his mouth.

Pam balanced on another downed tree and looked around. "No, for the same reason none of us quite took in how preposterous it is to try to inspire a mind in fear of being wiped. Denial, my lad. Denial and again denial. In our own way we're no different from them."

"I know that," Liam protested; he had said as much in that morning's session, after all. "I was just being rhetorical. And pissed about having been so stupid."

"Those old hellfire-and-brimstone evangelists? Scared everybody shitless? Their converts used to backslide in droves when the terror wore off. I've known that my whole life and I still didn't make the connection, I'm at least as stupid as you." Pam pointed toward a grove of spindly trees beyond the welter of logs. "Hang on, isn't that it? Over there."

Liam squinted, then said "I do believe you're right," and began to work his way in the indicated direction.

They jumped down and stood looking about them, trying to re-imagine the spot as a clearing. "Yeah, see, the creek runs right down past that area, and over there's where the still was," Pam noted. "And those two trees, those are the ones they tied Humphrey between." It was the site of a critical event from their shared past. Liam had been shot full of buckshot here. Pam had prevented Humphrey from murdering the televangelist Otie Bemis. Instead, Humphrey had "convinced" Otie—using thought control—that the Hefn had been sent by God to save the world from drowning in its own effluvia.

In a sense the Gaian movement had been born that day, the day of the tornado. Profoundly impressed that Pam had been able to stop him from killing Otie, who had been literally about to skin him alive when the tornado interrupted him, Humphrey had begun to study the power of emotional bonds to change behavior: bonds between beings; the bond between a person, Pam, and a piece of ground, Hurt Hollow.

And now the whole structure of belief that had followed upon that day was to be gutted and remade.

They sat on a hickory log and gazed around them, separately remembering that other time. Finally Pam, led to the topic by a chain of associations, said, "So how's Eddie?"

"Eddie's great. You've never appreciated Eddie's finer points." Liam sat grinning while he watched her review and reject half a dozen replies to this outrageous remark. Finally she settled on, "Well, I've learned a lot of useful stuff from living among the Mormons. I guess I owe him that."

"Something that's going to help us out of this quagmire?"

"As a matter of fact," Pam said, "maybe so. But I don't like it. I don't like what I'm going to propose."

"Which is?"

"I'll tell you the full version when I tell everybody else, but for starters we have to get out of denial and just admit the Gafr are right."

"Artie and Raghu aren't gonna like that."

"And face up to the fact, and I doubt that any of us truly has, that they really are not going to lift the Ban if they're not satisfied. Humphrey can only do so much. Bottom line, unless we can get people behaving like stewards for their *own* reasons, nothing will change. We have to find out what those reasons are and sell them, somehow; the Last Generation has another twenty or so childbearing years left at best."

Liam had twisted sideways on the log to look at her. Now he said irritably, "Correct me if I'm wrong, but what do you think the missionaries have been doing for the *past* twenty years?"

"Preaching to the choir!" Pam stood up and started pacing in the cramped space between downed trees. "And that's something else we need to face, that Apprentices, and Gaians too by and large, are members of an elite—a well educated, ecologically committed, Hefn-loving elite. Most of the people in the world aren't anything like us! We have to quit preaching to the goddam choir of the elite, and figure out what all *those* people care about, that could make them want to practice stewardship, and appeal to that. Not what ought to matter to them, but what actually does."

"Look," Liam said, "I can see you've given this more thought than I have, and I certainly defer to your knowledge of ordinary people, but what makes you so sure there's some common something for us to appeal *to*? I mean, the missionaries have been at this a long time. You'd think they'd've come up with it already, if it was there."

"Oh," Pam replied, "not necessarily. I'm talking self-interest here, and Gaians are a pretty high-minded bunch. Too high-minded, and maybe naive, for our own good or anybody else's. We could use a little more of Otie's common touch." She checked her watch. "Uh-oh. We better start back right now or they're liable to start pondering the question without us."

Liam got up. "What's all this got to doing with living among the Mormons, by the way? Have you got something in mind?"

"Little Liam, you shall hear."

Soon after, Pam was standing with her back to the fire, discoursing to the Apprentices about the Church of Jesus Christ of Latter-day Saints.

"What I'm suggesting," she told them, "is that we think about the values of ordinary people by looking at the LDS Church. I know that to most of you the Mormons probably seem more exotic than ordinary, but the reality is that after polygamy ended, in the late eighteen hundreds, the Mormons turned into mainstream Republicans in every way that matters to a sociologist. Their values are about as middle-American as it gets, and just about as different from Gaian values. They view the Takeover pretty much the way Otie did before the tornado. So, to find out what ordinary Hefn-hating people care about, I propose that we consider the Mormons."

She glanced around. The Apprentices looked skeptical but seemed willing to listen. "If we absolutely have to," Will said.

"I'll try to be mercifully brief. Now, in Utah the politicians and business leaders have always been overwhelmingly Mormon, and before the Directive they had an appalling record on wilderness use. Development, mining, logging, overgrazing, off-road vehicles, road-building, the works. They allowed everything and protected nothing. Yet at the same time, the way they feel about Utah is, it's Zion—it's literally holy ground. To them, Salt Lake is as much a holy city as Jerusalem or Mecca."

Samantha said, "Then their ideas about what to do with holy ground must be wildly different than ours."

"Wildly," Pam agreed. "The Church's position has been that exploiting God's bounty was both appropriate and reasonable, because the world was about to end. They'd been expecting the end long before the aliens got here, that's the 'latter-day' part of their name. But here's my point: there are a lot of Utahns with a Mormon background who don't believe what the Church teaches at all, but whose emotional investment in Mormon culture and pioneer history is still tremendous. Especially if their many-times-great-grandfather hauled a handcart across the Rocky Mountains in 1853 or whatever," she said, thinking of A Thousand Miles. "There's no place else they'd ever want to live, and these are the same people who feel stifled by the Church's stranglehold on state government."

She had their attention, but several people were now moving restively and Artie said, "Not that this isn't interesting, but what's it got to do with our situation?"

"I'm getting to that." She paused to organize her thoughts. "Okay. I won't go into this too deeply right now, but for theological reasons LDS families were *big* before the Ban, six or eight kids were common in Utah when the birthrate in the rest of the country had dropped to like two point three." Briefly she described the phenomenal Mormon machinery of genealogy and "Temple Work," baptisms for the dead and "sealings" of husband to wife and parents to children to grand-children to fifteenth cousins dead for a century.

"So Mormons are family-oriented and proud of their state history," Will put in. "And?"

"*And* I think the belief behind all this busy family piety—that 'families are forever,' that family ties continue after death—just basically reflects a universal human yearning that the LDS Church has turned into dogma. Which is why I think they represent ordinary people everywhere so well. Yes, they're family oriented. Yes, they're proud of their state history. That's what I'm trying to tell you: they've lived into a piece of land they consider sacred, and they're linked to that land by powerful family ties. And their missionaries have made a hell of a lot more converts than ours have during the past two decades."

Liam sat up alertly. "Aha. Very clever. You're about to suggest that the Gaians de-emphasize the model of an individual selecting a piece of Ground to bond with after careful study and thought, and construct a new model emphasizing family ties to native soil."

"Yes," said Pam with relief, "I am."

"Based on a hunch that if a piece of land already matters to some-body because of family ties, then the Gaians could work with that."

"As in, 'My family's been farming this land for four generations,'" Raghu offered helpfully.

Artie snorted. "Four generations? Get real. Apart from Mormons, how many people in this or any country stay in one place more than a couple of years?"

"Actually, a whole lot of them do," said Pam. "Not on the family farm, no, but somewhere, especially now. And plenty of people actually do have a family tradition about a piece of land, 'the old home place' type of thing. The old country."

"Okay. Okay. Okay," said Will, "you might be onto something at that. Start with the old home place, whip up some zeal for taking the right kind of care of that, teach them a little organic gardening in the process, and then—I guess generalize along the same lines. Get people taking care of all the parks in their hometown, or all the natural areas in their home county or home state—"

"—or any place that's theirs by birthright, where the emotional resonance is high. Yes."

"We'd be, like, appealing to their civic pride, or their patriotism or something. Their team spirit."

"Their self-interest," said Liam, not looking at Pam.

"Okay, I see real possibilities here," Raghu chimed in. "Think how native peoples feel about the burial grounds of their ancestors. The Chinese inter their parents' bones according to the principles of Feng Shui, the landscape features have to be just right . . . we'd be tapping into a vein that runs really deep."

"But doesn't it leave a lot of people out, too?" Roger asked. "Lots of people are estranged from their families." He meant himself, for one. Some of the others (Pam included, of course) had family problems. Working for the Hefn, always controversial, had lately become more so than ever. A lot of parents and siblings were unhappy.

Pam had stepped back, letting the discussion catch fire and blow about without her, but now she spoke up. "The old approach would still be out there for anybody that wants or needs it, and for everybody already committed to it. But there's more family piety out there than we've ever allowed for. A *lot* more, and it cuts right across the lines of class and culture. And it's even transferable, you don't even need the old country necessarily. I remember reading something about the Cherokee Indians, the tribe that was force-marched from Georgia to Oklahoma 200 years ago, over what they call the Trail of Tears? Apparently, leaving their land and their ancestors' graves was a religious catastrophe for the older ones, like Raghu said—but *now,* a lot of the Cherokees in Oklahoma feel about Oklahoma the way their foreparents felt about Georgia. What matters is living into the land of your people, wherever that is."

"I hate to be a spoilsport," said Samantha, "but if the Gaians start whooping it up for family ties, how can that not get people even more worked up about the Baby Ban?"

Their faces all turned toward Alfrey, who'd been following the discussion intently. "Yes," he said in neutral tones, "that would appear to be a true danger. You would say, 'Achilles' heel'?"

"I'll tell you another," Karla said. "What about people who think they've lived into a piece of native soil that somebody else considers *their* native soil? Ireland, the Middle East, Bosnia, Burundi. Isn't there a risk that those ethnic struggles over land, that have cooled off so much since the Hefn came, would be aggravated?"

That thought hadn't occurred to Pam, but after a moment she said, "I don't think we should not try this because of what might or might not happen. Things are too desperate now. Won't most people care less about their ethnic grievances than about vouchsafing the next generation? Wouldn't that be a really good incentive to keep a truce?"

Will snorted. "Right, they can always go back to killing each other *after* the Ban's been lifted."

"Yeah, that way they can breed replacements, anybody can appreciate *that*." When Artie got tired he got snide. They were all getting pretty tired.

Alfrey said coolly, "Success in any case would depend on very artful introduction of the new idea."

They discussed how the revamped mission might be launched to minimize the chance that it would backfire. Liam, thinking out loud, repeated the idea that had occurred to Pam while viewing Lexi's show: that the emotional force of the Baby Ban had less to do with the fear that, within their own lifetimes, the number of fertile humans could drop to a few hundred thousands, than with individual families being deprived of grandchildren, a stake in the future. "To make this work, we'd have to put the idea of caring for family land across in the light of that being the way to get the Ban lifted. It has to be a package."

Samantha said eagerly, "Homeland. Call it *Homeland*."

"Good, Sam," Liam said. "Let that be the new buzz word. Every missionary should say 'Homeland' several dozen times a day. 'Care for your Homeland, which you want to do anyway, and get the Ban revoked.' They can make a slogan out of it."

Raghu said, "I thought 'homeland' meant your nation, your native country, like 'Homeland Security' after 9-11." He twisted around in his chair. "Pam?"

Pam leaned forward. "It can mean local or national land, depending on the context, but everybody knows Gaians are madly anti-nationalistic. I think it's an excellent word for us to appropriate right now and put to work. We can make it mean whatever we like."

"And the Gafr need to *back off*," Artie, suddenly fierce, said to Alfrey. "No telling people to care for their Homeland or else. No stick, just the carrot, for now."

"Artie's right," Liam said. "We've seen the stick and nothing but the stick since the riots. The Gaians have enough to live down after yesterday, without any new threats from the moon." It was the only allusion anyone had made to the wipings and displayings—to get into that with Alfrey now felt unwise to everyone—but faces hardened all around the room.

To work all this up into a pious and palatable bundle, family heritage and tradition would be as important as venerable ties to place. The missionaries could encourage people to make genograms, do genealogical research (the transceiver *and* LDS databases would be useful there), dig up family documents, throw family reunions, organize tours and transport to wherever forebears had come from, open adoption records and records of the surrogates and plasma donors that most of the small number of living children owed their existence to.

And, since family relationships continued to be determining even for those estranged from their families, people should be actively urged to resolve conflicts through therapy. The Gaian Temperamentals, the psychology specialists, could be very helpful here. Groups and individuals could draw upon the resources of Murray Bowen's Family Systems Theory and other family therapies to promote family-of-origin work. The well-heeled might even buy a bradshaw, the Hefn vitual-intervention technology made possible by the time transceivers. There was already a whole psychological industry serving humanity under uniquely stressful circumstances; this industry might be expanded and further specialized.

Excited now, they went on scheming and planning with a will. At no point in the discussion did one person, even Artie, express skepticism as to whether—in view of Humphrey's performance, the riots, and the sickening newscast of twenty-five bewildered, wailing, terrified adults—it was at all likely that ordinary people were going to let Gaian missionaries convince them of anything. What Samantha had said was all too true: BTP Apprentices, trained to study the past, were perfectly terrible at foresight.

~

When the boat arrived to take them back to Scofield for the night, Pam strode up the gangway and went and stood in the stern by the paddle wheel, leaning on the rail, while the others went below-decks out of the cold wind.

While the gangway was being hoisted and secured, Alfrey came and leaned on the rail beside her. "It went well," he said in his deep, deep voice. "You have cheered them up, they think they see a way to proceed. Humphrey will be pleased. I believe we may have bought ourselves a little time."

Pam said flatly, "If it works."

Never one to varnish the truth, Alfrey simply repeated, "If it works," and went below.

The plan did have some good things going for it, she thought, but Pam knew that Humphrey would be no more truly pleased than she was herself about the decision to emphasize kinship over choice. He'd made himself clear on that score at Carrie's service. Humphrey, chief advocate for humanity's cause among his own people, had from the first been deeply stirred by the notion that an intimate friend or a lover, or a patch of Ground, could be freely chosen.

As was Pam, who—uneasily mindful of her oversight work in Utah, and especially, right now, of Lexi Allred—had nevertheless stood before the distraught Gaians and urged the Mormon example upon them.

But Pam, like her mother, was an only child. Her parents, both dead now, had created a family as dysfunctional as any she knew of; she'd already done a ton of therapeutic work on that. Her father's two half-sisters were still living, and there were some cousins scattered about, in Louisville and elsewhere in Kentucky and Indiana, though she didn't know any of them very well.

Partly that was because she had grown up from the age of fourteen in Washington and Santa Barbara, with the other Apprentices and the Hefn. Mostly, though, it was because she and they had absolutely nothing in common *but* kinship. The aunts and cousins were all, in fact, good examples of "most people"—the kind for whom the new mission should by rights have far more appeal than the old. Pam felt more genuinely related to that old stuffed hair shirt, Alfrey, than to any of her actual relations.

Though truth to tell, her experience with "families" of affiliation had also exposed the weaknesses of choice.

Jesse Kellum, no relation, had been a father to Pam in every way that mattered, and had left Hurt Hollow to her as a father bequeaths property to a child. But Jesse was the exception.

Liam's mother and Carrie Sharpless had for years made her feel like "one of the family," entirely accepted and welcome, but both were dead now and there'd never been much love lost between Pam and Liam's sisters, Margy and Brett. Liam, naturally, was still included in his own family circle; Pam was not, and nobody thought that strange, not even Pam.

Then there was the BTP. For years her right to a place in the family of Apprentices had been taken for granted by everyone. But the loss of her intuition had exposed the truth that being a math intuitive was, in fact, a requirement for full family membership.

And now the Gaians. To be effective she was going to have to practice what she preached, they all were. She pictured herself sitting at a computer station in the Family History Library in Salt Lake, dutifully looking up the antecedents of the Pruitts, Proctors, Morgans, and McCrays, and groaned aloud. She imagined visiting the Louisville cousins and aunts, making earnest attempts to get to know them better, and groaned again. Yet they and they alone were her "real," or birthright, family! This birthright required no further credentials, love or talent or anything else. No power on Earth could take it away. No power on Earth could get rid of it, either.

Followers of the old Gaian way might continue to make up a sort of ragtag community, but Pam understood that the course she herself had set the movement on would now, inevitably, begin to define her out of the Gaian family too. It made her feel like howling. She would have no family at all. "I am *such* a total jerk," she said to the splashing paddle wheel. "The last thing I want to do is what I always do do."

"You *are* a total jerk, I've often said so," came Liam's amiable voice out of the darkness.

Pam jumped and spun around. "Don't *sneak up* on me, goddammit!"

"I wasn't sneaking, I was moving quietly. What the hell are you *doing* out here, mumbling to yourself in the dark? Is this the terminal dementia we've all been expecting but dreading?"

Pam's anger abruptly drained away. She gave a sort of snort, almost a laugh, and Liam came and leaned beside her, careful not to touch her. "So," he said presently, "you were saying what a jerk you are?"

"Oh," she heaved a sigh, "just feeling low. I couldn't see any other possibilities, Alfrey thought it was worth a try, but the whole family-piety thing makes me gag."

"I know." He did know; he'd put in time with her parents.

"You even picked *your* Ground for family reasons."

He looked round at her sulky tone, then replied quietly, "Mm-hm, but as you'll recollect, my Ground is radioactive. At least you've got the Hollow."

Shocked out of her brown study, Pam blurted, "Oh God, I'm sorry, Liam, I'm so sorry. I don't believe I said that. I'm sorry as I can be." For a moment there she had actually, incredibly, forgotten about Jeff. They watched the water for a moment, Pam's face burning invisibly in the dark. "But, you know, you've got the Hollow too in a way," she finally managed to say. "I don't mean because it's a Hot Spot or a shrine, I mean because you lived into it when you were a kid, as much as any Mormon immigrant ever lived into a Utah town."

He ducked his head. "I guess I did at that. I miss the park though. When we took Carrie's ashes to the Ragged Rock after the service? I thought, it looks almost okay if you didn't realize. Like it used to in winter, bare trees, leaves on the ground. You know. Normal."

Pam's face still felt hot. She didn't reply. They watched the paddle wheel pull water over itself and let it fall into the dark. Finally Liam said, "We'll have to call a virtual conference right away—the gafrs of the major population centers worldwide. Then later in the summer, a live conference. You'll have to do your Mormon number a couple more times at least."

The Hefn and their Apprentices determined Gaian policy; passing policy decisions along to the rank and file of the stewardship fell to the Mission gafrs. "Yeah. I'll work on it. It's a hell of a lot easier to preach what you really believe in than what you think other people need to hear."

"You're a pretty good preacher though."

"But a pretty bad liar."

His head came up. "Why think of it as a lie, if it saves the Earth and gets the Ban lifted? Hey, if ever an end justified a means—" He bopped her shoulder lightly. "Anyway, who was just lecturing me about how we had to stop preaching to the choir?"

"Who was just informing you that she didn't like what she was going to propose? But never mind that now. This isn't about me."

The wind had picked up, and Liam hunched his shoulders and flipped up his jacket hood. "How about we go below? They've got hot drinks down there."

Pam shook her head. "You go ahead. We'll be at the landing in ten minutes."

"Okay, then," said Liam O'Hara, brother of two perfectly viable sisters, virtual son to a powerful Senator, child of devoted parents now deceased, doted on by his father's favorite cousin to the end of her life, skilled operator of time transceivers, valued member of the Bureau of Temporal Physics, lover of the unctuous Eddie Ward of the ethereally beautiful tenor voice, particular human friend of the incomparable Hefn Humphrey.

And narrow survivor of a loss that had cut his heart out.

Listening to Liam's (now distinctly audible) footsteps retreating, Pam asked herself how she could have let that unconscionable thing about his Ground slip out. *Because I'm such a total jerk.* The moral advantage between the two of them, an unstable quantity, usually belonged to Pam, but not this night.

She was damned if she'd let it happen again. There was no room inside her for any more guilt of any kind. She had to reconcile herself to what had become of the Gaian hope.

Wasn't there *some* way to make common cause with the "family" enterprise? An ancestor she'd never heard of, with whom she might identify? The little bit Pam knew about her forebears was unpromising—some had been slaveholders, several had fought for the Confederacy, a number had died young, in childbirth or of TB—but she'd never actually looked very deeply into her family background. "I am going to give this a shot," she told the cold night wind, "Somehow or other I'm going to come up with a way of belonging to my family."

And just like that the answer came.

CHAPTER 5

The Red Diary

28 MARCH - 4 APRIL 2037

When she died, Frances Pruitt had bequeathed to her daughter the house on the Scofield College campus, her father's guaranteed pension with six years left to run, and a bradshaw.

The bradshaw had been a surprise, to put it mildly. Frances Pruitt, like Phoebe O'Hara, had been very taken with Humphrey but had had nothing good to say otherwise about the Hefn or the Takeover. And besides that, anything to do with alien technology was so horrendously expensive for an average citizen. Pam figured she had to have scrimped for nearly a decade to buy it, starting not too long after she'd been told the truth about Pam's father, Shelby Pruitt, which was several years after he died in 2023. Afterwards Frances had remained deeply vested in her own version of their marriage, and except for that one occasion had refused to discuss the subject. The bradshaw was Pam's first clue that, over time, Frances might have begun to acknowledge that there could have been something to what she'd been told.

Not that she hadn't already known what her husband had done to their only child, or a lot of what he'd done. But her own father had died when she was little. Neil Reeder-as-Neil would have recognized her error: Frances had believed all her life that just having a daddy must be the most wonderful thing in the world, and taken it on faith that whatever Pam's daddy did to Pam was normal. He was her father, wasn't he? For all she knew, any father might take an obsessive interest in his daughter's large breasts and talk about them incessantly. Or assume a spraddle-legged stance before his daughter and her girlfriend, both young teenagers, to ask if they could tell whether he was wearing briefs or boxers under his trousers. Or zestfully describe to this daughter the circumstances (after school, creek valley, big flat rock, older boys) under which he'd been shown how to masturbate.

After Shelby's death, Pam had been mortified to learn that his obsession with her breasts had been aired outside the family circle. "I think it's terrible the way Shelby talks about Pam's boobs all the time, and I don't understand why Frances just laughs," a friend of her parents' told her own daughter, who eventually told Pam. "Remember those tight sweaters your mom used to stuff you into?" Betsy had added, recalling a certain deep-pink lambswool number with short sleeves and a little round collar, and a row of pearl buttons down its swollen front.

Pam remembered, all right. Why hadn't she refused to wear those sweaters, chosen for and pressed upon her by Frances, Shelby's former sweater girl? Considering how she had loathed her very large breasts as a teen, why oh why had the sweaters she bought for herself fit the same way? After years of therapy Pam sort of understood the storm of conflicting feelings present in every member of a family like hers, but thinking about it was still queasy-making. Considering that what had happened to Lexi Allred was far more extreme on the face of it than what had happened to Pam, the damage done seemed out of all proportion to the crime; but the damage had been immense. Which was why Liam, who knew all about these matters, had thought assigning Pam to child oversight a bad idea.

There hadn't been a graduating class at Scofield College, or a full-time standing faculty, since 2028. But Scofield was popular with conference organizers, and Pam's house, the one her mother had left her, was used regularly by the college as conference lodging. During the BTP conference, naturally, Pam had been staying there herself, and so had Liam. She'd invited him for auld lang syne—he had visited several times when they were kids—and he'd accepted, probably for the same reason she had offered: nostalgia for a distant time they both preferred, in certain ways, to the present. She had considered inviting Alfrey to join them—she would have invited Humphrey as a matter of course—but had decided the mix would not be comfortable.

For Liam to be there, however, was both comfortable and practical. By the end of a week of late-night brainstorming the two of them had hammered out a plan for introducing the refocused Gaian mission to the public, and the plan, with a few additions and emendations, had been approved. This, or a version of it, was what Alfrey would read as a conference report to the global community of Gaians.

And all week long, without saying anything to Liam, Pam had thought about the bradshaw, whether she wanted to make it, what incident to record if she did, whether it might reconcile her somehow, even a little bit, to her family and thus to the movement's altered orientation.

On the morning they both planned to leave, she went up to Liam's room, her parents' former bedroom, and found him packing and contemplating the framed pictures crammed on top of her mother's big mahogany dresser. "Look at us, would you," he said. "When did she take that one?"

The picture he meant was a holo of Liam and Pam at Hurt Hollow, shot in the spring of 2014, a couple of years before the Gaian recruitment disk Lexi had viewed had been made. For several weeks that spring, the year of the tornado, they had lived at the Hollow. The place had been a working homestead then, the goats, bees, and big organic garden had still been the basis of somebody's livelihood and not yet the teaching model it would soon become, or the untenanted museum/Gaian shrine it was now.

During Liam's first visit to Scofield the homesteader, Jesse Kellum, had been bitten by a copperhead. Liam and Pam had kept things going at Hurt Hollow while he recovered, and Humphrey had dropped by at Liam's suggestion to check the place out, as it was so powerful an evocation of the sort of lifestyle the Hefn had been trying to encourage. Pam had a treasured memory of Humphrey on the terrace one morning, in a chair that tried to make his legs bend the wrong way, pausing in the rapid spooning of blackberries and yogurt into his mouth to ask, "Do you clever children know, either of you, how to cook a 'cobbler'?" Cobblers figured large in Humphrey's emotional life. Pam could still see his spoon clutched in a tong-like hand, two short hairy digits opposing two others, and the gray hair around his mouth sticky with honey and stained with berry juice. At that moment Humphrey had been one happy Hefn.

In this Hollow holo, Liam was standing on the same terrace with a brimming pail of goat's milk in each hand, grinning at the camera; he was wearing shorts and a ratty tee shirt and old sneakers without socks, and looked as if he hadn't a care in the world, which was far from true. Pam had started ahead of him down the steep path to the spring house. All you could see of her was a blur of light-colored clothing and another of straight, brown, shoulder-length hair, but even so she had contrived to look both furtive and embarrassed, an impression emphasized by Liam's own sunny, open good looks.

The picture made Pam feel something between angry and desolate. "That was that day Mom and Dorothy What's-Her-Name stopped by, when we had to close the time window, remember? Listen, how long does it take to set up a bradshaw?"

Liam looked up sharply from this ambiguous image of their shared past. "A bradshaw? I never handled one, I dunno—couple of days? Why? *Oh*," he said before Pam could answer. "The one your mom left you! Thinking of shooting it while you're in the neighborhood, are you?" He folded his arms and smirked at her across the bed.

"Just tell me, how do I arrange to set one up on short notice? I need to get back, I probably shouldn't take more than an extra day or two out here."

Before Liam could reply, his phone dinged. Pam leaned against the wall while he talked to Bureau Headquarters, glancing back and forth between the live Liam and the holo of the Goatherd and considering how that handsome, cheerful-looking kid had been transformed into the balding, restless, dissatisfied, thirty-eight-year-old person in the BTP uniform, perched among tumbled sheets on her parents' old four-poster, making notes on a Landfill Plastics pad.

As the conversation wound down he glanced up and caught Pam at the back-and-forthing. "Hold it a second, Johnny—do you know how to set up a bradshaw on short notice?"

The little squeak of John Wong's voice came through while Liam looked at her. "Pam Pruitt," he said, eyes on hers, "in southern Indiana. Or maybe northern Kentucky?" Pam nodded. "She inherited one from her mom, and she wants to get it shot while she's out here—she's here for the conference too."

Johnny's voice squeaked again. To Pam's ear it had a surprised sound, and she imagined him saying, "Pam's there? How come?" and felt her face get warm.

But actually he was asking something else. "As a matter of fact, I do," said Liam, "Haven't used it, though, the weather's been terrible all week." He listened. "Come on, they can't all have left already. I know Artie and Will were still here last night, we saw them at dinner. I've never done a bradshaw in my life."

"Let me talk to him," Pam said.

"Pam wants to talk to you." Liam clicked the speaker button and aimed the phone at her.

"Hi Johnny."

"Hi." His tiny face on the screen grinned a tiny grin. "I never knew you owned a bradshaw."

"Listen, I don't want Liam put in charge of this, if that's what you've been leading up to."

"'Fraid you haven't got a lot of choice if you want to shoot it now," he said. "Artie and Will left this morning for Canada, and everybody else, including Alfrey, is en route to DC. Anyway, bradshaws are tricky, we usually get a couple months' advance notice. What was this, a spur-of-the-moment decision?"

"Yeah. Scofield is where I'm from, you know. I don't get back here very often, and I've been busy as hell."

"Thing is, Liam's got a transceiver with him," Johnny said, a fact that was certainly news to Pam. She darted a surprised, offended look at Liam, who shrugged. "He's your only hope. We can spare him for a few more days, that's all, and I wouldn't go that far for anybody but you. Humphrey wouldn't, I should say. If you don't want him to shoot it, you'll have to wait and go through the usual procedural red tape."

While she hesitated, trying to assess pros and cons, Liam clicked the speaker off and clapped the phone to his ear. "Hey, before you start disposing of my weekend, I need to get back, I've got plans and I'm beat. Pam can do this bradshaw some other time . . . okay. *Okay.* I'll let you know. See ya tomorrow. Bye."

He snapped the phone shut and slipped it into the inside pocket of his uniform jacket. "Don't look at me like that. There wasn't any reason to tell you. Humphrey thought it might come in handy."

He'd been hiding the transceiver in her own house. "Listen, blockhead, I don't want you tiptoeing around sparing my feelings. The more you do that, the more you rub it in that the rest of you consider me a tragic victim, and that's not how I want to think of myself, so do me a favor and cut it out."

"You da boss." Liam reached under the bed and pulled out a transceiver in its case, along with a family of dust bunnies; the housekeeping staff was getting sloppy. He didn't look at Pam.

It was when her father died that Pam's mathematical intuition had abruptly deserted her. In Liam's view this *was* a tragedy; it embarrassed him that his gift was still vital when hers was not—that he was a starter and she now only a bench warmer at the highest level of the world-saving game Humphrey had trained them both to play. Julie, Pam's therapist, hypothesized that her intuitive ability had developed as a means of escaping her father's attentions, and that when she hadn't needed it anymore it had simply shut down. This "instrumentalist" view of things horrified Liam, to whom the thought of losing intuition, the means to attunement with the time transceivers, felt like losing some essential power, eyesight or sexual potency.

Since Pam put a lot of energy into denying that it horrified her as well, and since she was dead serious about not wanting to think of herself as a Poor Thing, this attitude of his was intolerable.

Had she not lost her gift, of course, Pam would also not now be in the humiliating position of pleading with Johnny Wong to order some other tech to drop everything, requisition a transceiver, and make his way overland to the Ohio River Valley to do a job she could once have done herself. She needn't have even *considered* allowing Liam to make the bradshaw, let alone trying to persuade him to, let alone—the ultimate humiliation—exploiting his pity to get him to agree.

It was all too much. Pam wasn't that certain she even wanted a bradshaw. She was opening her mouth to say so when Liam suddenly relented. "Okay, I'll do the shoot, but that's all. I'm on that plane tonight whatever, I'm not crossing the whole freaking continent by rail. You can keep the recording and have the virtual program written after you get back to Salt Lake. Take it or leave it. That's my best offer."

~

Beginning about the year 2025, in the fifteenth year of their presence on Earth, the Hefn had gone into the bradshaw business in a small way by making their time transceivers available to individuals for personal use. Somebody might give a bradshaw as a gift for a really special occasion, or make one for herself to use therapeutically. Those who'd tried therapy a la bradshaw mostly raved about the results—Pam had seen a viddy documentary to that effect—but not many people had tried it; apart from celebrities and corporate moguls and the like, hardly anybody could afford the things. Hefn time transceivers were very expensive to run. Pam and the other Apprentices had used them so routinely that they'd seldom thought about the fortunes being spent on their training; but the media always emphasized the staggering price tag, whenever yet another glittering personality arrived at the decision to buy a bradshaw.

A time transceiver was the rarest object on Earth. The bradshaw-making process—and expense—began when one of these priceless artifacts was liberated from its usual function and removed to the site where the event to be revisited had occurred. Then somebody had to set coordinates, a Hefn or a BTP tech, because nobody else knew how. Then they needed someone to record the event, somebody to write the virtual program, and usually a therapist to guide the client through the experience of running the bradshaw after it was made. A Hefn might also be required, to wipe memories if anybody back in the past happened to be in the wrong place at the wrong time.

Thanks to their conviction that "Time is One, and fixed," the Hefn didn't worry at all about changing the timeline by doing this. Theoretically, there could be alternate universes; but for any given universe, theoretically, there were no alternate realities.

The potential for abuse, by pornographers and sadists and the like, was obvious; to prevent it the Hefn kept scrupulous track of every completed program. Each had to be filed at a public VR parlor and played only there. You could never be sure, while running your bradshaw, that a Hefn Observer wasn't looking over your shoulder.

The fellow who gave his name to these virtual interventions was a late-twentieth-century self-help guru called John Bradshaw. All too often this character, a Texan, was dismissed by casual viewers of his very popular media series as a cross between a sleazebag televangelist and a snake-oil salesman. In fact, Bradshaw had possessed an uncommon gift: he could synthesize the ideas of major psychological theorists, without distorting them, and communicate the practical side of these ideas to the sort of people who might never, otherwise, have access to psychotherapy.

On TV, and in his workshops, he would have his audiences do an exercise. They were to choose a painful scene from their childhoods, one in which they had felt particularly helpless, miserable, betrayed, and—Bradshaw's special buzzword—shamed. They were to close their eyes and picture this scene vividly. Then they were to imagine walking in upon the scene as their adult selves, and doing whatever was necessary to protect the helpless child they used to be.

It wasn't unusual for workshop participants to break into violent weeping as they followed their leader's instructions; and these interventions were "merely" imaginary. The effect of using the Hefn transceivers to capture actual events, making virtual interventions possible, was phenomenal.

The actual event captured when the bradshaw was made sometimes proved to be very different from the way the event had been remembered. But nailing the exact cause of misery mattered far less than promising the miserable virtual child that he would never again be alone, defenseless and terrified, in the face of torment. You couldn't, of course, make the promise good to the actual child who had suffered long ago. But you *could* make it good to that same child, still alive and still feeling helpless, inside the adult you.

Besides the visual dimension of the event, shadow memories were also captured and recorded. The transceivers couldn't manipulate memory as well as specialized Hefn memory-control equipment did, but they could get something; how much varied with the individual and the context, and other factors that weren't yet understood, not at least by humans.

Transceivers had to open the time window upon the actual site of the event. A person couldn't sit comfortably in Boston and look in upon one of her father's alcoholic rages in Topeka; she had to *go* to Topeka, to the actual house she'd lived in at the time, if it was still there, or to whatever building or abandoned freeway or rubble field presently occupied the space, and set up the equipment there. That alone could present a major challenge. When King William V made a bradshaw to replay a certain painful scene with his father, he'd had to sail the royal yacht *Britannia II* to California, pick up a transceiver and a techie, then sail on to New Zealand. The Hefn decided who got to fly in a plane, and a king's desire to experience a virtual intervention in his own past was no reason, in their view, to authorize a flight.

Until the moment Frances's will was read, the idea that Pam herself might ever make a bradshaw had never crossed her mind; and after she owned one—or a voucher that could be exchanged for one—she hadn't been sure what to do with it. On the one hand, conventional therapy had already helped her confront and deal with her feelings about her abusive father and unprotective mother; on the other, despite the relief she'd derived from that, in some ways she was still pretty much of a mess. Obviously there was more work to be done; but her several attempts to dig deeper had produced killer anxiety and no further information, and left her fed up with the whole struggle.

The Hefn didn't offer employee discounts; Frances couldn't have gone behind her daughter's back to buy one from Humphrey for cheap. Frankly, had the bradshaw not represented a posthumous admission that Frances had taken her allegations seriously after all, Pam would probably have sold the thing.

But even if she'd been downright eager to make this bradshaw, Scofield, Indiana—where her father had been Director of Libraries at the college, where she'd lived the first fourteen years of her life before the Hefn had whisked her away to DC and safety—was a long, weary way from Salt Lake City by train. She had seldom gone back even while Frances was alive.

But here she was, with a compelling reason to peer again into the reeking cauldron. If a bradshaw, by resolving something or removing some obstacle, would let her connect with her biological family in a positive way—and thus let her stay centered in the Gaian family—it would be worth whatever it cost.

~

"I could make the damn bradshaw!" Pam had said out loud while steaming back to Scofield, on the first night of the conference to overhaul the Gaian Mission. And now she was doing it, she was making the bradshaw. She and Liam had caught the noon packet and asked the pilot to drop them off at Hurt Hollow. Liam was standing just off the terrace, in almost the exact spot where the Goatherd picture had been taken, fussing with his instruments.

Pam sat on the stone step, munching a sandwich, looking around. She had first brought Liam to Hurt Hollow at almost exactly this time of year, mid-April. The trees were bigger now, of course, but their leaves flourished forth the same bright varieties of green as before, and were as full of noisy birds. Unlike those of the western species she'd never gotten to know very well, the songs of these birds were intelligible to Pam. Beyond the fence the pale-blue river spread out forever, as it had through all the springs of her life, though the beach where she and Liam—and Humphrey—had gone swimming in 2014 had been scoured away completely. "Thanks a lot for coming back over here," she said. "The weather's been so lousy all week, I didn't really get a chance to take all this in, and we were too busy anyway."

Liam didn't look up. "I'm too busy *now*. Don't talk to me for ten more minutes."

"Sorry."

He was rushing, bound and determined to make that plane. He'd pressed her to pick an event that had occurred back at the house in Scofield, or someplace on the campus, but Pam had held out for the Hollow at the cost in time of a five-mile taxi ride and a boat trip, and he'd grumpily given in.

She finished her sandwich and got up. "I guess I'll walk down to the dock. Yell when you're ready."

Thanks to the conference, all sixty-one acres of wooded river bluff were closed to the public till Monday; they had Hurt Hollow to themselves. Descending the steep path, Pam thought, as she did every time, how different this country was from the mountains and deserts of Utah, and how the Hollow was still and always the one place on Earth that she belonged to heart and soul, mind and strength—the one place that was absolutely hers, though the deed was registered now in the name of the Hurt Hollow Trust and she so seldom came back anymore. Pam would not have used such language to a living soul, Liam least of all, but here—cluster of buildings, wooded hillside, stretch of river—was her heart's home.

She unlocked the gate and walked down to the river, keeping back from the bank, which the past winter's currents and storm waves had undermined to the point where the trustees were considering moving the fence to higher ground. The dinged-up metal buckled and boomed as she walked out to the end of the dock, shrugging off the thought of sunblock, and sat down to watch the river roll massively by, letting the motion evoke feelings of calmness and clarity. It wasn't recommended that a bradshaw be undertaken in a rush. The candidate was supposed to ready herself with counseling and meditation before embarking upon her personal time-travel adventure. Pam wouldn't be running the virtual program for some time, but she was going to watch through the window while Liam made the recording, and knew that what she saw would be unsettling. Pointless to throw a bradshaw away on a comfortable memory.

Knowing it would be a waste of time, Liam hadn't even tried to talk her out of watching. He didn't have time to waste, and it was her own lookout anyway.

"Ready!" he called finally; and when Pam had mounted again to the terrace and joined him, "Okay, what are we looking for?"

The transceiver, a contraption of molded black metal and meshwork spread like a cobra's hood, had been erected on its tripod. For all Pam's brave talk it hurt her to see it there, see Liam's casual competence as he moved around it adjusting things, unthinkingly at home in a country where she had once lived and been happy and could never return to.

She looked away. "April 2013—I don't know the exact date, you'll have to scroll. Start in the middle of the month and work forward, scanning for Dad and me coming out the front door. We were looking up into those trees over there, up the bluff. The time window'll open behind us, I don't think we'll notice a thing."

"Righto." Liam slipped his hands into indentations on the sides of the cobra's hood, and almost at once the area directly in front of it began to shimmer and then swirl, forming a pattern in the air.

Pam moved off the terrace and around the corner of the house, ready to flatten herself against the wall when the window opened. She hadn't watched a temporal field form in years, but she could still read patterns, and followed as the field shaped itself around the early twenty-first century, then 2013, then spring, then April.

Liam was concentrating, leaning into the transceiver's field with his eyes closed, deepening his trance. When the pattern entered his mind and became visual, he would free his hands to finger the quincunx, the little abacus-like device the Hefn used to calculate coordinates. Then he would set the coordinates mentally, by hurling each number into the pattern precisely where it needed to go.

There had never been a feeling quite like that absolute mastery, being so in tune with the shimmer pattern that the numbers snapped into their places without conscious effort, the way a lacrosse player snatches the ball from the air and hurls it into the net. Pam would never feel that mastery again. Desolation seized her, and again she looked away.

When she looked back, Liam had stepped away from the transceiver. The window had opened; the silent recorder was running.

Anyone on the other side, where it was 2013, would have needed a sharp and knowing eye to spot the open time window. It was April afternoon on both sides, and fine weather on both, and Liam and Pam were watching from positions where they could look through without being seen from the other side, if Pam's father or Pam's own younger self did happen to glance their way.

Voices were murmuring inside the house, a pot banged on a stove top. Presently Pam heard what she'd been waiting for: a loud and piercingly sweet ripple of birdsong from a tree on the hillside behind the house. She got a grip on herself in time not to move or react when the screen door swung open with a squeak, and a girl came down the steps followed by a man: Young Pam at twelve-going-on-thirteen, and Shelby Pruitt at thirty-six.

The bird's song had stopped her breath; the sight of these two figures, though she'd been expecting them, stopped her heart. Pam could feel Liam's head turn to look at her. She hadn't been much older than the girl in the window when they'd met in Washington to begin their studies with Humphrey.

Her father passed the field glasses to Young Pam, who raised them and scanned the treetops. Almost at once she smiled; she'd spotted the singer, a rose-breasted grosbeak, high in a tossing beech tree full of flowers. "Is the female this pretty?" she asked, and at the word *pretty* a stab of pity and loathing pierced Adult Pam. That poor, homely kid with her potent binoculars! Her nose was much too big for her face, and her hair hung limp and mousy to her shoulders, but the thing that struck you was the rounded mass of her breasts, bulging forward beneath the red-and-blue flannel shirt with the rolled-up sleeves.

How Young Pam had loved that shirt—the boyish plaid, and the belief that it blurred her proportions! It hadn't of course; you could see with ghastly clarity how the breast mass strained at the buttons and the fabric between them. Really, the most that could be said for the shirt was, it wasn't a tight pink lambswool sweater.

"No," said Shelby thoughtfully, considering her question. In the round frame of the window he stood there younger by a year or so—astonishing thought—than Pam was now herself. "No, the female's duller, like most of the other female finches. Looks kind of like a great big song sparrow, but a duller brown."

Young Pam held the glasses tight on the vivid bird. From Adult Pam's hiding place the grosbeak was out of sight, but no matter; she remembered perfectly how actively he had moved through the foliage, eating flowers and pausing every so often to proclaim his territory. He was so pretty! Black above and white below, with a triangular bib the color of raspberry sorbet beneath his chin, and a powerful finch's bill.

The rippling song poured forth again. Pam's father suddenly chuckled. "You know something," he said, "you and that bird up there have a good deal in common—he's got a big strong beak, and he's got a pretty pink breast!" He laughed again, the innocent-sounding laugh of a person unaware of being cruel. "And I expect he likes both of his better'n you like either of yours, don't you?"

Again she felt Liam swivel his head in her direction, and this time she glanced back. His face had filled with indignation; he understood, now, why she had pushed for shooting this incident.

Young Pam seemed to falter—

—and precisely in that instant, the split second between the faltering and the hesitant lowering of the binoculars, a strange thing happened. Before Adult Pam's eyes flashed the image of a small book bound in red, with gilded page-edges, gold lettering on the cover, and a strap and gold lock. The image, suspended in midair, brought with it a whiff of feeling gone almost too quickly to register.

Then the image had vanished too. Young Pam lowered the glasses halfway and stood stock-still. Without a word, without glancing at her father, she handed him the binoculars and went quickly up the stairs into the house.

Shelby Pruitt stood looking after her, holding the field glasses awkwardly. Unbalanced as she'd been by what she'd just seen and felt, it still astonished Adult Pam—who hadn't, of course, witnessed this part of the scene—to see that her young father's boyish, handsome face now wore a baffled, even a bleak look, a look that plainly said *I did it again, but I don't even know what I did.*

Presently he lifted the binoculars again to scan the treetops. Pam signaled Liam to close the window.

This he accomplished quickly and neatly. The lens that formed the window spiraled out from the edge, went opaque, and disappeared. Liam shut down the recorder, pulled the cartridge out, and flipped it to Pam, who fumbled it, squatted to retrieve it—and couldn't stand up again. "Bastard," Liam said, genuinely outraged. "That stupid bastard. That son of a bitch. I'm sorry I never punched him out when I had the chance." He scrubbed his hands through his hair, watching Pam. In a minute, when she hadn't responded or risen, he said, "So—did you get what all you needed?" And then, sharply, "You okay?"

As Liam said this, Pam sat down abruptly on the paving stones of the terrace, clutching her temples; a headache had come on like a crack of lightning, making her stomach heave.

He came and hunkered down beside her, asking again, "Are you okay?" She shook her head, truthfully; she felt ghastly. "No wonder. I'm pretty thrashed myself. God, this bradshaw stuff is playing with fire, I had no idea! I think what we just saw actually hit me harder than that realtime thing in the canoe, when he was going on about your swimsuit being too small . . ."

He stood and reached for Pam's hand as he spoke, pulled her up. This put their eyes on the same level. "Right after he said that about me being like the grosbeak, did you—this sounds crazy—but—did you see a little red book in the air?"

"See *what*?"

"A red book. In the air," she repeated lamely, already knowing the answer.

"In the *air*? No. What are you talking about?"

Somebody jabbed an ice pick into Pam's right temple and wiggled it around.

"Liam—" she grabbed his arm so frantically he was dragged off balance, forced to take a step toward her "—I'm so, so sorry, I'm sorry as I can be, but this wasn't it."

He looked baffled. "What wasn't what?"

"I made a mistake. This wasn't the right time."

"Right time for what—the *bradshaw*?" And when she nodded, "What are you *talking* about? It was a classic!" Then, realizing where she must be leading, he started to get mad. "Hey, you don't *get* a second shot at a bradshaw, just because you rush into it without thinking carefully enough beforehand." He'd yanked his arm free.

"I would have made exactly the same mistake no matter how long I'd thought about it beforehand. I didn't know this wasn't the right time till I saw *this* time."

"That's not the Bureau's fault, Pam! You had one bradshaw coming, you were hell-bent on making it today, and you worked on me till I caved in and played along. But that's it. That's all you get. You're gonna have to settle for this one." He turned away and started to collapse the transceiver.

"I know all that," Pam said, trying to sound reasonable and placating though she felt like hurling herself on the ground and howling, "but this one won't get me where I need to go."

"And where's that?"

"I don't know yet, but I know for sure how to find out now."

The transceiver had been folded into itself; Liam snapped the case open and stood it on end. "Because of this red book you saw and I didn't?" He began to detach parts one by one and to fit them, in a necessary order that Pam remembered exactly, into the lined sockets of the case, like some bizarre musical instrument being readied to be carried home from practice. His hands danced among the pieces of molded metal with unconscious tenderness and grace.

Pam gulped. "It was a diary," she said, and heard her voice wobble. "A kid's diary, that old-fashioned type you were meant to keep in longhand. *My* diary. From when I was in the sixth grade. I threw it away." She took a step toward him, then another. "I've regretted it a million times, but I always thought I knew why I did it, till now."

He glanced at her, but without breaking the rhythm of his work.

"I was reading this library book, about a Navajo girl. She and her family lived in a hogan, where space was tight, I guess, and her mother was talking about her one day, and she said something like 'That one! She has more possessions!' and I thought, '*I* have too many possessions,' and started poking around my room to see what I could throw away."

"You were one weird kid."

"I don't remember whether I got rid of anything else, but I grabbed this diary that I'd gotten for Christmas and been writing in all year, and decided to pitch it. And then I wasn't sure. I remember saying to Mom that I was going to throw my diary away, and she said, 'Don't you think you might want to have it later on?' and I said, 'No, it won't get interesting till I start having dates.'"

Liam snorted. Pam watched the delicate hood reduce beneath his gestures into a fan and then a spiral, and be tucked into its place. "She could have stopped me," Pam said sadly. "If she'd said, 'Oh, don't do that, you'll be really glad to have that diary someday,' I would have kept it. But anyway, I think—this is what I just realized—I think throwing it away because of that Navajo-girl book is a cover story."

There was a brief silence while Liam slipped the last pieces of the transceiver into the case and snapped the locks shut. He looked at his watch. Then he walked across the terrace and decorously sat down on one of the low chairs Orrin Hubbell, the original Hurt Hollow homesteader, had built so long ago. "Okay. Enlighten me. Why *do* you think you threw it away?"

This, the big question, had only just dawned on Pam. She more or less made up an answer as she went along. "Maybe there was something in it that I needed to get rid of. . . something somebody didn't want me to tell anyone about. Maybe the person threatened me—I'd get sick and die if I told, or whatever. It wasn't Dad," she said, sure of this much at least. "He did what he did, and it was horrible enough, but all of a sudden I'm wondering if somebody else didn't get to me first."

"In that same way, you mean?"

"I don't know. Maybe, maybe some other way. Maybe I saw something I wasn't supposed to see." She knew as she spoke these words that they were untrue, that her mind had skittered away from the truth. It wasn't the residue of any "other way," different from Shelby's, that lay festering inside of her. Whatever the secret was, it was sexual and concerned Pam directly. An image of Lexi Allred, now back on location and carrying on bravely with her life, flashed in her mind.

Liam pondered this, then said carefully, "Well, if you're right, I can see why you'd have a hallucination of your diary right then. On the other hand I really don't see what's wrong with the Navajo-girl explanation. Why couldn't you have just taken a notion to throw the thing in the trash? People do throw stuff away, you know. Why does it have to be some heavy repressed-memory thing?"

But in Pam's mind, moment by moment, a conviction was strengthening. "No, think about it. I'd pasted some stuff in the diary—a straw from an ice-cream soda bought for me by a boy I liked, named Rick, a locket a different kid named Rick gave me, that had his name engraved on it. You know, souvenirs. Well, before I threw it away I carefully peeled the straw and the locket off the pages, to keep. Why would I *do* that—keep the trinkets and toss the diary? Why would I even *remember* doing all that? It doesn't make sense! I was a kid who *kept* things—I kept my *fifth*-grade diary, such as it was, I kept a piece of paper with the signatures of all the kids in my *fourth*-grade class on it, I've got diaries and journals from the age of fourteen up to and including right now! Julie says mine is the most thoroughly documented life she's ever dealt with in her entire career!"

Liam made pushing-down motions with his hands. "All right, all right. Calm down. Do you remember what you did with that souvenir stuff?"

"I've still got it! All of it!" He repeated the gesture, more broadly this time. Pam sighed heavily and said "Okay. I'm calm."

"Do you mean you could go straight to where it is and put your hand on it?"

"That's exactly what I mean. That stuff is all in Salt Lake. The straw and locket are pasted into a scrapbook labeled 'Memorabilia,' which is on a shelf in my study."

"Hmm. And the fifth-grade diary?"

"In a bookcase with all my other diaries and journals, above my desk. At the far left of the row. They're all in chronological order."

"I'm sure they are." He asked one last test question: "What color is it?"

"The fifth-grade diary? Brown, dark brown. Smaller and skinnier than the others. Flexible cover."

"Pam," said Liam, "Humphrey might okay shooting a second bradshaw, since the virtual program for this one hasn't been written yet—for you he might—but I'm getting on that plane."

"It would have to be Alfrey's call," she responded, but things had stopped. They stared at each other. Pam was now supposed to back down, though both knew that, in Liam's place, she would already have groaningly accepted that the plane would be leaving without her. And suddenly this time she wasn't having it; the stakes were just too high. "I can't stop you," she said, now very calm indeed, "and I wouldn't exactly *blame* you, I know you've already disrupted your plans as a favor to me. But. If you'll do this one more thing . . . well. I'll never forget it."

Liam's expression gradually altered. Moving slowly, he got up from the chair, so their eyes were again on the same level across the terrace. "Meaning that if I don't do it, you'll never forget that, either." In her hypervigilant state, his pupils seemed to shrink into sharp, hard pinholes. "And the next time I call you up at midnight or the crack of dawn, to vent about my problems, you might not answer the phone."

"I'd say that's probably a pretty shrewd guess."

"So it's a crisis."

Both understood that nothing less than the fundamental balance—or working imbalance—of the relationship was on the line. If Liam went home now to Eddie and his heavy weekend, and left Pam in this particular lurch, Pam realized that not only would she never forget it, she wouldn't be able to forgive him for it. And he had to decide now whether he wanted to deal with that, because at this point in their long, complicated friendship, they both believed that Pam had less to lose than Liam did.

~

On the morning following this scene, Pam woke to the sound of a voice speaking inside her head. "Pinny's Hefn," said the voice.

She often woke with the impression that someone had just spoken aloud, typically a name or an innocuous word or phrase: "Carrots," "Pete!," "That's the target!" So in itself this was nothing remarkable.

This voice sounded no different; the difference was in what it said, which almost seemed an aural equivalent of the diary-in-the-air hallucination.

Pinny's Hefn was the title of a "novel" Pam had written the summer she'd turned fourteen. The novel dealt with the doings of a peculiar girl named Pinny (short for large-nosed Pinocchio) who much resembled Pam, and a Hefn named Comfrey. Having been extremely taken with the only Hefn she'd met in the flesh—her mentor-to-be, Humphrey, at her Bureau interview—Pam had modeled Comfrey on him.

The novel was set, and mostly written, at Hurt Hollow. She hadn't paged through the manuscript in years, though (naturally) she knew exactly where it was: in a blue folder, in a cardboard box in a Salt Lake City storage closet, among the Memorabilia (or possibly the Juvenilia): 164 pages scribbled in longhand on blue-lined paper with three holes punched down the side.

What she thought about after the voice had startled her awake, while her mind was clearing, was the loose-leaf binder she'd kept those pages in as they accumulated. She could visualize it perfectly, that binder: a ratty old thing even then, made of fake brown alligator skin, with a zipper around three sides. She'd liked that zipper; it made the story feel secure. The binder had been Shelby's; he'd passed it on to Pam when she'd started writing *Pinny's Hefn*, at the beginning of her last whole summer at home. . .

No. He'd given it to her earlier, maybe a year before that, because she had already possessed it when she needed a folder to put certain secret papers into for safekeeping. What secret papers? She could barely remember; and yet—like the image of the red diary—the thought of them carried a powerful emotional charge.

Concentrate now, Pam told herself: what papers? Some news clippings about horses and horse races—Pam had gone through a racehorse stage, during which she'd clipped things out of the sports section of the paper. There was one particular Kentucky Derby when she had known who all the horses and jockeys were and who was favored to win by how much. That had been the fifth grade. She'd been ten. What in the world could have seemed so secret and private about racehorses and horse races? She had always supposed, when she remembered this at all, that she had made a secret of it just to *have* a secret; but it struck her now as peculiar.

What else? Pam lay perfectly still and cudgeled her wits, but all that came to mind were some sheets of computer paper on which a code had been worked out by her and a couple of guys named Charlie and Steve, her best friends since earliest childhood, no offense to the two Ricks. They had made up this code with a symbol for each letter of the alphabet so they could write encrypted notes to each other in school and leave them under the pedal of the drinking fountain out in the hallway. They did that in Mr. Hopper's class . . . so that had been the sixth grade, when they were eleven.

Lying there in bed, it drifted back to her. She'd kept those clippings and the code key in the alligator-skin notebook, tucked into pockets inside the flaps. When the notebook had been needed for *Pinny's Hefn* she had transferred the other papers to a big manila envelope, and kept the envelope in the bottom bureau drawer, under the tee shirts. Then at the end of that summer, before leaving for Washington to start her apprenticeship at the Bureau of Temporal Physics, she'd put the completed novel into the blue folder and the clippings and code key back in the notebook, placed both into a larger box, and stashed the box up in the attic in her parents' house in Scofield—*this* house. Pam's room was to be the guest room while she was away, and she hadn't wanted people poking through her stuff.

She could remember debating whether to keep the notebook at all. The prospect of the new life ahead had made her feel like making a clean break with the past. But she did keep it, at some level perhaps remembering the red diary and beginning to understand the moth hole its loss had gnawed in the fabric of her life.

Later, when Pam and Liam had graduated from the BTP and were preparing to move out to Bureau Headquarters, relocating that year to Santa Barbara, Pam had made a farewell trip home. It was right after the adventure with the bear. On that visit, acting on a vague wish to get them out of her parents' house and into her own safekeeping, she'd boxed up all her books and belongings. In the course of this packing she had climbed up a ladder through the trapdoor that was the attic access. Sitting up there cross-legged under a naked light bulb, Pam went through all her stored cartons and divided every-thing into two piles: *keep* and *chuck*. She vividly remembered lifting out the alligator binder and holding it in her hands. She remem-bered dragging the zipper pull around the edge, with a sound like heavy cloth ripping, and leafing through the yellowed paper scraps within.

Several times over the years Pam had winnowed down her stash of "possessions" in the attic. Each time she'd considered throwing out the papers in that notebook, but had always held back. This time she did it. The odd thing was that she *knew*, as she sat there in the dust making the decision, that someday she'd be sorry.

This precedent suggested that even had Frances Pruitt persuaded her daughter to save the red diary, another day it would probably have gone the way of the alligator-skin binder.

~

What the Sam Hill *was* it about that sixth-grade year, Pam wondered, that she couldn't afford to remember or keep any evidence of? The Hefn had returned to Earth in October; but that wasn't it; she'd felt only intense interest, untinged with fear, when the news came that they were back to stay. She had loved her teacher, her school, playing Tarzan on the wooded bluff above the river with Steve and Charlie; had anyone asked her, Pam would eagerly have affirmed that that year, her last of real childhood, had been the happiest year of her life.

It still seemed true. Eleven years old. No period, not quite yet. No breasts yet to speak of, though Pam had already been presented with her first training bras, two of them in soft cotton, a birthday gift from her grandmother Cranfill just before the start of the new school year; Frances had, obviously, discussed Pam's nascent "development" with her mother-in-law. Not with her daughter, though; the first Pam knew that there were going to be bras in her immediate future was when she'd opened the package, with both parents looking on, and there they were.

Maybe, Pam thought, I resented Grandma for forcing the development issue, and that's why I never wanted to go over to her house when we went to Louisville.

But that couldn't be right. Pam remembered sitting in a rocking chair in her other Granny's parlor one evening, rocking and reading, engrossed in a Tarzan book, when her mother touched her shoulder. "Time to go to Grandma's now. You're sleeping over there tonight, get your pajamas and toothbrush." She remembered clearly how, at these words, her heart had sunk like a stone with dread. But she hadn't been more than eight or nine at the time—much younger than eleven.

Old enough, however, to understand that she wasn't to object or whine or say she didn't want to sleep over, didn't want to go over there at all. Pam wasn't supposed to say how she felt about things, unless the feelings were the sort Frances wanted to know about, and Pam didn't have to be told she didn't want to know about these ones. Or hear about them, rather; because she did know. She just didn't care. She cared about what Pam did, not how she felt about it.

Gradually Pam became too agitated to lie still. She rolled out of bed, pulled on her robe, and padded down the hall. Liam's door was open, his bed stripped, his neatly repacked suitcase open on the mattress pad. The time transceiver, in its case, stood on the floor by the door. Pam trotted down the stairs and found her reluctant guest drinking hot cider at the kitchen table. He was dressed for overland travel, not in uniform but in a loose light tunic and trousers, and his scalp gleamed through his neatly combed hair. "Hi," Pam said. "Are you speaking to me today?"

"No," said Liam. "There's a Louisville packet at two-sixteen from Scofield Beach, and a train tonight that will get me to California Wednesday afternoon. I put my sheets in the washer, which isn't working very well, by the way, you'd better have it serviced. I've ordered a taxi for one-thirty. Eat something and let's get it over with."

His last hope for getting off the hook Pam had hung him on had been dashed the day before, when his request for permission to re-record her bradshaw had been instantly approved by the Hefn Alfrey, already back in California. After that he'd had to choose for himself. Pam glanced at the clock: 7:45. "I can eat later. I'm ready now if you are."

"Fine." He scraped back his chair and pushed past her, taking the stairs two at a time. Pam trailed him, thinking. Diary or alligator binder? If she couldn't have both, which was more important?

Liam grabbed the transceiver as he passed the door and said over his shoulder, without looking back, "Where do I set up?"

Both were important, but the diary mattered more. "In the doorway of my room, I guess."

His head snapped around. "Don't guess, all right? Decide and tell me where."

"Oh, knock it off," Pam said mildly. "The doorway of my room, then, *decidedly*." He was furious with her, but she didn't mind so much about that; what mattered was, he was here, and that meant the two of them were fundamentally okay, or would be again in time.

So, walking stiffly to make sure she understood how angry he was, Liam carried the transceiver down the hall and set it up in her doorway. From that position the lens could take in the whole small room. Though furnished sparsely enough now, it seemed crammed by contrast with the time they were about to revisit. Pam's parents hadn't figured that a child's room needed furniture; this room, painted pale blue, had held a bed and a bureau, and nothing else: no desk, no chair, and—astonishing in a librarian's household—no bookcase. Frances had never seen the point of kids owning books. Once you'd read a book, why keep it around, when you could check books out of the library for free? If Pam had appealed to her father, Shelby would probably—no, certainly—have intervened; it had simply never occurred to her to ask him for help.

Her few books had been arranged neatly on the floor, along the baseboard of one wall, an arrangement she'd accepted without question; the first bookcase she had ever had the use of was the one in her room at the BTP. There was a ceiling light and a bed light, but no lamp. She'd done her homework on the dining-room table.

Where had she kept the diary? She didn't remember. In the row of books on the floor, in a bureau drawer, maybe under the bed? She did remember sitting on the bed to write the daily entry. There wasn't anything else to sit on. When the window opened they would at the very least see that.

To hide the transceiver was going to be impossible; unless she happened to be very engrossed in her writing, the eleven-year-old kid Pam used to be would have to be mindwiped, as Liam pointed out while setting up. The possibility didn't worry her. Time is One. (Lost gift or no, Pam probably believed this doctrine more deeply than Liam did.) If she'd been wiped in 2011, that experience had been part of her life ever since. If she hadn't, then it hadn't been. Either way, nothing would change.

"Ready," Liam said finally. "Dates."

"Summer 2011. Late summer." The sixth grade would be over and the diary account of it completed. He was to scroll for prepubescent Pam sitting on her bed, reading or writing in a book. Liam nodded once, slipped his hands into the dimples, and began.

Their first problem was an embarrassment of riches. Prepubescent Pam had read in bed every night of her life; that was the point of the bed light hooked over the headboard. A bewildering jumble of girl, bed, and book, not images but ghostly implications, replaced one another in the shimmer pattern. Pam couldn't watch; the visual mayhem hurt not just the eyes but the brain of an observer not attuned to the transceiver. Even Liam, in perfect attunement, moaned a little with the mental effort of searching a haystack for one particular type of golden stalk.

So she sensed rather than saw him arch back out of the field. She looked, and the lens had dilated. A skinny, scabby girl perched on the edge of the bed, on the side near the window so her back was mostly toward the door, writing in a red book with a pencil. She was dressed in yellow shorts and a plaid halter. Her left foot in a white running shoe was tucked beneath her, and her long bare leg, bent double, stuck out over the foot of the bed like the hind leg of a grasshopper. Limp brown hair fell forward, screening her face. But for her leanness she could not have looked less like Lexi Allred, who was only a few months younger than this girl.

It was afternoon of a bright, breezy, hot-looking day; sunlight streamed in through the open window and the curtains were blowing. The bed was made up with Pam's favorite of several old quilts made by Granny and her spinster sisters, with a pattern of silhouetted Dutch girls in bonnets and wooden shoes. Looking upon this scene, Pam had to brace herself against waves of difficult feeling. Heartache. Longing. Nostalgia that without much pressure could have dissolved into anguish, grief for a lost joy impossible ever to know again, shimmering in the sunny room beyond the lens.

And something else, a sinister potential—dire, inescapable, but for the moment far away.

At the sight of herself, of everything she'd been just then, just there, extreme two ways at once, Pam's ears rang and the edges of her field of vision went black. But Liam, watching her react, had started the recorder, and Pam leaned against the door jamb with her head down till the ringing stopped and her vision cleared.

When she looked again, the girl had closed the red book and turned sideways on the bed. Her face and body in profile—fleshy nose that nobody'd yet realized hadn't healed correctly after being broken, little tethered breasts pointing beneath the halter—tightened Pam's throat. The girl clicked the diary's strap into its lock and held the book in both her hands, a moment of utter privacy, before reaching under the bed to pull out a scuffed navy-and-white saddle oxford, a school shoe. She shook something out—a key chain,that fell into her hand with a little clink. And at once Pam knew what was on the key chain: a four-leaf clover embedded in plastic, and a tiny gold key.

The girl pushed the key into the keyhole with two long fingers and turned it, locking the diary. She dropped the key chain into the toe of the shoe and stuck the shoe back under the bed. Then she started to stand up—and Pam signaled Liam to pull them out. She didn't need to see the diary's hiding place, not at the cost of having to call in a Hefn to wipe the girl. They had what they needed.

CHAPTER 6

The Bradshaw

1 - 28 MAY 2037

Four weeks later Pam sat hunched forward in a private cubicle of a VR parlor in Salt Lake City, the virtual program disk of her bradshaw in her lap. The therapy session was almost over. Pam's therapist, Julie Hightower, was seated in a big upholstered chair in her Washington, DC office—actually a room in her own house in Georgetown—looking as calm and composed as Pam felt anything but. They had had four weeks already to prep for this, but she and Julie had spent this session talking about the pros and cons of proceeding now versus more preparation.

The hectic nature of the past four weeks argued in favor of postponement. Launching Homeland had been an all-consuming business for everyone concerned; but Pam, as originator of the idea, had found herself cast as its chief promulgator. The conference report had been composed and approved at Hurt Hollow, and broadcast live in realtime, by Alfrey, to the global Gaian community over their special frequency. But the minute the Lexi Allred situation had been managed, Pam had gotten down to work preparing a series of retraining lectures for the mission gafrs and the missionaries under their supervision. As she completed and posted each of these, the other Apprentices braced to process the huge volume of queries and objections that immediately arrived in Santa Barbara from these same gafrs and missionaries, many passed along by them from rank-and-file Gaians; and since the Apprentices were themselves on a learning curve, a lot of the questions had been referred back to Pam.

When the computer had grouped the first barrage of mail by theme, the results showed that about 85% of it concerned just a handful of sticking points, all of which the Apprentices had anticipated and Pam had prepared detailed responses to. "I've lived into my own Ground for ten years, am I supposed to switch to family land now?" was one. "I liked it the old way better!" (a flood of those). From the missionaries: "What do I say when I teach Homeland and people get worked up about no babies?" And "Right after the riots they used to slam the door in my face as soon as they saw who I was. Now they let me in, but I'm trying to tell them about kinfolks and native soil and they're glaring at me with total hate."

Pam's reply to this last was especially full and carefully worded. The mindwiping of the twenty-five rioters had hurt the Gaian Mission more than anything else in its entire history. A conference for mission gafrs was already being planned for the Fourth of July weekend, specifically to address the problem. Alfrey and the Santa Barbara-area missions were putting it together. By then, thank God, Humphrey would be awake.

At Pam's suggestion the Temperamentals—the psychologically-focussed Gaians—had brainstormed online and produced a guidebook of helpful suggestions, which had also been issued to the gafrs. Pam and Rhagu had planned, and Pam had facilitated, half a dozen seminars by videophone; these were supplemental to the lecture series and dealt with the same subject in greater depth. Attenders got an immersion course on family relations through history. The wealth of material Pam exposed them to, ranging from Navajo clans to Chinese dynasties to Muhammad's direct descendants (called by their own particular name of *Sayyids*) to Norse mythology, with dozens of stops in between, made it crystal clear that who your forebears were, and who belonged to your living family, had always been matters of surpassing importance to almost everybody.

As she researched material for these seminars, Pam herself had been constantly astounded at the extent to which this was true. In her teens she'd read a novel whose author had flatly asserted that the members of your own family "are the people you care about most, when all's said and done." She distinctly remembered how she'd looked up from the page and said out loud, in exasperation, "*No* they're not!" And in fact, the month of long days crammed with reading and discovery had formed a most disturbing backdrop against which to initiate a bradshaw. Sitting in the VR parlor, trying to make up her mind, Pam was disturbed to the point of queasiness.

On the other hand, nothing could make the wisdom of healing family rifts feel more urgent.

The primacy and urgency of kinship had also come as a shock to the Gaian missionaries, when all this was passed along to them. Unlike Mormon missionaries, they had not grown up hearing and believing that "Family is Forever"; and as a group they were every bit as far out of touch with "ordinary" people and their values as were Pam and the other Apprentices.

Really, why wouldn't they be? All the Apprentices and most Gaian missionaries had been recruited as kids and raised in training camps, like Catholic teens who'd declared a vocation and finished growing up in the seminary or the cloister. In camp the missionaries had been schooled and encouraged to care more about saving Gaia, by producing and distributing food and commodities in a certain reverent way, than about anything else. A missionary less than obsessively passionate about saving Gaia by the means spelled out in the Hefn Directive eventually burned out. You had to be that unworldly and care that much to keep preaching an unpopular message, year in, year out.

LDS missionaries by comparison—in Pam's position it was impossible not to make that odious yet intriguing comparison—traditionally served for two years in Rio or Chicago or wherever they could be sent under the Hefn's travel restrictions, and then came home, got married, and immediately began doing their best to fulfill the Prophet's urgent dictum to "Let the waiting spirits come." Since the Ban, of course, this had meant surrogates and germ plasm, which few could hope to afford, but the Church had its own fertility program and helped as many young couples as it could to have at least one child.

But unlike them, and like Catholic priests and nuns, Gaian missionaries had no expectations of a "normal life," or any life at all really, outside that passionate commitment to the belief that all the Earth is holy ground in need of saving. They were present-crisis oriented. They couldn't afford to be distracted by fantasies of a time when they might not be missionaries anymore, and might actually care about worldly things like careers and family. The missionaries formed intense friendships among themselves and were not expected to be celibate, but, as with other political revolutionaries, the Mission was the primary thing in all their lives.

Gaians in general might be slow to warm up to Homeland, but selling the missionaries themselves really hadn't been difficult, once they'd understood what they were being asked to do. Most had grasped intuitively how to integrate the new message into the old one, and had earnestly gone out to pitch it.

Only to discover, and they quickly did, that more people than ever before refused to give them a genuine hearing.

As the new approach to stewardship began to be better understood, the fever pitch of work had eased off for Pam and her colleagues at the Bureau. But only somewhat. Locally and globally the world outside the Gaian sphere had continued to be a smoldering volcano. Locally, the LDS Church—defeated on the issue of the two rioters (neither of whom had lost the lottery, however) and unaware of its role as exemplar for the reformed Mission—was making a huge fuss about jurisdiction in the Lexi Allred case. Pam had promised Lexi to stay in touch, and keeping that promise occasionally involved visiting *A Thousand Miles* on location in the mountains, which took a big chunk of time. Meanwhile another abuse case involving an older girl had been brought to the Wasatch Mission.

Globally, the elderly Pope and the Secretary General of the UN had requested a joint audience with a Hefn delegation at Thingvellir, their headquarters in Washington, a long, arduous journey by sea for His Holiness unless the Gafr authorized a plane to pick him up (unlikely). Terry Carpenter and his Senate Committee on Alien Affairs were working frantically to hold things together in the US, but a conviction persisted that the Gafr had decided to dispose of humanity entirely. Alfrey and Godfrey were doing their best to quell the rumor through their daily TV appearances, but neither was much of a diplomat at the best of times, and images of the wiped rioters were fresh in everyone's mind. They really needed Humphrey if the genie he had uncorked were to be put back in its bottle, but Humphrey would be sleeping for five or six more weeks at least. A summit with world leaders, like the conference for mission gafrs, would have to wait until he woke up. And now a new rumor had surfaced, about a terrorist resistance movement being formed somewhere in the American Midwest.

Under such circumstances it was almost impossible to have a personal life at all, let alone a personal crisis or epiphany. Also, owing to the press of events, Pam hadn't made time to process her initial shock at seeing the child she had been, in their bedroom of extreme and contradictory feelings. So there were lots of reasons for her to be jittery about running the program.

"I do think, if you want to go ahead and run it now, you'll handle it all right," Julie was summing up thoughtfully, "but I think you should be careful, and be ready to pull out and regroup if you start to feel the waters closing over your head. Remember, you can always have another go tomorrow, or next month, or any time you choose for that matter."

One of the things Pam liked about Julie was the judicious, respectful way she spoke to her patients. She was Liam's therapist too—he'd referred Pam to her—but she and Liam had stopped exchanging notes about Julie years ago; Pam had no idea how, or even whether, Julie talked to Liam these days. She grinned weakly and said, "I'll remember."

Pam had asked if she wanted to monitor, but Julie felt the value of the experience—especially this first time—might be compromised if Pam's concentration on it were less than total. On the other hand, given the circumstances, extra contact time was okay by Julie. "*Call me* if you need to," she urged. "You don't have to twist my arm," Pam told her.

They confirmed the next week's appointment, said their good-byes, and cut the connection. Then, before she could lose her nerve, she popped the case and fed the disk into the slot.

Pam was not a frequenter of VR parlors. Unfamiliarity and anxiety made her clumsy, but the boots, gloves, and helmet were designed to be user-friendly. Finally the light on the console glowed green, and a speaker instructed, "When you are ready, initiate the program by saying the word 'Begin.'"

Feeling as if she were about to be hurled from a plane at her own request, Pam said, "Begin"—and was standing in the doorway of her old room, ten feet from Prepubescent Pam in what appeared to be the living flesh.

Awkward with the gear, Adult Pam took a couple of jerky steps into the room and sat down heavily on the near side of the bed, opposite the girl absorbed in her diary. She sat right on the Dutch Girl quilt and felt its nubbly texture under her hand.

The girl looked up, startled, snapping the book shut and clicking the lock; and at this first full-face view of her—synthesized from her profile with the aid of a couple of old holos—Pam almost stopped the program.

But she didn't, she let it run. She let Little Pam scramble up, back away against the wall, say her first alarmed words, which were, not surprisingly, "What're *you* doing here? Who are you, anyway? Where'd you come from?"

They'd used Liam's Hurt Hollow recording to get the voice and tuned it to be slightly younger. This kid sounded exactly like an eleven-year-old who was a little bit scared. Adult Pam was impressed, and quite nonplussed.

But, again, she stayed with it, replying as she had planned to when asked this question: "I'm you. I'm the person you're going to be when you grow up."

She'd been apprehensive about how the girl would react, but all she did was look surprised and say, "Oh." No real child would have settled for such an answer. By accepting it, Little Pam identified herself as virtual, and let her namesake recover some sense of control.

But then the girl started giving her the once-over, her eyes widening in dismay as she took in the size of Pam's chest. "Nunh-*unh, I'm* not gonna be that big, no way! If I ever get as big as you I'm getting reduced!"

"You won't mind as much when you get to be my age," Pam said, and then wondered how true this actually was.

The girl glared back, suspicious now. "I will so! I mind already! I'm getting *reduced*, and I'm not waiting till I'm as old as you, either. What are you *doing* here, anyway?"

Pam had the answer to that one ready too. "I came to see the diary."

The girl glanced down at the little book, still in her hand. "This?" Pam nodded. "What for?"

"Because I can't remember what's in it, and I'm pretty sure I wrote something important in there."

"So why can't you just look it up?"

"I can't," Pam told her. "I haven't got it anymore."

Coloring, Little Pam clutched the book against her flat stomach. "I'm keeping this diary forever!" She shook her head so hard her straight brown hair whipped about her face. "I don't believe you. You're lying. *You're* not me."

Getting into the question of why she didn't have the diary anymore was the last thing Pam wanted. It was all going wrong. "Pause," she croaked, and the girl's figure froze in place, indignant expression and all, between the bed and the wall. Pam closed her eyes, realized she was sweaty and thirsty, that the back of her head was pounding, and that she wasn't going to last much longer.

Arguing with the kid was no good, and Pam knew instinctively that to wrestle the diary away from her wouldn't work. Little Pam would have to show it of her own free will, and for that to happen Big Pam had to convince her child simulacrum that she was who she said she was. She took some deep breaths and ordered herself to calm down. After a minute she opened her eyes and said "Resume," and Little Pam came back to life, glowering at her.

"Look." Pam leaned across the bed and placed her right hand flat, fingers splayed, on the Dutch Girl quilt. "Put your hand there, next to mine."

She did look, then looked up, then back at the hand. Then, reluctantly, she gave a kind of capitulating snort. "I don't have to. They're the same."

"Do it anyway, okay?"

The girl hesitated, but sat back down on her side of the bed, laid the diary on the quilt, and spread out her left hand, long palm and spidery fingers, nails tapering instead of wide and blunt the way she wished they were, beside Pam's right one. The turquoise thunderbird ring a house cleaner had stolen out of her closet, years ago, was on the girl's left little finger. Their two hands were nearly of a size, though the skin of one was wrinkled and veiny and the nails of the other were dirty.

"Convinced?"

"They're like a pair of gloves, only one's been worn a lot and one's practically brand new." Little Pam withdrew the hand and hid her bony fingers in a fist. "Becky said in church last week that having big hands is good, because you can climb trees better.

And I said, 'But yours aren't big for a woman. Mine are big for a *woman.*'"

Pam remembered that exchange. "Can't get hands reduced, hon, not even in my time." She might have added that she *had* had a nose job; but this girl would be thirteen before she realized there was anything wrong with her nose, and besides, Pam could hardly claim credit. The rhinoplasty had been done over her violent objections. Shelby was the one who *really* hadn't liked that beaky nose.

Now the girl flashed her eyes at Pam. "I'm giving you one more test, okay? If you can recite 'Lone Dog' all the way through without making any mistakes, I'll believe you're me."

Smart move. Pam rattled off the poem from their sixth-grade reader without hesitation or error, and added, "Want me to quote 'Now Chil the Kite brings home the night'?" It was a chapter-heading poem from *The Jungle Books*—the very first Kipling poem she had ever learned by heart.

"Never mind," said Little Pam, relaxed and grinning now, "you win. You said it exactly like I do: 'Oh, mine is still the *lone* trail, the *hard* trail, the *best!*'"

"I hung onto that, anyway." She nodded. "So how about it: can I see the diary?"

She looked down at it, shiny red, and up at Pam, and then she picked it up and reached it over to her across the bed.

Pam could hardly breathe. She held the red book a moment, feeling Little Pam's eyes on her, before clumsily pushing up the button that released the lock and opening it to the middle, June, 2011.

The diary had a lumpy feel because of the objects—straw, locket, folded notes—pasted into it. Pam flipped slowly backward, then forward. May, April. July, August. All the pages were blank.

~

Julie was sympathetic, but not at all discouraged. "I guess we should have known it wouldn't be that simple," she said, after they'd talked about how Pam had felt when she discovered the diary had no writing in it at all (crushed), and how she felt now (wildly agitated). "Look at what you accomplished, though. You figured out a way to establish your authenticity, and you won her trust. Not bad at all for a first encounter. Also, I think it's significant that the diary wasn't locked."

It hadn't been locked yet when Liam started shooting, but Pam didn't go into that. "Not literally it wasn't, but so what? I was locked out anyway." Despite Julie's efforts, this still felt fairly shattering. "That kid, my God, she really threw me. I didn't expect her to be such a tough customer. I can't imagine myself, at her age, standing up to a total stranger like that, bawling her out for not getting a *breast* reduction!"

Julie smiled demurely. "Well, hardly a total stranger. And besides, for what it's worth, that hasn't been my impression." Professional ethics forbade her to say that Liam, the jerk, had given her a different picture of Pam as a child, but she was pretty sure that's what Julie meant.

"So where do I go from here? Any ideas?" Pam felt fresh out of them herself. The whole experience of the bradshaw, so far, had been one rude shock after another.

"It would probably be more useful if the ideas came from you," Julie predictably replied. "*You* destroyed the evidence—all of it, the diary and the papers in the alligator binder. Undoubtedly you had an excellent reason at the time, but it would appear that your unconscious will let you *see* what you wrote in the diary only after being reassured that it's safe to reveal the secret now. How to reassure it is the challenge."

"I see that," Pam told her, "but isn't there more than one way to skin this cat? What about trying hypnotherapy again? It's been, what, four years? Lots of water over the dam since then."

Julie hesitated, frowning slightly. "Hypnotherapy is certainly still an option, and, as you say, a lot has happened since we tried it before, but I don't think I'd recommend it right now. Your history of resistance isn't the only reason I say this; I've also found that it's usually better to stick to one approach until you've given that approach a fair chance to work. If you should decide at a later time to abandon the bradshaw, temporarily or permanently, we can talk about this again, but for now . . . "

"I was considering abandoning it, actually." Despite what she'd done to Liam and their friendship to get it made, and what Liam would say if she quit.

"Well," said Julie, and Pam knew which side of *that* line she was about to come down on, "of course that's your decision, but you've been given a rare means of delving into your unconscious mind—something many of my patients would love to be able to make use of—and I have to say I hope you won't throw that opportunity away without giving it a fair chance to work."

Pam said wryly, "I suppose you had no ulterior motive when you said you hoped I wouldn't 'throw it away.'"

Julie grinned broadly. "Of course I didn't."

She waited, looking expectant, while Pam cudgeled her wits, but her mind was as blank as the pages of the diary had appeared. Finally she said, "Look, I know I was no great shakes as a hypnotic subject, but I'm not sure I'm cut out to be that much better as a bradshaw operator either. Couldn't you at least suggest a strategy for coming up with some ideas?"

She chuckled. "Come on, Pam, you don't need me to tell you how to do that. I wonder if by trying to get me to tell you something you already know, you aren't actually saying you feel a need for help and support."

Actually, of course, Julie didn't "wonder" this at all. And she was right, Pam did know what to do, really: keep a meticulous dream log, do focused meditations, the usual stuff.

But maintaining all that on the front burner took time and energy, and Pam was working long hours these days. Julie was right that she was asking for support; but till she said so Pam hadn't realized that, and was embarrassed. *Little* Pam never asked anybody for help. She glanced at the clock to see if the session weren't just about over.

"Of course," Julie went on when she didn't reply, "I have, and do, and will continue to support you in every way I can. I do believe that you can use this bradshaw to find out some things you need to know about your past. But whether or not you proceed with this, or proceed with it now, is entirely up to you. It was pure coincidence that the convention you attended was on your home turf. If you don't want to work on the bradshaw just at present, that probably means you're not ready, and that I was mistaken to think you were."

Halfway through this speech Pam started shaking her head. "No, no, you weren't mistaken. I *am* ready, and I don't think I believe in pure coincidence. I'll do it, the dream log and free-associative writing, the whole nine yards—but I still don't want to right now, I'm too damn busy!"

Julie stood up, smiling. "One day we must have a discussion about the meaning of the word *want*. We're out of time for today, though, so I'll limit myself to wishing you luck on your next trip through the time portal. And to reminding you of one more thing you already know: that every word you put down in that little book is still stored in your memory."

"You could remind me of something else I already know, too: why I went to such lengths to make the thing in the first place. I keep kind of losing my grip on that."

"Sounds like you've just reminded yourself." Julie punched a key and terminated the session.

"I thought it might be a way of connecting with the new Gaian thing—Homeland, the family focus, all that," Pam said to the blanked screen. "You know. Confront Dad in my own head, work out some kind of reconciliation—I thought if I could put it all behind me, maybe I'd feel like looking up Dad's sisters and their kids, see if we couldn't find some common ground if we really made an effort . . . ." She groaned. Aunt Ginger. Aunt Doro. The raucous gaggle of cousins. For the life of her she couldn't really remember why the bradshaw had felt like such a brilliant a response to the problem of Homeland.

~

The next week was a blur of conference calls, casework, and computer modeling. Things were continuing to go badly for the Gaian missionaries in the field. From everywhere the same complaint came in: *Why hadn't somebody come up with the Homeland concept before the riots made people so unreceptive?*

In between calls and meetings, Pam used whatever odd scraps of time occurred to prepare herself for her next encounter with the girl in the bare bedroom. To that end she got out the soft brown diary from 2010 and browsed through the entries for the summer before the beginning of sixth grade:

July 31. Today I got my cast off my arm. The mussle is little. dr. ogden said it wont hurt too long. We star gazed tonite. Pam [She'd broken her left arm falling out of a tree].

August 1. Nothing happened today. Hank [Hank? Trying out boys' names. . .]

August 2. My arm is better I went swimming. We star gazed tonight. Sam

August 3. Last nite I slept downstairs I saw a viddy, It scared me. we went to Madison to get a water melin. Sam

August 4. Nothing happened today. Pam

August 5. today was boring nothing happened [not even token punctuation, apparently].

August 6. Tonight I saw Dungeon of mutations. Hope I don't have nightmares, but bet I will. I did calculus with Doug [Doug Emmi, Pam's math tutor].

August 7. Dear Diary, today was boreing we had hamburgers for supper Harry

Apart from scaring herself with horror viddies, most of August did sound fairly "boreing." She stargazed; Shelby was teaching her constellations and planets, and to locate bright stars like Arcturus and Vega. She went swimming at the quarry, played Tarzan with Charlie and Steve (before the broken arm), played "Mumbley Peg" with Becky. Nothing the least bit remarkable there. Pam skipped ahead:

August 24. Today I packed for Louisville [She was going down to visit Granny, her "good" (maternal) grandmother, for a week that would end with her eleventh birthday on September 1.]

August 26 Dear D today I had fun sewing and playing dolls with Granny. [A dexterous child, Pam could stitch a neat seam from the age of five or six with those long fingers; and while she hadn't "played dolls" in the usual sense—a girly-girl thing to be despised and scorned—she had loved making little pants and jackets for her two diminutive plastic boy dolls with patient Granny, the only adult who ever actually sat down and played with her. And now the diary reported again and again throughout the week: *Today I had fun.*]

August 29. today I went to town with Granny & saw Churchill downs. I got 2 books, the son of Tarzan & Woof howe hob. Pamfrey [*Woof Howe Hob* was a book about the stranded Hefn mummified in a Yorkshire peat bog. Obviously, two months before their second coming, Pam was already interested in the Hefn, to the point of appropriating their *-frey* suffix into her own name games. Nobody yet knew, of course, that one of the Hefn actually was called Pomfrey.]

August 31. Dear D today Mom came. I missed her a lot. [Shelby had definitely come too. Nothing about missing him.]

September 1. Today Is my birthday. I am eleven years old. I got a boomclox, a tunic, a blue bedlamp [!]*, swimming goggles, and   . I blew out all the candles & wished for an elec. canoe. Pam* [And in very faint pencil, along the margin of the bound edge: *MOM & DAD WOULDN'T SING HAPPY BIRTHDAY TO ME THEY MADE ME CRY BUT THEY DIDN'T KNOW IT.*]

Oh God. Now Pam remembered that birthday.

Her parents' strange refusal to sing to her hadn't been the worst of it. Her Granny had bought Pam a boomclox they'd seen in a shop window on their ritual trip to town. When Pam and her parents got home to Scofield, Pam was shown the boomclox Frances had planned to give her—instantly recognizable as superior to Granny's in every way, smaller, cuter, pricier—and told it was to be taken back to the store, Pam couldn't keep it; Granny's clunky boomclox was the one she had to keep. It occurred to neither of them—certainly not to Pam—that the redundant gift might have been exchanged for something else. Or simply kept and used.

Pam could visualize her mother's "present" in perfect detail. The clock part of it was Swiss. Every hour on the hour a bugle blew and a little door flew open, releasing three adorable clockwork thoroughbreds, each with a tiny, crop-wielding jockey on its back. Horses and jockeys raced each other around a semicircle to another door that closed behind them. The programing was randomized; you never knew which horse would beat the others. Pam had been less besotted with the Japanese "boombox" part, but no doubt its sound quality was excellent.

She pleaded and begged to keep that boomclox, but to no avail: back to the store it went. Needless to say, her pleasure in her Granny's gift was a casualty of all this fuss.

The blank space in the list? Best guess: it was a placeholder for the unmentionable bras from Grandma.

September 2. Mom sang to me late last night, and dad sang to me this morning. Now all I want is the boomclox mom got for me. Pam

Big Pam was starting to feel queasy. She shut the thin brown book and put it away.

~

Homely, skinny Little Pam sat on the double bed covered with the Dutch Girl quilt—now sealed in a plastic bag in a closet in Salt Lake City—one long leg bent double, one foot tucked beneath her, scribbling in the red diary with a yellow pencil. To the left of the door, on top of her bureau, squatted the ugly boomclox, displaying the time and date in violet numbers. A little rack of disks squatted beside it, but no music was playing. The room was full of sunshine.

"Hi," said Big Pam, and sat down on the bed.

Little Pam looked up, then dropped her pencil and clapped the diary shut. "You came back."

"Mm-hm. How are you? How do you feel?"

"Fine. Why'd you come back? What were you so upset about?"

"I couldn't read your diary. Sorry I rushed off like that. I want to try again, but first I want to talk to you about your boomclox."

The girl's eyes turned toward it, then back to her visitor. "What about it?"

"Granny gave it to you last summer for your birthday." She nodded. "And Mom got you one too, but she wouldn't let you keep it."

"No. She took it back."

"Why'd she do that? Remind me."

The girl shrugged. "Granny bought me that one 'cause I asked her to. . . well, not exactly asked her to. We were walking along and I saw it in a shop window and told her I liked it, and she was like did I want her to get it for my birthday and I was like sure. But Mom, see, she'd already gotten me one herself, but I didn't know it, and I couldn't have two so I had to keep this one."

"So it's kind of your fault that you couldn't keep the one Mom got for you?"

"If I didn't ask for this one I could've kept the one with the race-horses, but I did, and Mom said it would hurt Granny's feelings, so . . ."

"Honey," Pam said, leaning toward her, "it wasn't your fault at all. *Not at all.* It wasn't anybody's fault, but Mom was mad at Granny for messing up her plans and she needed somebody to blame. And she couldn't punish Granny, so she punished you."

That stopped her. Her mouth fell open. "You mean, like, by taking it back to the store? The good one? But she said it would hurt Granny's feelings!"

Pam shook her head. "I really mean by showing it to you at all. You were happy with Granny's till you saw Mom's, right? There was no reason to show it to you at all, if she'd already decided to take it back to the store. She just did it to make you feel bad—to get even. It was mean, and you hadn't done anything to deserve it. I want you to understand that. I didn't understand it till I was a lot older than you are now, and I wish I had."

The girl stared at Pam, eyes filling with comprehension, then suddenly with shiny tears. "It *was* mean," she said wonderingly.

"You're darn right it was mean. And I'll tell you something else: she won't ever pull anything like that on you again, because I'm here now, and I won't let her."

"You won't?"

"I won't. I promise."

Pam rubbed the back of her bare wrist under her nose, snuffling a little. Then, without being asked, she handed the diary over, across the Dutch Girls.

Pam held it prayerfully for a moment. Then she let it fall open and looked down.

~

"It was all in *code*," she reported to Julie, "that code Charlie and Steve and I made up, so we could write secret notes to each other in school! I looked down at the page—dreading that it would be blank again—and there were these lines of spirals and stars and triangles and pitchforks, in pencil."

"Did you keep the diary in code?"

"No, no, in ordinary English! I might've tried the code for a page or two, but it would have been too slow for everyday, even if I'd memorized it, which as far as I can recall I never did."

"Well, that's fascinating. That's really fascinating," said Julie. Plainly, she meant it. The ways and means of bradshaws still hadn't been studied much—too few cases—so this was all psychological terra semicognita. Pam could practically see the preliminary outline for the article Julie was about to write coming together behind her eyes.

"So after I checked to make sure the whole diary was in code, I asked the kid if she would let me borrow the code key."

"In the alligator notebook!"

"Right."

"And?"

"She said, 'I can't. It's out in the hall closet, and I have to stay in my room.' And I realized that by setting up the transceiver in the doorway, we'd trapped her in there. Nothing outside that one room was available to either of us. Well, then I had a kind of desperate brain wave; I asked her if she could call Charlie or Steve on her phone and ask them to bring a copy of the code key over and pitch it up to her through the window."

Julie sat back in her chair. "I take it that didn't work."

"Nope. She did call them up, but both their phones just rang and rang. *They* weren't available. I don't know why not, actually; it seems to me that she ought to have been able to reach outside the room in that way."

Julie nodded. "Maybe there are factors embedded in the whole bradshaw phenomenon that keep you from proceeding in a way your own unconscious doesn't endorse. But it's like the shadow-memory phenomenon; we don't know why a virtual person can remember the things she remembers, but *only* those things, or why someone running the virtual program—like you—can accomplish some things and not others." She leaned forward, toward the camera. "So: how did you feel when Charlie and Steve didn't answer their phones?"

"Defeated for this round, but not as discouraged as before. But I realized the phone idea was a bust, so I shut the program down till I could hash things over with you."

Julie smiled cheerfully. "Well! It's encouraging, isn't it? First you get blank pages, then you get a code you once made up yourself. That feels like progress to me." And when Pam nodded, "Shall we start on the hashing-over, then? What was different about this run? What did you do this time, that you didn't do the first time?"

Pam could tell her that, all right. She'd done what John Bradshaw himself had recommended: in his own ooey-gooey phrase, she had "championed her inner child." She'd told the kid that their mother had punished her for something that wasn't her fault, and that showing her the pretty clock was mean.

She had also promised that this would never be allowed to happen again. In life it had happened many times over, and none of those meannesses could be undone. Still, to this eleven-year-old version of herself, she had made a commitment of protection. According to Bradshaw, this should help them both.

THE BIRD SHAMAN

But Pam had said what she'd said spontaneously. She hadn't been trying to do a "championing" exercise. Fresh from reading the earlier diary, she had glared at that clunky boomclox on the bureau and told the kid what she herself had needed to hear when *she* was Pam/Sam/Hank, but never had.

~

Dream Log, 5/9/37. I live in a duplex. There are bears next door. The Fire Dept. comes to take them away. The next day two cubs appear in the hallway of the half of the house where I live, and rush into the room. I shove them out, but now the mother bear is in the hall. She sticks her paw in the door, tries to get in. The hasp on the door is frail and she bends the plate with her paw; I have to hold it shut, bending it back with my thumb so the bolt will engage. I'm very scared of the mother bear.

She keeps attacking the door. Several times I discover that the door's not completely closed. When I close it she attacks, but not while it's ajar. Once the mother bear comes into the room, standing upright, and I escort her out. We both maintain our dignity during this scene—no unseemly panic or ferocity. Only when the door's between us does she become savage.

There's an antique table phone in the hallway, white, on a tall stalk. I rush out and grab it, run the cord under the door, slam the door. The bear attacks. I call the Fire Dept., and they come right away. The bears are hiding. One of the firemen wants me to sit on a bed beside him and read a book of stories for a purpose now unclear, except that it had something to do with catching the bears.

Dream Log, 5/12/37. I'm weeding the flower beds of some house I live in with Mom, and accidentally break several tulip stalks. Mom yells angrily, but I reply that it doesn't matter because we'll never sell this house or move out of it. Will we? She acts furtive and moves away. I run after her, shouting, screaming even, furious that she's walking away like that without answering me. She walks faster, then turns and brandishes a shiny black handgun that's warped; I think made of licorice. I wrestle it away from her at once—no question I can control her in this direct physical sense—but I realize then that she's sold the house, my home, right out from under me.

151

I have to go to an orphanage not far from the house. I'm crying and carrying on, terribly upset. We go past a gatehouse where Mom collects the money, big handfuls of bills. Then suddenly she's lying in the long grass nearby, reduced to a shadowy impression of her body and outstretched hands, fingers extended, nails long and blood-red.

The orphanage is horrible beyond belief. The next day I put my hand in my pocket and realize I still have my keys. I decide to go spend one more night in my house, but when I get there I see a light in the basement and open, empty boxes in back; the new people have already moved in. I'm absolutely devastated, and cry and cry. I'm about eleven in the dream.

Every night for years, before Shelby died, Pam's dreaming unconscious had displayed a magnificent kaleidoscope of fractal patterns, curling upon themselves like a forest of burgeoning fern fronds. Such was her intuitive sensitivity that her brain had created visual equivalents of the feedback loops of lighter sleep and REM sleep levels and projected them in reds, blues, and yellows, rich and various, impersonal and pure. She had taken the fractals for granted; they'd always been there and they always would be. But behind the curtain they created, other images and dramas had been playing all the time; and now that this lovely aurora borealis protected her no longer, now that her father was dead, now that her unconscious had decided she could bear to know what it had been concealing, there were times when Pam yearned to go back and be Little Pam and Apprentice Pam, rather than go on living one more day with the release that had "cured" her of her gift.

~

"Hi," Liam said when she'd ordered the screen to come on. "Just dashing in the door, were you?"

"Your powers of observation render me speechless." She had run in from the back yard and was puffing and flushed; they were having a smothering heat wave in Salt Lake. She almost hadn't bothered to catch the phone but was glad she'd made the effort now. She and Liam hadn't spoken in six weeks—not since Kentucky and the bradshaw ultimatum.

"What were you doing?"

"Feeding the robins, out back. At this moment, six fledgling robins call me mother." For the past couple of summers Pam been hand-raising orphaned and injured birds for the local aviary. It was interesting and fun, but this year she was really much too busy to be doing it. Although the four healthy babies were flying well, all six still expected to be fed several times a day. Pam would push open the screen door to the back yard and the quartet of good fliers would dive out of the apricot tree, straight for her head. Adolescent robins aren't little, tiny birds; Pam couldn't wait for this stage to be over.

"Feeding them what?" Liam wondered. "Worms and bugs? No wonder you're out of breath."

Pam grinned in spite of herself. "Dry dog food softened in water. High protein content? Comes in a bag? Also I was siphoning the water from the ducklings' swimming pool into the growing beds."

"Swimming pool?"

"An old bathtub with a ramp and a deck."

"Ducks can climb a ramp?"

"They had to be lured up with feed on the cleats at first, but yeah. It's Winnie and Frank's pool really, but they're sharing it with the rehab mallards till the babies get waterproofed."

"Oh," Liam said. "They don't come that way?"

Pam shook her head. "They have to work oil from glands in their skin all through their feathers, with their bills. Getting wet stimulates grooming behavior. Listen, what are you guys hearing back from missionaries in the field?"

Liam's expression changed. He shrugged. "Most gafrs seem to be recalling their missionaries, they're gonna just wait till after the conference now, to see if anything useful comes out of that. Everybody hates Gaians these days."

"That's been my impression too, I just hoped maybe you'd heard something . . . Jaime's still got people out on the Ute and Paiute reservations, but not in the Mormon towns and for sure not here in Salt Lake."

Liam winced. "No, I guess not!"

"Just between us," Pam said heavily, "how the hell are we going to turn this around? I spend all day every day sunk to the eyebrows in this stuff, and so far I can't see any way to get the message past all that hostility."

"That's what the conference is for," Liam told her, "but I know what you mean, everybody does, out here. Even if the Gaian Mission were to publicly assume responsibility for inciting to riot, and I think we should, twenty-five people would still be mindwiped."

"They shouldn't be, goddammit."

"No, and the Gaians shouldn't have demonstrated that day, and Humphrey shouldn't have lost it at Carrie's service, but here we are anyway."

"Maybe," Pam said, "with Humphrey back in action—"

"Yeah. Well, I won't keep you, I know you've got a lot to do. Actually, I was just checking in to see how the bradshaw was going."

They exchanged looks. "Slowly," Pam said, "since you ask. It does seem to be going someplace, but I can't tell where just yet."

"The second take hit the bull's-eye?"

"I think so. Hit the target, anyway. I really appreciate it a lot that you stayed to shoot it, by the way."

"Yeah." Liam regarded her thoughtfully. "You're welcome, I guess. Although to describe Eddie as pissed about it would be a feeble representation of the truth."

"Apologize to him for me. What about you—does this call mean you've decided to forgive me?"

"For making me admit that I can't afford to lose you out of my life? I'll probably never forgive you for that. But Eddie being furious, the *interminable* train trip I suffered through, etc., etc., that's all water under the bridge. I called because I was concerned. Really."

And because you miss waking me up when something's on your mind, Pam thought but didn't say. They both knew why he'd called. Things being what they were with her and Liam, one of them had been bound to call the other eventually. "I haven't got time to get into it right now," she told him, "but in a nutshell, I can't read the diary. The first time I tried, the pages were completely blank except for the printed dates and lines. The second time the writing was all in code."

"Code?"

"A code Charlie and Steve and I made up to pass notes in school. Stars, triangles, spirals, pitchforks. I don't have a clue which symbols stood for what letters anymore."

"Codes can be cracked. Bring in an expert."

She shook her head. "I thought of that, but I've got this hunch that if the answer's going to be worth knowing, I have to discover it via the right process. Anyway, Julie wouldn't approve."

Liam laughed. "Let me guess. She'd be like, '*You're* the *real* expert, aren't you? You'll figure it out yourself when you're ready.'"

Pam laughed with him—Liam, a clever mimic, had nailed Julie exactly—before adding, "She's probably right, that's the hell of it. Listen, sorry to cut you off but I was supposed to be back in my office five minutes ago."

As usually happened when she tried to hang up first, this triggered a perverse refusal in Liam to end the conversation. "Okay, but just tell me, what about the straw and the locket, were they in the diary?"

"*They* were, just no writing."

"I get it," he said eagerly, "because you already *knew* they were in there and what they looked like. What you can't see is what you can't remember."

"I guess so." Pam looked at her watch.

"*She* remembers. You two kids need to learn to work together."

"Liam—"

"Okay! So long! Call me if you get a breakthrough."

~

Dream Log, 5/13/37. I'm sleeping upstairs, in the bedroom next to the laundry room. I'm awakened within the dream by the sound of a little girl crying in her crib, which is in the laundry room. The sink (actually full of Mallard ducklings in a cage at present) has vanished, and the crib stands in its place. Both rooms are black as pitch, but I get up, grope my way to the little girl, and put my arms around her. At the same instant I become aware that Dad is sitting in a rocking chair where the washer ought to be. He's facing the crib, and he's stone blind. He rocks in a gentle, regular rhythm, a little smile on his face. This doesn't sound terrifying, but I woke up terrified.

Later: another dream. I'm running the bradshaw. Pam/Sam/Harry and I are sitting across from each other on the bed. Again I ask her to try to get the code key for me. She activates her phone—in the dream she has a modern wall-mounted videophone—and places the call. At once a smiling Liam appears on the screen, looking as he did at fifteen. When Pam/Sam/Hank explains that we need his help, he reaches right through the screen and hands her a big iron key like a dungeon key from some old horror show. "You kids need to work together," he says.

~

Julie rubbed the sides of her nose with her extended fingers. "Let's go back to basics for a minute. We know your father was inappropriate with you. We know that he was "blind" to the effects of his behavior, which nevertheless made you so anxious in early adolescence that you developed a dissociative disorder caused by his sexualizing of your relationship—by the way, that rhythmic rocking is pretty suggestive, don't you think?" Pam rolled her eyes. "You've spent how many years now connecting feelings to events and doing the necessary grief work, so that at this point the abuse is old news to you, even though you're still dealing with some aspects of it. What I'm wondering is, where's all this sudden anger at your *mother* coming from? And why now?"

"From *her* always 'turning a blind eye' to what was going on?"

"Hm." Julie frowned slightly. "Perhaps."

"From reviving that business about the boomclox? I hadn't thought about all that for twenty years."

"Well, that too of course, but there's a lot of fear in these dreams as well." Pause. "Are you angry at her for leaving you the bradshaw, and afraid of what you might learn?"

"If I could read the damn diary," Pam said wearily, "maybe I'd know."

~

"Oh good! I was hoping you'd come back," exclaimed Little Pam. "I wanted to ask you about something." Her expression was serious.

Big Pam sat down on the Dutch Girl quilt. "Shoot."

"You know—you know that time when Steve and Charlie and I had a fight before church, and I didn't want to sit with them so I sat with Ninnie?"

Ninnie was a widowed family friend, older than Pam's parents, who occupied the same front pew every Sunday. Surprised that the program would let Little Pam bring up a subject Big Pam hadn't introduced first, she said "Sure I do."

"And before the service started, Dad made me leave and come home with him?"

Pam nodded. "He was furious, and you had no idea why. You were walking along next to him, trying not to cry. And finally he said, in this terribly angry voice, 'Why weren't you sitting with the boys?' And you said—" at this point Little Pam chimed in, and they chanted together, "I don't want to talk about it."

"And then," the girl finished, "he was like, 'I don't suppose you'll ever want to talk about things with me.'"

She brought it all so near. "He sounded disgusted. You were totally bewildered. The whole thing just seemed like some big craziness."

"Yeah. Then we got home and I ran inside and threw myself on Mom, bawling my head off. She said, 'What in the *world* is the matter?' But I couldn't talk, I couldn't tell her. And anyway, I didn't *know*."

They sat silent for a bit. Finally Big Pam said, "So what's your question?"

She looked up soberly. "Well, you knew why Mom showed me the good boomclox before she took it back. I thought you might know what Dad was so mad about that time."

Pam got up, went around the foot of the bed, sat down and put her arms around that tense skinny body, and pulled it close. The girl didn't resist, but neither did she respond. Pam didn't expect her to; Little Pam thought hugs were mushy, or thought she ought to think so. "I did figure it out, actually. He was mad because if you weren't going to sit with Steve and Charlie, he wanted you to sit with him."

The girl pulled back openmouthed. "With *him*?"

Big Pam knew, of course, that the idea of sitting with their father had never crossed their mind. For some reason Frances hadn't been in church that day; if she had been, they might have sat with their parents instead of Ninnie. But their father, by himself? It had simply never occurred to them. It would never have occurred to them in a million years.

"Now I've got one for you," Big Pam told her, releasing her from the circle of the embrace. "What happened next? After Dad came in the house. I don't remember."

"Mom just told me to go on up and change my clothes. They were talking downstairs. Then we had dinner."

So the episode had been dropped. Frances had probably remonstrated with Shelby for dragging them out of church, but neither parent had talked with them about it later to clear things up. Neither of the Pams had expected them to. Their parents backed each other up through silence, taking as an article of faith that if nothing were said, it would be the same as if nothing had happened. Big Pam tended to think of Shelby as "the problem," but all too obviously it wasn't only Shelby.

And suddenly she had a painful flash of insight into those recent dreams. She saw that *both* Shelby and Frances, in their very different ways, had been stupid and cruel about plenty of things, and that neither had protected their daughter against the stupidities and cruelties of the other.

She hugged Little Pam again, hard. "Dad wants to be closer to you, but he doesn't know how to make that happen. Then he gets frustrated and angry when he can tell you don't enjoy being with him. But it's not your job to fix that, honey. He's the dad, it's *his* job, only he doesn't know how to do his job—which isn't his fault, either, but it sure as heck isn't yours, and it was really, really wrong of him to blame you and scare you like that."

Little Pam's arms clutched back, then let go. She wiped her nose on the back of her hand, as before, and sniffed a couple of times. Their tears always mostly ran down their nose, where they were less observable.

Pam got up. "I have to go now, but I'll be back."

~

"We're kind of getting to know each other," she reported to Julie. "Reminiscing almost. It's nice. She's a pretty unattractive kid, I can't help noticing, but we sure do have a lot in common."

"And she needs you so badly, too."

Pam nodded. "I'd like to shake John Bradshaw's hand. All that hokey, cloying inner-child crapola? The hell of it is, he was right."

And a week later: "We're sitting on opposite sides of the bed, chatting about her birthday—in 2011 she's got a birthday coming up—and she hands me the diary. I let it fall open in the middle, not really paying that much attention for once, and then I see there's writing on the page, a pencil scribble, and my heart jumps into my throat. But then a second later I see what it is and start howling with laughter, and the poor kid gets upset—she thinks I'm laughing at *her*, at something she wrote. I had a job convincing her that wasn't it. Here, I keyed it out for you." Pam held the pad close to the screen so Julie could see, and read aloud: "*Kotar Tublat yud gom-lul kambo yang ta nala zor den. Kotar b'wang Tublat om zan dano histah, ho yummas Kotar tand gree-ah ho gree-ah histah unk lul.*" Julie's baffled expression made Pam laugh again. "You don't recognize it? It's Ape English—Tarzan talk!"

Julie leaned forward, squinting at the screen. "Tarzan talk? You mean, it's a language?"

"But of course! My pal Steve and I learned a whole list of words of what was supposed to be the language of the Great Apes, from the Tarzan books, and we'd talk to each other in Ape while we'd be playing in the woods. It's a grammar-less language, you just string words together. My name was Kotar, *ko* plus *tar*—Mighty White. Pretty braggy name for such a scrawny kid! Steve was Tublat—it means Broken Nose, but he just liked the sound of the word. Actually, *I* should have been Tublat, I was the one whose nose had been broken. Not that I knew that at the time."

"Pam, the suspense is killing me. What does this passage say?"

She laughed again, the Ape English made her feel so happy. "Sorry to disappoint you, after all the buildup, but not much. It basically just says we went to the river bluff and swung on the rope swing and played sex games—Steve used to let me play with his penis and watch him pee, and I'd let him kiss me."

"You're dismissing sexual play as 'not much,' given your particular history?"

"What I mean is, nothing *new*. I've always remembered going to the woods with Steve after school, and the stuff we did."

Julie looked quizzical. "Which is the part that says 'sex games'?"

Pam held the pad up again. "I'm paraphrasing. *Yumma* was our word for 'kiss'—we made it up, Burroughs didn't supply one. The Great Apes probably don't go in for a lot of kissing. It says 'I hold Steve's long skin bone snake, many kisses, I don't like *that* but I like watching his snake pee.' More or less. 'Pee' is 'go water,' literally—*unk lul*."

"Did you write in the diary in Ape English, or is this another involuntary translation?"

"Hmm." Pam considered. "Actually, something as purple as this passage I *might* have written in Ape, but I didn't ordinarily."

"And was the rest of the diary in Ape?"

She shook her head. "The other pages were blank, it was just that one entry on that one page."

"Well! This is all extremely interesting," said Julie with obvious relish. "Your unconscious is still protecting the diary's contents using a code from childhood, but now it's a code you're able to read. More progress!"

"You know," said Pam, "I believe it is."

~

"How are the robins doing?" Liam inquired. He'd called twice more, very late at night, waking her on both occasions; it was like old times. V-mail would have been far less intrusive, but he didn't like v-mail; he liked exchanging live comments with a face onscreen, even a grouchy, sleepy face.

That being so, it was clever of him to ask about the birds. "Wingy, Pesky, or Gimpy?"

"These names you give them stun me with their originality. Gimpy would be...?"

"The sick one—the one the dog roughed up, that's got everything wrong with her, leg, wing, eye, beak, *and* a bad cold. Ever hear a bird cough?"

"I didn't know they could."

"Me neither. Well, she'd been hobbling around for a week on one normal foot and one fisted-up foot. Then yesterday, all of a sudden the bad foot opened up and bingo: two sets of toes! And I know she has at least partial vision back in the bad eye. So the news on Gimpy is cautiously good."

"I had *no* idea birds caught cold."

"Well, it's a flu-like virus of some sort. I stick the dog food in and sometimes she spits it back out—her beak hurts, she can't swallow big pieces—and it comes out slimy. Yesterday she blew a bubble out of one of her nostrils. And she's always scraping her beak on things to clean it off. Then there's the cough, this little pathetic *hack hack*."

"You're breaking my heart," said Liam. "Actually, you sort of are.

160

She sounds like a wreck."

"She looks like a feather duster that got caught in a fan. Nobody thought she could possibly recover enough to be released, but after her foot unclubbed I started to hope."

"Well, keep me posted. And how does your garden grow?"

"Great. It's been dry, what else is new, but that's why God made mulch and rain barrels. Cabbages, corn, beans, tomatoes, sweet potatoes, red potatoes, onions, cukes and melons on trellises, straw-berries, blackberries for Humphrey, black currants, all looking good. Lots of fat healthy snails for Winnie and Frank. Good peach crop coming on but the apricots froze out again. I got everything planted but I don't have much time to fuss with it, the Utah gafrs have requested a pre-conference seminar, and I've been running that by phone every morning for the past two weeks, with no end in sight, on top of everything else. The crops seem to be doing okay anyway though."

"Probably the duck poop."

"Probably."

Liam stretched and yawned. "What's this seminar for? Can't they make the conference?"

"Oh yeah, they're coming. It's mostly anxiety management, they need to feel like they're doing something to support Jaime, and so do I, he's still awfully upset. Coming up with a dynamite idea to bring to the conference would help a lot."

"That wouldn't help just Jaime! I'm guessing nobody's had one yet?"

Pam sighed. "We'll all be talking, and suddenly he'll say, 'If only they hadn't mindwiped twenty-five people!' and somebody else'll say, 'It *worked*, goddammit, it stopped the rebellion cold!' and Jaime'll say, 'Drove it underground, you mean!' and off we go."

"Yeah, the main way we make ourselves feel useful out here is by sleuthing after terrorist rumors. Besides helping organize the conference and emailing updates to the mission gafrs."

"Our guys really appreciate those updates, by the way. It helps to know the Bureau's making a major effort to work with them."

She still hadn't mentioned the bradshaw. Sensing she was getting ready to hang up, Liam gave in and asked.

"There at least we *are* making some progress," she told him. "It's slow, though. If we get a breakthrough, you'll be among the first to know."

"Mind if I stick my, ah, beak in a little?" And when she grinned and didn't say no, "I don't mean to mess with whatever Julie's strategy is here, but I keep wondering if she's suggested that you ask the kid to help you."

Pam frowned. "No, I don't think so. Not even implicitly. Julie's been bending over backwards *not* to make suggestions, even when I request them. She does interpretive stuff, but she's maintained the position from the start that I'll hit on the right approach myself when I'm ready."

"Oh."

She waited for him to go on, but Liam screwed his face into a skeptical mask and just sat there. Finally she said, "Come on, say what you're thinking. How can she help me out? The kid."

"See, Pam," said Liam, "it never occurs to you to *ask* for help. You didn't ask *me* to help you, when you realized you'd picked the wrong event and needed me to re-record your bradshaw. Instead you put our whole relationship on the line. You *forced* me to help you."

Pam blinked. "I shouldn't have had to ask. You should have offered."

Liam shook his head impatiently. "Maybe so, but that's not my point. My point is, *you* help people without thinking twice, but you never expect them to help *you*, you always think you're supposed to do it by yourself. If help's offered you take it, but you never ask."

Pam had recognized this very trait in Little Pam, of course, and had been uncovering its roots in her family life. "Hunh. Okay, I accept that. But you kept repeating that you weren't going to miss that plane no matter what. Are you saying now that all you wanted was for me to ask you nicely?"

"To tell the truth," he admitted, "I'm not sure. Eddie was piling on the pressure, I might've felt you were asking too much. I'm not saying you were," he added quickly, "but that's beside the *point*. What I would've decided back then is about me; and the point I'm trying to make now, and want to stick to, is about *you* not asking for help."

"I did ask Julie," she reminded him.

"So you did. And she said you'd solve the puzzle by yourself when you were ready. But aren't you forgetting something? This kid isn't some other person, she *is* yourself! Julie's probably going nuts, wondering when you're gonna finally figure that out."

CHAPTER 7

Breakthrough

28 MAY - 7 JUNE 2037

At the end of May there was still snow in the Wasatch Range if you went high enough, snow on the ground, snow occasionally falling from the sky. Pam stood behind one of the cameramen and watched the actors haul the burdened handcarts, wooden wheels screeching against wooden axles, up the steep slope. Neil, in a tattered coat and britches, with a rag tied over his head and ears, was pushing a cart from behind while a man and woman strained backwards as they pulled on the handle. Snow swirled around them. As he passed the camera Neil looked directly into the lens, face contorted with effort and determination, heavy shoes slipping on the icy stones. The next instant a wheel came off the cart and Neil, with a startled yelp, went sprawling.

"We'll do one more take, folks," the director yelled. "Dave, move that mark two feet downhill, I want Neil to release the wheel a little sooner this time." The troupe of actors trudged back down the slope while props people reattached the wheel and rolled the carts down. Neil saw Pam standing with Lexi and waved, and they waved back. "Places, everybody. Neil, see the mark? About two feet sooner." Neil nodded. The director called "Ready? Roll 'em. And—action!" And the Mormon pioneers began again to toil up the mountainside, pulling and pushing their handcarts toward Zion and the cameras.

Pam glanced sideways at Lexi, who stood clutching a silvery emergency blanket over her long dress and shawls and, even in that getup, radiantly beautiful. Feeling Pam's regard upon her, Lexi looked up and smiled, and Pam smiled back, wondering as she often did these days what Little Pam and Lexi, if they could talk across the pattern of Dutch girls, would say to each other. Two kids the same age, in the same sort of fix. Would they hit it off? Would Lexi be able to pick up the diary and read it, just like that?

This time the director was satisfied with the detached wheel, and the actors regrouped to begin a different scene. "I'm in this one," Lexi said, and handed Pam the emergency blanket. Walking to join the others, she lifted her shawls and redraped them so they covered her head as well as her shoulders. Pam shook out and folded up the blanket, and handed it to RoLayne Allred, who came to stand beside her at that moment. "Can you take charge of this? I might get called away before they finish the scene."

"Fine," said Lexi's mother. She half-looked at Pam as she tucked the blanket under her arm, a look of mingled shame and resentment.

Her job had conditioned Pam to ignore such looks. "How do you think she's doing?"

"She seems to be doing all right," Mrs. Allred said briefly.

"Have you talked with her about it much?"

"That counselor you're making her see is the one she talks to," Lexi's mother said, and this time the resentment was unmistakable.

Pam wondered whether it would one day be this mousy woman's turn to buy her daughter a bradshaw. "She feels bad about getting her grandad in trouble, you know—she feels like what happened was *her* fault somehow. You could help with that, RoLayne. I know it would be a huge relief to her if *you* could talk with her about it. You know, reassure her that she did the right thing."

The director called for action, and they watched Lexi struggle up a different slope (with less trampled snow) at the front of a group of shawled women, heads bowed against the wind and swirling flakes. All the able-bodied women were helping haul the carts; these, as Pam and RoLayne could see on the monitor screen, were all too old, young, pregnant, or enfeebled to do more than totter along behind. Where the ascent was less steep, some would ride.

It wasn't a scene where the onlookers had to keep completely quiet, and Lexi's mother murmured, "Well, I can't very well say what I don't believe."

Pam murmured back, "That she was right to tell? But surely—"

"Tell you Gaians. I don't think that was right myself, so you needn't expect me to say it was."

Pam counted to ten. "But surely it's less important whether she told us or the bishop or her parents, than that she told *somebody*." When Mrs. Allred didn't reply, Pam added, "Kids often feel guilty at the upset it causes when they report abuse. That's why it's so vital that they be reassured by the people they love and trust the most. Lexi needs to hear that it's not her fault people are upset, and she needs to hear it from you."

"Tell her yourself," RoLayne said shortly. "I've already given her my opinion, which is that she should have come to the Bishop and let him talk to her grandfather. In the LDS Church even children have a responsibility to put the good of the Church ahead of their own good. Now as much as ever." She flashed Pam a look of pure hostility. "I don't expect you to understand that, but it's true."

"That's a wrap!" the director called. "Good job, everybody. Take ten. Neil, I need you for a sec."

The group of laboring women broke formation and headed for the hot drinks trailer, and Lexi, seeing her mother and Pam standing together, ran over to them. RoLayne shook out the silver blanket. As she wrapped it around her daughter, Lexi said, "Mom, could you fix this? I stepped on it and it ripped out." She held up the hem of her tattered dress with both hands.

RoLayne examined the hem. "Oh, I think so. Let's go see if we can't find a needle and thread." As she propelled Lexi toward the props trailer she slipped an arm around her shoulders and gave her a half hug. Pam she ignored.

Lexi, however, turned inside the hug to look back at Pam. "We'll be done pretty soon. I'm still coming home with you, right?"

"Right. It's okay, we've got time."

"Is Humphrey still hibernating?"

"Yep. It'll just be us tonight for dinner, but I thawed out another cobbler anyway."

Lexi grinned and turned away. RoLayne's stiff back was eloquent, but there was nothing she could do. Pam felt a twinge of sympathy. Only a twinge, though. If there was one thing she could not abide, it was a parent who protected her belief system and herself at the expense of her child's well-being.

~

They sat on the back porch steps before dinner, feeding the robins. "You're supposed to think about your *family*?" Lexi said dubiously.

"Your family, where they came from, where they live now. Like, all the LDS families that settled the Great Basin and made the desert blossom as the rose." She pulled a wad of dog food in half and fed the halves to Gimpy. Wingy sailed in to demand his share.

"Oh."

"*Your* family was part of that, right? Here, Greedy Guts." She poked a piece of food into Wingy, who gulped it down.

"On Dad's side. Mom's relatives came from Denmark later on. Dad's great-great-I-don't-know-how-many-times-great-grandparents came with a wagon train."

"But they've lived in Utah a long time."

"Yeah. Mostly."

"I was thinking up on location that making *A Thousand Miles* is a great way of focusing on the country that means the most to you and your family. You really know what a high price the first settlers paid to get here, and how important that makes this land to their descendants. It's their Homeland—that's the new term we're using." The soggy lumps were disappearing fast. Pesky hopped onto Lexi's knee, and Lexi, delighted, fed him a lump herself. She didn't push it far enough down his throat, but he threw his head back and managed to swallow it anyway. "Good!" said Pam. "Try to stick it a little farther in, like this."

"I wish they didn't change it. I know, Humphrey said they failed, that time. But I liked the old way better."

Stuffed, the robins withdrew. Pam snapped the lid back on the dog-food soaker, a little tub from Landfill Plastics, and smiled at Lexi. "Tell you the truth, I did too, but we think more people can relate to the Gaian mission if we do it like this, through family ties to land. But anybody that wants to can still go the Secret Garden route. We're trying to bring more people in, not push anybody out."

Lexi looked relieved. "What are *you* gonna do, keep on with your Ground in Kentucky?"

"Mm-hm, but I'm trying the new way too," Pam said. "I made a bradshaw—do you know what that is?"

"King William made one? And that movie star, Carole Cosby?"

Pam made a split-second decision not to tell Lexi that she herself had gone to grade school in Indiana with Carole Cosby, and had despised her. Carole Cosby and Lexi Allred were far more alike at eleven years old than were Lexi Allred and Little Pam Pruitt, who had the one dreadful thing in common and very little else. "A bradshaw is a VR program made with a time transceiver, of an incident in somebody's past. Mine is about a time when I was just about your age. I'm using it to work out some problems I had with my dad. That's part of the new Gaian approach, to smooth things out with your family members so that doesn't get in the way of connecting to your family land, your Homeland."

"I didn't know you had problems with your family, too," Lexi said in a voice so sad it made Pam's insides quail. "So is the bradshaw working? Are they getting smoothed out?"

"Mm-hm," she said, and then felt so dishonest that she added, "At least it's helping me understand them a lot better. Sometimes that's about all you can do about a problem. Sometimes it's all you need to do."

Lexi frowned. "But if the problem doesn't really get smoothed out, I don't see how it would help you connect to your family. The bradshaw."

"Well," Pam said after a minute, "in my case it's not going to make that much difference anyway—I was a grounded Gaian steward long before I ever owned a bradshaw. But it can be good to go at things from more than one direction." She grabbed the tub of dog food, stood, and smiled down at Lexi, sitting on the step looking worried. "So what about *your* dinner, are you hungry yet?"

Lexi got up slowly. "It doesn't make any difference in my case either. I mean the Homeland thing doesn't. I still want to be a Gaian, but for sure not a missionary. I decided. Everybody hates the missionaries now, and anyway I didn't want to be a farmer."

Pam flinched, but put her hand on Lexi's shoulder. "You be Gaia's actor, kiddo. Anything else would be a terrible waste of talent."

~

Little Pam looked up from the diary and beamed. "Hi!"

"Hi yourself," Pam said. "How you doing?"

"Great. I love it when you come."

Pam sat down on "her" side of the bed. The girl offered her the diary, but this time Pam smiled and shook her head. "I guess we both know by now that I can't read it by myself. So I've had an idea: how would you feel about reading it *to* me?"

The girl looked surprised, then uncertain. "Out *loud?*"

"Just the parts you don't mind reading out loud. You could skip anything you didn't want me to hear."

"It's not . . . I mean, I don't mind you knowing things. I mean, you already *do* know them. There's just some of it I don't like to say out loud."

Little Pam was almost morbidly sensitive to the power of the spoken word. "I know. You could leave those parts out though, and that would be fine."

"We-e-e-e-l-l . . . "

She wrinkled her fleshy nose, still not sure. Pressuring this child was the very last thing Pam wanted to do; she reflected that Liam was wrong and Julie right about not pushing things in this direction quite so soon. "You don't have to read any of it to me if you'd rather not, honey."

But Little Pam surprised her. "No, I do want to. Really. It's just, you know, embarrassing." She bent the covers back, ruffling the pages. "Where should I start?"

"How about just starting at the beginning?"

Whereupon, to her inexpressible relief, Little Pam flipped to the front of the red book and began: "January first, 2011. It's New Year's Day. We went to the candlelight service last night and I stayed up till midnight. Today I worked on linear algebra. January second. Today I went to Doug's and we did linear algebra. I got all the problems right. It looked like snow all day but it never snowed. January third. Today it snowed. I went sledding with Charlie on the scenic drive. There was a hefn on the viddy tonight, his name is Pomfrey! January fourth . . . "

Pam listened to the flat voice speaking these flat facts. After a while she shifted around and lay down on her back on the bed; and when Little Pam looked up inquiringly, "I'm just getting comfortable," she explained. "Don't stop, you're doing great."

"February ninth," she read obediently. "Today I went to Hurt Hollow with Dad. We walked in down the hill. I got to feed the goats."

Pam laced her fingers across her stomach, closed her eyes, and let this voice possess her. Time passed, or was borne along on the all-but-expressionless murmur she floated within. Once she opened her eyes and glanced over to ask, "Are you getting tired? We could do some more next time."

"Nunh-unh, I'm fine," Little Pam said, and went right on: "May 12. Today we came to Louisville. May 13. I went to the store for Granny and we played Chinese checkers. Aunt Maude isn't feeling too well. I came to Grandma's for supper. May 14. Today we came home. I slept with Granny the first night and I went to Grandma's the second night. I fell off the couch in the middle of the night. I found three four-leaf clovers and one six-leaf clover. May 15. Today I worked on fractals . . . "

—But the girl had gone on without Pam, who lay in the dark by herself, breathing in the hateful smell of her Grandma's living room, knowing that if she opened her eyes a tall shape would be looming over the couch, but if she kept her eyes closed she wouldn't have to acknowledge its presence.

~

"Who do you think it might be?" Julie asked calmly. Pam had called her from the VR parlor's public phone, whose cheap lens added ten years to Julie's age (though the late hour may have added one or two).

"I feel like all that's keeping me from dying of terror is that I still don't know." Just thinking about it, Pam shook like an aspen leaf. "But it must have been Rueben, Dad's stepfather, Rueben Cranfill. You remember I talked about him. A really bad alcoholic. Arrested for exhibitionism once. On our visits he'd either be sleeping it off in the basement or sitting at Grandma's kitchen table, all stubbly and reeking of whiskey, and I was supposed to kiss him and act like I was happy to see him."

Her teeth chattered as she said this. Julie looked concerned. "Time for a break? You could take a couple of weeks off, get used to the idea of what you'll be confronting—"

Pam shook her head. "No, I have to go right back in. The kid has no idea why I took off like that. One second I'm lying on the bed with my eyes closed and the next I'm halfway out the door. She had this jolted look on her face—I don't even remember getting off the bed, I must have levitated! I have to get right back, as soon as I catch my breath."

Julie nodded. "Sounds like you're getting the hang of the gear, anyhow. Listen now: call me after you end the program tonight. Don't try to prove how tough you are. I'm here, and I truly want to help, and I'm very concerned that you pace yourself appropriately with this, okay?"

"Okay," Pam said shakily. "Thanks."

~

"Let's go back to the beginning of May, all right?" Pam had apologized for bolting, and resettled herself on the bed. "I'd just like to go over that part again. We can do the rest another time."

"Okay, but I'm really not tired, so if you want me to keep going . . . " She found the place and began to read. "May 1. Charlie built a soap box racer, he gave me a ride but he pushed me too fast and it turned over. Mom made me come in. May 2 . . . "

Pam waited tensely for the trip to Louisville, but knowing it was coming left her too well defended. The replay was unrevealing.

Despite the kid's protestations that she wasn't tired, Pam stopped the bradshaw when they got to the end of May; she herself was shuddering with fatigue. She put a quick call through to Julie and was stowing the gear in the hall locker when the pay phone beeped and blinked on, and Humphrey's dear hairy face peered benevolently down upon her. "Hello, Pam Pruitt," he chirruped.

His was the very last face she had expected to see there. "Humphrey! You're still supposed to be hibernating! How ever did you find me?" She glanced up and down the hallway, but at this late hour they had the place to themselves.

"I *was* asleep," he said, "but someone woke me."

Having heard again and again how dangerous it was to wake a hibernating Hefn, Pam felt a thrill of alarm. "Why'd they do that, has something happened? Will you be okay?"

"I will be fine; I was to awaken in a few weeks' time in any event. Also, I had left orders that, should you initiate your bradshaw during my long sleep, and should it approach a climactic moment, someone was to wake me. My dear, you must not waver in your resolve. You *must* complete the bradshaw, as quickly as you can."

It struck Pam then that Humphrey had eavesdropped on this evening's session. The Hefn were within the terms of their sales agreement to do that at any time, but she didn't like it that he hadn't told her beforehand, and found it annoying to be urged not to quit when she'd had no thought of quitting. She said, a bit resentfully, "Why 'must' I complete it?"

"Because there is such important work to be done, and you are needed, now more than ever before."

"Humphrey," Pam said wearily, "you *know* I can't *do* the real work anymore, and what the Sam Hill has the bradshaw got to do with it anyhow? Did they brief you yet about what's been going on?"

"The rioting, the scapegoating, the hating of Gaian missionaries. Indeed, I have been briefed."

"Even Lexi knows everyone hates the missionaries now. We can't get Homeland off the ground—did they fill you in about Homeland?"

"They did. I fully appreciate that our situation is *in extremis.*"

"Well," Pam said, "okay then. I certainly mean to see *this* through, but you mustn't count on me for anything important."

He twinkled at her. "Go home and sleep now, my dear. I will be in touch."

~

He wasn't going to tell her any more, and she was too knackered to think, so she did as instructed: biked home and went to bed and to sleep.

In her dream Pam is lying again on the Dutch Girl quilt, afloat within the uninflected sphere created by Little Pam's reading voice. She can't make out the words, but behind shut eyelids she sees herself get up from Grandma's living-room couch and wander into the kitchen. Shelby is standing near the sink in the dark. He's aware of Pam but takes no notice and doesn't stop what he's doing. At first she doesn't understand what this is, but suddenly she realizes that his pants are unfastened and he's masturbating with his right hand, intending to ejaculate into the kitchen sink. In his left hand he's holding a metal bowl full of water and crushed ice, swirling the contents of the bowl gently, rhythmically, in time to the rhythm of his beating off.

Pam's reactions are two, and perfectly contradictory. She's frantic to get out of there. And she's very turned on.

In her panic flight from her monstrous father she tries desperately to wake up. She labors and groans, struggles to pry her eyes open, struggles against sleep with all her strength; but she's weak as water. Despite everything she can do she still lies supine on the bed, and Little Pam is still droning on, when out of the fog of words Lexi Allred's *Secret Garden* voice says clearly: *Take Two*.

—and Pam is back on the couch in her Grandma's house. It's the middle of the night, and she's lying on her back in the dark, on top of someone or something whose meaty hands she's holding. Terror has suffused her utterly. She gets up and walks into the bathroom, holding on with horror and loathing to the meaty hands. She's just about to look in the mirror over the basin to find out who they belong to—shrinking away in anticipation of the sight—when *Take Three*, says Lexi, and then *Take Four*, and each time the ghastly bradshaw of Pam's dream starts the program at the same place: on the couch in her grandmother's dark living room, in the middle of the night.

Every "take" is different, but again and again the same elements are worked in: a male masturbator; a porcelain fixture, basin or toilet or sink, usually full of water; herself as a very young child—much younger than eleven—in the role of participant-observer; and the emotional conflict of arousal and extreme fear.

~

"We're getting close," Julie said, stating the obvious. "How do you feel?"

"Terrible. Like horses have been kicking me all night."

"Have you had dreams like these before?"

Pam massaged her aching temples. "A few. Never a whole batch on the same night. There was, let's see, the one about my cousin Roland, Ginger's kid, standing naked in front of a bathroom basin full of water, while two 'pornographic hands'—that's how they were styled in the dream—came up out of the water to help him masturbate. And the one about . . . well, about me sloshing Liam's severed penis around in the basin of a hotel bathroom, while a strange man in a navy blue suit stood by with his shriveled genitals exposed, saying 'You can do anything you like with these.' That's all I can remember, there might be others."

"Affect of that last one?"

"Mixed. I wanted nothing to do with the icky man and his icky organs, and told him so, but still I touched his dick when he invited me to."

"Terror? Arousal?"

"Not that I recall. Just ickiness. Look, Julie . . . " She waited, holding perfectly still. ". . . would you consider monitoring my next VR session? I'm scared. Liam says I never ask for help, so, well, I'm asking. I'm scared to do this by myself."

Julie smiled and nodded, looking and sounding as positive as possible, to reassure the patient. "You probably can, but why should you? I'd say right now is an excellent time to bring in flank support. Did Humphrey agree to monitor as well?"

"I didn't ask him to. He said he'd keep in touch, that's all. I tried to reach him this morning in Santa Barbara but he didn't answer, and I'm not even sure that's where he was calling from. Something seriously weird is going on."

"Well," said Julie briskly, "Humphrey and I may have different perspectives and agendas, but we both agree that finishing your bradshaw is all-important. And whether he's there or not, I will be, whenever you want me."

So the next Thursday evening Julie was standing by when Pam entered the room of her childhood. That is, Julie was in VR hookup in Washington. She could monitor Pam's vital signs—pulse rate, brain wave patterns, skin moisture—through transmitters built into the VR equipment; Pam had connected herself up to them for this session. Julie could see everything in two dimensions on a life-size screen: Pam and Little Pam, the bed with its handmade quilt, the bureau and hideous boomclox, the row of books along the base-board, the window streaming with sun. She could hear what both Pams said, and if the elder were to address her directly she could answer through the helmet transmitters; but, unless she did that, Little Pam would be unaware of the third party present at their meeting.

Big Pam stood outside the doorway for a minute first, readying herself, watching the child write in the red book, trying to discern outward signs that she'd repeatedly gone through some horrific experience. But her surface seemed perfectly blank. If there was trauma there—and surely there was—it was very deeply buried.

She tapped on the door frame and stepped through smiling. "Hi, kiddo."

"Hi! Want me to finish reading the diary now?" She was all eagerness, relishing the attention.

"That would be *way* cool." Pam flopped down on the bed.

"June 1," the girl began promptly. "It was pretty today. I saw a yellow warbler and an indigo bunting at the Point. June 2. Mom wants me to take dancing lessons and I don't want to. I watched the Hefn program on TV. It was good. Dad got me a book at the library about the Hefn for my school report. June 3. I don't have to take dancing lessons, they cost money. Today Grandma came with Uncle Tommy. June 4 . . . "

Without even an instant in which to signal Julie, Pam is afloat upon the surface of the light flat voice—

—and watches herself get up from Grandma's couch and wander through the dark house to the bathroom. The door is partly closed. There's a light on inside, and a radio playing lively music. She reaches up for the doorknob and pushes the door open wider.

Uncle Tommy is standing at the basin, running it full of water. He's back late from the racetrack, he's been playing the horses. He jumps when he sees Pam peering around the door—she's startled him—but then he smiles. "Hi, hon. Wanna see somethin' nice? C'mon in here, I'm gon' show you somethin' real nice." Tommy is wearing his dark blue sailor uniform; he joined the Navy when he was sixteen, not very long ago. Pam comes closer, and now she sees that the front of his pants is unbuttoned and hanging down, and behind the square flap is a round opening like a cave, and coming out of the cave is a thing like a thick white snake.

Pam's eyes fill with the white snake, and two feelings seize her simultaneously. One is intense sexual excitement and fascination. The other is guilt: she knows she'll be punished if anybody catches her in here. She knows this from the sneaky way Tommy's talking. He smells like Pawpaw when he talks.

"See it?" Uncle Tommy says, and Pam can't help herself, she comes closer. She puts up her hands and holds onto the side of the basin.

There's a towel folded against the basin's front edge, and the snake is lying on the towel. "See, now, this is my peter. Ever see a peter like this before?" Pam shakes her head. "Well, it's kinda dirty so I'm washing it. Here, you can help. Let's just wet your hands and soap 'em up real good"—he holds her hands under the faucet and rubs soap on the palms—"and then you can help wash my peter for me."

She puts her slippery hands around the snake and Tommy says, "Oh Jesus." Then he says, "Just wash it off real good, just rub it up and down." She knows she's in terrible danger, but the snake feels hard and smooth. She loves the feel of it. She loves the silky skin of its pink head shaped like a blind frog's head, and the long shaft like a smooth enormous finger gloved in kid.

Pam leans her elbows on the sink and dunks the snake in the warm water and traces the lovely curve of its head with her soapy fingers, and then suddenly something happens. Tommy grabs her hands in his big ones and squeezes them hard around his peter, and stuff spits out of the end, clouding the water in the basin. He squeezes her hands on the peter and moans. Is he *crying*? She doesn't like this part, but Uncle Tommy is gasping like he's been running, he won't listen and he won't stop squeezing her hands. The sleeves of her pajamas are wet, she's trying to pull away and he won't let go, and she starts to get panicky, and she starts to cry. And then the door swings wide open and it's bare-foot Grandma in her nightgown with her hair all mashed flat on one side, saying "Tommy Cranfill, what in tarnation are you doin' to that child? Pammy, you git yourself back into bed right this minute."

She can't, though. In the shock of being discovered, to her intense horror and shame she has wet her pajamas.

~

Little Pam's voice came abruptly back into focus. "July 4. Today is the Fourth of July. We had a church picnic in Happy Valley. I climbed up the falls. Tonight they had fireworks at Scofield Beach and we watched them from the Point. July 5—You're *crying*," she blurted, sounding scared out of her wits. She couldn't stand to see people cry, even other kids. She'd never seen her mother cry in her whole life.

Pam lifted her head from the pillow and smiled shakily to reassure her. "Yeah, I am, a little. It's okay to cry if you're sad, you don't have to be afraid of it. Nothing bad will happen."

"Are *you* sad? What about?"

"I can't explain right now, but don't worry, everything's okay. *You're* not making me sad. Go ahead, keep on reading."

So she did, nervously at first, then relaxing as the diary reabsorbed her attention. Pam lay and felt the heavy rise and fall of her heavy chest, listening, accepting what she heard; and finally "August 25," Little Pam read, "Today I packed for Louisville. I'm going to Granny's tomorrow by myself on the packet. That's all! That's what I was writing when you came in!" She slapped the book shut and beamed at the woman on the bed.

Pam sat up groggily; she was drained. "You're going to Louisville tomorrow?" The girl nodded. "Will you stay at Grandma's part of the time?"

Her face slipped a fraction. "I don't know. If Mom wants me to."

Again Big Pam circled the bed, sat down beside Little Pam and pulled the scrawny frame against her fiercely. "If you stay at Grandma's, here's what I want you to remember. You don't have to do *anything* if it makes you feel bad. Not even if a grownup tells you to, and not even if you've done it before, and not even if Mom gets mad at you. If it makes you feel bad, *don't do it*. Refuse. Say no." Pam leaned back and looked into her eyes, brushing her stringy hair back from her face. "Listen to me. This is important. *You can say no.*"

The girl frowned, puzzled; she'd been conditioned all her life to believe that children weren't to bother, inconvenience, or disobey adults. Adults had never protected her and she'd never been taught to protect herself; and—since the abuse got consistently repressed, visit after visit—she had no idea why Pam was saying these things in such a serious way. She said as much: "What do you mean? I don't get it."

"Never mind. Just remember what I'm telling you. Promise."

"Okay, I promise." And then, seeming to take herself by surprise, she lunged against Pam and gave her an awkward hug.

Pam hugged her back, stood up carefully; she felt heavy as lead. "Time to go now. Thanks very, very much for reading me your diary, honey. Did you leave much out?"

"Only a little part, about a book."

"Was it *Shane*?" She ducked her head, cringing, but nodded. "I remember. I don't blame you a bit. 'Bye now. Have a great time at Granny's." Pam tottered to the doorway, smiled back at beaming

Little Pam, and closed the program down. "Julie? Did you get all that?"

"I did indeed. My phone's set up; we can talk right now, as soon as you're out of your gear." And five minutes later: "When Pam Junior read the entry for June 3, you slipped into deep trance. Pure alpha waves for six and a half minutes, then back to normal. What happened?"

Pam told her. "I don't think it was a dream. I think it was a memory, triggered by the reference to Grandma and Uncle Tommy."

"Do you realize that in all this time you've never mentioned an uncle named Tommy?"

Hadn't she? Pam reflected. "I suppose there didn't seem to be any reason to. He was Dad's half-brother, the son of Grandma and Rueben the Souse. Much younger than Dad. A very minor figure in my life, or so I thought. I'd totally forgotten this, but Tommy lived in Grandma's house during the years Mom used to make me sleep over there on Saturday nights. He was between marriages and probably out of a job. But that was later; in the memory—dream?—whatever, he was wearing Navy dress blues. And I couldn't have been more than three, I had to reach up for the doorknob. By the time I can remember having to sleep over there, four-plus years later, he wasn't in the Navy anymore."

Julie had her hot-on-the-trace look; her eyes were glittering. "As a child, how did you feel about Uncle Tommy?"

Pam made an effort to think. "Actually, I kind of liked him when I was little. He played with me some, and he gave me a ride on his motorcycle once. And I always thought he was good-looking— though funnily enough, when I cleaned out the house after Mom died I came across some old holos of him and was surprised at how …dissolute and seedy he looked in them. Not handsome at all. Even in a studio portrait made when he was about twelve you could tell there was something wrong, yet I remember thinking he looked so cute in that picture, when I was a kid." She leaned toward the screen. "So was it a dream or a memory?"

"Well, it wasn't REM sleep for those six minutes. As I said, according to the readings you weren't asleep at any time; you were in a trance state, a very deep involuntary hypnotic trance. Now, I know you're done in, and we'll stop soon, but I'd really like to hear anything at all that you can remember about Uncle Tommy."

At once, to Pam's surprise, a scene popped into mind. "Okay, here's something. One time—I was ten or eleven—I wrote, 'Souls I want to save: Uncle Tommy' on the fly leaf of my Bible. And I've always remembered I did that, because Mom *told* him I'd written it. According to her, Tommy said he appreciated it and he'd think about it real hard. She was *pleased*, she thought Tommy was pretty much of a bum. She was pleased with me for wanting to save his soul." Thinking about it, Pam got agitated. "I know exactly where I was sitting—in the living room, at the hallway end of the couch—when Mom told me she'd done this, beaming with approval. I pretended not to react, but I was embarrassed and stricken to realize she'd been snooping into my private stuff. I didn't want her to know I wanted to save anybody's soul."

Julie shook her head. "Why do you suppose you wanted to save *his* soul? That seems kind of unexpected."

A wave of exhaustion broke and sloshed around Pam; the volume of energy required in heavy-duty therapy was a constantly renewed astonishment. In the midst of this wave she sat and remembered how Little Pam had read out the facts of her encoded life, in terse declarative sentences, skipping over the one place where her feelings were so intense they'd forced her to try to put them into words. But out of this assembling heap of dry little facts a static charge had built up and built up until the bolt had struck Pam and stunned her. Only her; Little Pam felt nothing, as Pam had felt nothing when she was Little Pam. Her feelings had been shoved down into a place where they would fester in the dark for nearly thirty years, because for thirty years, as far as she knew, there was nobody in her life who wanted to help her not suffer so much.

Pam answered Julie as best she could. "I honestly don't know why. Maybe I thought, if he was saved, he'd leave me alone. There's something perverse about it, though, some kind of 'love your enemies' thing. Tommy had an awful life, both Dad's brothers did." Pam looked up, startled by a thought. "I just remembered, my Aunt Ginger once told me Tommy's first wife was an abused child, she'd been raped by her uncle . . . her *uncle*, by God!"

"Did Tommy rape you?" Julie asked quietly.

Pam shook her head. "No. Nobody ever raped me. Actually, Tommy was a diabetic; he may have been impotent as an older man. He had two wives but no children, *that* I know. But he must have gone for me, every time I spent the night at Grandma's while he was living there. Every time." She flashed on the menacing presence she'd sensed leaning above her on the couch, the first day Little Pam had read from her diary, and gagged with claustrophobia, though what he might have done to her then she couldn't guess. "Except," she added, "maybe not during the fifth grade, the year before this one. He might not have been living there that year."

Julie nodded alertly. "You kept the fifth-grade diary."

"Right."

"Is Uncle Tommy still alive?"

"No, not for years and years. He died of something to do with the diabetes. Dad always said he didn't take care of himself at all."

Pam's exhaustion was by now so obvious that Julie quelled her curiosity and pushed back her chair. "We can go over it some more tomorrow. You need to get to bed. Just one last thing I'm not clear about," she couldn't help adding. "Your uncle abused you sexually, that now seems clear. You hated going to the place where he had access to you. Yet you speak of him without anger, almost with compassion. The anger and fear are all directed at your mother. Any thoughts about that?"

"What she did was worse," Pam replied at once; and for the first time in all her years of off-again on-again therapy she broke down in Julie's presence, or at least her videopresence; she started to cry.

Julie had witnessed her exchange with Little Pam on the subject of crying, of course; but that was the bradshaw. This was just the two of them, therapist and patient, and Julie tried not to appear to gloat as the tough nut cracked at last before her eyes.

Pam, though, was past caring. "Tommy was an ignorant simp. He used me but he didn't mean me any harm, he didn't know I'd be damaged, I'd lay odds he was Granddaddy Rueben's play-pretty as a kid—probably all Rueben's own kids were, nobody in Dad's family knew a boundary from a turnip. But Mom loved me, and I loved her. She really loved me, and she betrayed me over and over and over. With Tommy the stakes weren't that high, there was no true betrayal, but with Mom—"

She choked and sobbed like a baby. "Take your time," said Julie, kindly if avidly.

"Mom *knew* I didn't want to sleep over at Grandma's," Pam said when she could talk, "but she made me go. She didn't care why I didn't want to, she only cared about not offending Grandma by letting me stay both nights of a weekend visit at Granny's house. We'd all three get in the taxi and drive over there, and we'd have dinner, and then Mom and Dad would get back in another taxi and go back to Granny's in the dark, and leave me behind. And pick me up for church the next morning." By now she was bawling again.

"And you don't blame your father for allowing this to happen."

Pam mopped her face with a handful of tissues and blew her nose. "Whew. No. Well, *yes*—but not in the same way. He didn't care whether I went over there or not. Mom was the one who cared about preserving appearances—and, to be fair, about not hurting Grandma's feelings."

"But your feelings didn't matter."

"I guess they didn't," she said, and in spite of everything still felt surprised at this sign that somebody (Julie) thought they did. "Dad didn't stop her, but if I'd appealed to him . . . if I'd pleaded with him to stick up for me, if I'd told him how much I didn't want to go, he might have intervened with Mom."

"But you didn't appeal to him."

"It never, ever occurred to me. Like it never occurred to me to sit with him in church that time, or to ask him for a bookcase, or to let me keep the nice boomclox. On some level of my childhood, he just plain didn't exist."

~

The next morning, a Friday, Pam called in sick. Then she called Julie and put her off till after the weekend. Felled like a tree by the bradshaw's revelations, Pam lay all day on the living-room couch in her pajamas and bathrobe, the tattered Dutch Girl quilt tucked round her. She turned off the phone, kept the blinds closed, ignored the mail, and generally treated the reaction she was having like a bad case of flu, rousing herself only to fill the duckling feeder and give the robins their disgusting lumps of soggy kibble. The fantasy that mending family bridges might lead to membership in the Homeland effort lay in pieces all over the room.

Nobody in such a family gets away unscathed. Everyone had been massively damaged by Rueben Cranfill and his unclean ways.

Hindsight showed Pam this truth, mercilessly reflected in Pawpaw's children, stepchildren, and grandchildren living and dead. Images assailed her; facts, known vaguely for years, formed new and devastating patterns; she tossed and groaned as they lined themselves up for inspection. Shelby, Harold, Doro, Tommy, Ginger. God only knew what each had gone though as children growing up in that household. Which might actually be a unifying force among siblings with little else in common, except that none of them *knew* what they knew. None of them did. Like Pam, they had deep-sixed the worst of whatever had happened to them. Pam remembered Shelby and a canoe, Shelby and a grosbeak; Aunt Ginger remembered a shaming revelation and Aunt Doro the shaming public staggers and DT's—all horrific enough, no doubt, but no match for what must fester below the level of conscious memory.

Until it broke out and wrought havoc. Diabetic Tommy and schizophrenic Harold, and the daughter Harold had abandoned to be raised in Pawpaw's house of horrors, all long dead of drink and their diseases. Shelby, the crown prince, the one who escaped and made his mother proud, exposed anyway by his emotional absence and sexual benightedness. Epileptic Doro and *her* daughter took antidepressants; life went on, for them. How the family legacy had affected Ginger's five children Pam didn't know. She didn't want to know. The Ban, thank God, had prevented it from being passed down any farther.

They had each other, some of them did; but any thoughts Pam had had of invoking her birthright and joining this collective had been utterly wiped out. Her links to them all were stronger than she'd dreamed or they would ever know, but the gulf of unknowingness could not be bridged.

And this new and most appalling truth—that her mother had thrust her repeatedly into the ghastliness, when she might have kept her safe, might have stood between Little Pam and the menace—that truth lowered above all, more monstrous than anything Tommy and perhaps Reuben had played at, not knowing what they did.

~

Pam was napping when the doorbell sounded. She glanced at the clock: nearly midnight. Whoever was out there must be on urgent business, but she simply didn't care. Another long *brrrring!* ripped through the house, and another, while she lay wishing the importunate caller away. Instead, brief silence was followed by the scrabbling of a key in the lock. Before Pam could bestir herself enough to rise from her bed of misery and confront the intruder, a stumpy figure in a hooded cloak had slipped inside and closed the door. "Hello, my dear, hello. No no no, do not get up."

Hefn could see perfectly in the dark, but Pam couldn't; she sat up and reached above her head to switch on a lamp. And there, of course, was Humphrey, his gray visage bristling and peering out of the draped maroon folds of his cavernous hood. He made a hilarious sight, but Pam wasn't in a laughing mood. "You look exactly like one of Tolkien's dwarves in that getup. What brings you here at this hour?" Or at all, she might have asked, wondering why he wasn't in Santa Barbara.

"I am traveling incognito." (This did make her smile.) Throwing back the hood, he shrugged off his cloak and stepped over it to straddle the Hefn chair she kept around the house for him. "Did I not say I would stay in touch? And has your phone not been turned off all day? I was not speaking idly, Pam Pruitt. There are things I must now tell you. Immediate things."

She would not have believed it possible, but the main thing Humphrey had to say made Pam feel worse than she felt already. It turned out that her mother hadn't sacrificed and saved to buy the bradshaw. The bradshaw represented no vote of confidence from beyond the grave, because Frances hadn't given it to her at all. He had.

"I always found it you would say hard to swallow, that a mathematical gift like yours, so powerful, so elegant, could be *only* a means of escaping a painful situation. I did not believe that such a gift could simply be discarded when escape was no longer required," he explained, all unawares, while Pam clutched the quilt tight around herself, blindsided by this final grief. "When we began to market the bradshaws, it came to my attention that a bradshaw, used effectively, could re-empower people who had for various reasons of trauma lost their power. And the more attention I paid, the more it seemed to me that some of these people were not unlike you, and some of this lost power was not unlike your own.

"But I saw also difficulties. The frontal attack was not a way to success. Nor could the customer be coerced. In every instance, the lost power returned incidentally, a byproduct of a freely chosen confrontation with the *source* of trauma. Unhappily I was forced to conclude that to press a bradshaw upon you and urge you to use it, in a deliberate attempt to regain what you had lost, must probably result in failure."

As far as Pam knew, this was more by a good deal than human psychologists had figured out about bradshaws. While most of her mind struggled with anguish, some small piece registered Humphrey's summary, aware of how much it would mean to Julie.

"I schemed therefore, I plotted. The Bureau needed you back. The work needed you back. *I*, most urgently, needed you." His wide flat eyes gleamed and his oddly jointed arms made stabbing gestures; Pam had rarely seen him so excited and never so thoroughly pleased with himself. "There were other reasons why I could not openly, directly, as the Hefn Humphrey, make a bradshaw available to an employee of the Bureau of Temporal Physics—you understand?— but when Frances Pruitt became ill I saw an opportunity. I obtained a copy of her will, and I altered it."

She felt a stab of hope. "Did Mom provide you with the copy of her will? Did she know what you were up to?"

"No no no, indeed not, my dear, she knew nothing. I never spoke with her of this. But when she died, I acted. I substituted the altered will for the genuine one, and supplied a voucher for the bradshaw. There was then nothing more to do, but to hope that you would use the bradshaw soon, and that using it would restore your gift."

Humphrey crowed on about arranging for the conference to be at Hurt Hollow, in case Pam should decide to make the bradshaw while she was there—the excellent chance that remembering what Tommy had done would now indeed unblock his protégé's intuition—how he would set about testing her to find out. Pam sat hunched in the semidarkness, so angry at last that she didn't trust herself to speak. Telling him how she felt was pointless; the delicate, outrageous crime he'd perpetrated, the raising and dashing of false hopes, wasn't the sort of thing a Hefn understood. By his own lights he had done well; and Pam partly realized, even then, that the hope of discovering her mother had believed her had helped her fight past the obstacles and tolerate the terrors of running the bradshaw.

But if she refrained from remonstrating, still it was impossible to forgive Humphrey, that evening, for his stupendous presumption.

She did refuse to submit to immediate testing, as he would have preferred. But after he'd swirled the wizard's cloak around himself and stumped upstairs, to work at her computer complex till morning, she had no heart to put herself properly to bed. She fell on her side, pulled the quilt up under her chin, and fell asleep where she lay.

~

Liam was quick to claim credit for the part he'd played: "Didn't I *tell* you you and the kid should work together?"

"You did. You were right, O Genius. Thank God you stayed and shot that second bradshaw. I can't honestly say I *feel* better yet—I feel like shit, actually—but I think in time . . ."

A look passed between them, establishing that Liam was by this point actually happy he'd given in but wasn't going to come right out and say so. Instead he said, "What you *know* can't hurt you *nearly* as much as what you *don't* know," in a wickedly accurate imitation of Julie.

Pam managed to laugh. "I've often wondered what repressions she ever dug up out of her own cellar, to be so certain of that."

"God knows. But you agree?"

She sighed. "Yeah, I guess I do. It's better to know."

"Even if what you find out is so awful it ruins your life?"

Pam considered this. "Actually, if there are things it would be better not to know, in the sense that your life gets worse instead of better when you find them out, I bet you'd know that unconsciously and let sleeping dogs lie. Me, I went into this with guns blazing, as you'll recall, so I'm guessing that eventually it'll feel like a good thing." Though it was still pretty hard to believe that. She'd said nothing to Liam about Humphrey's role in the bradshaw, and now wondered for an instant if that might in fact be one thing it *would* be better not to have found out.

"You were hoping to get on the Homeland bandwagon though."

"You know," Pam said, "I wonder now if I really was. It was such a farfetched notion all along, maybe I just used that to trick myself into making the bradshaw." She stretched, groaned, sighed. "Probably doesn't matter anyway. From everything I hear the bandwagon's lost a wheel and turned over sideways." An image of the cart losing its wheel on the *Thousand Miles* set flashed in her memory.

"Pretty much," Liam said. "Stuck in the mud for sure, the way people feel about Gaians right now." He paused. "Amazing how the personal life just perks right along regardless, while the world goes to hell—speaking of which, I meant to tell you first thing, Humphrey showed up here this morning."

Pam said, "Yeah, I knew he meant to," then immediately regretted not pretending to be surprised.

Liam certainly was. He said accusingly, "You've talked with him *already*? Why didn't you say so? When?"

"Yesterday." This was true, if misleading; but evidently Humphrey was keeping it a secret that he'd been up and about for more than a week, in which case where had he been hanging out? "I would've called you if I hadn't basically been turned into a cabbage by developments in the personal life." This was also at least half true. "That summit with the Pope's been called for tomorrow?"

"Right," Liam said, still a little miffed. "Humphrey and Alfrey leave for DC this evening. They *woke him up*, I'm sure he told you that—that's how bad things look to the Gafr I guess. They wanted that meeting to happen ASAP. They actually ordered Ormelius to send the UN plane to Rome to pick up the Pope."

"So what do the Gafr expect to accomplish?" And at Liam's look, "I was a cabbage, remember? He didn't tell me much."

"He didn't tell us much either, but from the sense of urgency I'd guess they're hoping to put out a few fires anyway. Actually, the atmosphere around the Bureau is pretty positive. At least something's being done to address the mess, and at least it's a discussion and not an extermination. Also, Humphrey was amazingly cheerful, which bucked us up of course."

"So I guess we'll know more in a day or two."

"I guess we will." Then—sensing Pam's wish to get off the phone, and not so miffed that he was quite ready to let her—Liam said, "So, uh, how's *avian* life perking along in a world gripped in crisis? How's Gimpy?"

Mired though she was in personal crises, on this subject Pam didn't much mind Liam's transparent manipulations. Her voice became eager. "Gimpy, my lad, is the greatest success story in my entire career as a US Fish and Wildlife Rehabilitation Permit sub-permittee. I told you her foot opened up and her eye was better? Well, just in the past two days she started eating by herself—and *whole* pieces of dog food, so her beak must have healed up."

"Ever figure out what was wrong with it?"

"Broken, I guess. Sprained? The upper and lower halves didn't meet right. Anyway, that's not all. Her broken wing had healed too, she'd started flying a little, but just low to the ground. Well, because of all the cats I'd been making the other robins sleep in the apricot tree—"

"How do you *make* a bird sleep in a tree?"

"You grab it and throw it up in the air as hard as you can, right at dusk. It'll come down in a tree and stay there. Anyway. Gimpy couldn't fly *or* perch, so she'd been spending the night on the porch, on the back of a folded lawn chair. Then yesterday afternoon she went missing."

"And you went looking for a corpus delecti."

"I did. But I finally found her next door, way up in a big lilac bush. She looked like she'd climbed up there using both wings and both feet, but she was up higher than my head in the thing, and I figured if she could do that, maybe she *could* perch on a tree limb. So last night I stuck her up in the apricot tree, to see what would happen. And she held on! She spent the whole night up there, and flew down out of it this morning when I went out to serve breakfast, looking for all the world like a normal bird. Well, a normal bird who'd been through a truly terrible experience." Pam laughed. Gimpy's recovery was the one delight in her life just now; what a relief to escape for a minute into something delightful. "And she gobbled up her dog food, and I haven't seen her since. I think maybe she's taken off. Two of the others have. She finally got over her cold."

~

On the following day, the seventh of June, 2037, Pope Miguel I and Claes-Göran Ormelius, Secretary General of the United Nations, met with three Hefn—Humphrey, Godfrey, and Alfrey—at Thingvellir, the Hefn base in Washington, DC. There, Ormelius stated bluntly that the resources of the UN were wholly inadequate to contain widespread social upheaval of the sort that had resulted in the recent mindwipings, and that worldwide societal breakdown and worldwide terrorism were now inevitable unless the Baby Ban were lifted. The tense calm that had followed the display of the wiped rioters had eroded and was on the verge of snapping.

And mindwipe, he said, could no longer be expected to work as a deterrent. Enough people had now reached the point of suicidal desperation that violence was certain to break out, with a high likelihood that Gaians—missionaries above all, but all Gaians, and for that matter anyone suspected of being in sympathy with the aliens and their goals—would be systematically tracked down and executed by the international terrorist consortium now in the process of organizing itself. Even the Apprentices and members of the Senate Committee on Alien Affairs, tight as their security might be, could become targets. The Hefn themselves would not be safe. And at the grassroots level, plots had sprung up to defy the Directive in every possible way.

"The people of Earth have come to a collective decision," he concluded. "They have said: 'We are ready to declare all-out war. We refuse to appease you any longer, in hopes of winning back what you have taken from us; instead we mean to fight you by every means we can devise, and there aren't enough of you to wipe us all.' They have reached a point where many would rather see innocents killed, or even see the world destroyed, than live one more day under the Baby Ban and the Directive.

"Humphrey, Godfrey, Alfrey, surely it is time for you to face the fact that environmental salvation cannot be imposed upon a people determined to stand or fall by their own actions! The three of you have done your utmost, but the will to self-determination is fundamental to human nature. And neither you nor we can change that, neither you nor we can 'save' us from our own truest selves. And, this being so, you must also see that the Baby Ban is pointless, a torment that can never bring us where the Gafr wish us to arrive. I therefore beseech you, by all you hold most dear, to plead with the Gafr: Lift the Ban! Lift the Ban! Lift the Ban!"

For his part, Miguel declared that he could no longer in good conscience counsel the faithful to patience and restraint. He too, predictably, urged the lifting of the Baby Ban. He didn't add "or else," nor did he have to.

The three Hefn consulted with their Gafr. That evening, on the regular Hefn news broadcast, Humphrey reported the gist of the summit and the Gafr's response.

"Our lords the Gafr," he announced in his best stentorian voice, "have decreed that the sixth of June, 2038, one year from yesterday and twenty-five years to the day since the Baby Ban was first imposed upon humanity, shall be a Day of Reckoning.

"Our lords have graciously allowed humanity one last year to prove the Secretary General wrong, to show them that humans are capable of being reasonable in their own self-interest.

"For the length of that year, the Hefn are charged to be merciless in enforcing the Directive, and to be ruthless in punishing any who attempt to injure our own selves or any of our friends.

"Succeed in convincing our lords that you are able to live sanely and sustainably upon this planet, and the Ban shall be revoked and the people of Earth again be fruitful. Fail, and the Ban shall be declared permanent. Revolt, and earn a penalty more dire than mindwipe.

"Regardless, on June the sixth, one year from yesterday, your proving time—and a quarter-century of uncertainty—are at an end for us and for you."

Pam's Journal

12 June 2037, Saturday, SLC. In the office all last week, reviewing the May reports on Homeland that came in right before Thingvellir and never got filed. In most senses an exercise in futility at this point. The basic idea still seems potent, but in hindsight it's incomprehensible how we could have failed—AGAIN!—to recognize that after the riots and wipings, nobody anywhere was going to listen to one word from anyone connected with the Hefn, unless it concerned when the Ban would be revoked. The reports all say the same thing: "Good idea, terrible timing." "If only we'd been given this a year ago."

Day before yesterday a call came in from the gafr of the Manchester Mission, a guy called Nigel Sutton. He had the May summaries for the North of England, which jibed with the reports from London and Birmingham. "To be brutally frank, I'm afraid Homeland never got off the ground over here." If we'd started promoting family land sooner it might have caught on, but after the riots . . . blah . . . blah . . .

I said, "You know, we're kind of in an ivory tower situation here, but you mission gafrs are out there on the front lines, and I can't help thinking it must have struck some of you that after the March 25th display—"

Nigel looked embarrassed. He admitted he'd heard a few skeptical remarks—I bet it was more than a few—but that I'd put the case "awf'ly persuasively" and he personally had felt it was worth a go, and What We Never Know Is How, etc. etc. Then he said, "Now, obviously, everything's going to be different."

Because of the summit, he meant. People might now do an about-face about the Gaian Mission—might actually join, in an effort to convince the Gafr it's safe to revoke the Ban. He thought Homeland might appeal to some of those types. "I expect we'll be a lot busier in the months to come, and a lot more popular. Instead of us knocking on their doors, in fact, I expect they'll come knocking on ours!" He actually sounded chuffed at the prospect. I rang off as soon as I could; I didn't want him to realize how much his words, his very tolerance for compliance without conviction, appalled me.

All the Gafr really did at the summit was repeat what they've been saying since they got here, but that one-last-year thing has yanked the rug out from under just about everybody. Really it was very clever of them, it shows an understanding of human psychology that I wouldn't have given even Humphrey credit for. The air's been let out of the terrorist balloon. Who's going to commit suicide to kill aliens and Gaians, when a year from now it'll all be settled anyway?

They've never lied to us. They imposed the Ban by trickery, but whenever they say they're going to do something, they follow through. So everybody believes in One Last Year, including me.

Here's what I see happening. People will make a big show of pretending to go along with the Directive cheerfully for this one year. What's a year? Nigel's probably right, the missions will be swamped with fake wannabe converts to stewardship.

And while the multitudes go scurrying around planting potatoes and making soap, and singing "Gaia Is Our Ground" in four-part harmony, with big phony smiles on their faces, an underground movement will be using the year to hatch a plot for taking out the Gafr ship, as soon as we're sure we've got our fertility back. All that pent-up outrage will be channeled into a top-secret dead-serious effort by experts to get rid of the Gafr once and for all. Rocket scientists of the world, come out of retirement! You have nothing to lose but your impotence! Without the Gafr, the Hefn wouldn't pose that much of a problem even if all 18 of them should happen to be on Earth when the ship blows.

It's a *radical* shift for me to think along lines like these. I can't be the only one. Everything suddenly looks simple: first get out from under the Ban, then get the aliens off our backs for keeps. As soon as you put the situation inside a one-year frame, things fall right into place. I'd almost be disappointed, in a perverse way, if people didn't try.

If they succeeded, if they actually got an armed rocket to the moon, what a story it would make. "Underdog species outwits its oppressors though stealth, coyote-cleverness, brilliance, raw courage, and heroism that does not shrink from the final sacrifice." I've heard that story lots of times, its plot is classic.

Do I want to hear it again?

The truth, now.

The truth is, I'm not sure. Right now, of much of anything.

14 June 2037, Monday, SLC. Yesterday Humphrey canceled the conference for mission gafrs that Alfrey called while he was hibernating; it's not needed now, he says. Instead, over the Fourth the *Apprentices* are to brainstorm in Santa Barbara about how best to use the final year.

He wants me there too, though it doesn't make much sense. When he tested me the day he left for Santa Barbara, I couldn't initiate a trance—even a light one—let alone set transceiver coordinates; I couldn't even do the kindergarten quincunx exercises he set for me. He was all crestfallen about it. But still hoping, he says now. It might come back more gradually. Anyway he wants me there.

What with one thing and another I don't much want to see Humphrey again quite yet, but I don't think I'm prepared to refuse a direct request. And I'm queasy about this final year thing, I want to ask him face to face what the Gafr expect to accomplish by it.

15 June 2037, Tuesday (just barely), SLC. It's 2:14 a.m. but I can't sleep, my brain's buzzing with radical-shift ideas. I seem to see something steadily and whole for the first time, and it's not good, in fact it's devastating.

Here's what I keep thinking. After 24 years of occupation, Earth may be a cleaner and . . . less brutalized place, but not because enough of us have had a change of heart, and started behaving like the trainees on that poster Lexi doesn't like. Gaia's healthier only because we're sterile and afraid of the HefnGafr. We remain a captive people, not a convinced one. We still think Earth is all about what *people* want. Released from the Directive, fertility restored, fear of mindwipe canceled, we'd go straight back to our old wasteful, arrogant ways. (And if my cloak-and-dagger rocket scientists blow up the Gafr, that's exactly what'll happen.)

So face the rest of it. The work of the transceiver techs, the work I yearned to be part of for so long, has been pointless for a decade. Up to now, every traditional pre-industrial culture they've found that "struck an ideal balance" with nature, every single one, lost that balance sooner or later in one of two ways. They're all hunter-gatherers to start with. In model one—the one we admire and idealize, and try to imitate with the homestead-ing analog—somebody domesticates a few goats, or plants a garden to supplement the game and berries. But if nothing inter-feres with the process, the herds and gardens always get bigger, things always progress from enough to surplus. Next thing you know you've got exponential population growth, social stratifica-tion, concentration of power, armies, mathematics, astronomy, and fine arts; and the culture's using up more resources than it's putting back in.

Gaians want to freeze that allegory at the Crux, where the gardens, herds, and population numbers are still small. Mission-aries have to believe that if people can be helped to realize how things always go, they'll sensibly choose to avoid the trap. Only people trained as they've been trained could be that innocent.

The other model is when primitive peoples are contacted by a culture with a superior technology. The superior culture may simply conquer the more primitive people, but instead (or first) it may offer to trade its stuff for their stuff, and the primitives always say yes. The elders may be cultural conservatives, but the kids are always eager to chomp into the techno-apple and get themselves thrown out of Paradise. You can see it perfectly well without a transceiver, in the Amish, for instance, or the Maori; with a transceiver you can watch Narragansett trappers trading beaver pelts for copper pots and rifles, and pretty soon nobody's left who remembers how to fletch an arrow.

The Hefn failed to allow for this, and so did the Gaians. They looked at Inuits in down parkas and dark goggles, driving their snowmobiles to the seal-hunting grounds, and saw only something to forbid. They ought to have seen a classic model of a human culture confronting a higher technology and choosing dependency. No—grabbing dependency with both hands!

We've known all these things for a long time, but haven't put the pieces in this order and drawn this conclusion. If we had, how could we not have given up? But the truth as I see it tonight is that a real answer to environmental exploitation was never there for the techs to find—not in prehistory, not in the human genome, nowhere except in the tiny minority that finds the Gaian model appealing.

So trekking out to California now, to brainstorm with the Hefn and Apprentices about how to use that final year, is totally futile. There's nothing left to try. There really never *was* anything to try. Ormelius is right, you can't save people from their truest selves. Which is exactly what we've been trying to do: save them, convert them. Lead them to renounce their sinful ways and be redeemed, born again as Gaia's stewards. We all believed it was possible, and even saw it happen often enough to go on believing. But "redeemed by the blood of the Lamb" has a pizzazz to it that "Homeland" (for instance) just doesn't. *We never found our transforming myth!*

Rather, the Eden myth has been there in plain sight all along; what we never found was a way to tailor it to the Gaian message so it would strike as deeply into people as the myth of the god who becomes a man and dramatically sacrifices himself to redeem humanity from the wages of their wickedness. Baptists and Mormons love the mythically transformed Jesus "because he first loved us and gave himself for us." What did Gaia do? Brought us into being and sustained us there; but a lot of people don't even believe that, and anyway evolution lacks the mythic punch of the Easter story, the victory over death. Does Gaia love me? Then why should I love Gaia? It's sacrilege to say this, but the real answer might actually be: If you have to ask, you'll never really know.

In which case the Mission has all been for naught, and we are even more guilty of denial than I used to think. *We* said that in so many words, ten weeks ago at Hurt Hollow, and then we turned right around and followed Artie (and me, oh yeah, I led the freaking *way!*) straight into another blind swamp. All that work, all those years of school, Humphrey's exhausting intercessions with the Gafr, setting the missions up, selecting and training the mission gafrs, the field work, the Apprentices' long, earnest scrutiny of the past to locate the model cultures and identify the Cruxes. Even Homeland; even the bradshaw.

The bradshaw! Oh God, right now (at 3:30 in the morning) I'm ready to confess that there's more real value in hand-rearing a bunch of ducks and robins, some of whose genes will probably flow into the Mallard and robin gene pools next spring, than for a woman who'll never raise a child to spend all those hours with her own Inner Child, facing up to repressed feelings in hopes of claiming a place in her abusive father's family of grotesques. And after all that, Homeland ends up in the toilet.

No, no, be fair. There are reasons besides Homeland to have faced those feelings, and maybe I *did* use Homeland as a prod to get myself to make the thing. I meant it when I told Liam it's better to know than not to know.

(I'm pretty sure I meant it.)

21 June 2037, Monday, SLC. Six days later I believe a little of the above can be chalked up to midnight angst. Specifically, I'll always wonder how things might have gone if we'd introduced Homeland several years ago. Liam says everybody's moaning about that out at the BTP, even the ones who liked it least.

But we didn't, and nobody's had any other brainstorms this week; and if they did I'm pretty sure it would be too late to try them out. I fear that on the evidence we have, and we have a lot of it, converting enough humans into willing Gaian stewards, within the context of the Directive and the Ban, would have been very, very difficult no matter what; but I'll still always wonder.

Now though, within that last-year frame, it's no longer a question of genuine conversion. The missionaries are out of the business of reaching hearts and minds, and into the business of teaching classes in organic gardening, and how to walk and quack like Gaians. A soul-destroying change for some, I don't doubt, and I bet a lot of them quit. I would.

How can we do *anything* real with a year? Doesn't a space that tight make real change impossible? Sure looks like it to me.

All I can think is that the Gafr have something up their sleeve that we'll hear about in Santa Barbara in a couple of weeks. Thank God I didn't argue with Humphrey about coming. At this point wild horses couldn't keep me away from that conference. I need to know what's really going on, and I need to hear it from him.

Also—much as it galls me to admit this—if the time's come to confront the failure of everything we've tried to do, I want to confront it in Liam's company. Maybe that's because things with Humphrey are strained right now. Or maybe I'd feel like that in any case.

Tomorrow was supposed to be my day to visit Lexi on location, but the prospect of an encounter with RoLayne Allred, on top of everything else, makes my stomach muscles scrunch up. When I mentioned it to Julie she said why not call and cancel, saying I'm sorry but just can't get away from the office right now, and make it up to Lexi some other time, maybe after the trip. So I did. She was pretty disappointed, I had pangs of remorse, but I just don't bloody well want to have to be civil yet to anybody's complicitous mother, not even hers.

CHAPTER 8

Betrayals

2 - 3 JULY

Liam met her at the station. "It's such a damn shame about Homeland," was the first thing he said. "The more obvious it gets that it won't work now, the more I keep thinking it might've worked wonders say two years ago."

"We'll never know. But thanks."

"I guess not. Let me take that." Liam hoisted her backpack over one shoulder and led the way out into the sunshine.

Awkward but relieved, Pam trailed along behind him through the bright California afternoon. She was shockingly glad to see him. When they had boarded the tram and found two seats together, she asked, "What's Humphrey had to say about One Last Year?"

"We haven't seen much of Humphrey at the Bureau these last couple of weeks, I don't think he's been in town. Everybody's down in the dumps. We're all hoping to hear something this weekend that'll make sense of this one-year thing, give us something to focus on, but till we do—how're the robins, by the way?"

Pam smiled. "Gone, gone, gone altogether beyond. Not everything ends in failure."

"No—though it does seem ironic, working so hard to save a few birds, when a year from now, odds are the human race will begin going through a bottleneck that'll turn the gene pool into a teeny puddle."

She shrugged. "The truth is, I feel like rehabbing those birds is the most useful thing I've done all year. Everything *but* the robins just seems meaningless right now."

"What about the bradshaw?"

Oops. Of course, Liam had a stake in that. "The bradshaw was totally and completely successful, as you know. The problem is how to evaluate micro-successes within a macro-catastrophe. Oh, and the ducklings, they're gone too. Winnie and Frank are empty-nesters again, being fed by the saintly Jaime while I'm here."

"How's Jaime doing, anyway?"

"Better," Pam said. "Working maniacally and joking less, but he's had some counseling and that's helped. We've got another abuse case that he's been handling, that's helped too, ironically enough. He's very good at that. How's Eddie?"

"Speaking of macro-catastrophes and meaninglessness?"

"You said it, I didn't!" They smirked at each other, and Pam breathed a little easier. "He's great, actually," Liam said with quiet satisfaction. "We went to San Diego over the break and watched whales." The Apprentices had been given the previous two weeks off, except for the few too involved in conference-organizing to get away. "He's got a concert Sunday afternoon. Bruckner's *Grosse Messe*. Want to come, if we're free? There's some terrific solo parts."

Eddie was a paid tenor soloist at local productions of big choral pieces. "Maybe. Sure. Let the personal life go on, as you so correctly said it always does."

They rode in amiable silence for a bit. Pam's mind, undistracted by chitchat, began to fill with certain heavy thoughts she had not yet decided to share. Looking out the window, then around the tram, she noticed a man across the aisle who was reading Arthur C. Clarke's old science-fiction classic, *Childhood's End*.

She nudged Liam so he would see it too. "Jeff loved that book," he said wistfully. "I bet it's had a big revival."

"Lexi told me somebody wanted to make the movie. Maybe they still will."

"With computer-generated kid mobs."

The humans in Clarke's novel had lost *all* their children, not through infertility but through an evolutionary leap to a higher form of existence, midwifed by aliens who looked exactly like devils. Technically it was a happy ending, but the book was sad to read.

People too old to make the leap had suffered a psychological blow so devastating that they lost their desire to reproduce, ultimately leaving the planet devoid of human life.

"BTP," said the electronic voice, "The next stop is BTP." They got off right in front of the building. In the instant before they entered it, Pam saw sunlight glinting on the distant ocean, and thought that if they had any spare time at all she was going to take a barefoot walk on the beach. You needed to *make* time for such things, especially now. On the screen inside her mind she saw herself kicking through sand, her cuffs rolled up, her expression tragic but calm, while in the background an orchestra played *"Waltzing Matilda."*

"Hi, Pam," said Johnny Wang as they came through the doors into the entryway. "Good to see you life-size."

"Thanks, you too. What are you doing manning the desk?"

"The receptionist called in sick. I'm only filling in till the replacement gets here. You're in 113, if you want to go and freshen up or whatever. Humphrey just announced the meeting for 7:30 in the Big Room. Dinner's at 6:30. Liam, there's somebody waiting to see you."

"Who?"

"Some woman. Young, nice-looking—has Eddie got anything to worry about here?"

Liam grinned. "I don't know any nice-looking young women. What's her name?"

"Search me. Why don't you ask her?"

Liam's mouth twisted sideways, considering. To Pam he said, "If you're going to your room now, I'll walk you as far as the lounge."

They went along the corridor of this building, constructed rather than converted, as the one in Washington had been, for the Bureau of Temporal Physics and its needs. It had been designed primarily as a boarding school for the training of successive classes of Apprentices. When the supply of fourteen-year-olds had run too low to matter, the rooms in the dormitory wing had gradually been turned into guest rooms for times, like now, when the Hefn summoned their human collaborators to Headquarters. The old Apprentice rec room on the first floor had been turned into a lounge that served as a waiting room—access to the offices and labs being, of course, restricted. Had their summit been held here, and had they arrived early, even His Holiness and the Secretary General would have had to wait for Humphrey in the lounge, which was, however, comfortably furnished and well lighted.

As they approached it, Liam unslung Pam's backpack from his shoulder. "See you at dinner?"

"Right." Pam groped blindly for the strap while trying to sneak a glimpse at Liam's mysterious visitor. At the sound of their voices a slender young woman with short thick black hair had pushed herself out of an overstuffed armchair. She smiled hesitantly—and the backpack crashed to the floor; Liam had let go before Pam could grab hold of it. He'd gone completely white. At the unexpected crash, the young woman fell back into the chair she had been getting up from. For a moment the three of them formed a tableau of lost composure; and then Liam braced himself with one arm against the wall, and the woman stood up again and said, "I'm sorry, I'm Gillian Jacoby? I'm waiting to see Liam O'Hara?"

Liam's face had now become suffused with blood. "Gillian—"

"Jacoby. *You're* him, aren't you? I've seen pictures from a while back, that *Time* magazine article about Hot Spots?"

She was confused and embarrassed; Pam on the other hand had stiffened, flooded with perfect comprehension. But no more than Liam was she capable of speech.

When Liam didn't say anything, "My mom passed last month," this person said, "but when she was in the hospital she told me you used to know my brother? My half-brother, actually, he died before I was born? Jeff Carpenter?"

And now Pam was rushing in slow motion along the corridor toward room 113, teleported out of the moment with no memory of how. She was never going to make it all that way before throwing up. The world around her brightened and turned plastic while she labored and fought—as if trying to wake from a dream—to reach the sanctuary of the room. But when she actually did make it after all, and slammed the door behind her, it turned out that the inevitable inner explosion wasn't what she'd thought. Instead of veering into the bathroom, she found she had hurled herself face down on the bed, was gripping the pillow in her fists, was making horrible lowing sounds that some part of her held back from in amazement.

The sounds when on and on. Then, fierce pressure in her forehead, clogged sinuses, soggy pillow. Time had passed, she must have fallen asleep. She rolled onto her side, gasping. The holding-back part of Pam also woke and observed this shattered person, herself, with fear and incredulity. It was like being flattened by a falling chunk of space debris.

Someone was knocking on the door—knocking again, Pam realized; the first knock was what had woken her. She tensed, willing the person to go away. Another series of raps; and then, oh God, she heard the latch click—she had not, of course, locked the door behind her. It was intolerable, how people kept walking in on her without being invited. "Pam?" said Liam's voice, and then the door swung inward, and there he stood, a short, graceful, balding man made entirely of plastic, framed in the plastic doorway.

At the last instant she had turned face down again; she saw the plastic Liam from under the crook of an elbow thrown hastily across her face. Go away, go away, go away. The light in the room was dim; he might believe she had slept through his racket.

Whether or not he believed it, Liam appeared to accept the apparent version of Pam's condition. He stole into the room and set her backpack on the floor, then scribbled something on the desk slate and tiptoed out.

When the door had clicked behind him, Pam reached to pull a handful of tissues out of the box on the bedside table, flopped over on her back, and blew her nose juicily again and again, dropping the damp wads on the floor. No need to get up and read the message; it would say "I won't be at dinner, see you tomorrow." She closed her burning eyes and listened to her blood pound in her temples, *ba-wham, ba-wham.*

What dreadful thing had happened? What other dreadfulness could possibly still be left? Pam's unconscious, but only her unconscious, had recognized the event's significance at once and reacted convulsively, hurling her away from the charged instant of encounter between Liam and the sister of his dead friend and into this room and this bed and this state of dishevelment. She had come completely to pieces and didn't yet know why.

Why had she been dissociating en route to the room, and why still dissociating when Liam opened the door? The world had not turned bright and artificial like that since before her father died; she had believed it never would again.

Pam fought down an upsurge of panic, forced herself to concentrate on her breathing. After a blank interval of deep, slow mouth breaths—no choice, her nose was now completely stopped up—a thought floated into her mind: *This is how he felt when Jeff died.*

Then another thought: *She looks exactly like him. Liam must have thought he'd seen a ghost.*

She hitched herself over onto her stomach again—and abruptly knew what she'd been dreaming in that position when the knock had come at the door. Into visual memory flashed a kaleidoscope of richly patterned reds and blues, undulating, rippling . . . Pam thought with stunned amazement, *I was dreaming fractals when he woke me up.*

She clutched her pillow. Breathed. In a while it occurred to her to wonder whether she might still be dissociating; she sat up and turned on the bedside lamp, but now the room looked normal.

Fractals—

As soon as she felt able to, Pam rolled off the bed and wobbled into the tiny bathroom, where she pulled herself together as best she could. Washed, combed, and fairly kempt, shirt changed, bed spread up, signs of calamity eradicated, she activated the phone. When Johnny Wang's round face appeared on the screen she said, "Can you get a message to Humphrey? I need to see him ASAP."

Pacing, waiting for the callback, Pam glanced down at Liam's message: "I brought your pack. Not coming to dinner, might see you at breakfast. L." Hissing as if burned, she snatched her damp washcloth out of the bathroom, wadded it up, scrubbed the slate clean.

The phone pinged. "He's on his way to your room right now."

"He is in fact standing outside of your door right now," came Humphrey's muffled voice from the corridor.

Pam pitched the washcloth into the basin and pulled the door open. Where the plastic Liam had stood an hour before, Humphrey stood now. He conveyed an impression of bursting with excited questions, though he was simply standing there, a stubby figure upholstered in gray horsehair. Pam looked at this figure, loved for most of her life more intensely than all but a very few of the human beings she had ever known, and felt nothing. She was numb. She said, numbly, "Hi. I think you might want to test me again."

~

"He ran the exact same tests as three weeks ago in Salt Lake," Pam reported to Julie onscreen—poor Julie, who quite reasonably must have assumed they'd finished dealing with crises for the time being. "In Salt Lake I flunked them all. Tonight I immediately got an excellent trance, induced the visual, handled the quincunx, placed coordinates, got the spin started—basically did everything I used to do twenty years ago, and it was all as easy and natural as pie. Humphrey is turning somersaults of joy and taking all the credit; he thinks the bradshaw did the trick."

Julie, wearing her "professional" face for this emergency midnight mini- session, said predictably, "But you don't."

"Of course I don't, and neither do you." (Julie let a little smile crack her mask for a second.) "I didn't think my intuition would ever come back after Dad died, because that threat was gone for good. But it looks like Liam and Humphrey have been standing all this time, without my realizing it, between me and some other threat, and now suddenly they aren't anymore."

"What other threat?"

"I can't decipher the code." The weak joke failed to conceal the degree of her distress. "But, okay, first Humphrey betrays me with the bradshaw, and then, when I see the look on Liam's face the second he lays eyes on Gillian, I know instantly that I've never been anything but a stand-in for Jeff. And Jesse's dead, so now there's nobody left between me and—" She lifted her hands and let them fall, unable to supply the word.

Julie frowned. "There's a lot you can't be sure about, Pam, such as, to take an obvious example, how things will work out between Liam and Gillian. You don't how Gillian's going to feel about Liam."

Pam shook her head stubbornly. "Julie, I'm a substitute for Jeff. What difference does it make how *she* feels about *him*?"

Being Liam's therapist as well as Pam's had complicated things for Julie before. She became positively pokerfaced. "I'm wondering whether the fact that Gillian is a young woman could be having an effect here. I mean, you've never sounded this . . . implacably bitter about Eddie, even though you've always felt a lot of hostility toward him."

Pam nearly choked on her impatience. "Male, female, what's the difference? Liam's not straight *or* gay in a truly determined way, you know that as well as I do! What he is, is Jeff-obsessed. If Jeff had lived, who knows how all that would have played out? But Jeff died when he did, at twelve, and Liam's been stuck there ever since. It's not about gender per se, it's about how much you remind Liam of Jeff, how successful a stand-in you are." Incredible how absolutely clear this was to Pam, though she had never put it into words, even to herself, until that moment.

Julie's mask had slipped a fraction, but she only said, "That's not quite what I asked you."

"You want to know if I'm jealous of Gillian because we're both female, and she's pretty and young and I'm not? All I can tell you is, I don't think I'd feel one bit less grotesque right now if she were Jeff's half-*brother*."

"'Grotesque'?"

"Like a damn fool, then. Not least for hauling you out of bed to listen to this ridiculous caterwauling, waa waa waaah."

"Steady on." Julie looked at the offscreen spot where the clock was. "We do have to stop, and we should certainly take this up again, but—you haven't said how it feels to have your intuition back! You've suffered terribly from the loss of it, and now after all these years you're back in the Bureau family with your faculties restored. I'm not underestimating the pain of feeling abandoned by both Humphrey and Liam, but isn't there cause for rejoicing here as well?"

~

Humphrey certainly thought there was. In fact he'd been rejoicing noisily all evening, and since he wasn't sleeping nowadays, nothing stood in the way of nonstop celebration.

Pam wasn't sleeping either. She thrashed from side to side, plagued with distant sounds of revelry, tossed by incongruent and violent emotions. Every time she dropped off to sleep for a minute, fractals swarmed beneath her lids.

She had never expected to feel again the grace and mastery, the oceanic bliss, of oneness with universal truth expressed mathematically. And now against all odds this gift had been restored, perfect as if the two-decade hiatus of impotence had never been. How could she not rejoice?

Suppose someone had said, "You can be an intuitive again whenever you like, all you have to do is sacrifice your abiding faith in Humphrey and your deep connection with Liam. Deal?"

It was no deal at all. Life without intuition had been bleak. But life not grounded in the bedrock of her relationships with Humphrey and Liam?

Pam groaned aloud and fought the sheet and blanket. *I knew this, I knew it. I knew if I was being mauled by a bear, Liam might run away and leave me, but he wouldn't leave Jeff—I* knew that. *I knew how clueless Humphrey could be, I thought it was part of his alien charm!*

This was the third time in three weeks that Pam had wrestled with the bedclothes while being relentlessly blitzed by her own intolerable conclusions, the second time she'd spilled her guts all over poor Julie, who had behaved impeccably but probably felt like screaming *For God's sake, get over yourself!* Pam wouldn't have blamed her one bit. Her chest swelled tight with self-loathing.

Finally she threw off the covers and wrenched herself out of bed. She switched on the lamp, put on the robe and slippers provided by the Bureau (so Apprentices could travel light), and opened her YellowPad.

When she closed it an hour later and fell back into bed, she couldn't have said then whether what she'd written was a defiant lyric or a suicide note.

FORTUNATE FALL
—for Jesse Kellum; Liam O'Hara; the Hefn Humphrey

Precarious as Moroni on his spire,
Minus the gold leaf hide, the golden horn,
And the sweet certainty of being upborne
By an angelic nature or a stout wire

Harness come earthquakes, twisters, gales that blow
Fiercest up where the wingless angel stands,
Above you, mortal trinity of friends,
I played my trump and balanced on my toe.

But now, O father, brother, alien,
None kin to me, whose three lives propped so long
Their tripod spire beneath me, it's gone wrong,
The steeple's come to pieces. Hurricane-

Force winds of change blew through and shattered things.
I slipped. The ground flew up and knocked me silly.
So much for balance now! I'm on my belly,
I can't get up—wait—where'd I get these wings?

~

She'd missed dinner, but by morning everybody—with the likely exception of Liam, who had not, in fact, made it to breakfast—knew Pam's math intuition had returned. She was so besieged with congratulations she could hardly eat her grapefruit. "High marks for timing!" Raghu yelled across the room. Samantha gave her a hug, saying "Pam, I am *so* happy about this! Welcome back."

She bore all the fussing with adequate grace and firmly did not say what was in her mind (*Humphrey can think what he likes, but me being back doesn't change a damn thing!*). But it was a relief when they adjourned to the big classroom and he called them to order. "Where is Liam O'Hara?" Humphrey asked the group when they were seated. "Does any of you know where Liam is? Do you know where Liam is, Pam Pruitt of the restored mathematical intuition?"

Nobody knew. "He came in yesterday afternoon, with Pam," Johnny reported, "but I haven't seen him since. He wasn't at dinner."

"Or breakfast," said Artie.

To miss a session of such critical importance was so unthinkable that Humphrey sent Will to check Liam's room. Will came back with the news that Liam wasn't there and his bed hadn't been slept in. This caused a stir; but when Humphrey, greatly alarmed, started instructing Will to put through a call to Eddie, Pam took him aside. "Somebody turned up here yesterday looking for Liam. He's probably with her."

"Her?" Humphrey sounded baffled. "What *her* could cause Liam to be absent from this meeting?"

"Only this one, if that's where he is. Remember that after Jeff Carpenter died, Jeff's mother divorced Terry and moved out here and remarried? Well, she had a daughter. Yesterday the daughter was here waiting to see Liam. Her name's Gillian Jacoby, and the thing is, she looks exactly like Jeff."

The Hefn became still, and something flickered behind his eyes; Pam saw that in his own way he was as shocked as she had been. Both of them thrown over for a slip of a girl! Remote from him as she felt, the long habit of their intimacy moved Pam to say, "Still, there might be a perfectly good reason why he hasn't turned up yet. Maybe he just got held up. I think we should proceed with the meeting."

Humphrey gave her an icy look, turned away, spoke briefly to Alfrey, and left the room.

While Alfrey was calling the Apprentices back to order, Pam sat down and considered her feelings, or rather her lack of them, with mild wonder. None of it seemed to *matter*. Liam's absence was just a fact. Humphrey's "alien" glare had failed to stop her heart. It seemed there was truly now nothing of a personal nature left to lose. Overnight, somewhere inside herself, Pam had crossed Humphrey's and Liam's names off a list that had had only three names on it, ever.

She looked about her in bafflement. Here she was, qualified to be a member of the BTP family again, as Julie had pointed out, and she didn't care, she simply didn't *care*—not if membership could be lost and gained by forces altogether outside her own control, not if Humphrey and Liam could be traitorous in the pursuit of their own passions without even noticing the effect they were having on hers. Forcing Liam to shoot the second bradshaw didn't come close to being in the same league, or so she felt this morning. That the intuitive power itself had so little value to her now seemed past belief, yet it was so. She had moved beyond anguish or joy, into a region of eerie calm. Last night's hysterics felt completely unreal.

Dull from lack of sleep, dissociated in a brand new way, she stared at Alfrey, pointlessly willing him to begin the pointless meeting.

~

Stretched full length on his left side, head propped on his open palm, the cause of all this agitation lay in the semidarkness watching Gillian sleep.

Short dark hair, rumpled on the pillow . . . thin face, lips slightly parted, long dark lashes feathering her cheeks . . . twenty-seven years ago, asleep in a mummy bag in a small canvas tent, Jeff Carpenter had looked like this. *Exactly* like this; in the dim light, the facial likeness of Jeff at twelve and Gillian at twenty-three was simply uncanny. Liam had pored over this face for hours the previous evening and

206

made love to it for much of the night. Morning had broken, and still he could not stop devouring it.

Since yesterday his emotions had been in such turmoil that despite Julie's training he could get no perspective on them at all. Sometime during the night, one semi-coherent idea did form within the maelstrom: that he was living out a kind of realtime bradshaw: his Inner Child's miraculous recovery of the lost love of his life. With the thought came the briefest glimmering, instantly thrust away, that Gillian was being pushed along unwillingly by his own ravening need.

Helpless in the grip of this need, he lay now and watched her sleeping countenance.

Eventually the dark lashes fluttered and Jeff's blue eyes opened in Gillian's face, banishing thought entirely. Liam smiled down at her. "Hi," he said softly and bent to kiss her.

She didn't return the kiss. Pulling back a little, he was surprised to see that she looked confused, even alarmed. She sat up and pulled the sheet around her. "What—"

"You invited me to spend the night. Remember?"

"I've got the most awful headache. We—did I have a lot to drink?"

She looked more alarmed than ever, but also, in a tousled way, more beautiful than ever to Liam. Smiling to reassure her, he reached over and stroked that unruly hair. "We split a bottle of wine, that's all. Do you really not remember? We had dinner here in your hotel and then we came up to the room, and—"

"I shouldn't drink wine," Gillian said distractedly, "I haven't got the head for it, I . . . get silly."

"You didn't get silly last night," Liam said soothingly, and gave her hair a little extra tousle. The truth was, he had no idea how she'd behaved or what she'd said, or for that matter exactly how they'd wound up in bed together. It had felt so inevitable that the details seemed irrelevant.

Gillian didn't appear to agree. Abruptly she leapt naked out of the bed and rushed into the bathroom. He could hear her being sick, which made him frown, then the sounds of flushing and water running. He rolled over onto his back and folded his arms behind his head.

A few minutes later she came out wearing a bathrobe. In the fluffy white robe she looked less like Jeff, and Liam sat up, suddenly uncomfortable. "You better go," she said. "I'm sick and I've got a terrible headache."

He pushed back the covers. "Hey, I can get you something for that, I'll get dressed and run down to the lobby—"

"No!" said Gillian. "I want you to *go!*" Abruptly she burst into tears. "I don't know what's going on, I'm sick, I don't want you to *be* here. *You shouldn't be here!*"

Finally alarmed, Liam swung his legs over the side of the bed. At that instant there was a brief clamor of voices in the hall and the door sprang open. Gillian uttered a wailing cry, bent her arms around her head and leaned away from the commotion, as Humphrey—shouldering aside the hotel manager and a couple of cleaners—burst through the doorway. All his body hair was fully erected. "Oh indeed he should not be, young woman," he proclaimed in the ghastly metallic voice that afflicted Liam like fingernails on a chalkboard. "Mark William O'Hara, you should not be in the Radisson Santa Barbara sitting on this bed. You should be at BTP Headquarters, helping to plan our strategy."

From his perch on the side of Gillian's bed, Liam looked up at the bristling Hefn. "Strategy," he said stupidly. From a distance he observed the ridiculous tableau formed by the three of them: his own naked self; Humphrey imitating a porcupine in the doorway; and Gillian with her white terry-cloth bathrobe and bare white feet, clutching her head and sobbing wildly. *She's never seen a Hefn up close*, he realized, and then: *This must be that thing that happens to Pam, dissociation. Whoo. Can't say I care for it.*

But when Humphrey slammed the door to, breaking the moment, releasing him, Liam snatched his knickers and pants from the floor; and as he was climbing into them, Humphrey finally took a good look at the hysterical Gillian and froze where he stood. He seemed to shrink bodily as the corona of grizzled hair deflated. "Gillian Jacoby," he said, quite tenderly. "My dear, do not cry. Oh, do not cry! Oh, oh—"

She glanced up at him, and Humphrey did something Liam had not seen a Hefn do in more than twenty years, not since the *Delta Queen*: without moving his body at all, he locked eyes with Gillian and reached without permission into her mind with his own alien mind. Gillian stiffened and cried out at the instant of connection; but then she drew a deep shuddering breath and stopped sobbing. And Liam, watching, correctly guessed what Humphrey had done.

Humphrey did not, of course, remember Jeff, who had died just before the alien ship arrived; but he had lifted Liam's own memories of Jeff when Liam was fifteen, restoring them little by little as Liam, working with Julie Hightower, had become able to tolerate them. Because the memories had remained in Humphrey's mind as well, the sight of Gillian had told him at once what Liam felt at his own first sight of her. And, in a spontaneous act of intrusive compassion, he had passed some of this knowledge along.

It worked. The hysterics and chaos of a moment ago vanished. Gillian mopped her face with her sleeves and blew her nose on a tissue. "That was—" she said shakily, then stopped and tried again. "Okay, I'm cool? Like, I get it? But," looking at Liam, "I'm sorry, I still want you to leave."

"He is leaving," Humphrey assured her.

Liam froze with his shirt pulled on halfway. "Strategy! The meeting this morning! I forgot the meeting!" He crammed his shirttail into his pants and sat down on the bed again to tie his shoes. "God, I forgot completely, I can't believe it." He jumped up and started picking things up off the floor, shoving them into his pockets. To Gillian he said, "When can I see you again? How long will you be in town?"

Gillian looked at Humphrey, who informed Liam, not unkindly, "Gillian Jacoby is going home to Oakland *today*."

Liam froze again. "Today? But—"

She shook her head vigorously. "I don't want to see you at all for now. I'm really mixed up and I feel terrible, and I guess you really, really loved my brother, but I'm not him, you know? All this—" she gestured around the room—"it's too much, I feel like a herd of elephants just stomped on me? I don't know what I'm going to tell my boyfriend, he wanted to come with me? And I said no?"

"*Boy*friend!" Liam exclaimed. The idea could not have seemed more bizarre.

"Liam O'Hara," Humphrey stated firmly, "you will come to BTP Headquarters now, and Gillian Jacoby will return to Oakland and her boyfriend. And you must respect her wish not to be pestered by you."

Liam rounded on him. "The hell I must! I'll go to the meeting, of course I will, but if I want to see Gillian later on, that's my business!"

Humphrey became rigid. Liam, taken aback by his own outburst, was aware of a quality he had experienced in Humphrey's presence just once before, at Carrie's memorial service: menace. And this time, unimaginably, directed at himself.

Abruptly Gillian darted between them to yank the door open. "I can't *stand* this, I can't stand it! Just go! Go! Go! Please?" she beseeched Humphrey, "Just get him out of here?"

Humphrey reached for Liam's arm. Liam shook him off and stalked furiously toward the open doorway. "I'll see you soon, I promise you that," he said to Gillian, and leaned to kiss her. When she pulled sharply away he flung up both arms and stormed from the room.

~

"—frankly, I don't see why—*there* he is," Marshall said.

Everyone turned to watch Liam stride across the Big Room and throw himself into a chair. "Sorry, everybody. Sorry, Alfrey. It's a long story."

Alfrey said, "Humphrey found you?"

"He found me," Liam replied shortly. "He'll be along."

Samantha said, "Eddie's been trying to reach you. He says your phone's turned off."

Liam nodded, carefully expressionless, but his face became warm. He hadn't given Eddie a second's thought since inviting Pam to the Bruckner performance, however many hours ago that might now be. "What were you discussing?" he said, to direct their attention away from himself.

"The Mission," Raghu said promptly, "how people are already joining up now in droves to get instruction on how to behave exactly like the Gafr want them to, since it's only for a year. We figure hardly any of them will be true converts, but Alfrey says the Gafr don't care what they believe as long as they follow the Directive. So even if *we* care, as far as the HefnGafr go it's not an issue. So he says. I'm having a little trouble with that."

Will took over. "Yeah, so then we started on how to use our year, and Artie was like, number one, if the Gafr don't care what people believe, why do anything? I mean, in that case a lot of us can't see the point of even having this conference. Including me, I mean it doesn't add up. If people aren't truly changed, they'll go back to the old ways after the Ban gets lifted. The Gafr realize that, so how can they not care? I'm like Raghu, I think something else is going on."

Artie said, "And my second point was, even if they did care what people believed, what could we try that we haven't tried already? We've been talking about it for weeks, and nobody's come up with anything they think might succeed where Homeland failed." Liam nodded; before the break, this had indeed been a constant topic of discussion among the Apprentices.

"So," bottom line," Marshall said, "I was just asking Alfrey why the Gafr would call an unnecessary conference purportedly to get us to do the impossible. Or, in other words, what are we doing here?"

"I've got a better one," said Karla, who seldom spoke up. "If the Gafr don't care what people believe—and if we can't convert them anyway—why give us this final year?"

That was something Liam wanted to know too. He faced around toward Alfrey with the others, expecting to be enlightened. Alfrey would now reveal the true story, the story the public wasn't in on, that would make sense of things and explain what they were really being asked to accomplish.

It didn't happen. Instead of projecting sympathy or patience or respect for their acuteness, or any of the emotional states he was so skilled at suggesting, Alfrey now stood before the assembled Apprentices an image of inscrutability. "Our concern today is neither with reasons nor with judgments," he said in neutral tones. "Our concern is how best to employ the year we have been given."

An uneasy stir followed the baffled silence that greeted this statement. Finally Marshall said, "Excuse me, Alfrey, but does that mean you're not at liberty to say?"

"It means," said Alfrey in the same neutral voice, "that my focus remains fixed on the matter at hand. In one year's time my lords the Gafr will judge whether humans in sufficient numbers are willing to live on Earth with their planet's welfare foremost in their minds. Should the Gafr judge today, no child of parents under the Ban would ever be born into this world. We have one year. Must we not now consider what might be done with it?"

Gradually the room filled up with tension. The Apprentices were accustomed to taking Alfrey and his support for granted. This speech not only avoided Marshall's question, it had an edge; it made Alfrey sound neither as boring nor as friendly as they had always supposed.

"Alfrey has hit the nail on the head," Humphrey's deep voice declared from the back of the room. None of the Apprentices had heard him come in, and their heads snapped round wearing smiles of relief—short-lived relief; Humphrey sounded, if anything, even less friendly than Alfrey had. "Are you ready to give up, then, with a year of opportunity left to you? Is a fresh approach impossible to imagine? One that might succeed in the new circumstances? Is none of you ready to fight to the finish?" As he made these remarks, Humphrey passed among the chairs and stood before the group. Alfrey stepped back a pace, tacitly yielding the floor to him.

Pam had been following, from a distance, what Alfrey and the others were saying. Her own thoughts and questions were being expressed by others, she had nothing special to contribute to the discussion. Liam's showy entrance—unshaved, uncombed, uniform unchanged since yesterday—had broken her detachment only a little, and only momentarily.

Now her mind became alert. She grasped that the two Hefn were deploying their scoldings and insinuations to divert the Apprentices' attention from the fact that Karla's question—the same question they'd all been working toward, the only one worth asking—was not being addressed.

Whatever had happened between Humphrey and Liam had completely altered Humphrey's mood; his delight over her regained intuition had been snuffed. He had spoken with rancor on numerous public occasions, but never, never, never had he addressed his own Apprentices, assembled or singly, in the voice he was using now. The Apprentices sat astounded and stricken; but Pam's mind, clear in its detachment, readily distinguished tone from content and thought, *If he hadn't quarreled with Liam he would be charming us, not berating us, but he'd still be ducking this issue.* She glanced about, wondering who else had realized that Alfrey and Humphrey were now putting on a performance meant, not just to refuse to answer, but to deceive them.

Somebody had. Liam spoke into the silence: "Humphrey, please answer Karla's question. Why did the Gafr really give us a year? What are they really trying to accomplish? If they want our help, we need to know what's up."

Humphrey looked at his beloved Liam the way a cleaner might look at a cockroach. "Our lords the Gafr have their reasons. Alfrey has told you, our concern is not why. It is what. What to *do* with the year. Have you nothing to offer, any of you?" As he spoke, his left hand made the motions of Hefn agitation and his voice acquired metallic highlights.

"*Are* you just not telling," Liam said, "or don't you know?"

Pam found herself on her feet. "Stop this," she said. "Both of you. Let's call a break. Whatever's going on here, let's don't let it go any farther."

"I agree with Pam," Johnny Wang said at once. He stood up too. "Everybody in favor get up and leave the room, right now. We'll reconvene after lunch." Pam smiled at him gratefully, and the Apprentices, with a hushed bustling, pushed out of their chairs and headed en masse for the door.

Except for Liam, who stubbornly stayed in his seat, legs extend-ed, arms folded across his chest. "Liam," said Pam sharply, "you too. Please."

He glanced over at her, then slowly drew his legs in and stood, mouth a grim line.

And now, finally, Pam looked at Humphrey. A long moment passed before he nodded, or did whatever a being without neck vertebrae did to suggest a nod of concurrence.

Pam checked to be sure Liam was gone, then said, "I'm going to call Terry."

"No. *I* will call Terry. I will do so at once." Humphrey spun round, swept Alfrey up, and exited the room through the little door in the side wall. At least he did it on two legs, not on four.

~

Amazing to be able to think and act when you didn't feel a thing. While Humphrey was calling the Chair of the Senate Committee on Alien Affairs, Pam went back to her room and checked her messages: a brief one from a calm-looking Jaime that boiled down to "Every-thing's under control"; an even briefer one from Lexi in a tattered sun bonnet, evidently sent on a break between scenes: "Hi, sorry to bother you on your trip but could you please call me right away?"

Pam sagged with sudden sleepiness. Shoving this aside, she sat—not lay—on her bed and rummaged in her pack. Maybe food would help. She got out a chunk of cheese, an apple, and a denim drawstring bag containing several dozen Hurt Hollow hickory nuts and a nutcracker, and shelled, nibbled, and chomped her way through some of these items methodically, while staring unseeing out the window. She unscrewed the cap of her canteen and drank several long drafts of bio-filtered Salt Lake City tap water. Methodically she then replaced the cap, pitched the apple core and nut shells into the composter, rewrapped the cheese, and stowed it and the nut bag in the pack.

She felt no brighter. Sighing heavily, she got out her phone and pushed the recall button.

The face that flickered onto the screen was that of Marcee Morgenstern, producer of *A Thousand Miles*. "Hi," said Pam. "I'm returning a call from Lexi."

"From Lexi? Lexi's gone AWOL again!" Marcee looked angry and flustered. "You say you're *returning* a call? When was this? What did she say?"

Startled out of her funk, Pam checked the display. "Nine twenty-six, Utah time. I was in a meeting and I'd left my phone in my room, I didn't know she'd tried to reach me till a minute ago. She just asked me to call her, nothing else. What do you mean by AWOL?"

"She finished her last scene and I sent her to get out of makeup. Half an hour later here's RoLayne having hysterics, where's Lexi, has anybody seen Lexi. Which nobody had—including makeup, she never showed up over there. We all dropped everything to look for her, but so far no luck. I'm going to tan her bottom when we get ahold of her, this has played holy heck with the schedule and we were already half a day behind—"

She was going to do no such thing, but Pam understood how she felt. "How long have you been looking?"

"I don't know, an hour maybe, or a little less."

"An hour?" Pam relaxed. "That's not very long. Maybe she went for a walk."

Marcee glared. "Apart from the shooting schedule, she's under strict orders not to wander off, *remember*?"

Pam herself had given those strict orders. "Yes, of course she is, I'm sorry. She didn't say anything to Neil?"

"He's as surprised as the rest of us, he hasn't got a clue where she could have gone." Marcee's voice slid up dangerously. "And *I* haven't got a clue how she managed to slip off, there are people everywhere up here keeping an eye on her!"

A real pang of alarm shot through Pam. "Okay, I'll notify my office. If she doesn't turn up soon, Jaime Rivera will call in the police. I can't get away for another couple of days, we're doing some crisis management here, but I'll come back as soon as I can."

"If she calls you again—"

"I'll handle it. Let me know the minute you find her, okay?"

Pam hung up, perfectly certain in her own mind that one of two things had happened: either the Church authorities had snatched Lexi, or she'd run away to *escape* being snatched by the Church authorities. Brother Parker, the infuriating creep, had agents everywhere; he knew all about the Gaian crisis and that Pam was in California, and had not been slow to seize his moment. Pam reviled herself for not anticipating this. Remorse smote her also; had she not canceled out of that visit to Lexi on location, she might have picked something up.

The main question now was, were people holding Lexi, or was she all by herself somewhere up Emigration Canyon, scared to death? *I'm going to sic Humphrey on RoLayne Allred, by God I am*, Pam thought. *If she's played a part in Bro Peckerwood's plot, Humphrey will have it out of her.*

This thought jerked her back to the here and now. Siccing Humphrey on somebody wasn't going to be so easy to do just at the moment. Humphrey was walking a tightrope of mysteriously conflicting loyalties and trying to make his Apprentices believe otherwise. If Terry couldn't get things patched up between Humphrey and Liam . . .

Pam sat and thought a minute, then punched her phone. When Humphrey appeared on the screen she said simply, "I need to go home. Lexi's in trouble, and I'm not any use here anyway."

Humphrey projected negative affect. "Not so. You were of great use this morning. Also, Terry Carpenter is coming. He will deal with Liam and speak with Gillian Jacoby. Liam will listen to him. Stay here and be of use to me! Now that you are whole again, you can be more useful than you know."

He was not in the habit of issuing orders to Pam, nothing in that line having ever been needed before, but this sounded very much like an order. A warning flashed in Pam's mind: *Tread carefully.* "Humphrey," she said quietly, "you and Alfrey put on quite a show this morning, but *you know* there's nothing to be done with an extra year, so why are you trying to make us think you think there is?"

Long pause. Humphrey whickered softly, the Hefn equivalent of heaving a sigh.

"You see? It's better if I go back. Anyway, Lexi's disappeared and I have to try to find her, that's my job."

He chuckled, a thick, unconvincing sound. "You have, my dear, if I may say so, a great many jobs."

"I know. But right now protecting Lexi seems like the only one of them I might actually be able to do. If I go now I should make the 14:58 express."

Humphrey didn't protest. He said soberly, "When we have finished here, I will come to Salt Lake if you have not found Lexi."

"If we haven't found her, I would love it if you could interview her mother. But come either way," Pam said. "I shouldn't leave Utah for a while now, and I think it's time you and I talked some turkey." And as Humphrey's countenance lighted with irrepressible curiosity, and he opened his mouth to ask about the origins of *that* remarkable expression, she cut the connection. Then she called Jaime.

~

"Gillian," said the Senator, "it's so good to meet you. Thank you for turning right around and coming back. I was so sorry to learn of your mother's death. We hadn't been in touch for years, but I loved her very much when we were young. Is your father still living?"

Gillian shook her head. "He passed about six years ago? He had a massive coronary?"

Terry, with the full force of Humphrey's authority behind him, had summoned both Gillian and Liam to his rooms at the BTP. He'd placed them across a table from each other and seated himself at the head, like a mediator in a contract dispute.

"So you're alone out there in Oakland, then?"

'Oh no, I'm with Wayne,' Gillian said quickly. Wayne, the boyfriend, had made the trip too this time; he'd been left glowering in the lounge. Jeff's little sister plainly resented being ordered back to Santa Barbara, but was intimidated by the famous Senator who'd once been married to her mother.

Opposite her, Liam sat in a kind of angry stupor and stared at Gillian's slender face in its frame of black curls. Through his self-absorption he was aware that Terry too, though far too cool a customer to stare, had been badly shaken. Now he was taking a long, frank, full-face look and saying, "Your resemblance to my son really is extraordinary—almost uncanny. Now, it's late, and I know you're tired, but I'd like you to look at these pictures if you would." As he spoke, he lifted a large envelope from his attaché, removed half a dozen holos, and laid them out on the table in front of Gillian.

Liam could tell exactly which pictures Terry had grabbed off the wall of his new Georgetown condo, even upside-down. Liam himself was in most of them. While Gillian picked up one after another, the two men—one openly, one covertly—gazed with identical hunger at her face.

When she glanced back up there were tears in her eyes. "I looked *exactly like this* when I was seven? I mean exactly, it's like looking at a picture of myself? It's just so weird. I always thought it would be so way cool to have a brother, but this, this is like having a clone, a dead male clone?" For the first time that day she met Liam's eyes. "I can see what a shock I must have given you, I can tell what good friends you were from these pictures, well, I knew it already from what that Hefn did, but you have to understand, I may look like him but I'm not him. I don't know anything about him, I didn't even know he existed till my mom was dying! I don't know if him and I even have anything in common."

Not good grammar anyway, Liam thought, not that he cared; he found everything about Gillian captivating. "Well, let's see. Jeff and I both went to a Quaker school but he was serious about the Quakers, more than I was. He didn't play sports. He was an Eagle Scout. He got straight A's in history."

Terry picked up the litany. "He liked fantasy fiction. He had a complicated model train setup in our basement, and a big bubbling tank of tropical fish. He made animated films, really clever ones."

"And he had a beautiful singing voice, he did a lot of solo work with the Philadelphia Boys' Choir."

Gillian had been frowning, but at the phrase "singing voice" she looked up sharply from the pictures. "I sing, I'm a singer," she said.

"I'm the lead singer in a band?"

"Well then, I guess both you and Jeff got your looks *and* your voices from your mother." Terry smiled at Gillian the way he did at the TV camera during interviews, when it was important to give the impression of being firmly in control. "I brought along a disk of the last performance the Boys' Choir ever made, just before the tour when everyone on the bus was killed, you know. If you don't mind, I'd like to play it for you."

He wasn't really asking. Gillian said without enthusiasm, "I don't know too much about classical, if that's what it is."

"You're under no obligation to like it," Terry assured her, "just listen." He started the player.

But as soon as the music began, Gillian snapped around wide-eyed to stare at Terry. A few measures into Jeff's solo, almost in spite of herself, she began to sing with him, the recorded voice and the live one melding into a single tone, high, pure, otherworldly:

Alma dei creatoris,
sedet rei peccatoris,
mater, mater clementissima!

It was as if the dead boy's spirit were being ventriloquized by his physical double. To Jeff's best friend and to his father this was almost unbearably moving. Soon Terry's eyes and then Liam's were streaming.

By the time the recording had ended, Gillian's eyes were streaming too. "My mom asked me to learn that piece," she said shakily. "She said it was always one of her favorites, even though it made her cry? She said it made her cry because it was so beautiful and I sang it so beautifully . . . but she was hearing my brother, just like you were, she was hearing *Jeff.*" Gillian began to sob. "I wish I would've never come to see you! I was better off not knowing about all this!"

Had she been present, Julie Hightower could have told them how stern-faced Pam had sobbed in exactly that way, after realizing that Humphrey, and not Frances Pruitt, had given her the bradshaw. But even Julie might have refrained from saying, at just that moment, "What you *know* can't hurt you *nearly* as much as what you *don't* know."

Liam had no thought of saying any such thing. He had not been told about Humphrey's role in the bradshaw, but he and Pam had been almost morbidly close for a very long time, and knowledge of Pam's complicated difficulties with her own mother came to their rescue now: he saw, between one breath and the next, what he'd been doing to poor Gillian, whose only crime was that she shared so many dominant genes with his dead friend. As the truth struck home he shoved back from the table, hanks of scanty hair clutched in both hands, blurting, "Oh my God, I've been acting like a total asshole! Oh, God, Gillian, I'm sorry! I'm so sorry! You're totally right, I *have* been pretending you're Jeff come back to life. That's exactly what I've been doing."

Nodding, Gillian blew her nose. "That's what I've been trying to tell you. I'm not him, I'm a completely different person."

Liam smoothed down his hair and wiped his face with the heels of his hands. "I know. I know *now*. I honestly couldn't help myself, last night or this morning, but I get it now and I'll stop, I've stopped already."

Gillian said, voice wobbling, "I guess it's just a really mean trick on everybody that I look so much like him, and then here I'm a singer too."

Terry wiped his face with his handkerchief, blew his own nose, and assumed charge of cooling things down. "*That's* not a mean trick on anybody, least of all on you. You're a fine singer. I take it you learned the Mozart as a favor to your mother. What kind of music does your band like to play?"

"We're hopped-up retro," she said, still shaky but more brightly. "The Lunatic Fringe? We do, like, ragtime, calypso, soft ozone rock sometimes, Fifties pop—"

Liam broke in. "I *love* Scott Joplin! To tell you the truth, much as I hated to admit it, Jeff's music wasn't really my thing either."

"Nor mine," said Terry. "Anne truly loved sacred and classical, but Liam and I just learned to like whatever Jeff was singing because he was singing it. But what *I* truly love is ozone rock! I wish you could see my collection."

Gillian looked happier. "Wayne, my boyfriend, he plays guitar in the Fringe? He's a big ozone rock man, he's the reason we do it."

"Hey, *I* play piano and keyboard," Liam said. "Maybe we could— before you guys and Terry take off tomorrow—" Then, catching her expression, he amended, "but you're probably not really up for that right now."

Gillian had stood, shaking her head, pushing back her chair. "I just want to get some sleep and then get back home."

Terry stood too. "Gillian, thank you again for coming back to Santa Barbara. And for being so understanding. I should probably tell you, you have a legal case against Liam here if you want to press charges."

She shook her head again. "No, I, I just want to go home."

Liam heard Terry and Gillian walking back to the lounge, heard Terry exchange a few words with Wayne and give them a voucher for another night at the Radisson. When he came back to the conference room, Liam was still standing where they'd left him.

His gaze focussed when Terry came in, shutting the door behind him. "I need to find Humphrey and apologize."

"Yes, you do. Sit down." Terry pointed to Liam's chair and pulled his own up to the table. After a minute Liam did the same. "You've had a bad shock, I know that, but this is about the worst time I can imagine for you to break down. Humphrey's beside himself over this, he feels you betrayed him."

"I guess I did betray him in a way. I think I went a little crazy for a while." The Senator raised one eyebrow and didn't reply. "But he's betraying us, too, Terry, he's trying to distract us, he was stonewalling this morning. We're not being leveled with."

"That much is obvious. I spoke with a few of your colleagues."

"Do *you* know what's going on?"

Terry looked sober. "No, and if Humphrey stops trusting the people he cares about, we'll find out the same time everybody else does, when it's too late. So tell me now: can you pull yourself together?"

"You know, I was just observing to Pam," Liam said, "that it's amazing how the personal life keeps right on cooking even when the world's going completely to pieces."

Terry nodded ruefully. "Where is Pam, anyway? I'd like to see her before I go back."

"She was at the meeting this morning. Actually, she cleared the room."

"I heard about that."

"But I haven't seen her since, I've been hanging out in my quarters, avoiding Eddie and going nuts." Liam looked at Terry. "What happened this afternoon?"

"Answer my question first: can you carry on?"

"I think so. Realizing you've been a totally selfish vicious asshole has a way of clearing the sludge right out of your brain."

"If you said that in hopes that I'd tell you you haven't been behaving like one," Terry said drily, "think again. I'll ask again: can you set all that aside for now and focus on your job?"

Liam sat up straighter. "Which is chiefly getting my relationship with Humphrey back up to speed? I can do that, I want to."

"All right then. Let's go find him, I'll fill you in while we walk." Terry began sliding the holos of Jeff carefully back into the big envelope. "And then I want to find Pam and congratulate her."

Liam stood and stretched. "On what?" he asked through a huge yawn.

Terry glanced up. "On her math intuition—you didn't know? It's back."

CHAPTER 9

Wings

3 - 4 JULY 2037

The sledcar had been fitted with hard rubber tires for summer, which made for a bumpy ride. Barefoot, in her raggedy dress, Lexi sat shoved up against the car's passenger door, as far away as the seat belt would let her get from her grandfather. She was trying not to make a sound as they jounced along, but her makeup was streaked with tears.

Her grandfather was making the sledcar labor up the mountain at its top speed, which was not that fast but was still way too fast for the condition of the road. Both of them were being thrown around, but Lexi had no way to hold on; her hands were tightly tied behind her with a leather bootlace. Granpa's face wore a funny look of grim satisfaction. Once he and Lexi's mom had got Lexi bundled into the car, he'd paid no attention to her at all, except that when she had asked—careful not to sound panicky—"What's happening? Where are we going?" he stopped the sledcar just long enough to pull her arms behind her and whip the leather thong around her wrists.

"That's in case you should take a notion to jump out," he said. "We're going someplace no Hefn and no Hefn-lovers would ever think to look. And by the way," he added in a mean voice, "don't you worry about me lovin' on you anymore. The very idea of lovin' on a little brat that would go and tattle to the Gaians makes me sick." He whirled on her suddenly. "You ought to be ashamed! Embarrassing me, that's bad enough—do you know you got me put in *jail*?

Your own grandfather? But slinging mud at the Church, now, that's beyond anything."

Granpa looked a little crazy while making this speech, glaring at Lexi, spit spraying, face working. The car lurched wildly. She shrank away from him in fear. Also in guilt. Despite what the counselor kept telling her, and Pam and her dad and even Neil had told her, LDS conditioning went bone-deep in Lexi.

They ground along in silence for a while. Finally she asked timidly, "Do Mom and Dad know where you're taking me?"

Granpa smirked. "Your mom knows where I told her I was taking you, but that's not where we're going. And your dad, he's a know-nothin' from the word go. Now I want you to sit still and shut your mouth."

This was a side of Granpa Lexi had never seen, or even consciously suspected. All her life he had treated her like a princess, in a kind of overly sweet, artificial way, even when he was doing things to her in the dark. She had dreaded spending time with him alone, but she hadn't exactly been *terrified*, like afraid for her life. But this crazy-seeming stranger frightened her so much it was hard to think.

The one hopeful thing was that she'd left the message for Pam after catching a glimpse of her Granpa, who wasn't supposed to be anywhere around her, through the window in the wardrobe trailer bathroom. She'd come out, gone straight to the phone, and made the call, somehow knowing better than to say in her message what she was calling about. Then it was time to do a scene, and then another scene that had required multiple takes, and after that Marcee said she was done for the day. Lexi'd been on her way to get out of makeup when her mother, sounding happy and excited, called to her to come and look at something out behind the trailer she shared with Melva, who played her mother on the series. By that time she'd forgotten about Granpa, and that was when they'd tossed the blanket over her head and shoved her into the car.

"Mom!" she pleaded when she'd been strapped in and the blanket came off. RoLayne looked over her shoulder furtively. "Honey, everything's fine, don't worry. Just mind Granpa, do what he tells you. I'll see you real soon." She squeezed Lexi's arm through the car window, and they started moving.

Remembering all this gave Lexi an idea, something to grab onto mentally in the dizzying terror. "I have to go to the bathroom," she said in a whiny voice. He'd called her a brat, okay, she'd play a brat.

"Then I guess you'll just have to hold it." He sounded calmer now. He didn't take his eyes off the road.

"No, I really have to go *bad*," she said in a high, complaining voice. A little more nasal quality? Maybe just a little. "I already had to go when I was going to the trailer. Granpa, I'm gonna wet my *pants!*"

"I told you to shut up," he snapped, but he looked uneasy all the same. He must have borrowed the sledcar, and what sledcar owner was going to be thrilled to find the seat had been peed on?

Things seemed to be taking a promising turn, but just then Lexi realized that even if she prevailed, Granpa wasn't going to untie her hands and let her go off into the bushes on her own. He would keep hold of her, and pull her dress up and her pants down himself. He'd claimed that the thought of "loving on her" made him sick, but what if getting into that kind of situation made him change his mind? Lexi felt a thrill of a sicker sort of fear. "I guess I can wait a little while," she said in a sulky voice.

"You do that," said her grandfather, though he looked over at her in a way that made Lexi glad she had changed tactics. "It's not that much fu'ther anyway."

"But this leather thing's really hurting my hands, they're getting numb."

"Like I said, it's not much fu'ther. "

At that moment the sound of a helicopter made Lexi's heart leap with hope. Pam might have returned her call by now; by now, everyone would realize she was missing. Maybe that Jaime at Gaian headquarters had called the Salt Lake Police. The only choppers allowed in the air were official ones. The police were probably hunting for her right this minute. She strained around, trying to see, just as the racket got much louder and the chopper suddenly appeared from behind the slope of a mountain.

It wasn't a police helicopter after all. The lettering on the side said THE CHURCH OF JESUS CHRIST OF LATTER-DAY SAINTS. As she was realizing this, Lexi also realized that Granpa was looking up with interest, not concern. In fact, the chopper was landing behind some trees above the road, and he was turning the car into the parking area at one of the abandoned picnic sites that used to be popular back when people could take private cars up into the canyons east of town.

Lexi's heart plummeted. This wasn't rescue, it was rendezvous. Granpa was handing her over to the Church. He hadn't kidnapped her for some reason of her parents and his own, he'd done it with the cooperation, maybe even on the orders, of the Church leadership.

Her grandfather quieted the car and came around to pull Lexi out. "Up there," he said tersely, and started pushing her ahead of him, up a trail that wound among derelict picnic tables set on terraces.

The trail pretty much went straight up the side of the steep canyon. Part-way up, Granpa had to stop to catch his breath, holding onto Lexi's arm and bending over to pant. She could probably have wrenched herself loose while he was preoccupied with panting, but there wasn't much point, the terrain was way too rough and her bare feet, toughened though they were by all that traipsing over rough ground while the cameras rolled, would slow her down, even if she could keep her balance with her buzzing hands tied behind her. She would never get away. "If you untied me I could walk by myself," she said anyway.

"Don't make me laugh," he growled. They started up again.

Lexi expected to see Brother Parker, but the person standing by the chopper was the bishop of her own ward, the one who was Granpa's friend, the one who always used to say how wonderful it was that their ward had a real family with a real testimony.

Bishop Erickson gave Lexi a big smile, then frowned when he saw that her hands were tied. "Was it necessary to truss her up like that, Ed?"

"Trust me," Granpa puffed, very red in the face. "It was necessary. The kid can run like a rabbit."

Bishop Erickson leaned over Lexi's bonds. He *tsk*ed sympathetically, and Lexi made a strategic tear slip down her right cheek, already streaked with actual tears. "Oh dear, it's digging into her skin, look. Jared," he said, turning to a person inside the chopper, "will you take a knife and cut this child's hands free?"

"At least put her in there first and lock the doors," Granpa said. "You don't know her like I do, Carl."

The bishop nodded. "All right, Lexi, up you go." The man called Jared swung to the ground, picked her up like a sack of flour, and boosted her onto the helicopter behind the pilot. He climbed in after her and opened a clasp knife, and Lexi's hands were free.

Numb as they were, if she'd still been on the ground that wouldn't have mattered, she'd have been off like a streak of lightning. Granpa

225

was right about that. Vividly she saw herself squirm into a hidey-hole in the rocks and crouch low while they lumbered past, kicking at the scrub oak, failing to find her. Later she would tear strips from the dress to wrap and tie around her feet, make a little shelter, stay cleverly hidden until Jaime or Pam could spring into action. There was plenty of water in the mountains. She had perfect faith that Pam would save her. All she would have to do would be not get caught until that happened, and put up with being hungry.

But it was all pointless; she was sealed inside the helicopter and the pilot was making the rotors roar.

~

Pam sat at a table in the concessions car, on the bullet train from LA to Las Vegas and Salt Lake, sipping hot cocoa. The Nevada desert zipped drearily past her window. Her YellowPad lay on the table in front of her; she was making an annotated list, trying to put the events of the past few days into graspable order. For a while she had tried to do this mentally, but her brain was too sleep-deprived and there were too many events.

1. Lexi's missing, almost certainly abducted by the LDS Church. Why am I so sure of this? RoLayne's attitude? Probably. Unconsciously I think I was already worrying that Church authorities might get to Lexi through her. The Church had motive (deprogram Lexi, discredit the Gaians) and opportunity, and nobody else had either, let alone both, so far as I know. The Mormons aren't going to pretend to go along with the Gafr, then, for the final year. Well, good for them. Whatever else they are, they're not hypocrites.
2. Humphrey and Alfrey are lying to us—the worst sign imaginable.
3. Humphrey sold me down the river re: the bradshaw. Knifed me in the back?
4. Gillian Jacoby turned up and Liam revealed his true colors.
5. My math intuition is back as a direct result of (3 + 4).
6. Incredible but true: now that I've got it back, I could care less.
7. Humphrey does care, a lot, about the intuition being back. Why? No idea.

Pam stopped here and reread her list. She watched Nevada—or Utah, they'd probably crossed the border by now—whip along for a while. Then she turned back to the YellowPad and slowly typed what she most needed to understand:

WHY ARE HUMPHREY AND ALFREY LYING TO US?

At once things rearranged themselves in her mind. In the same way she'd known who had abducted Lexi, Pam knew why the Hefn were lying to their human friends: because their lords the Gafr had now arrived at a final decision never to revoke the Ban.

An anguished groan burst out of Pam, so loud and sudden that other people in the car looked round. When they'd gone back to what they'd been doing, she held her breath and keyed:

THEN WHY GIVE US ANOTHER YEAR?

Instantly the answer was there: the *Gafr* needed that year. The Gafr—by concealing their decision—hoped to keep humanity under wraps long enough to do something they still needed to do. Pam stared at the letters of her question on the screen, as certain of this mysteriously acquired knowledge as she was of her own name.

The new frame thus set around events transformed their meaning. If Humphrey and Alfrey had been acting under orders from the Gafr—and weren't they always, in a way?—the confrontational charade at Santa Barbara took on a different aspect. Maybe even the bradshaw—?

Not now. Pam shook her head to clear it. On the YellowPad she typed:

WHY DO THE GAFR NEED MORE TIME?

She listened and waited. But the answers had stopped coming.

~

Finding Lexi remained the first priority. If the Church was indeed holding her, there was no need to be concerned about her physical safety. But the leadership would work on her to renounce the Gaians, and otherwise try to guilt-trip her back into the fold, which—not knowing that the war had already been lost—they would consider a great PR coup if they could bring it off.

Lexi had enough problems without being put through deprogramming. Pam intended to find her fast, with Humphrey's help if necessary. And from now on, however often she would have to encounter the odious RoLayne, Pam intended to play a more positive role in Lexi's life. The world as they had known it might be about to end for everybody, but this one child was not going to be forced to live in constant fear of having her private world turned inside out like a sock if Pam could help it.

As if activated by these thoughts, the TV screen above the forward door of the car crackle-flickered to life—and Pam gasped and half-rose, for there stood Lexi herself, in her Kate dress and sunbonnet and bare feet, arms folded across her chest, looking proud and defiant despite her streaky makeup. As Pam sank back in her seat, a news announcer began reading a report: "CBC-TV has learned that Alexis Allred, eleven-year-old star of the popular television series *A Thousand Miles*, was kidnapped earlier today by agents of the Church of Jesus Christ of Latter-day Saints, more commonly known as the Mormon Church.

"The network received this disk about an hour ago from a spokesperson for the Church, which is claiming credit for liberating Alexis from what they term 'the corrupting influence of the Gaian Movement.' Church agents are holding the girl in an undisclosed location. Here is the actual recording received by the station."

The still image of Lexi on the screen now began to move. Someone said, in a voice Pam didn't recognize, "Lexi, go ahead now, honey, tell the folks you're all right." The girl glared at the camera and lifted her chin, and Pam's insides weakened at this show of courage. Lexi might be intimidated, or even scared to death, but—professional to the core—she wasn't going to let it show. The speaker chuckled. "Alexis doesn't want to tell you herself, but as you can see she's absolutely fine. We're going to take wonderful care of her. But we're going to keep her tucked away safe in a secret place till the Hefn agree to give her back to us. This child was a wonderful Mormon girl until just a few months ago, when the Gaians got hold of her and brainwashed her into believing their lies about the aliens and about the LDS Church.

"So now, while we're waiting to hear back from the Hefn, we'll also be trying our best to undo the evil visited upon this innocent child. Every single child is precious to us, all the more precious now that the aliens have stolen a whole generation of our children." All the time the unseen speaker was holding forth, Lexi stood very still but her mobile face expertly conveyed her disdain. ("Precious my foot . . . *what* a load of crap . . . you people don't *believe* any of this, do you?") Pam was so proud of her that her eyes prickled.

"We ask for your prayers and support as we endeavor to force these creatures to renounce the crime they committed against us all a generation ago. We demand not only that they give the Church jurisdiction over this child, but that they restore our ability to obey the commandment God first gave to Adam and Eve: that we increase and multiply and replenish the earth."

The newscaster's face replaced Lexi's on the screen. "CBC has learned that six months ago, the Gaian Mission in Salt Lake City filed a complaint against Alexis Allred's grandfather, on a charge of sexual abuse of a minor. The grandfather, Edgar Young, is a member of the Mormon Church and a direct descendent of the Prophet Brigham Young. Alexis has been under Gaian oversight ever since the allegations against Mr. Young were filed. *A Thousand Miles*, which is financed and produced by the Church, was filming on location in the Wasatch Mountains east of Salt Lake when Alexis was abducted."

They put the disk back up, while the newscaster promised to keep viewers informed of developments, and read a statement from a citizens' group denouncing the Church's provocation of the Gafr during the sensitive one-year probation period. Then the screen went dark; but just before it did, Lexi—arms still folded left over right—slipped her right thumb over the middle fingers of her right hand and stuck her index and little fingers out in a broad V, like horns. There were several Gaians in the car, and they gasped and exclaimed at this signal the LDS kidnappers had evidently not noticed, or not understood.

It was the goat-horn salute of the missionary trainees. Lexi was telling them—telling *me*, Pam thought—that she would not give in.

~

It was nearly midnight when the train pulled into Temple Square. TRAX had stopped running at 11:00, but a few horse cabs were still parked at the curb. Pam shouldered her pack, climbed the stairs to the street, then stood dithering. Office or home? Home first, then office? Or vice versa?

From habit she glanced up at Moroni, guyed to his spire, and for the first time that day remembered her anti-Moroni poem, written in dead-of-night angst after talking to Julie. Something about falling and wings, a fantasy image. At least it had put her to sleep.

The search for Lexi was both official and personal, but the Gaians would need to put a public face on their efforts to find her. It would be best to get a statement out tonight. "Office," she decided. She hailed a horse cab and climbed in.

The night air was delightful; the driver had folded down the top of his cab, and Pam sat back to watch the angel, bathed in light far above the darker streets, as the horse began to clomp forward on its rubber shoes. Moroni did seem to be in flight, as the figurehead of a ship appears to fly above the waves. From the high vantage of his perch a person might very well be able to see where Lexi was being held. The great slab of the LDS Office Building dwarfed the Temple, spire and all; if they were holding her there—a very good possibility—then Lexi could look down on Moroni instead of the other way round, or maybe look him in the eye. Supposing they ever let her near a window.

"Where to, lady?" inquired the driver, who sounded Mexican.

"The Gaian Mission on Fourth South."

He whistled. "Wouldn't go nowheres near that place if I was you."

"Yes you would, if you were me. Just take me there, okay?"

"You the boss." He flapped the reins and the horse picked up the pace a bit; and Pam, who had scooted forward to speak to the driver, leaned back against the seat and closed her eyes, inhaling the lovely smells of horse and leather, letting her mind go briefly blank.

Inside the Mission, lamps were lit. Good, dear, faithful, dependable Jaime. Pam climbed out and paid the driver, who got his first good look at her under the streetlight. "Oh, hokay, you that lady that works for them Hefn. Workin' late tonight, tryin' to fin' that little girl on the telly, now I get it."

Pam hung her pack from one shoulder, waved with a noncommittal smile, and hurried up the walk. The cab didn't move. As she was unlocking the door the driver called to her, "*Esas creaturas son diábolos!*"

"*Esperámonos que no,*" she called back. Let's hope not.

Jaime jerked the door open before she could finish unlocking it. "Thank God you're back. Who're you yelling at?"

"My cabbie. He thinks the Hefn are devils." She shrugged out of her pack and sank down on the couch beside it. "I heard the news on the train. I'm mighty glad to see you too. What have you found out?"

"Not a freakin' thing. That kid, that Lexi, we spend all our time trying to find her!"

"Did you see her give the missionary salute, like flipping the bird to Brother Whoever-It-Was that was recording the broadcast?"

"Yeah. She's a great kid, you know? But damn if I know where to start this time either."

"What'd the cops say?"

Jaime blew through his lips in disgust. "I called 'em right after I talked to you, but the minute they found out who it was that had her, that was the end of that. The Church is zipped up tight on this one. I worked through the whole list of contacts and nothing, not a peep, nobody's talking."

Pam rubbed her eyes. "There may only be a handful of people who actually know anything. You have to give them credit, the ones involved are putting their lives on the line, they know they could be wiped for doing this if it doesn't go their way. Mormons have never been cowards about their convictions."

"Yeah, well, I think it's pretty cowardly to kidnap a little girl and use her as a hostage," Jaime muttered. He threw himself into the chair opposite the couch. "Not to mention pretty dumb, like why attack the Gaians *now*, with everybody else bending over backwards pretending to *be* Gaians . . . look at us, we're sitting in the same places we were last February, brainstorming about how to find Alexis Allred, it's like a freakin' time loop!"

"Time is One," Pam said drily. "The Church's timing with this is just like ours with Homeland. Look, I want to brief you on the conference, and some other stuff, but not right now. But things were tense when I left, and I don't know how the Hefn will respond to this—whether they'll respond at all, actually, they're more likely to just act like it didn't happen, leave it to us to fix if we can. Or no," she said, "Humphrey's fond of Lexi, he won't leave her in the clutches of the Church. He's coming out in a couple of days. If we haven't found her by then, he'll get it out of them where she is, and not by negotiating either."

"Well, I'd a hell of a lot rather not wait that long." Jaime looked down, then up. "Boss, one other thing? Your intuition's back?"

Pam's head snapped up. "How'd you hear about it?"

"Raghu called. Last night. I found the message this morning."

Jaime looked a little hurt, and Pam smiled around a pang of remorse. "I'd have called you myself right away if things hadn't gotten so crazy out there. Sorry."

"No problem." Embarrassed, he scrubbed his fingers through his hair. "Congratulations. You don't look very happy about it. Too worried about the kid?"

"Not really that, but it's complicated. I'm *not* that worried about Lexi, since we know it's the Church that's got her. She won't crack, but she'll be counting on me to get her out of this, and I absolutely have to not let her down this time—I'm with you, I don't want to wait for Humphrey, let's get her out *now*." Despite these words Pam yawned and stretched, pulling herself almost horizontal on the couch.

"So, do we want to issue a statement?"

"Yeah, we do. That's why I came straight here from the station." Saying this, Pam heaved herself up and trudged into her office. "Computer on." She plunked into her desk chair. "I liked what you said before. How's this: 'Abducting a child to use as a bargaining chip is a cowardly deed. The LDS Church, whose history is replete with acts of sacrifice and courage, has betrayed herself today.'"

Jaime read the screen over her shoulder. "Fine, but say 'filled' instead of 'replete'?"

Pam frowned, reread the statement. "How about 'abundantly figured'?"

"Too literary, boss, it's a sound bite. Just say 'filled,' so I can issue this and get to bed! We're both too tired to think."

~

Jaime recorded the statement, dispatched it to the *Tribune* and CBC, then left to walk the half mile home. Pam had intended to go home as well, but the couch in her office suddenly seemed to sing a siren song. She scrounged her toothbrush and a tee shirt out of her luggage, washed the sunblock off her face, flicked off the lights, and crashed.

THE BIRD SHAMAN

She slept heavily, done in by the past few days. Fractals came, went, came again. At dawn, weightless in the pure light, she stood transfixed upon the spire of the Temple and beheld the burning sliver of the sun poised to lift above the Wasatch Range. Birds came to her: finches and sparrows, robins and mallards she had nursed and released; black Cayuga ducks she had butchered and eaten; all shining, whirling about her head. Gimpy swooped in and hovered at arm's length before her face, wings beating, strong and whole, and then a stunning bird larger than Gimpy, with black wings and a breast the color of raspberry sherbet, and as she stretched forth a finger to touch the grosbeak's breast feathers the realization struck home: *I'm dreaming! I'm having a lucid dream!*

She had read about this but never experienced it, till now. In a lucid dream you're aware that you're dreaming, you can take the dream wherever you like. *I'll find out where they're keeping Lexi!* she decided at once, and launched herself from the high spire of the Temple.

Flanked and buoyed up by the spiraling flock of ducks and songbirds, Pam circled high over the city. *Show me where Lexi is!* she commanded, and was immediately soaring south, the Great Salt Lake to her right and rear, the Wasatch Range and the sunrise to her left. The birds flew with her—silent, even the mallards, except for the stroking of their wings. All together they swept past Point of the Mountain and flew over Orem and then Provo, the silver tracks of TRAX flashing far below.

They went like the wind. The birds had stopped weaving in the air and settled into a mixed flock with Pam at the center, holding a flat smooth trajectory, higher and far faster than natural birds can fly. *I hope I don't wake up before we get there*, she thought; but the landscape streamed beneath her and the dream went on.

Pinned to the wall of the office where Pam's body lay asleep was a huge relief map of Utah. Now this map lay spread below her, showing her the green peaks through which she was being guided. Above Spanish Fork, with the tip of Utah Lake in view, the flock turned east of south, leaving the shiny rail tracks and the Salt Lake Valley behind. The terrain abruptly changed; they broke out of the peaks, and now beneath them deep meandering canyons cut through scrubbly mountains, where the dark green of vegetation grew thickly scattered against a ground of red and yellow-tan. A road wound through and they followed that, flying high and fast. Clustered buildings—Price?—flashed by. They were moving still faster now, veering south again, and now the land-map lost definition in a long broad valley vaguely and distantly flanked by ranges, and Pam was aware of little but dizzying speed and the energy of the birds, bearing her up, sweeping her along. Till suddenly there was the tiny twisting of a river dead ahead, dirty green within the wrinkled flatness of the valley, and they were speeding down, down, down, circling, swooping low above a line of tall flat-topped cliffs and the flash of bright water to a wider road, a long low building, a child looking up, holding her left hand high in the Gaian salute.

Pam gasped awake. Her legs swung off the couch by themselves, rushed her to the wall and the relief map. "Lights!" Her head was clear as a bell, but she had to prop herself with both hands on the wall for balance while she made sure.

Then she pushed off and spoke to the phone in a high tense voice. When Jaime answered, "How fast can you get over here?" she said to his puffy, stubbly face onscreen. "I know where she is!"

~

"Green River?" He peered at the map doubtfully. "How would they get her there from Emigration Canyon? We'd know if they'd taken out their chopper after the news release. They haven't. They probably can't."

"No, they'll lose their chopper now. TRAX to Salina, then overland?"

"Overland how? By public bus? It's less than twenty-four hours since they snatched her." Jaime rubbed his face, making a raspy sound. "They could put a Church car on the train without attracting attention, I guess, they do that all the time, but—look, Boss, tell me again about this dream?"

Pam said, "No matter how many times I tell it, it's not going to sound any more plausible. I can't even be sure it *was* a dream. I was sound asleep, but . . . ."

He made a face. "Okay. Fine. Then explain about getting your intuition back. Maybe this has something to do with that."

Startled, she stared at him. "Maybe it does, I never thought of that." Her mind veered to the unreasoning certainties of the train ride, then skittered away. "Listen, I'll tell you all about it later but right now we have to get down to Green River. Humor me, Jaime. I know that's where she is, even if I can't explain how I know."

He looked unhappy but resigned. "I'll go along, but I gotta say, it's not like you to do things that don't make sense."

"I know it's not. I agree with every word you've said so far."

"Well." He paused. "Okay. Here's what we do. We call down to Moab and have Parley send some people up there."

The other strong Gaian Mission in Utah was in Moab, not far beyond Green River but farther than Pam had flown in her dream. "Of course we do! That's brilliant! Thank God one of us still has his wits about him. Better not mention the dream thing, say we've had a tip, and to check out all the motels that have rows of rooms on one level. Probably an older motel, maybe abandoned."

"Phone on," yelled Jaime, striding toward his own office.

"And tell him to be careful! The Church has staked an awful lot on this."

Jaime sat at his desk and punched a key. "People go back and forth all the time between Green River and Moab on the old rail line through Crescent Junction," he called to Pam. "I've got cousins in Crescent Junction so I know about this. They fixed up just that stretch of freight track, fifty miles, for the tourist trade, the rafting and the big parks? In spring and fall they even use open cars pulled by mules for part of it, like the old canal boats, only on rails. Summer and winter they put on regular engines, though. We can have a posse up there by lunchtime—what the devil's the matter with this phone?"

The problem was an incoming call from Santa Barbara. "If it's Humphrey I don't want to take it right now," Pam said, but at Jaime's astonished look she pulled herself together. "No. All right. Put it through to my office." She went in and shut the door, and there on the screen was the familiar face, all beard and fuzz.

He looked fairly normal. Pam wondered fleetingly what had happened since she'd cut and run from the conference, but her mind was filled with other things. "Hi," she said. "Can I call you back in five minutes? We're sending out some people to pick up Lexi and we need to contact them."

"Lexi has been found?"

"Not yet, but we think we know where she is. I'll explain when I call you back."

"You can explain when you see me," said Humphrey, "this evening. I am coming to Salt Lake as you requested. So that we can talk some turkey."

The conference had ended early then. There was a slight pause while Pam's stress meter registered dismay. She said, "Well, but I may be tied up with this rescue, you might want to wait a day or two."

"I do not want to wait a day or two. If you are not at home I will let myself in and wait for you, or I will come and find you."

"Okay then." He nodded and hung up. "I'm off," she called to Jaime; and while he was placing the call to Moab she gazed soberly at the blank screen. If you took the view that Humphrey had been lying under duress, that changed—not everything, but a good deal. But she needed time to think before discussing it with him or with Jaime. And before anything else she was by God going to rescue Lexi, come hell or high water or alien inconvenience. Thrusting Humphrey out of mind, she hurried into Jaime's office in time to hear Parley Kroupa describing how he would organize and move his troops. "Be careful!" she told him. "Don't you guys get taken prisoner, or we'll have to bust you out too."

"You *sure* they've got her in Green River? Seems like a funny place to pick."

Jaime started to answer but Pam drowned him out. "That's what we hear. No guarantees, but it's our best lead, and if there's any chance at all—"

"Gotcha. We'll do our damnedest. An old motel, you said, just a strip of rooms like a train of cars?"

Pam hesitated; it *was* like that, but not exactly. But—"Yeah, I think so."

"Might be any of a bunch of 'em. Well, those ones are all on East Main, we'll stake 'em all out."

"Great. If you can bring her back as far as Salina, we'll meet you there. There's a train in an hour and a half."

Jaime cut the connection and swiveled in his chair to look up at Pam. "*We* will?"

"I will, then. You don't need to come, O thou of little faith; I know you think it's a wild goose chase." Her own words made her shiver; a wild goose chase it was indeed, but not in any sense that felt ordinary. "Anyway, somebody should stay here and mind the store. We'll probably get some business today, people not wanting the Gafr to think *they* approve of the Church doing this, just because they're Utahns."

~

Lexi came out of the little bathroom of the swaying bus and made her way back to her place behind the driver, holding onto the other seats to keep her balance.

She was no longer in her *Thousand Miles* getup. Back in the huge bathroom of the fancy house in Little Cottonwood Canyon, where they'd shot that viddy, she had washed off her makeup and changed into her own jeans, polo shirt, socks and sneakers. Her mother had put these items in a bag for Granpa, and Granpa had given the bag to the Bishop after they'd hauled her into the helicopter. There was a sweatshirt too, but she'd taken that off. Even with all the windows open it was warm on the bus.

She'd been sleeping with the seat tilted back as far as it would go, and felt dopy and strange, and now she was hungry. She glanced across the aisle at the young man, Jared, who'd been in the chopper with Bishop Erickson and who had bundled her onto the special car at Midvale while everybody looked the other way. He was reading, a book that looked like *Doctrine and Covenants*. It went against the grain to ask a kidnapper for any favors, but the more she thought about food the harder it got not to. She was mentally practicing "I don't suppose you thought to bring any *food* on this getaway bus," in haughty, disdainful tones, when Jared closed his book, stretched, looked over at Lexi, and said, "How about something to eat?"

"You don't mean to say you actually brought any *food* on this getaway bus," Lexi said in her best withering voice, hoping her relief didn't show.

He grinned. "Sure did. Let's see here." He got up and opened the lid of a cooler on the seat behind him. "Ham and Swiss with lettuce and mayo? Coke?" When she nodded he handed her a sandwich wrapped in wax paper, and a green bottle, then took another sandwich and bottle for himself and slid back into his seat.

Except for the driver, they had the whole big bus to themselves, a shockingly unGaian waste of resources. Lexi couldn't remember getting off TRAX and boarding the bus; she'd slept right through the whole thing and had been sleeping off and on for hours while the three of them roared along through the dark. *I bet they drugged me,* she thought darkly. She'd had tomato soup and a grilled cheese sandwich for dinner on the train. *I bet they put ground-up sleeping pills in that soup. So I wouldn't yell and give them away when we switched. I would have, too.*

Now it was morning. They were deep in mountains Lexi didn't recognize, heading toward the sun. She unwrapped the sandwich avidly, wondering who had made it, and twisted the cap off the Coke bottle with CAFFEINE FREE stamped in raised letters right in the glass.

The sandwich was heavenly; Lexi tried not to wolf it but she pretty much did. The Coke was cold and delicious. "Want a cookie?" Jared held a round tin box across the aisle. "Oatmeal raisin?" The cookie was *very* good. Lexi ate several more cookies and started to feel a lot better. Cookie by cookie, the dopiness was dissolving out of her head. She stared out the window, wondering where the heck they were taking her.

It couldn't hurt to ask. "Where are we going?" she asked above the roaring of the motor.

"Sorry. Can't tell you that." Jared smiled when he said this, but Lexi could tell he wouldn't budge; probably he had orders from Bishop Erickson, and probably the bishop had orders from somebody higher up.

Would he maybe relent and tell if she sobbed and begged him and acted distraught? After watching her gobble a sandwich and seven cookies? Not likely.

It didn't matter much right now anyway. When the chance came to make her break, she'd take it. After that would be time enough to figure out where she was.

At least Granpa wasn't on the bus. Not on the train either. Lexi figured he'd gone home. Not only was he not supposed to come anywhere near her, he was also not supposed to leave Salt Lake. When Pam found out about the part he'd played in this drama, Granpa was going to be in big big trouble, that much Lexi knew for sure.

Time dragged by, and they were still on the mountain road, not going very fast. She hadn't been able to deduce anything from looking out the windows except that the road was in pretty good shape, so this was a regular bus route, not an unmaintained highway carrying no traffic. Once in a while a vehicle—an ambulance, a recycling lorry, another bus—would pass them going the opposite direction, but all were unrevealing except for the bus, which said SALT LAKE EXPRESS on the front. *That* wasn't very helpful. All the road signs had long since rusted over or disappeared from their posts. Nobody had replaced them. In a world where private cars were forbidden, what was the point of signs?

Lexi leaned her head against the window and thought about Pam. If Pam had been in Salt Lake, instead of Santa Barbara, her mom would never have dared get involved in the kidnapping, not in a million years. Thinking about how her mom had helped Granpa shove her into the sledcar, Lexi's eyes filled up; but she blinked hard and swallowed, and decided to be mad at Pam instead. Pam had no business going to California! Pam was supposed to stay here, making sure stuff like this didn't happen, that was her job! Righteous indignation swelled Lexi's chest. She thought about the scathing things she would say to Pam after Pam had rescued her from the kidnappers—I'm not speaking to you!—and how sorry Pam would be, how she would apologize over and over and promise never to go away again. This line of thought was deeply satisfying, for a while; but then Lexi remembered sitting at Pam's kitchen table with Pam and Humphrey, all three with big plates of spaghetti in front of them and big red circles around their mouths, and how Humphrey had talked about what Pam used to be like when she first went to the Bureau of Temporal Physics as a kid not much older than Lexi herself, the only girl in the first class of Apprentices, what a gifted mathematician and quick study she'd proved to be, the first Apprentice to learn how to place the numbers in the time transceiver fields, how she used her mind to do this with such beautiful precision. Lexi had seen Pam watching Humphrey while he was explaining all this, she knew what that look meant. Pam loved that weird-looking, hairy old Hefn. When Humphrey ordered her to go somewhere, she had to go. That was her job too, doing what Humphrey said.

The swaying of the bus made her drowsy. In spite of herself Lexi dozed off again. Till they got wherever they were going there wasn't much else to do.

Then it was later, and the bus had slowed even more as the driver geared down. Outside were drab-colored flat-topped mountains under puffy, flat-bottomed white clouds. They were coming into a town. Jared had moved over next to her, and one of his big hands had a grip on the back of her neck; that was what had woken her. "Stay right like you are, Alexis. I don't want to hurt you, but I will if you try to yell or signal out the window."

Saying this, he pushed her head down nearly to her knees and ducked down beside her. Grinding its gears, the bus moved slowly through the town. From her bent-over position Lexi couldn't see out at all. Being pressed down made her panicky; her heart thumped while she struggled desperately not to struggle, to master the panic. If she gave in to it and started to fight Jared, whose hard breathing was a rasp in her right ear, he would hurt her. He had said he would, and she believed him. He'd said he didn't want to, but she wasn't so sure she believed that.

After a few minutes the bus turned right, into what felt like a driveway. It changed directions several times, then stopped.

Jared sat up cautiously and looked out, then took his hand off Lexi's neck. "Okay, Alexis, we're getting off now. Now, what I'm gonna do is, is I'm gonna hold your hands behind your back. Now, don't you make one sound, okay? Not one single sound. Just do like I tell you and you'll be fine. Okay, come on."

He pulled her up and clamped her again, gripping both her wrists together in the same hand that had held her face to her knees. "Ow!" she said—though it was more uncomfortable than painful to be held that way—but all he did was grip her tighter and hiss: "*What did I tell you*? Not one sound, not a one! Now get going."

He thrust her ahead of him, not ungently, to the front of the bus and down the steep steps, one at a time. Through the windows she could see that the bus was parked between two identical long, low buildings. As Lexi stepped the last long step down to the ground, she caught a glimpse of deep blue sky and tall pinkish-gray cliffs that did look a little bit familiar, and thought, *I bet we're somewhere near the parks.* The driver had maneuvered the bus so that the door was only a stride away from a door in one of the long buildings, which Jared now opened with his free hand. He started to push her inside—

—and let out a startled yelp, and Lexi was jerked backwards. She hit the ground on her left side, hard, hard enough to knock the wind out. While she fought to breathe there was a commotion overhead—scuffling—the thwacking sounds of a fist-fight, also the sound of the bus roaring and screeching away.

She got her breath back finally and tried to roll onto her hands and knees, but something was wrong with her left hand. She heard herself yell. Then a woman was helping her up, saying "Are you okay, Alexis?"

"Something's wrong with my arm," said Lexi. A few feet away, a group of people she'd never seen before were holding onto Jared. One of them had Jared's arm bent behind him in a way that looked to Lexi like it must hurt. Abruptly, humiliatingly, she threw up.

The woman who was examining her arm seemed unperturbed by this. "Looks like you broke your wrist when you fell on it. Ever had a broken bone before?" Lexi shook her head, feeling extremely strange. A moment later she was lying on the ground again. "Keep still, honey. You fainted. We need to get you to a doctor."

Somebody brought her some water. In a little bit somebody else helped her stand up again, and held her up while the woman arranged her arm in a makeshift sling. "We'd better get you down to Moab, the medical facilities are a lot better down there."

The sling helped. "Where's Pam?" said Lexi. Not for an instant did she doubt who had brought about her rescue.

The man who had helped her stand the second time said, "Pam's on her way to Salina. The plan was for us to meet up at Salina, and she'd take you back up to Salt Lake. I'm Parley Kroupa, by the way—I'm gafr of the Moab Mission."

"The Gaian Mission?"

"That's the one." He grinned. "Hey, we were all mighty proud of you, Alexis, the way you gave the missionary salute on that viddy. Grace under pressure, that's what that was."

She remembered to say "Thanks." It felt like a long time ago. "Where are we? What's this place?"

"This is Green River," said Parley Kroupa.

"Oh. I was here one time. We went rafting. Oh, so that's the Book Cliffs then."

She glared at Jared, wilted and sullen in the custody of the victorious Gaians, and back at Parley. "Is Pam coming to Moab too?"

"We'll have to see. Let's us get over there and get Jaime on the phone; I expect he'll know how to reach her. And you might as well let this fellow go," he told the man who was holding Jared in a half-nelson. "Let him get on back to Salt Lake whatever way he can. I expect he'll be wanting to speak to the President."

The Gaians all laughed, and the man holding Jared turned him loose. Jared worked his shoulders and looked down at Lexi. "Listen, I'm sorry you got hurt, Alexis. If these goons hadn't of interfered, not a thing would've happened to you, you'da been fine."

"When you were holding my head down," Lexi said, "I wasn't fine. I wasn't fine *at all*. I bet the Hefn are going to wipe you and I hope they do."

CHAPTER 10

Moab

5 JULY 2037

There was no faster way to get from Salina to Green River than the way Lexi and Jared had come, but at least the twice-weekly public bus continued on to Moab. Parley Kroupa met her at the station, a converted film lab. "Great to see you," he said, shaking Pam's hand vigorously. "They pinned her wrist this morning. She's sleeping off the sedative. She wouldn't settle down last night till we told her you were on your way." He shouldered Pam's backpack. "The Mission's just a couple blocks along here."

They started walking, past a cluster of small gift and snack shops with CLOSED TILL SEPTEMBER 15 signs in their windows. Pam formed a dim impression of turquoise jewelry and tee shirts lurking behind the glass. It was the same on the other side of the street. A tourist town. Hot as it was in Salt Lake, here it was hotter; dry as it was, Pam could feel the sweat pop out on her back. The wide sun-washed street was all but deserted. They crossed at the corner: more gift shops, more small eateries, a motel. In the rush to leave Pam had forgotten her hat, and the ferocious light stabbed her eyes. Shading them with her hand, she asked, "How bad is the wrist?"

"Not very, just a hairline fracture. She'll be fine, but I reckon they might have to write her out of the series for a while."

She smiled. "That won't do the series any harm. Nothing's better for telly ratings than a little notoriety. So Jaime tells me."

Parley Kroupa laughed. "That Jaime is a character." He turned serious. "I get the impression he's perked up some this past little while, but we've been mighty worried about him down here."

"He's better. Working too hard, talking to a counselor. It'll take time, but I think he'll be okay." Pam smiled up at Parley, a lean, weathered man with a drooping mustache, in jeans and boots and a ten-gallon hat. They had conferred often by phone; this didn't feel like a first meeting.

"Well now, we've been wantin' to get you down here for a good while. Not quite what we had in mind. You've never been to Moab at all before, have you?"

"No," Pam said, "and I've always wanted to, ever since I read that Edward Abbey book, *Desert Solitaire*."

Parley nodded emphatically, grinning. "*Ed* Abbey. He's always called Ed."

"*Ed* Abbey," Pam agreed. "Not quite what I had in mind either, but now that I'm here I'd like to take a look around before heading back. It would be nice to see Delicate Arch. The bus went right past the entrance to the park."

"Not a problem," Parley said with laconic enthusiasm. "Take you up there myself, tomorrow, if you don't mind an early start. It's a good little hike, slickrock'll burn the soles right off your boots in the middle of the day. Or we could go later, around six."

"Thanks, I'd like that, either way." She slid a glance up at his impressive headgear, which he didn't wear while making phone calls. "If I can I borrow a hat."

"Hat, canteen, whatever you need."

"Way cool," said Pam. "Coming in from Salina instead of Salt Lake, I got to see the San Rafael Reef. That was a first too. What a sight." Their spiraling descent through the red astonishment of the reef, like a series of colossal stone thunderclaps, had briefly startled everything else from Pam's mind; but now she was one hundred percent back on the job. "So the rescue went off without a hitch, apart from Lexi's wrist?"

Parley ducked his head, looking sober. "We all feel mighty bad about that, Pam. I keep going over and over it, wondering if there wasn't some way we could have grabbed him without her gettin' knocked down."

"Well," said Pam, speaking in her role of Child Oversight Liaison Officer, "I won't deny it would have been better to pull it off without

243

anybody getting hurt, and especially without the hurt person being Lexi. Besides the effect on her, it gives the Church a stick to beat us with."

He nodded. "I know. They'll scream bloody murder about the wrist to distract people's attention from the fact they kidnapped her in the first place."

"And claim she didn't need rescuing anyway. It's bad luck, no lie. But you got her out, and I don't doubt you did the best you could in the circumstances, and neither will Humphrey, I'm sure. So, apart from the wrist, things went smoothly?"

Parley looked relieved. "Slick as a zipper—see, Green River's a pretty dead town most of the year. The town center's basically moved down around the newer motels, there's several of 'em down there on the Green, right where they launch the rafts, right across from the river museum. Plus the bus stop, the bank, the farmer's market, and so forth . . . but the train station's in the old downtown. Well, and the LDS church, that's the only church in town of course. Well this time of year there's nobody around as a rule if it's not Sunday, but if somebody happens to see a group of people gettin' off the train it looks suspicious. So we're keeping our heads down and checkin' up and down the street, there's several derelict motels on East Main. Well, so, we're checkin' out the ones like Jaime described and talking about what to do, and while we're doin' that we see this bus pull in at the old Book Cliff Lodge, and we're not even thinkin' about that one because it's got *two* rows of rooms, two buildings you know, one directly behind the other, but of course that means there's space between 'em to park a bus out of sight of the street."

Pam, who had been nodding encouragement throughout Parley's narrative, thought: *That's it. That's what I missed.*

"So soon as they drive behind the street-side building, all eight of us just hightail it across the street, and the minute they get off we jump the guy that's holding Lexi." He shook his head ruefully. "And down he goes, and down she goes with him."

"You couldn't have known she'd be on the bus," Pam said reasonably. "Actually, I can't imagine why they'd risk taking her out again—or taking the bus out again, for that matter, once they'd made it here without getting caught."

"Well—" Parley shot her a surprised look; but they had arrived. "Here we are, this is the Mission." Parley held a door open and Pam stepped ahead of him into the dim relief of a swamp cooler's breeze. Two women stood up from desks as they entered. "Pam Pruitt, this is Mercedes Kimball, my assistant—my gal Jaime, so to speak. She was a member of the very first class of missionaries to be recruited." He waited for them to shake hands. "And this young lady is Sophie Rodriguez, she's a volunteer at the mission, she was along on the raid. She's the one that took care of Lexi."

Sophie shook hands with Pam too. "I've had some medical training so I volunteered. They were mighty glad they let me come!"

"It's not a bad break," the other woman, Mercedes, put in. "Sophie did the X-rays herself."

"We all feel bad about it though. We know the Church will make hay out of it."

Again Pam went through her acknowledgment/reassurance routine: Yes, it's a pity; no, nobody blames you; don't worry, we'll deal with it. "I'd like to see her as soon as possible. Right away, if the doctors don't object."

"I can take you to the clinic now," Parley offered. "You can leave your stuff in the guest room and freshen up if you like, and you can use Mercedes' bike. It's about a mile from here, you passed it on the bus coming in. Several of our guys are standing guard—they wanted to do something to make up for letting her get hurt."

"Sounds good." Pam's eyes had adjusted to the low light in the room, and she saw now that the walls were covered with posters of monstrous attenuated figures, obviously primitive, very striking, a bit disturbing. The figures had the massive stillness of Easter Island heads. "Would this be the local rock art?"

"Some of it, and fairly local," said Parley. These come from the Great Gallery in Horseshoe Canyon. They're thousands of years old. Mercedes is a pictograph expert, among her other virtues; she put these up."

"It's awesome art," Mercedes said. "We're not the first ones by a long shot to have lived into this land. The people who made these paintings were proto-Gaians for sure, and the Great Gallery itself is a Hot Spot of incredible power."

The posters made Pam curious to see the real thing. "Could we work the Great Gallery into our hike tomorrow, Parley?"

"I'm afraid it's not quite *that* local. We do have one site right here in Moab, though, pictographs made by this same culture—we might manage a little detour past that one."

Judith Moffett

~

The walls of the clinic's waiting room were plastered with more posters, some of rock art in different styles, some of stunningly gorgeous scenery from inside the parks. All the rock seemed to be dark red, or red and white, or red-gold and glowing in hard sunlight. The painted figures were dark red. There was a big picture of Delicate Arch in winter, red rock against white snow.

Lexi was still asleep but the nurse in charge said she should be waking up any time now, and it was perfectly okay for Pam to wait in the room.

"I think I'd like to be there by myself when she wakes up," said Pam. "Thanks for the escort."

"Sure thing," said Parley. "See you back at the Mission for dinner, then?"

"I'll have to let you know, but probably." She turned to enter Lexi's room.

"Oh, and by the way," he said, "you were saying about how we couldn't have known Lexi would be on that bus? I didn't get a chance to explain—they were just pulling in from Salina when we got there. We only beat them to Green River by a couple of minutes."

Startled, Pam turned back. "I thought they got there the night before, the night of the day they kidnapped her."

He shook his head. "Nope, not till yesterday afternoon. From what Jaime'd said we thought they'd be there already too, but they were only just hittin' town, and if you think about it, they really couldn't have gotten there very much faster. If they holed up somewhere close to Salt Lake to make that viddy, and then had to wait for a train, get a car put on, get hold of a bus to charter from Salina—you just got off one so you know yourself how long it takes an electric bus to get up and down those mountain roads, they only average about twenty-five or thirty. And there's not that many trains that come this far south either nowadays. We can check the schedule, but I'm pretty sure they got there about as fast as humanly possible."

"Pretty sure" was just Parley being tactful; he was obviously correct. "Of course you're right," she said. "I wasn't thinking straight. Thanks."

"See you later, then. Hope the little girl's doin' okay."

The room held six white hospital beds, five of which were made up flat. Pam went in quietly and shut the door behind her. Lexi lay in the sixth bed, the one closest to the door. The head of the bed had been elevated, and Lexi's long blond hair lay loosely mussed over the pillow. Her left arm was swathed in a white sling with an ice pack tucked inside it, and there was an IV line taped to the back of her right hand. The line led from a beeping bottle of fluid hooked to a pole on the right side of the bed.

Lexi looked little and pale in all that whiteness. The sight of her struck Pam's solar plexus a blow that felt physical. Carefully she drew up a chair and sat in it, watching the child's sleeping profile while her mind grappled with the wild new information from Parley.

If Lexi had arrived in Green River at the same time the posse did—then Pam's lucid dream had showed her, not where Lexi was, but where she was going to be in eight hours or so.

She sat and thought about this. After a bit, she reached over and slid her hand, very carefully, beneath Lexi's left hand where it was sticking out of the cast. Seeing the two hands together triggered a memory of the moment, which felt distant now, when she had spread out her hand on a different bed beside Little Pam's spidery hand with the thunderbird ring on its little finger. That likeness of shape and detail was absent here. Lexi's hands were perfect, as beautifully formed as Liam's. Pam closed her bony, big-knuckled fingers lightly around Lexi's perfect hand and sat back.

Considered from the perspective of an ordinary person, remote viewing combined with precognition might seem no more remarkable than setting time transceiver coordinates mentally while in a self-induced state of trance. But several dozen BTP Apprentices from successive classes had been operating transceivers since they were children. For those with native talent, it was a teachable and learnable skill, which could be applied to existing technology. Pam didn't understand how her mind interlaced with the transceiver fields, anymore than she understood how her YellowPad did what it did. But both were familiar, part of the frame of reference of any BTP Apprentice.

Whatever she had done in the dream was not familiar. Jaime had suggested a possible connection between the dream and the return of her math intuition. The timing was certainly suggestive, but the lucid dream had not felt at all like hurling the numbers into a matrix. That was a masterful feeling. In the dream, she had stated her request and been immediately swept up and carried like a cork on a surge of energy. And nothing analogous to the time transceivers, or even crystal balls or mirrors, had been involved. Nothing! It was a dream!

She conjured up the moment of descent toward the long low building—double building—where Lexi stood holding up her hand—this hand, the broken one—and shivered. Had Lexi known where they were taking her, had Pam read her mind somehow? Some kind of psychic thing? Even that would be easier to accept than that she had glimpsed the future.

Though if Time were truly One, didn't it follow that the future is just as "there" as the past and just as available to be looked at, if you knew how to look? "But I *don't* know how!" she whispered, "It happened *to* me!" She was gripped by a craving for information. Studies had been done on precognition, she'd seen them referred to, somewhere, sometime. But involved so intimately with the past—first Gaia's, then her own personal past—Pam's curiosity had never before been quickened by the idea of the future. The future was the disaster they were fighting to head off.

The hand lying weightless in hers moved, and Lexi stirred, gasped a little, opened her eyes and saw Pam. As her lids fluttered shut again, she smiled and murmured, "I knew you'd come."

~

"I'm going to have to take a rain check on Delicate Arch," Pam told Parley Kroupa on the phone. "Lexi's fine physically, but she's pretty upset about everything that's happened. She doesn't want me to leave her, so I guess I'll stay here with her tonight, and then we'll start back in the morning on the early bus."

She'd chalked up Parley's obvious restlessness during this speech to disappointment over the canceled hike, but he quickly set her straight. "Understood. Listen, Jaime called; I was just about to call you. He wants you to get back to him ASAP." Parley paused dramatically. "*Humphrey* is on his way to Moab! He wants you not to leave till he gets here. He came to Salt Lake—well, maybe I should let Jaime fill you in himself."

This was a poser. "He's coming *here*? Did Jaime say why?"

"No, just that he seemed really determined about it. He'll be here—well—any time now I guess, he took a helicopter from the Salt Lake airport. Will he come to the Mission, do you think?" Parley's droopy face was flushed and transformed with excitement.

"He'll probably land in the middle of Main Street and wait for the Mission to come to him," Pam said drily. "Oh God. Well, okay, I'll call my office. When he shows up, please tell him I have to stay here with Lexi, but that he's very welcome to join us. And maybe you could send us in some dinner? I'm sorry, there seems to be a lot going on at once."

"Sure, we'll rustle you up some dinner, I'll bring it over myself, bring your backpack too. Is Humphrey—is he partial to anything in particular?"

"Cobbler," Pam said. "Blackberry cobbler. I don't expect you can produce one of those just like that. Lexi and I aren't finicky, but we're both pretty hungry."

"I'll see what I can do."

He rang off, and Pam placed the call to Jaime, who flashed onto the screen with both eyebrows raised. "I take it all back, boss," he said. "You're a magician and I'll never second-guess you again."

"Good God, don't say that! I'll have to fire you and find somebody else to play devil's advocate!"

He grinned. "I hear from Parley that she'll be okay?"

"Completely okay medically, it's just a hairline fracture, but she's got some PTSD. Anxious, won't let me out of her sight, doesn't want to see her mother—RoLayne and Ed Young and the bishop of Lexi's ward were all in on the abduction. I'll brief you on the details, but anyhow something's got to be decided about custody right away, she can't go home. What's all this about Humphrey, though?"

"I'm keeping a list of all the things you're gonna brief me on when you get around to it," said Jaime. "Humphrey, well, he turned up here around 1:30, he'd flown in from Santa Barbara and didn't bother to call from the airport. I didn't say anything about your dream, I just described the situation, told him that when you took off you were expecting to come right back, then Lexi broke her wrist and had to be doctored, you had to go to Moab, blah blah blah. I said you'd probably bring her back up here tomorrow, and did he want to make himself at home at your place till then, and he said, I swear to God, 'I will not wait at Pam Pruitt's house if Pam Pruitt is in Moab. I will go directly to Moab. I will not pass Go. I will not collect two hundred dollars.' Where did Humphrey learn to play Monopoly?"

"Oh, we used to play board games a lot at the BTP. He loved all those corny old ones like Monopoly and Clue."

"I guess he went back out to the airport, I heard a chopper take off about, oh, two hours ago? I assumed it was him, coming straight there."

"It was," said Pam, "I hear the chopper now. Did he say what was so urgent it couldn't wait?"

"Maybe he's always wanted to see Delicate Arch," said Jaime. "He didn't say word one about the conference either. I thought Raghu or Liam might call last night, but no. I suppose messages might be waiting for you at home."

Pam groaned. "Let's keep the focus on the custody question for now. Lexi's got aunts and uncles in Salt Lake and Ogden, but they're all Mormons and she doesn't want anything to do with Mormons right now. She hasn't come right out and said so, but I know what she wants is to stay with me. Which is fine, for a while anyway, but if she's going to go on acting in *A Thousand Miles* she's going to need two things: a different responsible adult on location, and a full-time gentile bodyguard. Can you get rolling on all that?"

Jaime's mouth twisted sideways. "Hm. Custody and bodyguard I can do. Responsible adult, I don't know. What about her dad, could he take over for RoLayne?"

Pam realized she knew nothing whatever about Lexi's father, not even his first name. "It's a thought, but I'd better ask Lexi how she likes that idea. He's her dad, but he's a Mormon too; Ed Young is his stepfather. Hold off on that one, I guess. Did you call Marcee?"

"Yesterday afternoon, soon's I knew something to tell her. The writers are already beavering away on a script about Kate's broken arm."

"Lordy, they didn't waste any time! Well, then I guess we'll see you tomorrow. Good thing you *were* minding the store. Do much other business?"

"I passed out a couple dozen Homeland brochures. Person after person made a point of telling me *they* didn't approve of the kidnapping. It's gonna be a long year."

"You got that right."

Pam cut the connection, apologized to the nurse, whose name tag read MRS JACKSON R.N., for keeping the phone tied up so long, and went back into Lexi's room. The patient was sitting up in bed; she had taken her arm out of the sling and was examining her cast. "Dinner's on the way," Pam said, "and guess what else is on the way? Humphrey! Did you hear the helicopter?"

Lexi nodded, beginning to smile. "Was that him? Cool! Why is he here though?"

"Jaime wasn't sure. Maybe he'll tell us himself. How do you feel? Want to get dressed before he gets here?"

"Can I?"

"I don't see why not, if we can get the nurse to take your IV out."

Mrs. Jackson checked with the doctor by phone, then came in and disconnected Lexi from her drip. The band-aid she plastered over the insertion point had ducklings and bunnies on it, and Lexi slid her eyes sideways at Pam, saying more plainly than words, *What does she think I am, a baby?*

Pam grinned behind the nurse's departing back. "Where's your stuff? In the locker?"

Lexi didn't know, but Pam opened the locker door and there were Lexi's jeans and tee shirt on hooks, and her socks and sneakers on the floor. "I had a sweatshirt too, but I guess it's still on that bus."

"Hm." Pam took the the tee shirt down and considered it. "Let's see if this'll go on over your cast. Did I ever tell you I broke my arm when I was about your age? I remember what a hassle it was, trying to get stuff on over my head by myself."

"How'd you break yours?"

"Falling out of a tree." She sat down on the bed and untied Lexi's hospital gown. Underneath the girl was flat as a board, and Pam felt an involuntary surge of pure pity for Little Pam—the same age as Lexi and already cinched into that hateful bra. The shirt went over the cast without difficulty, then over the other arm and head. Lexi re-donned the sling, tugged her hair free, and pulled on her own jeans one-handedly, sitting on a chair to do it, but Pam had to button the waistband. Lexi did the socks and shoes herself and Pam tied the laces. "Teamwork is the answer. You'll get better at doing things for yourself, though. It's good it was your left wrist you broke."

The doctor, large brown envelope tucked under her arm, knocked and came in as Pam was brushing the tangles out of Lexi's hair. When

Lexi introduced her to Pam she added with proprietary pride, "Dr. Boniface is a *Gaian!*"

"It's Susan, and I certainly am. It's a great pleasure to meet you, Ms. Pruitt."

"And it's a great pleasure for me," said Pam, "to meet the person who fixed up my girl here." She shook the doctor's hand. "Would you want to stick around and meet the Hefn Humphrey? He's rumored to be headed this way."

"It's more than a rumor," said the doctor, a stout woman with a cap of brown curls. "Parley called me a couple of minutes ago. They were leaving as soon as Sophie had finished hitching up the team. Sounds like they're bringing enough food to feed an army."

"Dollars to doughnuts Humphrey will be driving by the time they get here," said Pam. "Anything I should know about Lexi's wrist? We're leaving in the morning."

Dr. Boniface laid the envelope on the bed. "These are her X-rays, the Salt Lake orthopedist will want to see them. Lexi, in a couple of months you'll be good as new. Your cast comes off in five or six weeks, then they'll give you a splint, that'll make things easier. Keep the sling on till then, okay? And no riding your bike no-hands." Lexi grinned.

There was a small commotion outside, that grew louder as they listened. "Here comes dinner," Pam said. "And every Gaian in Moab, by the sound of things. Quite a few of you, actually, aren't there? Jaime Rivera keeps track of the numbers closer than I do, but I do know that much."

"There *are* quite a few of us. If you live anywhere near the Golden Circle and don't get the message, you probably won't get it anywhere."

The door of the clinic burst open. Lexi bounced on the bed with excitement. Squaring her shoulders, Pam walked through the open doorway into the reception.

One of the truly endearing things about Humphrey was the way he gave himself up completely to simple pleasures. "*Hello*, my dear! Look, I am a driver of horses! Parley Kroupa gave me a lesson and put the reins into my hands! We *trotted*! It is very, very—it is very— *delightful*—to drive a team of horses!" He was literally wriggling with delight, and Pam felt her defenses melting treacherously; she had always loved him in this mood. While she struggled to keep her clarity, Humphrey looked past her. "Hello to you also, dear little

Lexi! Like you, I am now a driver of horses! Do you also find it very wonderful?"

Lexi had come and stood next to Pam. "Hi, Humphrey. I do find it lots of fun, I wish I got to do it more."

"On *A Thousand Miles*," Humphrey explained to the gathered Gaians, who doubtless already knew this as well as he did, "Kate McPherson had once to drive horses and a supply wagon through the North Platte River. I had *no idea* how delightful it could be." He made a visible effort to calm himself down. "How are you feeling this evening, little dear? I am very sorry about your broken bone."

"It's only a hairline fracture," Lexi told him; she'd being hearing people say that since yesterday. "It kind of hurts though."

Pam supported the arm and pulled the sling out of the way. "It's swollen. Better get that ice pack back on it. Can she have something for pain?" she asked Mrs. Jackson, who was standing at her station taking in the show.

Susan Boniface, who had come out to see it as well, said, "I'll take care of it. Come along, Lexi," and they ducked back into the room.

Parley and the other Gaians had by now crowded into the reception behind Humphrey, carrying covered dishes, picnic baskets, and coolers. The space filled up with good smells. "Here's what we'll do," said Pam. "Lexi and I will entertain Humphrey in Lexi's room, but there's enough food here for an Irish wake. Why don't you folks put those dishes on the nurse's station and have a potluck out here—if that's okay with you?" she asked the nurse, who nodded happily; things were obviously not this lively at the clinic as a rule. "Thanks. We'll all help clean up."

"Here's Humphrey's cobbler," said Mercedes, the "gal Jaime" from the Mission. "You can just take that in with you. He had the most wonderful time driving over here."

It really was a blackberry cobbler, still warm. Pam looked up from its purple surface with amazed gratitude. "How—"

"I had one left in the freezer. Humphrey is more than welcome to it. This year's crop will be coming in before we know it anyway."

~

"The great thing about so many Utah Gaians being ex-Mormons," Pam told him later, after everyone had gone home and Lexi had dropped off to sleep, "is that they can put on a first-rate potluck at the drop of a hat. Having to eat hunkered on the floor, out of sick-up basins with tongue depressors, just made it that much more of an adventure. The morale of the Moab Mission will probably never be higher than it is right now." She paused. "A pretty strange time for Gaians anywhere to be throwing a party."

Pam was sitting in the bedside straight chair, Humphrey on the bed nearest Lexi's—straight chairs were just about impossible for him—clutching the round glass cobbler dish to his torso and a large spoon in one of his forked hands. He had shared this treat with Lexi and Pam, but had eaten three-fourths of it himself, and now from time to time he scraped the spoon around the sides and scooped off the scrapings with his lower lip. "The Gaians of Moab have cause to rejoice without ceasing," he said mildly. "This land they have lived into, this is a place where Gaia shows herself without equivocation. This is the true Zion and well they know it."

"What they don't know," Pam said casually, "yet, is what the Gafr will say on June 6th."

Humphrey's spoon scraped the Pyrex dish. "On June 6th their Ground of splendid red rocks will be exactly the same as it was on June 5th."

"But when they find out the Ban is never going be revoked, it'll have an impact even here."

The spoon paused; Humphrey looked up, eyes fixed on Pam. In a moment he said, "This is the turkey."

"This is it. Not quite what I meant in Santa Barbara—but yes."

"I perceive that you speak in perfect certainty that the Ban will not be revoked. Artie, Liam, Will, they suspect this, believe it perhaps, but even they do not think they *know*." He gave the bowl one last scrape-scoop and set it on the bed beside him.

"I do know." Pam summarized for him her experience on the train from Los Angeles: of keying certain questions on the Yellow-Pad and receiving answers in the form of thoughts charged with conviction. Then she told him about the lucid dream. "Lexi didn't know where they were taking her," she finished. "She asked the guy in charge of her on the bus that very question but he wouldn't say. *He* knew, the Bishop knew, RoLayne thought she knew. Lexi didn't. So either I read one of their minds in my sleep, or I saw a little way into the future, or—what?"

In a swift blurry movement, Humphrey had leapt up and was standing on the bed. All his body hair bristled straight out. His large flat eyes were trained on Pam. The tension in the room had been building steadily; now it was overwhelming. "What is it?" Pam said again, and stood herself.

Humphrey made a noise she had never heard any Hefn make in all her years among them, a high gargling sound, as shocking in its way as the howling bellow he had uttered at Carrie's memorial service. His arms whirled in circles. In her own bed Lexi started awake. "What's the matter? What happened?" she asked in a frightened voice.

Pam shot Humphrey a warning look. "Nothing's the matter, honey. Humphrey just got carried away about something and forgot to be quiet. Everything's fine, go back to sleep."

"Nothing is wrong, Lexi Allred," Humphrey said in a high, strangled voice. "Everything is right. Everything is wonderful!" As an afterthought he sat down.

~

Of course Lexi didn't go back to sleep. Her arm hurt, she needed more ice, she needed more pills and a drink; what she needed more than anything was for Pam to pull her sheets straight, tuck her in, and generally reassure her. "Could you sing me a song?" she finally asked, half-apologetically. "My mom used to sing me to sleep when I was little."

"If you like. Got a request?"

"No. Just not Mormon songs. Do you know any lullabies? Like that one, you know—" she hummed a few notes.

It was Brahms' Lullaby. "Sure you wouldn't rather have 'Rock-a-Bye Baby'?" Lexi giggled. "Okay. My voice is kind of rusty." Pam sang the two verses of Brahms' Lullaby she knew in English, and one in German. Lexi was still wide awake. "More? Let's see." She racked her brain for lullabies and came up with "Now the Day Is Over" and "All Through the Night." After that she moved on to Christmas carols that were lullaby-esque, and during one of these Lexi's eyelids finally fluttered shut and her breathing became even.

When Pam turned her attention back to Humphrey, ready to remind him sternly to keep his voice down, the Hefn's mood had

again changed completely. "Do you remember how you and Liam
O'Hara would frequently sing a song together called 'Peace! Be
Still!'? At Hurt Hollow and at the BTP, when you were children? So
sweetly? I have not thought for a very long time of what pleasure it
was for me to hear you sing."

"I remember," Pam said, feeling a nostalgic pang of her own.

"Singing together! How strangely powerful it can be! In Santa
Barbara, Gillian Jacoby sang together with the recording of Jeff
Carpenter, the recording we played at Carrie's service. Liam and
Terry were greatly moved." Pam blinked; the drama of Liam and
Gillian, played out—was it only three days before?—seemed to
have happened at an enormous distance in spacetime. Was Gillian
a singer, then, like Jeff? (Like Eddie?) "Liam has recovered from his
infatuation," Humphrey said, offhandedly landing this bombshell.
"But let us not speak of this now. Let us speak of you, Pam Pruitt.
What you tell me fills me with joy. For out of near-catastrophe has
come your transformation."

He slid to the floor and beamed at her across sleeping Lexi. Pam's
patience, frayed already, gave out. "*What* transformation, for chrissake?"

His pelt began to erect again. "Behold, I show you a mystery.
That is from First Corinthians. Come." Spinning round, he walked
briskly through the doorway and directly up to one of the posters
on the wall.

He must have noticed it earlier. Pam followed and stood beside
him. The poster displayed two long, static, red figures, different
from, but also similar to, those she had seen in the Moab Mission.
The figure on the left had a flattened head with huge goggle eyes
and skinny arms held akimbo; it looked much more like a spaceman, in point of fact, than Humphrey did. The one on the right
also had skinny arms, but its head was small and surmounted with
what appeared to be a pair of rabbit ears or two upright, feath-
ery antennae; and around these structures a group of insects or
tiny birds formed a kind of vertical halo. "Look, my dear. Do you
see the little birds? This is a shaman figure. Do you know what a
shaman is?"

"I think so—a kind of sorcerer, a medicine man?"

"In traditional human cultures, a shaman is a person who travels
on behalf of his people into the spirit world. He enters the spirit

world in a variety of ways. Some of the ways, such as fasting, purging, going without sleep, and eating nasty substances, are not very agreeable, but many shamans have no other means of getting out of their physical bodies. They must do this if they are to seek a cure for an illness or an advantage in warfare. It is difficult and dangerous, but carries high prestige."

Pam looked at Humphrey with amazement. "How the dickens do you come to know all that? I wouldn't have thought it was in your line, so to speak."

"A very common reason for entering the spirit world is to find what has been lost. Valuable objects. Missing persons! Shamans also achieve entry in ways that are less unpleasant than purging or ingesting peyote buttons. Drumming, for instance, can effect the separation. Also, some of the most powerful shamans are known to be strong dreamers."

Pam stared at him, then back at the poster. Her heart began to thump in her chest. "These pictures are thousands of years old," she protested.

"This painted shaman does not portray *your* experience specifically, my dear." He trotted to the nurse's station and did some things to the computer, while Pam continued to stare at the unnerving rabbit-eared figure with its bird halo. "But these shamans of a different ancient culture," he said a moment later, "do." He turned the screen so Pam could see.

It was another pictograph, done in a different style. Against a whitish, uneven surface Pam made out a pair of shapes like identical red sausages, each with four stick limbs, placed horizontally at the center of the screen. Each arm and leg terminated in a three-toed bird's foot.

Sausages or not, stick limbs or not, there was nothing Easter Island-like about these figures. That they were in flight was unmistakable, partly owing to the fact that above and below them, and oriented in the same direction, a flock of birds was flying. These were no tiny creatures swarming like gnats around an immobile spaceman's antennae. Relative to the sausage figures these birds were large, and there were a lot of them—ten—and though they had been painted crudely, the arrangement was extremely dynamic. The shamans flew across the rock wall and the birds flew with them, supporting them, guiding them—Pam stepped to the station and leaned on it; her ears had begun to ring.

There was writing on the screen, a caption: "Escort Birds of Fate Bell." Below the label Pam read: "In this rare scene from Fate Bell Shelter, ten birds flank two flying shaman figures, illustrating their role as psychopomps or guardian spirits during the shamanic voyage of the soul."

Psychopomps? Wordlessly she looked at Humphrey, who said, "The people who made these pictures, called the Pecos River culture, lived in western Texas perhaps three thousand years ago, when the people in these reproductions we see around us were living here in Utah.

"Despite the distances involved, the rock paintings of these two cultures are amazingly alike in many respects. Not in how they are rendered, but in what they depict. No one is able to explain this likeness satisfactorily, or explain why it should be shared by a culture in Baja California, and by no others in between them or elsewhere. There are similarities elsewhere, remarkable ones, but not this duplication, as if three artists painted three pictures of the same visionary landscape.

"In one way, moreover, one astounding way, the Pecos River people were unique." He punched some keys, and a different picture flashed on the screen: a weathered oval figure outlined in red. The interior of its torso had been painted black, with red and yellow markings. Strikingly, the torso and outspread limbs were heavily fringed in red, giving it somewhat the aspect of a paramecium with arms. Even more strikingly, the figure was headless. Two straight red lines jutted up from the neck region and two other lines crossed them at the tips; to Pam it looked rather like a child's drawing of a trolley car's antennae coupled to a set of cables. The caption said: "FANTASTIC CREATURES, THE DART-HEADED FIGURES. Invariably, these creatures can be identified by the parallel lines crossed by one or two bars that substitute for its head. The cross bars often bear an oval motif that designates them as a sign for dart or lance. Some part of the body is hairy, whether just the appendages or the entire torso . . . this mythical creature is so consistent and common, it must represent a well-known actor in the Pecos River cosmological cast whose role in some way informed the audience, but the intent of this morality play is no longer evident."

Now Humphrey was making different versions of the monstrous creature flick on the computer screen. There were quite a few of them. "Dart-headed figure, Devils River." "Dart-headed figure, Pecos River." "Dart-headed figures, Panther Cave." Plainly the figures had been painted by many different hands, but virtually all were fringed in dark red, as if tricked out in Daniel Boone buckskins. Other figures in the same pictures—more obviously human, with heads—were sometimes also fringed.

Pam wanted to get back to the escort birds, but Humphrey kept methodically displaying pictographs of the hairy headless beings. Quelling her impatience, she said, "These look powerful, but creepy. What's the fringe, is it static electricity?"

"No," said Humphrey, and waited. After a bit Pam looked up from the screen. All his body hair was erected. As she stared, he raised his stumpy arms to the sides as if he were about to make the Gaian salute; and all at once Pam knew exactly what he was going to say.

He said it. "They dreamed us."

"They—"

"Dreamed us. Three thousand years ago, the Pecos River people dreamed the Hefn."

Pam stared at him, then at the screen. "The heads—the heads are *weapons*. Thought control. Memory excision?"

"Yes."

"That's—no, wait, wait a minute." She backed off, waving her arms as if to drive the thought away. "How can you know that? These could be anything, you can't be sure they're Hefn! Unless—was there a contact you never told us about, three thousand years ago?"

Humphrey bent his body and crouched in the nurse's desk chair. Ignoring Pam's question, he said, "I came across the pictures by sheerest chance, in a book I found in Terry's house, a book Frank Flintoft had given long ago to Carrie Sharpless. When I saw the pictures, I knew. No: when I saw them first, I *believed*. Then I saw these ancient images painted on the living rock with my own eyes, and then I did know. As you knew the Ban will not be lifted, I knew this."

"That they dreamed the Hefn."

"Do you remember when I came to Salt Lake, after Carrie's memorial service? On the way from Washington, I made a detour, I went to Texas. Del Rio, Texas. There is no airfield. I was driven to

Del Rio from Austin, Texas, in an ambulance, by a rock art expert who does not remember what he did that day."

Pam winced at this casual allusion to mindwipe, of Humphrey erasing a day out of somebody's life to satisfy his curiosity. She forced herself to remember that this had happened immediately after Carrie's service. He'd been so filled with fury at ungrateful humanity, on whose behalf he'd been struggling so long with his bosses the Gafr, that he might well have done something far worse.

Deliberately, she let go of it. "Hot Spots all over the place?" He nodded. "Did you take a transceiver?"

Humphrey twisted, a Hefn shrug. "What would be the point? We open a window, we observe a shaman painting a 'dart-headed figure' on a cave wall. What would this reveal to us? If he told stories about these figures, we would not understand what he was saying. As you observe, the figures could be anything. But," said Humphrey fiercely, "they are not 'anything.'"

Pam pulled up a second chair and sat down. "Did they dream the Gafr too?"

Humphrey considered. He turned the screen back toward himself and began to strike keys rapidly with two digits of each hand. "Not the Pecos River people. Not the people of Utah, called Barrier Canyon. Not in Baja California. But centuries later, in northeastern Arizona and southeastern Utah, there occurred another great dreaming."

He finished and turned the computer. On the screen was a white circle like a full moon, within which a curious humanoid being sat like an embryo inside an eggshell. Its arms and legs were spread and bent, its fingers and toes were splayed. While she tried to make sense of what she was seeing, Humphrey tapped a key; the screen split, and a different white circle appeared on a red wall. Inside stood a red figure—unlike the other, more familiar somehow, horned and square-headed, widespread fingers pointing not down but upward. They were not the same, and yet they were.

Pam looked at Humphrey. She cleared her throat. "The Gafr?"

"An impression only."

"But—of the Gafr?" He nodded. "Whose?"

"That of the Anasazi and the Fremont peoples. Both of whom were about to disappear from their ancestral lands, perhaps to migrate elsewhere, perhaps to vanish forever. They dreamed the Gafr, as you see. Only they, and only one pictograph each. On the Pecos River, many shamans dreamed the Hefn many times."

"Before I say anything else," Pam said, "I want to know if I'm going to remember this conversation."

Humphrey conveyed shock. "How can you ask me this?"

Pam thought of the several ways this Hefn of hers had abused her trust. She thought of the hapless rock-art expert from Austin. "How can I not? You're showing me the Gafr!"

Humphrey's flat eyes were turned on Pam. "Have you understood nothing then, my dear? That everything is different now?"

Pam stared back. "Maybe I *have* understood nothing. Why is everything different?"

"Because," said Humphrey, "the Hefn do not dream the future. The Hefn do not dream at all! Using a piece of finely calibrated equipment, and our mental abilities, we look into the past. But you, Pam Pruitt, one of our own from childhood, with no equipment at all, have dreamed an event before it occurred. Like the shamans of old, *you have looked into the future.*"

"Not very far into the future," Pam said lamely. "A few hours, maybe half a day."

Humphrey hit another key and the image of a dart-headed figure flipped back onscreen. "These humans saw three millennia into the future. You are a BTP Apprentice, a mathematical prodigy, you understand the behavior of irrational numbers and nonlinear equations. You understand how chaos overwhelms every attempt to predict the future mathematically. But Time is One! Like the shamans of old, you have overleapt the predictive models, you have *seen what will be!*"

Pam said, "I have to know whether you thought this might happen when you rigged the bradshaw," and held her breath.

The memory thief gave her a look that was a perfect simulation of innocent hopefulness. "Your mind, Pam Pruitt, your intuition, were different from every other in the first class of Apprentices. I thought at first that this must be a matter of gender merely, but saw in time that gender explained nothing. And then your gift left you, a fate that had befallen no other Apprentice in any class we trained. It was strange, bewildering, it cried out to be understood. You worked with Julie Hightower and reached one sort of understanding; I 'rigged the bradshaw,' as you say, and hoped for another."

THE BIRD SHAMAN

"Well," said Pam, "no matter what you hoped, the bradshaw isn't what brought my intuition back. But ever since I got it back, something very strange has been happening with my mind, that's for damn sure. I knew the Church had abducted Lexi. I knew about the Ban, and that you and Alfrey were lying about the extra year. I had that dream." Another thought startled her: "I wrote that *poem!*" Humphrey looked his question. "About—never mind right now."

Too absorbed to press the point, or to get into a wrangle about the bradshaw, Humphrey tapped a couple more keys and four figures shaped like bullets with arms and legs soared up the face of a cliff, trailed by a horizontal line of five large duck-like birds with outspread wings. The caption read, "Birds and anthropomorphic figures rising from a sawtooth horizon at Rio Grande Cliffs, Texas. Copy. Original inundated after the construction of Armistad Reservoir."

More escort birds, drowned ones. Another version of her own dream. Pam shivered; way beyond freaky though it was, she was frankly mesmerized. Another tap, and still another image: "Rotund shaman rising in a cloud of birds. Halo Shelter on Devils River."

Tingling excitement surged through Pam, a thrill of focussed energy. She was dying to know more. "These are all in Texas?"

"Yes. But many, many rock paintings and petroglyphs from many, many ancient cultures depict birds and shamans," Humphrey informed her. "Everywhere, birds are seen as symbolic of the flight of the human soul from the body, into the spirit world. I have delved deep into the subject of shamanism since my visit to Texas."

"Whoa," said Pam. "We're getting pretty far into a belief system I haven't got anymore, when we start talking about the human soul and the spirit world."

Humphrey twinkled for the first time since catching a whiff of the approaching cobbler. "It would appear to be unnecessary for the individual to embrace the belief system, if the belief system has decided to embrace the individual." But then he spoke in dead earnest. "You also, Pam Pruitt, must now delve deep into the subject of shamanism. Also into the subject of precognitive dreaming, which is the same subject *au fond*. At bottom. These matters were studied intensively by anthropologists and neurologists, before the coming of the Hefn and the Gafr. There is a very great deal to learn, whole libraries of information!"

"Look," said Pam, "I'll do it, I guess I want to anyway, but I wouldn't get my hopes up, I mean I wouldn't count on this being any help generally. It might be just something personal to me."

"Nevertheless I *shall* hope," he said fervently. "It may be our best hope. It may be all the hope we have!"

"Hope of what? It won't make any difference about the Ban."

"Yet in other ways it might. A great difference perhaps."

"For me to dream the future? How, if Time is One?"

"And *how*, my dear, is exactly what we never know!"

He looked so pleased at this perfect rejoinder that Pam laughed and let it drop. Excitement and energy had surged up in her again; suddenly she couldn't wait to get started. Her thoughts went racing ahead. "Well, now look, everybody will be expecting me to come back to Santa Barbara now that I'm fit for work again. But if I take this on I can't go back, not yet. I'm not sure I can even do my regular job right now. So what if I just"—she realized as she said it how good this sounded—"drop out for a while? Just go away and start learning? Jaime can take over in Salt Lake, he's ready for that."

Humphrey never skipped a beat. "Will you go to Hurt Hollow then?"

Her personal Ground: perfect. "I'd have to bring in a much better computer, I hate to do that in a way." But she had already decided. "You know, I'd rather the others weren't told till I understand this better. We can say I'm making a retreat, doing transceiver exercises or something. Getting used to having my intuition back—that's close to the truth anyway, and something everybody at Headquarters will buy."

"With the exception of Liam O'Hara perhaps?"

Incredibly, Pam had forgotten again that Liam was no longer smitten with Gillian. "Can't fret about that now, we'll figure something out."

The Hefn "nodded." "It is a good provisional plan. And I think you are right to tell no one. Telling could dilute the force at work in you."

Pam nodded with him. The mystery of what her mind was developing into clamored to be solved; and who could say that the solution might not bear upon the future of humanity and their alien overseers? Humphrey obviously believed it might, and really he had a point. Two decades spent mining the past had not resolved the conflict; if it were possible, why *not* seek a solution in the future, where Pecos River shamans had encountered the Hefn three thousand years ago?

"One more thing. Are you going to tell me why the Gafr need that extra year?"

"No," Humphrey said. "My dear, forgive me, I cannot tell you that."

Fine then; let Will and Artie keep the pressure on about the year while they settled on something to do with it themselves. Pam realized she had no idea what had been discussed and decided during the last day and a half of the conference. It seemed that the BTP and the conundrum of the final year were no longer her immediate concern.

Then with a jolt she remembered. "Oh my God—what about Lexi? I told Jaime to get custody papers ready for me to sign as soon as I got back to Salt Lake! Damn! It could take a while to find her another situation, if we even can." She paced the waiting room, passing back and forth beneath monumental or attenuated red anthropomorphs sublimely indifferent to her dilemma. "It won't be easy, she needs a lot of sensitive support. I don't think it's a good idea to put anything extra on Jaime and Claudia for a while longer. Maybe one of the other Gaians, or like a younger couple—"

"Couldn't I just come to Hurt Hollow with you?"

Humphrey and Pam spun around, and there, of course, was Lexi standing in the doorway, barefoot in underpants and tee shirt and her white sling. "They can kill me off. Or maybe leave me with the Pawnees till my arm gets better. I wouldn't be any trouble, honest," she pleaded. "I could help out!"

Shit! Before she could stop herself Pam had blurted, "How long have you been standing there eavesdropping?"

"I didn't *mean* to eavesdrop, I just woke up and heard you talking, and my arm was hurting, and then you said," her voice squeaked up, she was trying not to cry, "that it was a picture of the Gafr, so I got up, I was going to come out, but then I wasn't sure if I should, and then you said—" Two tears spilled down her face. Dismayed and stricken, Pam rushed to Lexi and hugged her, taking care not to bump the wrist. "Oh, sweetie. I'm sorry. You weren't eavesdropping at all, I shouldn't have used that word, it's our fault for talking where you might wake up and hear us." This felt eerily like explaining to

Little Pam why what *she* had done wasn't wrong, why the people who blamed her were being unfair. The girl sagged against her, crying openly now, not trying to hold it in. Inwardly Pam sagged too. Her bubble of excitement had been popped, but that wasn't all. Given a good enough reason, she had proved as ready to betray Lexi as any of them.

"Little Lexi, do not cry," Humphrey said, and quietly to Pam, "Shall I take this memory away?"

Pam shook her head furiously; but Lexi, her face muffled in Pam's teal-green uniform shirt, said, "Could I come to Hurt Hollow if I did?"

"You can come to Hurt Hollow anyway," Pam said firmly. "From now on we stick together. I promise."

PART TWO

Transformations
2037-38

...with bliss ineffable
I felt the sentiment of being spread
O'er all that moves, and all that seemeth still,
O'er all that, lost beyond the reach of thought
And human knowledge, to the human eye
Invisible, yet liveth to the heart,
O'er all that leaps, and runs, and shouts, and sings
Or beats the gladsome air, o'er all that glides
Beneath the wave, yea, in the wave itself
And mighty depth of waters: wonder not
If such my transports were, for in all things
I saw one life and felt that it was joy.

—William Wordsworth, *1805 Prelude*

Judith Moffett

CHAPTER 11

How Ya Gonna Keep 'Em Down on the Farm Now That They've Seen Paree?

6 JULY - 15 AUGUST 2037

Six weeks later, Pam and Lexi were still in Salt Lake City. They would have had to stay till after Pioneer Day in any case. Pioneer Day, July 24, was the day Brigham Young arrived in the Salt Lake Valley in 1847 and declared (or hadn't; the legend might not be historical, not that anybody cared): "This is the place. Drive on."

The Fourth of July—that crammed day beginning with Pam's lucid dream and ending with Lexi in the Moab clinic—had almost dwindled away as a celebration; where people bothered to observe it, they did so in a spirit of defiance. The Hefn presence made "Independence Day" ring hollow. But in Utah, Pioneer Day had always totally overshadowed the Fourth; and the Hefn presence had only goaded the LDS Church into celebrating its pioneer heritage more vigorously. This year, that would be truer than ever. Salt Lake would not bulge and bustle with a huge influx of pilgrims from around the world, as in the days before commercial flights were banned, but there would be a big parade, fireworks, a Tabernacle Choir concert, reenactments, speeches by members of the Church hierarchy including elderly President Wells, and a lavish public barbecue in Liberty Park. The cast of *A Thousand Miles* was going to ride on a float in the parade, and Lexi, naturally, wanted to be part of all that. She was on the outs with the LDS Church leadership, not with her dramatizing/idealizing series about its pioneer history or its cast and crew, and said as much in a couple of interviews.

Even had Lexi not been a consideration, Pam couldn't very well have been out of town on July 26. That date, just two days after Pioneer Day, happened to be the birthday of James Lovelock, the scientist who had first recognized that Earth's biosphere behaved like a living, self-regulating organism. Lovelock wasn't the founder of the Gaian movement—as several Apprentices had pointed out at Hurt Hollow—but without him it would not exist, and his birthday was always celebrated. Gaian social get-togethers were few and far between, a consequence of the focus on personal Ground rather than on human community. That made it important to reinforce such community bonding traditions as they had—and never more important than now, the most recent Gaian group activity having resulted in global mayhem and worse. Lexi's triumphant rescue had given the movement a badly needed morale boost—and, thanks to the popularity of the series, not just in Utah; even the media spin had been along the lines of *Gaians Outsmart Mormon Leadership Without Alien Assistance*. The local membership would expect Pam to lead the festivities, and she thought herself that she needed to make an appearance, partly to reinforce the celebration, partly to address the ranks of faux neo-Gaians that were expected (correctly) to turn out too.

After the 26th, though, forces of every sort had conspired to keep them in town. Or to keep Lexi there, and Pam had promised they would stick together.

The immediate thing, of course, was the broken wrist. The orthopedist had taken such a dim view of Pam's plan to spirit Lexi away to darkest north central Kentucky that she had let herself be persuaded; and removal of the cast was to be followed by weeks of physical therapy. Lexi's counselor had taken a view nearly as dim as the orthopedist's of Lexi's breaking off her sessions for a couple of months at this point in her counseling. Even her tutor raised objections, as if a BTP Apprentice and a computer program weren't capable between them of home-schooling one bright child.

There were other claims. On *A Thousand Miles* the writers, far from writing Lexi out of the script, had come up with a story about how Kate, indomitably high-spirited despite her hardships and deprivations, had tried to ride a colt born to one of the wagon horses way back in Iowa. The colt had pitched her over its head and down a steep slope of scree. Kate had been knocked unconscious;

besides the broken arm—a wrist having been deemed less dramatic than a whole arm—she got concussed, and had to be prayed over powerfully by the members of the priesthood, who brought her out of her coma by a laying on of hands. (This episode featured Neil as an emotional young elder who played the decisive role in restoring Kate to herself.) In subsequent episodes the camera was to make the most of her raggedy sling and wooden splint, while cast and crew struggled their way closer and closer to Zion, and Kate's stepmother's pregnancy came closer and closer to term.

The producers of the show, led by Marcee Morgenstern, raised a great outcry at the idea of not being allowed to use this material. Nobody had thought of breaking one of Kate's bones until Lexi actually broke one of her own, but now they were all excited by the dramatic possibilities, not to mention the real-life media tie-ins that were guaranteed to boost ratings, not that they needed boosting. Lexi had switched her own status from famous to notorious by defying her LDS abductors, yet continuing to work on the show. As Pam had foreseen, the Church was making a tremendous fuss about the fact that Lexi had been injured in the rescue. From the producers' point of view the entire episode of the kidnapping could not have played out better.

In the old days, a cast member of a Church-sponsored series who defied the Church would swiftly and certainly have been canned. But for obvious reasons canning Lexi was neither possible nor desirable now.

With Lexi's cautious, then more enthusiastic, approval, her father, Martin Allred, had taken on the job of responsible-adult-on-location. He and RoLayne were separated now, but Lexi had moved in with Pam as soon as they got back from Moab. It was not a casual arrangement. Lexi had her own room upstairs, with her own furniture, a bed and bureau moved from her parents' house, plus two bookcases and a chair and lamp that were presents from Pam. There were fresh calico curtains and a matching bedspread. Lexi had picked the paint herself (Custard), and she and Pam had hung the pictures she wanted on the fresh yellow walls: sepia posters featuring handcarts and the *Thousand Miles* cast in costume, and a *Secret Garden* illustration of Mary, Colin, and Dickon doing their "magic" ceremony against a background of a stone wall smothered in roses. These had been brought from her old room. She also asked for and received another picture: a framed twentysomething-year-old holograph of Pam with Humphrey, taken at Hurt Hollow.

The room had come out pretty well, Pam thought. Ever so much nicer than her own childhood bedroom where Liam had shot the bradshaw. Small wonder Lexi wanted to stay in Salt Lake and live in it.

The Mormon bigwigs behind the kidnapping had not been charged. In child oversight matters in Utah, decisions about anything to do with molesters was left to Pam; and Pam, backed by Hefn authority, had judged the public humiliations of their failure and fecklessness to be an exquisitely just and adequate punishment for Bishop Erickson and the Church authorities behind him. RoLayne and Jared, however, out on bail for the time being, would be tried for conspiring in the kidnapping. Edgar Young was back in jail awaiting trial with a non-LDS judge and jury. Lexi was the primary witness in all these cases. When the trials began her presence would be required in Salt Lake, and until the court dates were set, planning when to be away was awkward. Lexi's counselor also pointed out that *she* was going to be needed before and afterwards, to help Lexi deal with testifying against her mother and facing her grandfather in court.

No more abuse cases had come in. The Gaian Mission was adjusting to its new double role of keeping the true faith while distributing information to those only interested in going through the motions. Not even Jaime minded much whether Pam went on retreat; but everyone else, including Lexi, didn't want Lexi to go *anywhere*. Until Lexi was both able and ready to leave, Pam couldn't leave: it was that simple.

So she chafed, but made the best of her confinement: she got some materials together and started to read about shamanism. Nearly all of what was available had been collected and analyzed before 2010; anthropology, like so many other fields of human endeavor, had suffered a catastrophic loss of confidence when the Hefn and their time transceivers took control of Earth. But in print and online there was plenty of older stuff for someone unfamiliar with the field to look at, and Pam dug in.

In early August she called Jaime into her office. "I'm promoting you, buddy," she told him. "As of now, you are chief Hefn liaison for child oversight in Utah, and I'm demoting myself to two days a week, till we can hire you an assistant. Your job won't change much, you'll just be better paid and you won't have to go along with the crazy things I tell you to do. How about it?"

By the time she'd finished, Jaime was beaming. "We can for sure use the money, and I'm very happy that you still have that much confidence in me. And I couldn't work any harder anyway so that part sounds about right—but why, boss? I mean, why now, in the final year?"

"I'm not your boss anymore, big shot. We'll have to start calling you *'jefe.'*"

His grin got wider, if possible. "Long as nobody starts calling me 'Hefn'! But really, b-, uh, Pam, why do this now? Is this about your intuition coming back? Are you going back to Santa Barbara?"

She hadn't put it to herself in those terms, but— "I guess you could say it's about that in a way. But no, I'm not going anywhere for now, I just—" She lifted her hands and let them fall. "I need more time."

~

Until that night in Moab with Humphrey, Pam had given no thought for many years to what might be called the supernatural aspect of spiritual experience. To the best of her understanding, there *was* no supernatural aspect. In spiritual terms, "Gaia Is Our Ground" was as deep as it went for Pam. The intense religious feelings of her childhood, that had felt so true, had betrayed her. Evolutionary biology and modern biblical scholarship together would have made being a Fundamentalist Christian impossible for a person like Pam, even had the actuality of the Hefn on Earth not altered the meaning of everything she'd been taught in Sunday school.

She thought of Otie Bemis before his re-conversion, how poisonously he had hated the Hefn, how he had stirred a congregation into a mob that had tied Humphrey between two trees and tried to skin him alive. The same self-righteous certainty that had sustained the Crusaders, Inquisitors, and genocidal *conquistadores*, that turned good Baptists into screeching furies when schools in the American South were being integrated, and good German Catholics into voting Hitler into power, had twisted like a viper in Otie Bemis that day. The Vatican had excommunicated Communists for being Communists, but not Nazis for being Nazis. Many flavors of Chris-

273

tians were guilty of many centuries of gay-bashing. A spirituality able to coexist with so much evildoing was of no use to Pam. She had painfully missed the good side of the Baptists for a long time, but not anymore. For years and years, the sense of transcendent rightness about being Grounded at Hurt Hollow, of how she fit into the Hollow and how the Hollow fit into the web of the living Earth, had been enough.

But now, here was this new experience that neither science, nor biblical scholarship, nor history, nor Gaian mysticism, seemed to shed any useful light upon.

The subject of shamanism opened so widely and quickly into related fields of inquiry that Pam felt overwhelmed almost as soon as she'd scratched the surface. Her study at home stood layers deep in a wild collection of disks, books, and printouts. Several of Jung's works, including *Memories, Dreams, Reflections* and *Man (sic) and His (sic) Symbols.* Several of Swedenborg's brambly texts. *Synchronicity* and *Blackfoot Physics* and some other titles by an offbeat quantum physicist, F. David Peat. The *I Ching* in translations by Wilhelm and Baynes, Alfred Huang, and Stephen Karcher, and an encyclopedia of divination, also by Karcher. A treatise on *Feng Shui* from the Compass School perspective. *The Varieties of Religious Experience* by William James. Poetry collections by William Butler Yeats and James Merrill—two modern greats, the latter a particular favorite of Pam's—and the more obscure Vachel Lindsay, all of whom had written extensively about their experiences with what was customarily labeled "the occult." Books and assorted articles by literary critics *about* the occult experiences of Yeats and Merrill. Biographies of all three poets. Three books on lucid and precognitive dreaming by Robert Moss, a twentieth-century Euro-Australian who claimed to be a shaman. *Black Elk Speaks.* Robert A. Monroe's 1971 classic, *Journeys Out of the Body* and its sequels. Mircea Eliade's 75-year-old study *Shamanism*, still the bible referenced and reverenced by everybody who delved into the subject of its title. *The Ancient Science of Geomancy.*

Except for the works by and about the poets, and a couple of texts about quantum field theory, every bit of this was new to Pam.

Material directly concerned with shamanistic rock art, a field she had been ignorant of a mere month ago, had already overflowed the small bookcase Pam had emptied to receive it and piled up in ragged stacks on the floor. Most of the rock-art books were oversize, with color plates; they took up a lot of space. Apart from the Lascaux murals, rock art had seemingly never penetrated very far into the imagination of the general public; but like other arcane subjects this one clearly had its devotees whose interest bordered on obsession.

She read obsessively herself, sponging up lore like a blotter.

Pam was sitting cross-legged on the floor one afternoon, poring over a book of rock art photographs, when the phone rang. She stuck her finger in her place and scrambled up and into camera range. "Screen on."

It was Liam. They hadn't communicated since Santa Barbara, and the sight of him on the screen—paler, balder, thinner, *older*—made Pam realize with a small shock that in the weeks since Moab she'd scarcely given him a thought.

"Hi," he said wearily. "Busy?"

"Kind of, but that's okay."

"I just thought I'd look in. I've been having a bad time, Humphrey probably told you."

"He told me you and Gillian weren't, uh . . . together, that's all."

"Really? He didn't go into the gory details?"

"A lot's been going on out here, too. Has he filled you in on any of *that*?"

"Not really." Liam looked skeptical, as if he had a hard time believing that anybody else's gory details could possibly be as compelling as his own. (Pam felt a familiar flash of irritation.) "*All* the Hefn Observers are out here, all eighteen of them, Hefn I haven't laid eyes on in years, Jeffrey, Innisfrey, Saxifrey, Pomphrey—and old Godfrey, remember him? the one that put Nancy Sandford into cold storage till they found a cure for AIDS? She died last year, by the way, of something else entirely, something to do with her heart. She was around Carrie's age. Care to guess what the Observers are up to?"

"Trying to reconfigure the transceivers."

"Humphrey told you that, I thought he might've. I suppose he told you why."

He'd told her two versions of why, one genuine, one diversionary: to seek another way of seeing into the future, as backup for the approach Pam was taking; and to keep the Apprentices busy. Pam didn't want to have to steer a safe course between versions. "Listen, we do have a lot to catch up on, but we need to find a better time. Lexi gets home in less than an hour and I haven't even thought about dinner."

"She's *living* with you?"

"Since the kidnapping. You must've heard about *that*."

"After the tumult and the shouting died out here I did."

Clever clever Liam, to quote Kipling. Despite herself Pam felt something yield. She gave him a grudging smile—*No fair!*—and he grinned back sheepishly. "Well, okay, when do you want to talk? Tonight?"

"Actually," Liam said, "I thought maybe I might come out for a while. I mean, I was going to suggest that. That's why I was calling. If you don't have plans or anything."

"You mean—to Salt Lake?" Pam was nonplussed. Liam had never expressed the faintest desire to visit her here. Eddie would have put his big fat foot down had he even hinted at such a thing. So did that mean— "Have you and Eddie split up?"

"*Oh* yeah. I'll say we have. Gorily. Not that I blame him, after the Gillian fiasco." He actually looked ashamed for a moment, as well as woebegone. "So, what about it?"

"Well—when? When were you thinking of coming?"

"I thought, for our birthdays? A joint party, but split the difference?" They'd always had a joint party at the BTP, alternating between August 25 (Liam) one year and September 1 (Pam) the next.

Pam's gears whirred. "Look—let me call you back. That's pretty soon." The 25th was all of ten days away. "I need to look at the calendar and check with Jaime."

"Humphrey said you'd promoted Jaime and cut back on your days, so I thought . . ."

He knew more than he was owning up to. "I cut back because I had so much to do. But it still might work out, I just need to check. I'll call you back. What were you thinking, like, a week?"

"On that order. Long enough to catch each other up."

He meant something more serious than just catching up. Pam's defenses went up automatically—but if her own entire concept of reality had had all the wind knocked out of it since the Santa Barbara conference, maybe his had too. Maybe a visit was a good idea. Was it possible that something of their friendship could be salvaged? The Humphrey-bond, after all, which Pam had believed hopelessly damaged, had been reforged, in a way that was different but perhaps as powerful.

Suddenly, with a treacherous little flutter of hope, she *wanted* Liam to join her in this new reality, wanted to tell him what had been happening to her and hear what he thought about it. She even admitted to a prickle of curiosity about Gillian and Eddie. Before these stirrings could lead her to reveal too much, Pam said quickly, "I'll let you know tonight after Lexi's in bed. She has an early call, so . . . around eight my time?"

"Fine. Talk to you then."

~

After corn on the cob, tomatoes, and green beans, all picked fresh from the garden by Pam, after sliced peaches picked by Lexi who had climbed the Mormon peach tree one-handedly to get them, after the reading of the chapter from the first *Jungle Book* and Lexi's recitation of the Kipling poem of the week ("The Lullaby of the White Seal") from memory, Pam called Liam back to tell him he could come on the 24th.

Then she called Humphrey. "Liam's coming out for a visit," she said to his onscreen image.

"Indeed he is. At my suggestion."

"Really?" She was vexed to feel a small sag of disappointment that the visit hadn't been Liam's own idea.

"He had thought of a visit, but feared you would not care to see him. I suggested that this fear might be exaggerated and urged him to risk bringing the subject up with you."

Relief seemed to be as vexatious as disappointment. "Then you probably agree I should fill him in?"

"If *you* are so inclined, yes, I think that you and Liam should fill each other in, though you may wish him to understand that what you tell him cannot yet be shared with the other Apprentices. He will agree to that, I believe. Since the Independence Day conference he is feeling much anger and shame, he is feeling sadly apart from the others—apart from me also, regrettably—and Eddie Ward has shut him out as well." This Humphrey said deadpan, but Pam understood him perfectly. No more than Pam had Humphrey ever taken to the unctuous Eddie.

"Okay. But if I tell him, and he talks after promising not to—no lifting those memories, Humphrey! I don't mean you would, I'm just saying you mustn't. There mustn't be anymore of that now."

"Then do not then tell him the Ban is not to be revoked. That one thing."

"And if he asks me straight out?"

"Then you must lie straight out, if you do not wish his memory to be altered."

Liam would see straight through a lie; but these terms were clearly nonnegotiable. She nodded reluctantly. "Deal."

~

16 August 1937, Tuesday, SLC . Okay. Even allowing for the limits of what rock art and ivory carvings can communicate across the millennia, pre-Hefn-era anthropologists seem to pretty much agree that a lot of "primal" art, from Africa to Australia to the Americas to the Arctic, was meant to be a shamanistic record of supernatural experience—"the birdlike flight of the soul," as somebody puts it. Okay, I acknowledge that the pictographs Humphrey showed me in Moab and the rock art in these books, taken together, make an impressive case for my lucid dream being the same type of experience. Of course there's a lot of mystery about archaic art, you know almost nothing about the cultures and can't interview the shamans, but still, I'm impressed. More like wowed (some of the time).

That's the archaic stuff; there's also the work of Mircea Eliade, this big guru of cultural anthropology of the mid-twentieth century whose name I'd never heard in my life till now. He collected and catalogued huge amounts of info from every extant culture he could find that was still calling upon the services of the shaman. There were a lot more of 'em than you'd think, and those shamans could be interviewed, they were fine with that, they would talk quite matter-of-factly about flying to the moon, being transformed into animals, their spirit guides (walrus, narwhal, bear, seal, loon), and how they could leave their bodies whenever they liked and move back and forth across the boundaries between life and death, male and female, present and future.

And their cultures expressed shamanic experience in art, just like Barrier Canyon and Pecos River and the Aussie Aboriginals from the Dreamtime and the Chinese before King Wen. People working with Inuit groups found the exact same images in the carvings and drawings made by the people they were studying, as I've got here in front of me in these books of archaic rock art.

It's astonishing to me that the same sorts of images appear in art made by native peoples with no knowledge of one another, across thousands and thousands of years and miles, in deserts and the Arctic, in temperate forests and tropical ones—everywhere and everywhen! They appeared to Black Elk, the famous Lakota shaman, in a vision during a deathlike illness when he was nine years old in the late 1800s. The same images! Skeletonization, snakes, spirals, horns, feathers, flight, the number 7, the colors of the cardinal points, the world tree, the omphalos, and dozens more. How come nobody knows about this? Why didn't it make headlines when archeologists first put it all together? What does it mean?

Actually, as to that, there's a theory that shamanistic experience and art can be explained in terms of Jungian archetypes. My work with Julie has basically stuck to Freud and Murray Bowen; I knew almost nothing about Jung till now and his approach would have struck me as wackily irrelevant before the lucid dream. Before that, I would have had no patience with stuff like "spirit traveling," that's for damn sure. Doesn't mean Eliade's informants knew what their experiences "really" mean either, but I've got no choice but to be open to lots more possibilities than I would have been earlier. Lexi was *there*, in Green River.

According to these informants, a shaman was typically born to his calling—usually his, rarely hers. His early life, like Black Elk's, was often marked by trauma—critical illness, coma, seizures, being struck by lightning or bitten by a venomous snake. He might grow up to be a sickly adult. He might manifest gender or sexual deviance; and I read somewhere that one Eskimo shaman acquired great power after (shudder) having sex with his mother.

All of which makes me wonder, grumpily: why shouldn't Liam have to deal with this too (or instead)? He lost Jeff, plus his home and Ground, in the meltdown; he's been shot full of buckshot and mauled by a bear; he's gay, or at least bisexual. Seems to me he's got as many qualifications as me, if not more.

But no, he wallows in self-pity out in Santa Barbara while I sit here day after day with these books and disks, earnestly seeking to learn whether I've been called by some "power" to be a "shaman," and what that would mean if it turned out to be "true." How am I supposed to explain all this to Liam when he comes, or to any living person who's not a complete fruitcake, when a lot of the time it seems crazy even to me?

Only I keep coming back and back to the dream, superimposed on the picture of that Pecos River anthropomorph flying at the center of a flock of giant birds. Coincidence? Maybe so, but then what about what happened on the train? And round and round we go.

~

Pam's garage—now garden shed—had been built for one car but given a two-car-garage-sized roof, half for the garage and half to cover the concrete patio. Normally by late afternoon the patio was way too hot to sit on in August, but it had been sprinkling and a few clouds made all the difference. The three of them carried out trays—even Lexi, balancing hers on her cast—and took their tea on the patio. Lexi's bodyguard, a bulky young man with a shaved head, named Jack, had carried a lawn chair to the other side of the yard, to give them privacy. It was pleasant. The garden was bushy and full, beginning to decline a bit; the ducks, Sir Francis Drake and Winnie, who'd been prevented from raising a family this year, sat peacefully grooming themselves with their black bills in the muddy shade of their bathtub swimming pool.

In the morning Lexi was going on location for eleven days, so she had today off, and was showing off a little for Liam by performing her way through some of the Kipling poems she'd learned. Her presence was helpful to the adults, who might otherwise have been fencing warily with one another. Instead Pam listened with satisfaction and Liam with gratifying amazement as Lexi, the consummate professional, worked her way through the poems in the first third of *Puck of Pook's Hill*. "Mithras, God of the Morning," she was reciting now with reverent intensity, using her *Secret Garden* accent, "our trumpets waken the Wall! Rome is above the Nations, but Thou art over all!" She had Liam's complete attention. She finished the four stanzas, then sat forward and helped herself to another blueberry tart with her left hand, the hand sheathed in the cast.

"Wow," Liam said. "My cousin Carrie, my second cousin—she was older—used to read those poems to, uh, my sisters, and my friend and me." His stumbling over the allusion to Jeff alerted Pam to the probability that the wounds from the Gillian incident were still pretty tender. "We all learned them, a lot of them—I learned that one, actually—but I definitely never learned how to say it so you could downright smell the soldiers sweating."

Lexi grinned. Pam said, "She's a pro, remember. If you'd ever seen *A Thousand Miles* you'd be less wowed."

"He could see it tonight. Want to? It's a good episode, it's the one where I break my arm." Lexi's arm would come out of its lavender cast as soon as she got back, but on the show the ordeal was only about to begin and the fans could hardly wait.

"We'll all watch it, that's this evening's planned entertainment," Pam said, "but we need to get you all packed and ready for bed first. No malingering."

"No, I won't. Cool! I thought you might want to watch it later because, you know, you've got company." Her sliding glance at Liam held just a trace of resentment; Lexi still had bouts of being cling-ingly possessive of Pam.

"I want to see it with you, and so does the company," Pam said firmly. "He's in for a treat. What time is your dad picking you up?"

"Five. I'm already packed, pretty much. I have to do this all the time," she explained to Liam.

"If you're done with your tea, why don't you go get finished with that, and then take your shower and put on your PJs. Any special requests for dinner on the eve of your departure?"

"Deviled eggs and cole slaw!"

"That cabbage on Saturday was the last Savoy. Would you settle for beet salad?"

"Yuck." She made a face. "I know! Potato salad—no—*scalloped* potatoes!"

"Okay, I can handle that." It would heat the kitchen up, but oh well.

"And peach cobbler!"

"That too."

Lexi ran inside, Jack the bodyguard folded his newspaper and followed her, and Pam and Liam collected the trays and followed more slowly into the sanctuary of swamp-cooled air. Liam said quietly, "For a kid who's been through what that kid's been through, she seems to be pretty together."

Pam sent him a grateful look. "Thank God for *A Thousand Miles*! Everybody connected with the show has been absolutely terrific, that's the stable, supportive element in the picture and I think it's the reason she's doing as well as she is. You should have heard them all when it turned out she'd been abducted off the set! It's a Mormon show with a Mormon cast and crew, and Mormon money is paying for it, but they were behind Lexi one hundred percent and furious at the Church leadership for what happened. Also, her counselor is first-rate."

"Also," he said, "much to my surprise, you're not half bad at the mothering thing. Where'd you learn? Not from *your* mother."

"Probably from yours. Thanks, I'm kind of flying by the seat of my pants in that department, but so far so good, mostly. The hardest part is thinking up *meals* all the time. Could you wash this up while I start boiling and peeling?"

"Yeah, in a minute. I brought something for you, I want to get it."

Pam could hear him rummaging in his luggage in the guest room next to the kitchen. In a minute he was back with a paper-wrapped object, obviously a book. "It's from Carrie, I mean she left this to you. It's that book of old Swedish paintings, remember? The one Jenny Shepherd left to Carrie when *she* died? Terry brought it when he came out to Santa Barbara to sort out the, uh, Gillian incident."

Pam was surprised. "Gosh, it was nice of her to leave me something, I wouldn't have expected her to, but why that, I wonder? I barely remember flipping through it at the house."

"I think there's a note. I'll just put it on your bed, okay?"

When he reappeared, Liam started stacking cups and plates in the dishpan. He turned taps and swished to make soapsuds. "At this precise moment our smooth kitchen teamwork is reminding you of Hurt Hollow, am I correct?"

"As a matter of fact," Pam said, "you are. Maybe you've got the second sight too." She opened the icebox door and removed a tray of large, grayish eggs. "How many of these will you want? Never mind, I'll make it an even dozen and we can snack on them later if we like."

"Gray eggs? Oh—from the ducks. How come no little duckies?"

"Because when the little duckies get bigger you're supposed to kill and eat them. I tried that last summer. Never again." She got out a saucepan and ran some water in, rather self-consciously bumping elbows with Liam at the sink.

"I can see it would be a little confusing, rehabbing wild ducks with one hand and murdering tame ones with the other. So what's all this about the second sight?"

Impulsively she started to tell him. Not caring to mention the very earliest inklings in Santa Barbara, which involved him, she began with her certainty that the Church was behind the kidnapping. Lexi reappeared, damp and hungry, before she'd gotten very far, but after dinner, *A Thousand Miles*, *The Jungle Book*, the poem of the week, and the tactful disappearance of Jack to the upstairs sitting room next to Lexi's bedroom, where he was bunking, she took up the thread again.

It was two in the morning when she finished, exhausted with talk and emptied of her story. "Humphrey said I could tell you all this, but that you'd have to promise to keep it a secret from the others for now. Sorry, I should have told you that before I started."

"No worries." They were in Pam's study, surrounded by the books she had shown to Liam at various points in the narrative. He had listened attentively, without arguing or interrupting, but under the fatigue his face was a mask of skepticism. "Well. I guess that sheds some light on this 'future' mania of Humphrey's, anyway. I'm too tired to get into it tonight, but I gotta say, right now I kind of feel like you've fallen back into the Baptist baptistry and dragged Humphrey in there with you."

Pam snorted. "I don't blame you for thinking that, but *I* gotta say, if anybody dragged anybody, Humphrey dragged me. I'm just the one it happened to, he's the one that stuck the label on it all. I knew exactly zip about shamanism till I started reading all this stuff."

Liam waved his arm in a gesture that took in the heap of open books. "Well, obviously there's a lot to know, I mean it's a big subject with a lot of scholarship and so on, but it seems like something you study, not something you, like, do."

Pam stood up, groaning. "I've got to go to bed. I have to get up with Lexi in less than three hours."

"Listen," said Liam, "I don't want to be a bad guest, or seem like I'm insulting you or anything, but—remember that time you came to dinner at College Park, the very first time, and we talked on the train about your being a Baptist? I'm having this sense of déjà vu."

"*I've* actually been realizing," Pam said, "that if it weren't for the Baptists I wouldn't have any way at all of relating to all this, so you better hope it never happens to you, hot shot, but don't worry. I'm not insulted. Two months ago, if anybody'd told me such a cockamamie story I'd have looked at them exactly like you're looking at me right now. Oh, and Happy Birthday, by the way, you're thirty-nine."

~

Over brunch the next day it was Liam's turn to fill Pam in. "I behaved like such a jerk I can't believe it," he said at the end. "I can't stand to think about it. Eddie was perfectly right to dump me, it was never really him I cared about. It was never really *you*. It was never really Humphrey either, and he knows it, too. It's whoever reminds me of Jeff, it's always Jeff, that's the beginning and end of it all. A twelve-year-old boy! Thank God I never met a *boy* who looked and sang like Jeff, I'm scared to think what might have happened." He looked terrible, making this confession.

Pam had, of course, arrived at this conclusion back in Santa Barbara, and subsequent events had allowed the anguish to fade out of it. "Well, look," she said reasonably, "why not just admit to yourself that you'll never care about anybody else as much as you cared about Jeff, and then realize you've got a job to do anyway, and a life to invent, and just—get on with it."

"You say that like it's something I could like just up and decide to do," he said, irritated. "I thought about starting back with Julie again. Maybe she knows how a person could turn the best feelings he ever had into something as ugly as what I did to Gillian. Oh, shit, let's talk about something else." He got up and started to clear the table.

"No you don't, Birthday Boy," said Pam. "No working. I'll do that. You can sit back down and tell me what's been going on at the BTP these past couple of weeks. And then I thought we might take a little chopper trip. Humphrey's cleared me to use a chopper. It's going to be hot as blazes but we won't have to walk very far and it should be interesting. You up for that?"

"Where to? Walk where?"

"Up some canyons, to look at rock art sites. I've got pictures but there's a bunch of sites I think I should see for myself, since they're right here, and I picked out a couple to start with. But it's your day, if you don't want to spend it like that I can start next week."

He shrugged. "What else is there to do?"

"Visit Temple Square? Attend a rehearsal of the Mormon Tabernacle Choir? Drop in on a course Jaime's leading at the mission, for people learning to behave like stewards?"

Liam looked horrified. "Anything but that!"

"He does it with a better grace than I could. Be taken out to dinner at the Old Salt City Jail, a restaurant that used to be a prison, where they seat you in cells with iron bars?"

"Oh God. Fine, I'd love to see some rock art sites." Liam pulled out a kitchen chair and straddled it backwards, while Pam started clearing up. "Okay, the BTP: you know Humphrey's got all the other Hefn down here, trying to make some of the transceivers open windows in the future. All of a sudden the past is passé, it's now desperately important to know what lies ahead, but he won't say why."

"Same reason he wants me to *dream* the future for him, no doubt, and he won't tell me why either. What's he got the Apprentices doing?"

"Learning to make the field spin clockwise. Trying to, anyway."

"Hunh! Really!" Pam twisted round at the sink to look at him.

"Yeah." Liam kicked out of his chair and strolled to the window. "They've managed to get one transceiver adjusted so Sam and Walt can use it, kind of—nobody else can at all yet, I get a headache just thinking about it. Everything's ass-backwards. They get the shimmer all right, even I can do that, sometimes they can get the swirl to go clockwise, once in a while they even get into sync, which I guess is killingly difficult, and if they get that far the quincunx does provide coordinates. But neither of them has managed to sink a single number yet, and if they keep at it too long they start throwing up and passing out."

"Good grief!" Pam turned round again. "Why is anybody going along with this? Why are you? Did he threaten you?"

Liam shook his head. "No threats, no lies. Humphrey said straight out that he can't tell us why he's doing this and whoever doesn't trust him anymore can quit. So that was disarming," he said, "and the truth is, we're all pretty curious about whether it can be done. Everybody stayed, even Artie and Will. When push came to shove, I think we all pretty much realized there was no place else we wanted to be, given that it's the final year."

"Hunh." Pam grabbed a handful of silverware out of the rinse water and clattered it into the drainer. The diversionary tactic had worked well; but the Hefn were also dead serious about what they were attempting. "I always thought it was theoretically impossible to use the transceivers like that. Humphrey as good as said so."

"Well, now he's hoping he was wrong. If Time is One, theoretically the future should be as fixed as the past."

"I don't have a problem with *that*," Pam said. "I figure what I saw in my dream about Lexi *was* the fixed future. But using transceiver technology and retread Apprentices to try to see into it, I don't know. Maybe if you could start fresh with a batch of new kids." She put the last pan in the rack and dried her hands on a dishtowel.

"I was wondering last night by the way, after I went to bed, if you'd had any more of those lucid dreams."

She made a face. "Nope. Just fractals and flotsam—I thought the fractals might stop again, but they haven't—but no, the whole time I've been reading up on shamanism, no lucid dreams and no strange 'knowings' of the future. I've formed a kind of theory about it."

When she didn't elaborate, Liam said, "Which is?"

"Which is, that in the one dream I did have, I got information I needed really badly, so maybe that's how it works. The shaman's job is to help the community, that's what ecstatic trance is for, so they say. But no desperate need, no spontaneous shamanic flight." She hung the towel on a hook and dumped the water from the dishpan into a bucket. "Or, you *can* induce a trance with drugs or mortification of the flesh, but I haven't really wanted to go there till I've tried a lot of other things first." She hefted the bucket by the bail. "They say you can get a trance with drumming. I'm not much for drumming, but I recorded a couple of music loops, the second movement of Beethoven's Second and one of Bach's cantatas, pieces with really insistent rhythms, and tried those a couple times. Nothing happened though, I couldn't seem to get into it."

"What about a transceiver trance? You can get a trance now, right?"

Even the memory made her queasy. "That was terrible. That didn't work at all."

"Have you tried setting coordinates since this happened?"

"To look into the past?" Pam set the bucket back down. "You mean, now that I can predict the future, can I still use the transceivers in the old way? That's a good question. No, I haven't tried, and

Humphrey hasn't suggested it, he seems to be totally focussed on the road ahead nowadays."

She picked up the bucket and banged through the storm door, Liam trailing behind. The bone-dry heat slammed into them. "Whew," he said, "you sure about this rock-art-viewing caper?"

Pam was pouring the water slowly around the tomato and cuke stems. "We'll wait till the sun gets lower, it could be even hotter than this in the canyons right now." She finished and straightened up, and gazed with devotion upon her raised boxed beds and netted trellises, at the garden's foliage, lush and green despite the staggering heat. "You know the thing about shamanism that's almost the hardest for me to accept in a way? That it was the hunting cultures that expressed it so sort of stunningly in their art."

"So? Why's that a problem?"

"Well, because it seems that whenever a culture hit the Crux—i.e. at the exact cultural moment *we've* identified as the ideal human lifeway—their rock art started to go downhill. How weird is that? I mean, the art might still be very impressive, and aesthetically interesting and appealing and all that, but not . . . not like what I showed you pictures of last night. Haunting. Profound. Overwhelming."

Liam took her point, but not its import. He gestured toward Pam's trained thickets of stalks and vines. "You mean, the Gaian model—this—doesn't produce the most powerful art? Art's not the be-all and end-all, surely."

She gave him a wry look. "Hunh. You've never been religious."

"What's that got to do with it?"

They wandered back inside. "Something, I'm not sure what. I only realized this a few days ago, but it's been bothering me."

~

It made sense to Pam that the religious practice of sedentary people living chiefly by farming (Cain) and herding (Abel) would differ from that of people who lived chiefly by killing game. It made sense that, as society stratified and religion moved indoors, people would come to depend more on a priest class, and less on the unique abilities of a singular individual—one of themselves, yet different—who could leave his body and enter the spirit world on their behalf (supposing for the sake of argument that he could really do that). A tamer lifeway would require a tamer religion.

Still. As Pam had explained to Lexi, months before, the Gaian movement had been grounded from the start in a conviction that homesteading, a lifeway transitional *between* hunting and farming, represented the ideal way for people to live on the Earth. They based this conviction on things the Apprentices had observed by looking back in time; and they based it on the "life on the fringe of society" modeled by Orrin and Hannah Hubbell, seventy years before, at Hurt Hollow. Not many modern humans could actually live a homesteading life, of course, but the Hollow remained the perfected model, the ideal.

Orrin himself had idealized not the garden plots of the Shawnees and Cherokees, which much resembled his own, but the small, diversified farms he had known as a boy in Kentucky. He wrote that they represented to him "the life of man in harmony with nature; a brief flowering between the primeval wilderness that was gone and the urban blight that was to come." Orrin and these farmers both aimed at self-sufficiency. The only important difference was that the farmers grew more than their families consumed and sent the surplus to market, but both systems were sustainable in a sense the Hefn approved of.

Orrin was an artist whose rural paintings and riverscapes glowed from within, as if by lamplight, with a reverent love for his subject. Not only his paintings but everything he had turned his hand to, from woodcuts to cutting wood, revealed this deep spirituality. Orrin's work was wonderful to Pam, full of loveliness—but not haunting or awe-inspiring, not shamanistic. Good, very good even, but not great.

What did it imply for the Gaian Mission that religious art—an art more profound than Orrin's by any standard—had arisen within cultures that had lived by predation and a little seasonal browsing, in "the primeval wilderness that was gone"? Pam, a gardener-poet who had vowed never to kill another duck, wanted the "best" way to live on Earth to produce the best, or at least the most transcendent, art. That it didn't was disturbing; at some fundamental level it seemed to call the Gaian lifeway into question.

Lying on her bed now, sandals off, arms folded behind her head, ceiling fan twirling—she and Liam had separated to nap away the hottest part of the afternoon—Pam felt her brain click a notch forward. She grasped that the difference between Orrin's paintings and those of the Barrier Canyon Style artists could be simply put. Orrin's work was about human innocence in a benevolent landscape. The Barrier Canyon and Pecos River Style pictographs were about animals and fear. Fear of what? Not of the animals, certainly. Of something terrible and great.

The achievement of these artists in expressing their awe mixed with dread . . . was what imbued the *art* with greatness?

Uncomfortable with this insight, Pam flipped over and wrapped her arms around her other pillow. Take the other extreme of "urban blight," then. Orrin was too honest to deny the greatness of the religious art high civilizations had given rise to. He'd probably never tried to reconcile his rejection of the one with his genuine appreciation of the other; for all his contemplativeness, Orrin hadn't really been an intellectual, or terribly widely informed. It was unlikely he had ever tried to work out the contradictions.

Pam, however, felt compelled to try. Take some easy examples from the Renaissance: Michelangelo and Leonardo. Paintings, frescoes, sculptures. The greatness was obvious. Where was the fear? You would say nowhere, and yet . . . could you look at a painting of the Madonna and infant Christ without shrinking from what you knew was going to happen to them? The David seemed a wholly positive statement, and yet you knew the story, you knew Bathsheba and Absalom were lurking in the shadowy future. More to the point, Michelangelo knew.

Maybe the greatness was just there, in the fearful tension between the immediate impact of the sculpture and what you knew about the subject? Or was that nonsense? How could a complete Bible ignoramus fail to respond to the perfection of the David? How could calling a statue "David" alter its impact as an image of the idealized human form?

Take a harder example, then: Breughel. Some of Breughel's work was religious; all of it was scary, even repugnant. This was helpful; it showed Pam her mistake and her mind clicked forward another notch. *Not all religious art is great, but all great art is "religious."*

So where does fear come in?

As she thrashed onto her other side, Pam's eye lit on the package from Carrie, still unopened, on the bedside table where she had put it before falling into bed the night before. She reached for it and pulled off the string and paper. Inside was the big thin book, faintly remembered, full of early nineteenth-century Swedish cottage murals. Inside the front cover she found an unsealed envelope with *Pam* scrawled across it in Carrie's shaky old-lady handwriting. The note inside said, "You are the one person I know who is familiar with the stories these pictures are about. I hope you can think of somebody to pass it on to when your own time comes. Carrie."

Pam rolled onto her back and rested the book on her breastbone to leaf through it. The pictures were biblical scenes showing Elijah, Joseph, the Three Wise Men, etc. in Swedish peasant dress. She hadn't remembered the murals as being particularly interesting; now she saw that they had both quality and charm. The pages were crammed with vigor and color, green foliage, yellow pinafores and houses, blue uniform jackets, red rosettes, brown frocks, with big, curly designs spilling into all the empty spaces. Fear was altogether absent. A fine example of Gaian-model folk art, flowering cheerfully in its placetime between Barrier Canyon and the Sistine Chapel.

Orrin's idea of Kentucky smallholder life had been narrowly formed out of what the Ohio Valley had been like around 1700 when Europeans first entered the area, and what they'd been doing with the land ever since. Almost certainly he was unaware of what Pam's recent total-immersion study of prehistoric Indian art had revealed to her, that long before the "pristine wilderness" stage alluded to by Orrin, a phenomenal Native American civilization had flourished for three or four centuries in the Ohio Valley, not far at all from Hurt Hollow. Archeologists called these people the Ohio Hopewell. In every cultural way the Hopewell fell outside the sphere of Pam's research, but because they were "local" to her personal Ground she'd been curious about them, and what she'd learned was fascinating.

Pam had already been somewhat familiar with the Indians living in the Ohio Valley at the time of European contact: Shawnees, Delawares, Miamis, all following a hunting/foraging/corn-beans-squash lifeway close to the Gaian model. Their art was utilitarian, to the extent that it could properly be called art at all.

Pam closed the book of cottage murals, laid it back on the table, and picked up her YellowPad; she'd made some notes on the Hopewell, thinking to come back to them someday if there was ever time in her personal future for anything besides shamanism. Now she piled pillows against the headboard, pushed herself upright, and clicked the YellowPad on.

8/2/37 Ohio Hopewell 500 bc?-500 ad?, heyday +/-100 bc-200 ad
        centered in S Ohio bet Miami & Muskingum Rs (tribs of Ohio R)
        (towns: Chillicothe, Newark, Ft Ancient; C & N connected by Gt
        Hopewell Rd (cf Chaco, Nazca, preclassical Maya)—astronomy,
            geometry
        (how far from Hurt H by river in ad 100?—ck map)
        —mound builders (cf Adena—earlier & less stupendously
            skilled but centered in same area—Hot Spot? ask L to
            ck (nb Tecumseh born there too, near Lt Miami R!)
        —artwork excavated from OH burial mounds reflects web of
            trade routes from Rockies to FL panhandle (cf Chaco)
        —raw materials brought back from trading expeds (copper,
            mica, volcanic glass, silver, shells, grizzly teeth,
            metoeritic iron, obsidian) —> objects & ornaments of
            phenomenal beauty by H artisans
        —pottery & effigy pipes made from local clay and pipestone
            also v fine
        —amassed freshwater pearls by 1000 Ks
        ALL FOR GRAVE GOODS to send high-ranking dead into
            afterlife laden w/ wealth (cf Egyptians)

Judging by the color plates Pam had studied, Ohio Hopewell art wasn't eerie or awesome, apart from its sheer opulence; but to lavish so much effort on objects not made to be used or admired but to be buried brand-new under a thirty-foot mound of earth—the very idea had a dreadfulness to it. The ancient Egyptians, of course, had done much the same thing. But these were American Indians, who'd fanatically practiced their morbid religion two thousand years, but not more than two hundred miles by river, from the placetime where Pam had grown up and the Hot Spot where Orrin had carried out his experiment in living. They were "hers" by right of land.

You could see instantly that Hopewell society was sharply divided by class. To produce artifacts for so many thousands of burials would need an army of people working continuously, but only a small elite got the full treatment, the engraved copper breastplates and heaps of pearls and the rest. Who would have made up the elite? Kings. Priests. Important artisans? If so, that could explain why what they made reflected no awe or dread. Probably also the geometry-wielding engineers and astronomers who directed the construction of the immense geometric earthworks and the embanked causeway called the Great Hopewell Road, stretching straight as a ruled line for sixty miles to link Newark and Chillicothe, the two major astronomical centers of Ohio Hopewell culture.

All very well for the elite; but what did the workers who kept all this going expect of the afterlife? Did they have a stake in their death-obsessed society's goals, or were they afraid all their lives of dying destitute into an existence where wealth was all-important?

—centers prob ceremonial like Anasazi Chaco, w/ people living in ag
    villages—maize found in middens but v few village sites
    located; but wealth on this scale imposs to support w/o ag
—OH declined ca 450, cause unknown—sources suggest same list as
    for Anasazi & Fremont ca 1350:
        climate change —> crop failures—> famine, disease
        internal conflict (worker uprising?)
        invasion (Ft A one of several forts suggesting outside threat)
—ask Hump abt transceiver to rule out last 2? (not anytime soon!)

Cultural decline wasn't the kind of thing a transceiver could readily explain in any case, unless the language could be identified as belonging to a known group. The end, absent a slave uprising or a conquest, usually came too gradually. Pam thought the Hopewell, like other highly civilized prehistoric peoples, had most likely worn, hunted, and fished out their land. All those mouths to feed, all those people furiously engaged in non-food-producing work. That type of lifeway always proved unsustainable in the end, whatever other factors combined to bring a culture down.

The highest expression of Ohio Hopewell was not in the artifacts, though—stunning as they were—but in the burials themselves, the bodies having to be prepared just so and heaped just so with treasure, then fixed forever under tons of earth. You were safe only once everything had been done correctly, and that's where the anxiety came in.

Pam had never heard of the Ohio Hopewell before this recent

spate of research had turned them up. She was positive Orrin Hubbell had never heard of them either. The complex of Hopewell ceremonial centers and settlements probably wouldn't count with him as "urban blight" exactly, but he would surely have despised Hopewell values as demonstrating an urban type of decadence.

Pam's head was pounding. With a snort of exasperation she switched off the YellowPad, swung her legs over the side of the bed, and stared out the window at her apricot tree, massaging the back of her neck with one hand.

The best way to live on Gaia was not the best way for the human species to maximize its creativity or its standard of living—that much had been obvious long before the Hefn came. But this line of thought suggested something new: that the best way to give creativity free rein was to live in healthy terror of whatever had the power to kill you.

Reframe the Gaian message, then. Say that between the very real fear of starving in a harsh landscape redolent with power ("primeval wilderness"), and the existential terrors and angst of civilized tyranny ("urban blight"), there had occurred brief intervals in the human saga worldwide when existential fear had abated. A big-game-hunting people learned to grow crops, pen up a few goats or turkeys, clump together in villages, and for a little while life got less uncertain. And then, starting from a base of village life, the slow, inevitable ascent of kings and armies of conquest, powerful priests, hoarded wealth, slave labor, ritual sacrifice, works of monumental construction—and in a few years or a thousand the swollen population had worn out the place it had lived into, and fearful uncertainty had long since returned to the people, though in a different form.

So why, the Hefn had wondered with increasing frustration as the years dragged by, does humanity refuse to accept the homesteading model as a permanent lifeway, since everyone knows what happens whenever they advance beyond it? Why does an intelligent species cling to its freedom to make money and satisfy its curiosity and creativity, while its world runs out of air and water?

Because we're wired that way! Pam answered them in her mind. *Because we never believe we can't have the apple and the garden both! Because even if we can't, Gaians are the only ones willing to stay inside forever, finger-painting like children on the garden wall!* She stood with a sharp movement, got socks and boots from her closet and sat in a chair to pull them on.

Really, those farmers of Orrin's, of the "brief flowering," weren't all that innocent when you came right down to it. The Kentucky smallholders of Orrin's boyhood, over a century ago, may have lived decently upon the land—less decently than the native people their ancestors had displaced, but decently enough. But country people were racist to the bone in those days just before World War I. Rural northern Kentucky was Otie Bemis country. The Klan had been active there. The farmers' sons went off to fight in France and came home bedazzled for keeps by city lights. Most of the innocence in Orrin's art was simply personal, as he partly knew himself.

CHAPTER 12

Psychopomp

8 AUGUST - 5 SEPTEMBER 2037

L iam was positive he had never been this hot in his life. The canyon was a bone-dry sauna, turning his lungs to leather with every breath he drew. "'Mithras, God of the Noontide,' he intoned, 'the heather swims in the heat, Our helmets scorch our foreheads, our sandals burn our feet.'"

They were wearing broad-brimmed canvas hats and low hikers but Pam said with compunction, "Want to go back? It *is* your birthday."

But he didn't really, he just couldn't resist yanking her chain a little. "No, no, I'm only messing with your mind. I'm curious to see what you're up to here. Scout's honor." Then he started to mutter, in time with their pacing, "We're foot—slog—slog—slog—sloggin' over Africa, Foot—foot—foot—foot—sloggin' over Africa, Boots—boots—boots—boots—movin' up and down again—"

Pam groaned and Liam shot her an evil grin; he knew she didn't much care for the Barrack-Room Ballads, and this one was just too perfect. He continued to chant as they walked, mostly to provoke her, and for the birthday's sake she held her peace—plotting her revenge though, he figured; the boot would be on the other foot in five days' time.

The helicopter had set them down on a wide road of sand near the confluence of two rivers they'd spotted from the air coming down. The road hadn't been driven on by wheeled vehicles in a long time, and was marked by erosion, horseshoe and mule deer tracks, and tufts of grass, but you could tell it had been made by people. The wash it transsected had just as obviously formed naturally, through the action of water. Liam imagined a wall of water—runoff from the surrounding mountains—flash-flooding down the wash after a summer thunderstorm; it was as hard to visualize as water flowing in the dry red riverbeds on the surface of Mars. There was no water at all in the wash now, only sand mixed with clay that had hardened in places to a texture like smooth concrete. It made a fairly firm walking surface, but they were heading up the wash and the canyon floor radiated heat like the open door of an oven.

Pam was taking a long guzzle from the tube of her backpack canteen. "Keep drinking, every few minutes," she ordered over his barrack-room drone, "you get dehydrated in no time out here. The desert will suck you dry."

Liam complied, and decided to knock off the Kipling for now. "Okay, tell me what we're going up here to see. Who were these people anyway?"

"The ones who made the pictographs were the Barrier Canyon Style people, the ones who painted the Great Gallery—remember, I showed you last night. Hunter-gatherers. There are said to be ruins in the shelter where the panel is, Anasazi with an older culture underneath, no pottery in the lower stratum so probably BCS, but you can't get up there anyway nowadays. Look, there's a lizard!"

The lizard darted across the wash and disappeared under a pile of rocks. Liam said, "What's so special about this one panel?"

"Just a feeling. Plus, it's not that far. I didn't want to have to hike very far when it's this hot."

"So as not to embarrass the desert tenderfoot?"

Pam smiled. "That might have been a small consideration, but it's mighty hot for me too. I was just thinking, though, it's nicer than I expected, having you along. Do you realize how many hundreds of miles of trail you and I have hiked up and down together over the years?"

"Mm. Now that you mention it." *But not Life's Trail*, he thought, *we never quite got the knack of that.* He started to say so aloud, a knee-jerk defense against the flicker of wistfulness in Pam's voice, but shrank at the last instant from sounding sardonic. Anyway, he was pleased she liked his being along. So he only said, "This one beats the lot for hot and dry. I almost think I'd rather take my chances with the Kaiser Trail."

"Why choose?" Pam said lightly. "You won't see a sky this blue from the Kaiser Trail. Praise Gaia's variety!"

He pulled off his sunglasses and squinted up. "Righty-o, I concede the sky. Do we need more sunblock or is it late enough now?"

"Late enough for me. If Lexi were here I might put some on her."

"So—these Barrier Canyon people were Indians?"

"Who else was here three to six thousand years ago?" Pam snorted suddenly. "Did you know the Mormons call the Indians Lamanites—rhymes with 'ammonites'"—Liam grinned—"and believe they're descended from the Lost Tribes of Israel?"

"I didn't even know there *were* any Lost Tribes of Israel. How'd they get lost?"

Onward and upward they marched, chatting about this and that, sucking water. The wash was wide as a highway and almost as flat, but fairly shallow, its sides formed by great slabs and shelves of red or white sandstone exposed by ancient flash floods, and fringed with some small, skimpy kind of tree, maybe cottonwood. Runnel tracks cut through the hard, sandy, boulder-strewn bottom.

Soon enough though, conversation wilted in the helmet-melting heat. To Liam, baking in sunlight, the land seemed harsh and unlovely. He began to want to get the hike over with and get back to Salt Lake.

Right about then Pam slowed down. "We go left here, the alcove we want is up this way, see?" She held the map so he could look.

"Never mind, I believe you. How much farther?"

"Not very, but you're welcome to wait here for me if you like, in the shade."

There *was* a pool of shade, formed in the lee of a giant boulder by the lowering sun. It looked wonderful. Liam returned her smirk with a look both dirty and determined. "Just get on with it, boss woman."

They turned into a tributary wash, much narrower and sandier, with steeper sides. The footing became more difficult at once, but as they ascended the terrain also grew less barren and they started to see more shrubs and trees. "More water up here, looks like," Pam remarked. "In spring this might be pretty green." The red walls of the little canyon began to rise above its red floor into interesting shapes against that blue, blue sky. Liam felt a little interest kindle within the aura of his discomfort.

Then the canyon curved left and ended abruptly in a tall amphitheater of red and white stone, and they had arrived. Pam dropped her pack into the shadow of a tree, and then herself. "Whew!" She poured some canteen water into a bandanna and mopped her face and hands with it, then wetted it again and handed it to Liam, who'd settled thankfully into the shade beside her.

This was a box canyon; rain would collect here and be channeled down the tributary to the main wash. To himself Liam admitted that in a rough and rocky way this was a beautiful place. The canyon walls had collapsed repeatedly and the terrain was a tumble of boulders, a red field here, a white one there, the several waterfalls of rock pulled together by dusty vegetation. High on the wall opposite was a cave mouth like a long horizontal oval; that would be where the paintings were. As they sat puffing and fanning themselves with their hats, a green hummingbird buzzed over to check them out. The tiny thing's absolute fearlessness was comical; Liam felt himself grinning. Without taking her eyes off the indignant bird—"I think that's a black-chinned but I can't tell 'em apart for sure, boy is he mad!"—Pam pulled two packets of dried peaches and apricots out of her pack and handed one to him—"Mine, from last year. They're chewy but they're good." At that moment, with brief fanfare, the sun dropped behind the canyon wall and the air became instantly cooler.

Chewy they were, but the home-dried peaches exploded with sweetness in Liam's mouth. He sucked on his drinking tube and realized with faint surprise that he was enjoying himself now, happy to be sitting there, glad again that he had come. The hummingbird whirred away. "So," he said quietly, careful lest he jostle this fragile happiness, "what are we looking for?"

"The panel's on the roof of that rock shelter." She pulled a large pair of binoculars out of her pack. "They say it's impossible to climb up there now without equipment or a ladder, and there was no way I was gonna lug extra weight in here today, but we should be able to see the pictographs with these things. It's two small red figures grouped to the right of another figure. My directions say to climb up higher and sight straight across, into the alcove."

They stood up, and were in sunlight again. Pam went scrambling up the slope behind where they'd been sitting, with Liam at her heels. While she fiddled with the binoculars he stared at the cave opposite, a big empty eye socket eighty feet above the canyon floor, near the top of the cliff. The rock around the opening was white and smooth, like bone, but streaks of some black mineral had stained the rounded brow ridge above and run down unevenly into the socket itself. "There they are!" Pam said suddenly. She stared raptly, immobilized by concentration, and Liam seized the chance to fall back a bit, slip his camera out of his pocket and take a couple of quick pictures to surprise her with later.

But then she went on staring so long that he got bored. He was on the verge of breaking her trance of concentration, when just then she lowered the binoculars and held them out to him. "Here. Up on the roof, a little bit right of center."

Liam lifted the glasses and looked through them. The cave leaped toward him across the canyon; he could see inside. He swept across the cave roof impatiently, frowning, not seeing a thing; and then, scanning back more slowly, the powerful binoculars found the panel: three small, dark-red figures, cartoonish in their simplicity, painted on the surface of the white rock.

His finger pushed the focus wheel; the image sharpened. The figure farthest right, a tall attenuated human form in profile, stretched thin curved arms upward toward an animal form, shorter but much bulkier, standing in three-quarter profile close to and facing the backward-leaning human, its stubby forelimbs slightly extended toward him. Immediately behind the animal, two wavy parallel lines formed a vertical barrier between this intimate pair and a still smaller upright animal, also in profile, also with front legs extended. Its legs were slightly bent; from how they were jointed you could tell that the figure was an animal and not a child. Below its torso, a piece of rock had broken away and this animal's lower body and part of the wavy barrier were gone.

The panel socked Liam in the stomach like a fist, seized and suffused him. Words were forced out of him along with all his breath: "*Mine enemy Adam-zad!*" He understood instantly that the human on the right was himself, that the heavy animal was the bear that had attacked him on the Kaiser Trail in far-off New Jersey two decades before, and that the little animal beyond the wavy barrier was Jeff. The Liam-figure held out his arms and leaned away in an effort to ward off the bear, but Jeff's were lifted in supplication: *Come on! Let him send you through, so we can be together!*

Things blurred then. He had flung the binoculars away and himself to the bottom of the slope, half-sliding, half-falling, scraping his hands and bare knees on rocks he couldn't feel. Faintly he heard Pam yelling, but the only thing he knew was that he had to get up there, had to climb up the red rubblefall into the cave. There came a confused interval of struggle, being swept backwards in a hail of loose rock, fighting to climb, backsliding, fighting with Pam, pain, exhaustion, and at the end his own voice cracking, sobbing, screaming, "Why did you save me? Why didn't you let him kill me? I could have died, I could have died, why didn't you let me *die!*"

~

Keeping it light, Pam said, "If you'd busted these binoculars you'da been on my shit list for keeps."

Liam lay on the couch in her living room. He looked awful but had finally calmed down and become able to talk rationally about the rock art panel, what he'd thought it was telling him. Pam had called the chopper in to airlift them both, Liam still ranting, out of the box canyon. The pilot had radioed ahead; a medical team had been waiting on the helipad. And now, with Liam tranquilized and whitely bandaged, they were back at Pam's.

"I'm sorry. I don't remember dropping them. I must've just wigged out completely. I had no idea I was that close to the edge."

"Maybe it was heatstroke."

She knew better, but it made Liam give a little twitch of a smile. "Yeah, I wish. All I know is, I saw that panel and it was like some incredible Rorschach blot event, I knew that was our bear, and I knew it had been sent to bring me to Jeff, if only you hadn't butted in and spoiled everything—I *knew*, like in one bright flash of complete clarity."

He hadn't said that before, about her butting in. Pam, sitting backwards in Humphrey's Hefn chair, which she'd pulled over next to the couch, rested her chin on her folded arms and tried, unsuccessfully, not to let the words stab into her. "So ever since, you've unconsciously borne me a grudge for saving your life?"

"Maybe so." After a while he added, "I thought I'd worked out that suicide thing *years* before that, with Julie and Humphrey, but . . . I dunno, maybe this goddam Gillian mess stirred it up again. Or something."

Pam sat. It sank in, and sank in deeper, that Liam wished she hadn't saved him from the bear. Difficult to wrap the mind around this thought. There seemed to be nothing to say. She was trying to summon the energy to go to bed when a picture flashed in the gloomy blank of her mind.

Hm. Kind of risky, but— "Well, it's still your birthday for— another 87 minutes, even if you'd rather be dead, and I've got a cake in the freezer. How about it?"

"I don't think I could possibly choke any down. I thought we were splitting the difference."

Out of the blue, fury flared up in Pam, catapulted her out of her chair. "Liam. This visit was your idea, I agreed to it in spite of reservations, all of which look like being entirely justified. I am now going to make some tea and defrost that cake, and we're both going to eat some of it, and then you're going to unwrap your presents, and after that I don't care what the fuck you do."

She turned her back on his white startled face and stalked stiffly out of the room, into the kitchen. Fill the teakettle, plug it in. Teapot on tray, cups and saucers, two plates, two forks, two napkins. Take out the cake, shove it in the microwave, set the controls. She was seething with rage, so much so that in the end she banged through the storm door and stepped out on the back porch, gripping the metal railing, struggling to calm down. She drew in and expelled several deep breaths. The night air, cool at last, flowed into and around her.

The outburst had nothing to do with birthday cake. She was furious because Liam blamed her—had always blamed her!—for risking her own life to save his, and succeeding. This blame was not calculated; it was how he truly felt at the bottom of his soul. You could demand civil behavior from people, but not that they could change how they truly felt. Old Edgar Young, to take an extreme example—his crime wasn't lusting after Lexi, it was molesting Lexi. For incestuous feelings you got therapy; for incest you got jail (and maybe mindwipe).

Pam's own true feelings right now might be fury and devastation, but Liam was the proximal cause, not the culprit. Did she really believe that? Yes, goddammit, she did.

When she came back inside he was standing awkwardly between the fridge and the counter. "Can I help?" he said contritely. "I'm sorry, I honestly thought the plan was to split the difference on the birthdays."

Without meeting his eyes, Pam said "It was. I switched it without telling you. I'm the one who should apologize, I'm sorry I blew up."

"I guess we're both pretty upset."

Now she could look at him. "If you can pour some milk and take the tray in, I'll bring everything else in a minute."

He went off, balancing the tray between his bandaged hands, while her own hands flew about in the complex dance of tea-brewing. As she popped the cozy on the pot, the microwave pinged and she took out the sheet cake, a white rectangle, thawed but with icing unmelted: perfectly timed. She had baked and—with one of her rock art books propped against the toaster—decorated it herself. She had filled a paper cone with icing to which a lot of red food coloring had been added, and copied the picture of man and bear, wavy lines and zoomorph, onto the top.

This sort of thing was not Pam's strong suit, but the cake had come out pretty well. She'd frozen it for the joint celebration on August 28 or 29, but had had a clear hunch that serving up this image of the trauma done in sugar now, tonight, was the right move exactly. All the same she wanted Liam to be sitting down when he saw it.

She framed the panel in birthday candles, seven above, seven below, twelve on each long side, and stuck the thirty-ninth candle between the forepaws or hoofs of the little zoomorph that Liam in his wigged-out state had taken to be Jeff, to indicate that Jeff was in Heaven, beyond the wavy lines separating Heaven from the realm of mortal boys and bears. Then she lit the candles, using five matches.

Lifting the blazing pictograph with great care, she bore it into the living room.

~

A little after midnight Pam mounted the stairs to Lexi's room, her arms full of stuff she would need—toothbrush, towel and washcloth, sleepshirt, robe, shampoo. For the rest of Liam's visit she planned to bunk up here, so the two of them wouldn't have to share a bathroom or wake each other up prowling around.

She was also bringing up her music loops and the player. That telegraphed mental message about the cake, which had worked out so successfully and saved the near-disastrous birthday, had given her an idea. She wanted to see what would happen if she tried a little trance-inducing music before falling asleep. Or, more likely, actually fell asleep to the endlessly repeating rhythms of Bach or Beethoven.

Which loop? Brushing her teeth, she pictured Liam's face when he saw the cake. Whew. One of the best things about Liam had always been his ability to see the funny side, or at least the comical irony, of his own high dramatics. After one startled instant when she set it down in front of him, he had burst into delighted laughter, and rocked and snorted till they both were flushed with crazy hilarity. He got it instantly about the one candle, the only one he failed to blow out in fact; and when Pam said, "Aw, you don't get your wish, too bad," he answered. "We knew that anyway, didn't we?" with normal, familiar, Liamesque irony.

Indeed, while they were deciding who was going to eat which part of the pictograph, somewhere in there, she realized that things had come back into balance, that the revelations from the day's events had sunk from sight beneath the sediment of their shared need to get it out from between them.

Liam chose the bulky zoomorph, excising it neatly from the middle of the cake himself despite his bandaged hands. "Make ye no truce with Adam-zad—the Bear that walks like a Man," he growled, and drove in his fork. Pam ate Liam, with relish: "Matun, the old blind beggar, bandaged from brow to chin." Too bad not to have taken a picture of the uncut cake with Liam's camera, but by the time they'd thought of that it was too late.

Pam dried her face, shucked and hung her clothes on a hook behind the bathroom door—freeing her breasts at last from their sweat-stiffened bra—and went into Lexi's yellow bedroom. She pulled the sleepshirt over her head. Which loop? She went with alphabetical, and slipped in the Chorus of Bach's Cantata 104. The choral parts had been scored for recorders, clarinet, and oboe, and the retard at the end had been eliminated, producing one smooth rocking cycle of sound. She started the player, threw both windows open to the cool night air, flipped off the light, and fell into bed exhausted.

Too exhausted to sleep, or too keyed up. Pam thrashed around in Lexi's narrow bed, trying to get comfortable. The music wove its textured beauty against a base in 3/4 time, restful and regular as a rocking chair, but nothing happened. After a long time she craned around to check the bedside clock: 2:17.

Maybe not sleeping in her own bed was a bad idea. *If I'm still awake at 2:30 I'll take a pill and go back downstairs*, she promised herself.

She flopped down on her back. The player could stay up here when she went down; tonight it was no help as a sleep *or* trance inducer. Struggling to pull the twisted sheet straight, she yielded at last to an impulse and started to sing with the music, very softly, so Liam wouldn't hear. "*Erscheine*," she sang many times, "*erscheine, erscheine, erscheine*," three-one-two three-one-two, switching at whim between the soprano and alto lines, and finally something else to sing, "*erscheine, der du sitzest über Cherubim*."

That was how the Chorus ended, but of course the player went instantly back to the beginning without a break. *One more time through, then I can look at the clock.* She let the music rock her through the first bars toward when it was time for voices to come in, drew a breath, and made a three-point landing on the first alto note. At that moment she noticed a point of light in the room. Her voice continued automatically, "*Du, hi-i-i-i-irte Israel.*" A third above her, another voice had taken the soprano part.

Had she waked up Liam after all? Liam couldn't sing that high. Liam didn't know any Bach. "*Du hirte Israel, höre,*" she sang, hearing the other voice soar above her own.

Singing, she moved and sat on the side of the bed. The point of light floated in absolute blackness. When the fugue began with the oboe solo, she and the other voice dropped out and the light came nearer. It was the flame of a candle in a silver candlestick, a beeswax candle whose mellow light spilled across the rough brown shoulders and huge shaggy head of the bear, and lit from below the face of the young boy standing beside him, one arm thrown round his massive neck, like Mowgli and Baloo in the old Disney movie that Pam held in such contempt for how it trivialized Kipling's stories. But this boy, dressed formally in gray slacks and burgundy blazer and black tie, candlestick in hand, wasn't Mowgli. This boy, unmistakably, was Terry's long-dead son, Gillian Jacoby's look-alike dead brother, the love of Liam's life and—in one sense at least—the nemesis of Pam's.

Now came the moment for Pam to reinsert herself into the musical web. By now she knew; but Jeff gave her a nod that said *Go on,* and so she did; and Jeff came after and soared above. Candlelight filled the room now, the bear stood planted on all fours, filling the room a different way. The chorus ended and did not begin again.

They looked at each other. Jeff was grinning. Pam said, "It worked. I'm having another lucid dream."

"Hey, you called me, right? '*Erscheine, der du sitzest über Cherubim.*'"

The line meant something like *Thou that rulest over the cherubim, appear! Erscheine* was "appear." She had called him again and again. "So," she said, "you're in Heaven, then?"

He patted the bear's shoulder. "This is Adam-zad, obviously. He got to be a nuisance bear, hanging around campsites, and they didn't have the staff to relocate him so they had to shoot him."

Pam's head felt clear as a bell. This was the bear from the Kaiser Trail, right here in Lexi's room, check. This was the near-sainted Jeff Carpenter, check. And this was her second lucid dream. Check and mate.

She needed to ask questions, she might wake up any second! "Am I a shaman?"

Under the flop of black hair his grin got wider. "Do people usually see bears in their bedroom?"

"Well—what am I supposed to do?"

A shrug. He didn't go in for straight answers. Worried about waking, she rushed on: "What about Liam then?"

Jeff took his arm from around the bear's neck and shifted the candle to his other hand. "Gillian's preggers."

What? Impossible. "How can that *be*?"

"She'll think it's her boyfriend's baby but it's our Liam's. A girl. Jiffy, because she never keeps still and because it's kind of after me. He needs to know, but wait for the right time—you'll know when."

Wait a minute. This was way too much like Terry's famous story about the time window. Suddenly skeptical, Pam said, "How do I know I'm not making this up?"

Jeff laughed, leaned forward and blew out the candle. Pam snapped awake, supine on Lexi's bed in a pool of daylight, Cantata 104 still looping away on the bedside table, her gut in a twist.

~

Humphrey agreed the story was virtually a version of Terry's. "Terry Carpenter learns of the future birth of Liam O'Hara via time window. Pam Pruitt learns of the future birth of Jiffy via lucid dream. What is foreknown is kept secret, family connection in both cases, yes yes yes."

"With Jeff as the linking figure." Pam sketched it on a pad, which she held so Humphrey could see:

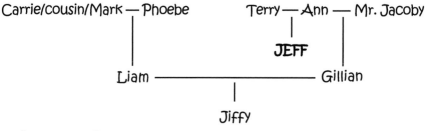

"Yes yes yes."

But he was tremendously excited. If Gillian Jacoby gave birth to a hyperactive baby girl in seven months' time and called her Jiffy, there could be no doubt that Pam had had precognitive knowledge of those facts. And if a DNA test proved Liam to be the father—

Pam steadied her voice and said, "Humphrey, would you please explain why you're not surprised that she *could* be pregnant with a child by Liam?"

The Hefn made throat-clearing noises. "Ah. Of course, you would not have been aware—it was not in fact understood for some time"—he actually looked embarrassed, however a Hefn managed a look that subtle—"but we have found that when a Hefn reaches into the mind of a particular human, the hypnotic infertility, ah, mechanism, is neutralized in that human." He paused for a response but Pam was dumbstruck. "Liam, for instance," he continued, "has been fertile since he was fourteen; but since he had no fertile female partners, indeed no female partners at all apart from yourself, my dear, it had never seemed necessary to reestablish . . ."

Details she'd learned at brunch the day before took on sudden meaning. "Oh. And when you were calming Gillian down in that hotel room—"

"Liam's semen still inside her may certainly have contained viable sperm, yes. We will verify the DNA, but I do not doubt that the child is Liam's, and is not against all odds that of Gillian's boyfriend Wayne Gillespie."

Pam said through pain like sheet lightning, "*If* she's actually pregnant she'd be fifty-three days along, she might not have noticed anything yet, but in another month or so—but you do have to wait, Humphrey, no poking and prying, now, I mean it!"

Humphrey said serenely, "I do not doubt that she is pregnant. A shaman sees what will be true—a Hefn, a Gafr, a kidnapped child, an unborn infant."

"I don't know yet whether I'm a shaman and neither do you! *Jeff* didn't say I was, he answered all my questions with questions." Jeff had not in fact told her a single thing she craved to know, Pam thought bitterly. He'd only told her the news, if that's what it was, about Gillian's baby and its paternity. Which she fervently wished he'd kept to himself. So much for being able to control the content of a lucid dream.

"If the future proves out as you have dreamed it, my dear, you are a shaman. Let that be enough for now. I will not poke and pry, be easy on that score, is that correct? 'on that score'? Yes? I will not snoop. Like a wise virgin I will wait and watch with plenty of oil."

Some virgin. "Good. Thanks."

"And now I say goodbye. Tell me if more dreams come."

~

Pam had already realized that the shamaning business was going to be like Uncle Tommy and the sexual abuse, in that most of the time she knew with certainty that the abuse had taken place, had in fact gone on for years; but then, despite the bradshaw, she would suddenly realize that doubts had crept back in. It was a common problem for abuse victims when there were no living witnesses and a family history of looking the other way. At such time she could call up Julie for validation; but Pam had ventured now into a realm where Julie's expertise would be no help. In Moab, peering with Humphrey at the Pecos River pictographs on the computer screen, she'd been sure of herself; but lately it had been getting harder to keep that version of reality in focus. Liam's skepticism was something she often felt herself.

Now here was this new dream so unlike the first, making her guts knot up, making her hope there was nothing to focus *on*. Who wanted to be a shaman if it meant being privy to such secrets and feeling such pain? She stared at the screen of Lexi's computer, where an old movie adaptation of *The Secret Garden* endlessly played, glimpsing for the first time why some of those interviewed shamans had spoken of their calling as a curse that had befallen them unsought.

Still, if she *hadn't* spoken with Jeff in the dream, she was *not* a shaman. And it was still reasonable to hope that the dream had been only a regular dream, with a totally plausible interpretation: Liam's reading of the pictograph copied onto the cake, a picture come to life, like the *Jungle Book* cartoon feature. Rich cake consumed at midnight might do that to anybody. (Pam suddenly thought of Scrooge telling Marley's ghost that he might be nothing but a bit of underdone potato—not a comforting analogy.) But even Humphrey had admitted the "prophecy" echoed the story Terry had been running for office on for nearly thirty years.

On top of that, while she couldn't deny that singing with Jeff had been, well, heavenly, he was a damned irritating kid otherwise—not a bit like the wonderful person she'd heard described by Liam and his family, and by Terry, ad nauseam if the truth be told, for the past quarter of a century.

Anyway, Pam hadn't believed in an afterlife since the age of eighteen and was by no means prepared to accept that Jeff Carpenter, candle in forepaw, arm around his bear familiar, had actually spoken to her from beyond the parallel wavy lines of death.

Weird, though, that Liam, equally if not more so an unbeliever in life after death, had looked at the panel and instantly understood that in it Jeff was imploring him to let the bear kill him, so they could be together on the other side of those same wavy lines. Just like that, Liam had flipped into the alternate viewpoint Pam now yearned to invalidate. Very weird, sinister in fact. She shoved back from Lexi's desk and headed for the shower, face scrunched into a frown of displeasure.

~

Fierce jealousy, not felt *within* the dream at all, had struck with vicious force the instant she awoke. No fear of being tempted to tell Liam anything! The problem was going to be not letting him realize that something else had upset her, and getting through the next five days.

This however turned out to be unexpectedly easy, thanks to Liam's being totally preoccupied with his mini-breakdown. He wanted to talk and talk about that, unravel its meaning, its probable causes, its implications for the future, and the evidence that his self-destructiveness, long thought exorcized, was still capable of being roused. The people he had always processed such issues with were Julie and Pam, and here was Pam, right here, and she wasn't charging. This was not pure narcissism, he had done as much for her in the roles of novel critic and bradshaw commentator, but it was narcissistic enough to make him unobservant of anything but the crisis bubbling merrily away on his personal front burner.

So they talked for hours about what had happened at the rock art site, and Pam had no trouble keeping the site's manifestations as cake and as dream scenario completely out of the discussion. She let Liam moderate and followed his lead, holding up her end without difficulty. It was a welcome distraction, really. The suicide question, for instance: she was genuinely interested in that, and found she didn't at all mind talking about the real Jeff Carpenter who had once been a living child. Liam himself didn't want to talk or think about the Gillian episode, so that was no problem either.

Pam had planned a second rock art expedition for Liam's second day, but clearly that was a non-starter for any number of reasons. Instead she spent the whole day coddling her guest, conversing, changing bandages, fixing some of the nice little meals she had learned to make for Lexi, anything to keep his mind busy and herself out of contact with her feelings. Knowing better than to try to take a nap while Liam was taking his, she spent that hour on the phone with Jaime, catching up first on office matters and then on the big picture.

"It's shaping up, like, gafrs from all over say their missions are bustling with people wanting to find out how to do this last-ditch turnaround. A lot of gafrs have started courses like this one I'm doing. Morale is actually pretty good, it's nice to be teaching motivated students again, I'm kind of enjoying myself. I slip in little lessons on how to follow the spirit of the Directive, not just the letter."

"Even if all the students care about is the letter."

Jaime said eagerly, "Well, but you know what? Some of 'em are getting it! Not too many, I haven't had anybody here in Salt Lake, but Parley's got four or five genuine converts, and that's not that uncommon for a given mission."

Pam was surprised, and said so. "Any sign that some of this will carry over past the deadline?"

Jaime shrugged. "Who knows? When you're cramming for a final, who looks past the deadline? That's the mentality, that's what all the hustle and bustle is about, the short time horizon. This course is pass/fail, they have to focus on passing."

They had already failed, of course. They were being kept preoccupied a little bit longer with hope, for some unknown purpose of the Gafr. To hold this knowledge in mind made it too difficult to keep up the pretense with Jaime. Hoping events would allow him to forgive her, somewhere out beyond the deadline, Pam changed the subject.

"Well, I figured there would be a run on the missions," she said, "but not that some who came to scoff would remain to pray. But another thing I figured was that there would probably be some people, scientists and engineers, that type, who'd like go underground and start plotting to take out the Gafr the minute they lift the ban. Heard any rumors like that?"

The idea seemed new to Jaime. "Even if there were, I doubt that kind of rumor would circulate where Gaians could pick it up."

"I thought maybe some of these new converts might have heard something before they converted."

Jaime looked dubious. "Not that I know of. How could they take the Gafr out? Bomb the moon?"

"I just had a hunch that some rocket scientist or like that might decide to get a few friends together and see what they could figure out. A Manhattan Project kind of thing."

"I'd think it would be impossible to get the materials, but I don't know squat about rocket science. But if I hear anything I'll let you know. This isn't something you dreamed about, is it?"

"No, no," Pam said, "it's the plot of a hundred formula thrillers. People besides me are bound to have thought of it, but making it happen is something else entirely."

They talked for several minutes more about their last abuse case, a teenager called Carmen Petosky. Then, as they were starting to wind down, Jaime thought to pass along the latest word from Santa Barbara. "The Apprentices who can't interface with the refitted transceivers, meaning most of 'em? Well, now Humphrey's got 'em logging placetimes where windows have opened in the local present *from* the future. How's that even possible?"

This was interesting. Liam hadn't mentioned it. "A window leaves a signature for a while. What've they come up with?"

"So far, just what you'd expect. Besides the training ones and the way-back ones, and the bradshaws—all those had already been logged—there's the ones that opened in Hurt Hollow in the 1960's, three from '14, one from '26. And there were some in England and Sweden, from when the Hefn were scanning for survivors. The one Terry Carpenter saw, in 1990 was it? That one's not on the list, I looked for it."

"That one opened in the area affected by Peach Bottom, radiation would have erased the signal."

"Oh. Why are they doing this, do you know?"

Pam said, "I would imagine they're trying to find out if a message was sent through from our future and somehow missed the target. If nobody even tried to send Humphrey a message, knowing how frantic he is to have one, it could be a bad sign."

Jaime said, "Maybe they just haven't sent it yet. But I was thinking, the marooned Hefn in England and Sweden—the hobs and the other ones—they waited a couple of centuries for a window to open and it never did. Why not? I forget."

"The ship malfunctioned, they couldn't get back here for a long time. By the time they did, the only message would have been, 'Sorry, mates, turns out you're stranded for life. Goodbye and good luck.' They did raise that one last Swedish Hefn, remember, but he was dead when they found him. And of course that hob of Jenny Flintoft's—but no, they didn't use a transceiver on him." Thinking of Jenny, Pam remembered the book of cottage murals.

"Oh right, right. I was wondering if maybe the transceivers quit working, meaning maybe they've quit working up there in the future."

"Well, maybe they have. Maybe all this tinkering damages them for normal use."

"Maybe so. How's the visit going, by the way?"

Pokerfaced, Pam said, "Fine. Yesterday we went for a hike. Tomorrow we're making spaghetti sauce."

"A hike, in this heat?"

"It *was* pretty hot. We're sticking close to home today. I thought we might drop in on you maybe Friday afternoon, if you'd be up for that."

"Sure, that'd be great!" He really did looked pleased. "I've got Gaia 101 at ten and two, and a meeting with Carmen's counselor at 4:30. Come by for lunch?"

"Okay, thanks. We can bring a jillion tomatoes and some peaches."

Jaime grinned. "Any more dreams, if you don't mind my asking?"

"No more dreams," Pam said firmly.

"Heard from Lexi?"

"A call just came in from her while we've been talking. I should probably get off and call her back. Keep me posted on developments, okay?"

"You bet." He rang off. Pam placed the call to Lexi, smiling because in a conversation lasting almost an hour Jaime hadn't once called her "Boss."

THE BIRD SHAMAN

~

The more Pam kept herself from thinking about the dream she'd told Jaime she hadn't had, the more preposterous it seemed. This was a strategy to encourage. She popped a sleeping pill at bedtime and went to bed in her own room, explaining to Liam that Lexi's was just too narrow for a person used to rolling around in a wider one. She slept soundly, woke early, and by the time Liam padded bare-foot into the kitchen had already picked a bushel basket of dead-ripe tomatoes and a bowl of green peppers, and brought a sack of onions up from the root cellar under the basement stairs.

Liam's lacerated fingers were too sore for chopping onions, peppers, and mushrooms into little pieces with a paring knife, but he could quarter tomatoes and turn the crank on the juicer that separated skins and seeds from watery pulp. After breakfast Pam got him two plastic bags to wear like mittens, to keep his bandages clean and dry, and put him to work. She sat at the kitchen table, he stood at the counter by the sink. He talked some more, but it became clear he was starting to run out of gas on the subject of his freakout.

To top up his tank with a safe subject, Pam asked about the search for time window signatures.

"Oh," he blew out a breath dismissively, "it's part of their frenzy to find out what's going to happen after June 6 before it gets here, just like you're part of Humphrey's personal frenzy to do the same thing. They're leaving no stone unturned. They've had some of us systematically scanning for transceiver signatures in little geographic segments around the globe, but no surprises so far, nothing from *our* future, i.e. the future relative to the morning of August 27, 2037."

"That's what Jaime said. It's surprising."

"You think so? I don't." He tipped a bowlful of quartered toma-toes into the hopper of the juicer and picked up a wooden tool like a large honey dipper. "Ow. This is bloody awkward. I have to push this thing with the places on my palm that aren't wounded and the handle keeps slipping off and gouging me."

"Don't do it then, I'll take over. You keep on quartering."

"No, no, I'll manage," he said predictably, having established the martyrdom of his position. "Maybe if I take the bag off this hand."

"Good idea."

It worked, but it took all of Liam's concentration. Not until he'd poured the pulp into the big pot on the stove, re-donned his plastic bag, and gone back to washing and quartering tomatoes did he say, "About the time windows, not finding signatures is only surprising if you expect the Hefn to stick around if they don't lift the Ban. How likely is that? If I were the Gafr I'd just load everybody on the ship, or almost everybody, and go away for, oh, fifty years. Practically all the humans alive during the Take-over would be dead when they got back, and they'd find a rebalanced ecosystem and a very small, pretty young population of fertile people who've grown up knowing the aliens would be coming back to take over again." He glanced at Pam. "Who needs a crystal ball to figure that out? The mystery to me is why all the Hefn are in such a lather about it."

They were skirting dangerously close to the question of whether the Ban would be lifted, but Liam didn't seem to care. "What's mysterious about *their* being in a lather?" Pam had finished the peppers and started slicing mushrooms, grown in her basement by inoculating boxes of punky stuff with spores. "Even if you're right about the fifty years, etc., wouldn't they send themselves a message when they got back, if they possibly could? Right to BTP Headquarters too, all this scanning shouldn't be necessary, a window should open right smack in the middle of the transceiver lab: 'Relax, guys, everything's going to be fine. Time is One.'"

He looked up. "You're right, I hadn't thought it through. They don't know what it means that there's no message. They don't, and neither do I." He dumped another bowl of pieces into the hopper. "On the other hand, if Time is One, what difference does it make?"

Pam laid her knife down and smiled at him kindly. "What we never know is how, good buddy. There's lots of things it might mean. One, all this retrofitting messes up the transceivers beyond repair, or, two, something else happens to make them inoperable, but, which-ever, they *can't* send a message, but their mission goes forward as planned whether they leave or don't leave."

"Three, the ship leaves but never comes back, or doesn't come back for centuries like before. Another malfunction. The mission is a total bust."

"Four," Pam suggested, getting into the spirit, "also like before, there's a revolt while they're in space, and the new command decides to abort the mission. Pretty unlikely at this point, that one, I'd guess."

"Five," Liam said with relish, "a small but tightly organized revolutionary force on Earth finds a way to regain control of the planet. When the aliens return, they are immediately seized and rendered powerless."

"Six, a group of brilliant rocket engineers and nuclear scientists, working even now in some underground lab, sends an armed rocket to the moon and blows up the Gafr ship before it can take off."

They grinned at each other. "Nah," Liam said, "now we're talking science fiction."

The slicing and dicing went on until the tomato substance had risen to within an inch of the sauce pot's rim, at which point Pam turned the heat down, cleared off the table, and made sandwiches. Over lunch (eaten inside, so an eye could be kept on the boiling sauce) they talked about the extra year the Gafr needed but went on pretending not to need, even to the other Apprentices and Terry.

"And Humphrey hasn't even told his own personal crystal ball."

Pam shook her head. "Nope. I asked. He said he couldn't. It's something to do with needing to see the future despite Time being One, I'd bet the farm on that."

"So would everybody out in California, if they knew what you know," Liam said. "Don't look at me like that, I said I wouldn't tell. But if I did, nobody would be very surprised. It's pretty obvious that all this fuss over the future isn't about saving Gaia, or humanity's right to reproduce, or anything we've been trying to accomplish all this time. It's a HefnGafr thing—like we're a labor force for some goal of theirs, while our goals have been sidelined. They're letting people work their own fate out, they've stopped trying to help."

Rushing past her reaction to the word "reproduce," Pam said, "Yet you're all going along, even Artie and Will—even you—because when push comes to shove you still trust Humphrey, even though Humphrey doesn't seem to trust you, am I right?"

Liam looked at her, then looked away. "Chumps that we are, I guess that's right. And because we feel like he'd tell us if the Gafr would let him; and because we'd all kill to know if there's a way to make a window open up ahead, what the math would look like . . . and, again, as much as anything, I guess because we can't think of a better way to get though the year."

"I'm not sure," Pam said slowly, "how far I trust Humphrey myself these days. I don't think he would work against us—I mean, you know, use me or you guys to hurt humanity." As she said this Pam realized she was not in fact certain that Humphrey would understand co-opting the Apprentices as a betrayal. The emotional subtleties were a lot like those of tampering with France's Pruitt's will. On the other hand, if the decision not to lift the Ban had already been made, what would "working against human welfare" consist of now? "I tell you what though, I would really love to know what the Gafr are up to, that's one lucid dream I'd be happy to have."

Especially compared to that last one.

~

On the second-to-last day of the visit, September 1—Pam's birthday—Liam suggested that they finish the pictograph cake, which had been wrapped and returned to the freezer. Pam's first reaction, which she concealed, was to be horrified. Her second was more rational. She set the cake out to thaw and picked off the bits of melted wax, and after a big spaghetti birthday dinner they polished it off.

Pam rejected Liam's offer, to cram 38 of his 39 candles onto half a sheet cake with his scabby fingers, as being redundant. She served the Jeff zoomorph to him and the blank innocuous edges to herself. He gave her a book about strange attractors, which he hadn't wrapped ("Sorry"), and a pound of caramels covered in dark chocolate, which had been gift-wrapped at the store. These were pretty good presents. No dreams followed the cake-eating; in fact, fractals excepted, Pam's sleep had continued sound and dreamless throughout Liam's visit.

The visit ended the next morning, and with it her ability to keep her feelings contained behind a flood wall. The wall coming down all at once felt like flu. She got home from seeing Liam off at the station and went straight to bed—without calling Jaime or Lexi or Humphrey, without passing Go or collecting $200, without doing anything but pull the shades all the way down—and spent the rest of the day and night burrowed beneath the Dutch Girl quilt.

By morning, decisions had firmed up. One: if Liam was sorry she had saved his life, instead of grateful, Pam would have to accept that. Two: until they knew that Gillian was or was not pregnant, she would think no more about shamanism or rock art—about art of any kind, religious or otherwise, or its relation to the cultures that produced it. She would devote herself to the Utah Gaians and to Lexi.

From the moment she'd started reading, Pam had all but abandoned the Gaians; she'd dumped all that on Jaime, not even asking about the local ones anymore. But during the night she'd remembered Moab and the excited faces at that impromptu potluck for Humphrey. Morale had peaked for them at the very instant when the Hefn had switched their focus from a viable human past to an Earth where a human presence would be insignificant for a very long time. With the blow about to fall they could use her help, and she committed herself to helping them.

And Lexi would be home in a few more days; Pam would clean the house and tidy up the garden in honor of the homecoming. There was certainly plenty to do. Briefly, she would stay busy and wait upon events, keeping them out of mind in the meantime as best she could.

Pam Pruitt could follow a sensible regimen with as much determination and even zest as anybody alive. When Liam called to thank her for her hospitality, she exclaimed ungraciously, "I had no idea you knew about making bread-and-butter calls!" He wanted to discuss his recent session with Julie, but Pam said she really couldn't talk, it was still peak spaghetti-sauce-making season, sauce pot on the boil all day long, kitchen filled with heat, steam, and fragrance, plus she was working on a major address to the worldwide Gaians Mission, and making and freezing Lexi's (also Humphrey's) favorite desserts for when she got home. "I'm taking her on a little vacation trip next week, she's got a week off, for Labor Day ostensibly, what a joke, but I'll be back in touch right after that, okay?"

A bit miffed, Liam said, "I guess it'll have to be, won't it. So you don't want to hear about the fight Artie had with Pomfrey over using a transceiver to check something in Angkor Wat?"

"Not right now. Sorry, I really do have to go."

"Still working on that shaman stuff? Done any more rock art hikes?"

He was incorrigible. Pam hung up.

When Lexi and her bodyguard arrived home a few days later, they found the sand and gravel of the front yard neatly raked, gardens and flower beds weedless, rooms softly gleaming from the removal of dust, a freezer stuffed with spaghetti sauce and cobblers, a well-turned compost pile, and a big sign strung across the front porch: WELCOME HOME LEXI (JACK TOO).

Over dinner (spaghetti, salad, warm rolls, warm peach cobbler with homemade ice cream) Pam unveiled the prospect of the mini-vacation. Lexi's cast was coming off the next day; they had an appointment to get that done in the morning and one with the physical therapist in the afternoon, but then where would Lexi like to go? How about way up Little Cottonwood Canyon, where it would be cool and the wildflowers in Albion Basin were now at their most spectacular? They could rent a cabin.

Lexi, who had spent a lot of time in the mountains on location, clearly found that prospect not so thrilling. Anyway, she had a better idea. "I know where I'd really *like* to go, but it's too far prob'ly—Hurt Hollow?"

Pam's mouth fell open. She'd been thinking ever since Moab about going to Hurt Hollow, but always in terms of a prolonged stay, which of course had been put on hold along with everything else; but what about going just to go? Just to *be* there? To be at the Hollow with Lexi, show Lexi around the Scofield campus, maybe spend a night together in the Scofield house where they'd shot her bradshaw—all this seized Pam's imagination. "What a totally terrific idea! You're probably right that it's too far, it would take us a couple of days to get there and a couple more to get back, but let's check into it anyway."

For a retreat Humphrey would authorize a plane. Not for a one-week vacation, though—or would he? Would he fly them out there in the secret hope that putting Pam back in contact with her Ground, even for a week, would affect her in the way he wanted?

She shooed Lexi off to watch TV—no chores on her first night home—and did the washing-up, thinking how to put this request to Humphrey. The more she considered, the greater seemed the likelihood that he just might go for it. She finished, trickled the dishwater into the bed of young lettuce under shade cloth, then came back into her study and activated the phone.

Humphrey popped onto the screen at once, all his hair standing out in a nimbus around him, quite a startling sight. "My dear, a delightful coincidence! I was just preparing to call you!"

Uh oh. "How come?"

"To tell you the *wonderful! wonderful! news!*"

Pam's stomach fisted up. He didn't need to say it. "Gillian's preggers."

But he said it anyway—crowed it rather, an English-speaking

rooster jubilant to the point of hysteria: *"Gillian Jacoby is pregnant! I did not poke and pry into Gillian or her gynecologist,"* he added quickly, *"only into the records of the medical clinic of her gynecologist, whom she visited today."*

Obviously he'd been monitoring the clinic's computers since the morning Pam had told him about the dream. Gillian would have missed her second period by now, had probably worried that something was wrong, never imagining in her wildest dreams . . . Pam's queasiness suddenly flared into outrage at her own outrageous fate. "All right, fine. Here's what I was calling you about though: Lexi's got a week off. I want to take her to Hurt Hollow and I'd like to make the most of the time we've got by flying out there and back."

"Hurt Hollow? What a splendid idea! Pam Pruitt! is! is! is! a shaman, of course she shall travel in style—but a week only? I believe—"

Tensing herself against this outburst, Pam protested, "A week is all we've got!" But with Gillian's pregnancy confirmed, the jig was up and she knew it. "I'll be going back for longer, don't worry, I know it's necessary. But I really can't quite yet."

Bristling with avidity, Humphrey said, "Oh be very soon, my dear, be soon!"

"As soon as Lexi can leave Salt Lake. I promise."

Judith Moffett

PAM'S ADDRESS TO THE GAIAN MISSION
4 September 2037

Apprentices, mission gafrs, missionaries, stewards—everyone everywhere who is or wants to be Grounded in Gaia: in less than a year, we'll finally know whether the Baby Ban is ever to be revoked. The human race has been given a final year of reckoning, and for this reason many of you listening tonight have sought us out and asked to be instructed in Gaian stewardship. For the same reason, some committed stewards, longtime missionaries in particular, feel this ultimatum as a defeat.

I want to remind you all of what the Hefn say about time. First, they tell us that Time is One, and fixed. But they also tell us that no one knows beforehand just *how* events will play out to their fixed conclusions. No one does.

We Gaians, who've been so goal-directed throughout our whole existence as a movement, may also take to heart the words of another committed missionary, the Apostle Paul, a person I myself would ordinarily never cite as an authority on anything. "I have fought a good fight," Paul wrote in his second epistle to Timothy, "I have finished my course, I have kept the faith." His words have a force and truth that apply to Gaian missionaries in full measure—more, indeed, than they did to Paul himself. Paul was completely confident that his faith-keeping had won him a crown in Heaven, but from their beginnings the Gaians fought the good fight, more unselfishly and no less valiantly, without being assured of winning anything.

Now we are required to tolerate our uncertainty a little longer. It won't be easy. But it *will* help to bear in mind that Gaia is still and always holy ground, that the right way to live in the biosphere is still the right way, and that teaching Gaian principles to others will always be profoundly worth doing for its own sake.

And bear this in mind as well: that what we *never* know . . . is *how*.

CHAPTER 13

Trailing Bird

7 - 23 SEPTEMBER 2037

"As soon as Lexi can leave Salt Lake," Pam had said, but how soon would that be? The passing of time had removed other obstacles, but two things still had to happen before Pam could take Lexi out of town: her series had to conclude, and her mother and grandfather, and Jared Johnson, had to be tried for kidnapping.

A Thousand Miles would film its climactic final episodes on location when deep snow returned to the Wasatch. The surviving remnant of the Martin company would totter into Salt Lake City at last; Katy's mother would have her baby and name him Handcart McPherson. During the fall they could complete other parts of the filming on sets at the studio; but even if global warming should force cast and crew to shoot November 1856 in January 2038, Lexi would be free to leave town when the series was wrapped, and not before.

Humphrey could of course have stopped the show's production just like that, but doing so would hurt Lexi and alienate Pam, the very person whose cooperation he most required. So driven was he by the need to know whatever he needed to know, or such was the pressure being applied by the Gafr, that he might have resorted to force had that been possible; but none of his extraordinary powers had evolved to coerce a recalcitrant earthling to dream the future.

What he did instead was eliminate the trials. The Hurt Hollow retreat must be neither deferred nor interrupted; and so, the day before Pam and Lexi were due back from their week in the Ohio

River Valley—and without consulting Jaime—Humphrey returned to Salt Lake to pass and impose sentence on the criminals himself. RoLayne and Jared he terrified and then pardoned; the hard case, Ed Young, he mindwiped back to the year before Lexi was born and sent to a Mormon town in Idaho where there were no children at all, after implanting a phobia against crossing the county line.

They came in, and there he was, in the living room. Several minutes were taken up by greetings, and in admiration of Lexi's castless arm—Lexi took off her splint and worked her wrist back and forth, so he could see—but then Pam sent her up to unpack. She wanted to find out what Humphrey was doing there.

"I'm not complaining, don't get me wrong," she said when she'd been told, "especially not on Lexi's behalf, never mind society's. She said on the way home that she didn't want to testify at all, especially not against her mother. But it would have been courteous to consult with Jaime first."

"I would not have wished to proceed over his objections."

Provoked as always by this sort of oblivious Hefn highhanded-ness, Pam said crossly, "You know, I've never understood why can't you *repair* a person like Ed Young when you go rummaging through his mind."

"Repair?"

"Untwist him, so he doesn't hanker after little girls anymore. If you can implant a phobia against leaving the county, why not a phobia against abusing little girls? Why does it always have to be destructive?"

Humphrey, perched on his Hefn chair, peered at her owlishly. "Was it destructive to remove the memories of Liam until he could bear to have them back?"

That stopped her. "No, of course it wasn't."

"A memory is something that happened. A hankering is some-thing that is."

Lexi, excited to have Humphrey in the house, came racketing down from her unpacking. "Should I defrost a cobbler, Pom? Is he staying for dinner?"

"Oh, I reckon he is. Sure, let's defrost a cobbler."

"Blackberry? We've got cherry and peach too."

Pam had made quite a few cobblers in her denial-interval between Liam's departure and Lexi's return. She cocked her eyebrows at

Humphrey, who called "Oh, blackberry please!" as she had known he would.

"And then should I do a tomato pick? There's jillions of 'em out there."

"Great idea. Careful of the arm!"

"I will be!"

The freezer door banged, and then the back door. Humphrey said, "The broken bone is truly mended?"

"Not quite, but it's coming along well. We did mobility and strengthening exercises all week. She has to bend her hand at the wrist over the edge of a table, and squeeze a ball, and some other stuff. It hurts but she's good about it, she's in a hurry to get back to normal."

"And how did little Lexi enjoy Hurt Hollow?"

Pam smiled, a bit ruefully. "Well, she certainly enjoyed the visit. I'll let her tell you about it. You're distracting me very cleverly from the subject of mindprobe, by the way. How about what you did to Gillian? You intended to help her but now she's pregnant, very possibly by the wrong person." The steady way Pam said this showed the extent to which she'd come to terms with her situation.

"What we never know is who is the wrong person," Humphrey insisted. "What I did not intend, has proved to me that Pamela Pruitt is a shaman. Am I able to regret this? No. Now I attempt another diversion: What is 'Pom'?"

Pam smiled again, more openly. "She's never known what to call me, nothing felt comfortable, but lately she's been calling me that. She made it up—a combination of Pam and Mom. And she likes it that there've been Hefn called Pomfrey and Lexifrey, she likes the symmetry, and the implied link with you guys, God knows why."

"God knows why," Humphrey echoed cheerily. "This is irony? Yes? Does she know that Lexifrey, such a likable fellow my dear, was also called Lexi by those who knew him best, and that he and Pomfrey were kinfolk? relatives? I do not know precisely how to express the connection —"

"Maybe just 'family.'"

"Family, yes. Close family."

"Speaking of irony," said Pam, family-less originator of the failed concept of "family land."

~

Lexi had enjoyed the trip a lot. She enjoyed not having her body-guard, Jack Stanley, trailing along everywhere she went, and she enjoyed exploring the real place she'd seen first on the Gaian recruitment viddy. The Hollow, a Gaian shrine to the Hubbells and their way of life, was in full swing. By September things were winding down a bit; but people's determination to look like Gaians to the Hefn meant they were still visiting the Hollow in record numbers, as they'd been doing ever since the Summit in June, braving the heat and humidity to show their bona fides. A brace of full-time curators was in residence, and a staff of volunteer docents from Scofield and Madison in Indiana and Milton in Kentucky came in by the half-day. Months of tremendous daily turnouts of visitors and Ohio Valley summer had worn the staff to frazzles; by now they were more than ready to call it a season. But the unheralded arrival of Pam Pruitt, famous in one way, and Alexis Allred, famous in quite another, was a huge perk-up for everybody. The tourists, some of whom never saw a live child from one month to the next, let alone a child celebrity of uncommon beauty, queued up for autographs and followed Lexi with their eyes, something else she enjoyed.

The garden, now surrounded by an eight-foot deer fence which would certainly have taken Orrin aback—in his day there hadn't been any deer in northern Kentucky—had passed its summer apex, and the tomato and pole bean foliage was looking pretty ratty, but the fall veggies under their tents of shade cloth were spectacular. Lexi proudly named them: broccoli, cauliflower, bok choi, cabbage, kale, peas, three kinds of looseleaf lettuce; the only one she missed was the chard. She got to milk a goat. She got to put on a bee veil and long gloves (working the left one on very carefully over her splint) to help inspect the hives. Child of the desert, she was astonished—as was Pam, every time she came home—by the green jungliness of everything. She absolutely loved having Pam's undivided attention all day every day.

They stayed in Pam's house on the Scofield campus, riding back and forth from Scofield Beach on the regular steamboats, and Lexi enjoyed that too. She requested and was given permission to sleep in Pam's old bedroom. Night after night, beside the bed where a different eleven-year-old girl had sat to write in a red diary, Pam read the *Jungle Book* chapter of the evening and heard the recitation of the poem of the week. "'Oppress not the cubs of the stranger, but hail them as Sister and Brother,'" Lexi chanted night after night, "'For though they are little and fubsy, it may be the Bear is their mother.'" In this way, night after night, the image of Jeff embracing the huge immobile bear that had filled Lexi's bedroom became superposed on this bedroom, Little Pam's. The feelings evoked in grownup Pam by this sense of layered times and children were strange past telling. "What's 'fubsy'?" Lexi asked, and Pam said, "Oh, like pudgy, roly-poly. I looked it up when I was your age. Mary Lennox would have known, though, she and Kipling were both the kids of civil servants stationed in India, and they both got sent back to England."

"Crikey, I never thought of that!"

But all week, while Pam was reconciling herself to being a person with a vocation she must not refuse—and this now appeared undeniable—Lexi was noticing and thinking too, and toward the end of the visit she said, "I can tell Hurt Hollow is your Ground. And I can tell it's not mine."

So now that Humphrey had eliminated one major impediment to Lexi's going to Hurt Hollow, another had arisen: Lexi didn't really want to leave Salt Lake, not to be gone a couple of months she didn't, not in the dead of winter, not to kick around by herself all day, keeping quiet, while Pam studied and meditated.

When this had become clear, Pam sat her down one evening and brought her up to date. Lexi hadn't known there'd been a second lucid dream, or that the Gafr were pressuring Humphrey and Humphrey was pressuring Pam. "So we need to figure something out, sweetie," Pam concluded, "because I have to go back out there as soon as I possibly can."

Lexi's lip quivered. "You promised we'd stick together."

"I know I did, and I meant it, too, but that was about you coming to the Hollow with me, remember? I'd still love to have you come, and I'm happy to wait till you get done shooting—but only if *you* want to come, and you don't really want to be out there that long, do you?"

Lexi looked down and shook her head. "I don't see why you can't just study the rock art here. I don't see why you have to go to Hurt Hollow."

"Yes you do," Pam chided her gently. She smoothed her hand over Lexi's fall of hair. "I'd much rather not be separated, believe me. If I could do what I have to do right here, I would, but you know it's not up to me. I really do have to go back and be there a good while, so we need to think about other ways to work things out."

While they were thinking—Pam at least was thinking, Lexi was mostly sulking—a coolish, brilliant late September day arrived when Pam woke up remembering all the Barrier Canyon Style sites she had never been out to see. Lexi had a point, the learning possibilities right here in Utah were far from exhausted. Over breakfast she studied her notes and a map. After breakfast she ordered a helicopter.

Just as she was heading out the door, Liam called. "Are you avoiding me or what? You said when you hung up on me before that you'd call me back as soon as you got home from your trip."

"Listen, I was just leaving for the hospital to pick up a chopper, I'm off to see a couple of rock art sites. Can I call you tonight? Or maybe tomorrow?"

"Or maybe next year? What's going on? *I* thought the visit was a great success."

Pam groaned inwardly. "I promise I'll call you tonight without fail, but right now I'm going to hang up on you again." And she did hang up, obliterating his indignant face in the act of opening its mouth to protest, and immediately called the Moab Mission.

Mercedes the rock art expert answered the phone. Recollecting her official position (and her manners) at the last possible instant, Pam asked how they were getting on down there.

"Since you ask, I'm afraid I'm kind of in the dumps," Mercedes admitted. Belatedly Pam remembered her decision to focus on the welfare of the Utah Gaians, and that in actual fact she'd done nothing whatever about the Utah Gaians, other than include them in the general address she'd written and delivered in the midst of her cobbler-making frenzy. "I'm sorry," Pam said contritely. "Is it something personal? Jaime tells me you folks have a booming business going on down there, and a few real converts among the simulacra."

"All true. Parley's very pumped about the classes and the conversions, but I can't help feeling it's all over but the funeral. I caught your speech," she added, "it was a good speech, I agree with everything you said, really, but I guess I'm just one of the ones who feels like the game's over and we lost."

"Well," said Pam, thinking fast, "of course we have lost in a way. We were out to convert the world. They called the game before we did it."

Mercedes said glumly, "Not that we were exactly winning at the time." And as Pam was opening her mouth to reply, "No, that's okay, you don't need to give your speech again. I'm sorry. What was it you were calling about? Did you want Parley?"

Her depression was about the failure of the Mission, not about the Ban. Pam suddenly remembered Parley's saying Mercedes had been a member of the first class of missionaries; for them the Mission itself was the be-all and end-all, not a means to ending the Ban. She breathed easier. "Don't be sorry. You feel like you feel. No, actually," Pam said, "I was hoping to speak with *you*. I'm off on a field trip by chopper to two rock art sites out your way, Dead Mule Canyon and Feet of Sinbad. Got any advice?"

That caught her interest. "I'd better fax you some directions. They're both a little hard to find, Dead Mule especially."

"Is Feet of Sinbad Barrier Canyon Style? The anthros are wearing long skirts and shoes."

"Yeah, but the groupings of the figures are like you find in other BCS panels, and the rain birds and horned serpents are diagnostic, though the placement is a little bit unusual. Remember, some people think this style may have been around for as long as six thousand years, in that much time you're bound to get some variation, even in a culture as static as Barrier Canyon. Also, Head of Sinbad is right next door, and that's definitely BCS. You must have been reading up on this since you were here."

"That," Pam said ruefully, "would be putting it mildly."

"If we had the broken-off part with the heads, a lot of the uncertainties would clear up. Why are you interested in Feet of Sinbad especially?"

Quickly Pam considered how much to tell her; it wouldn't do to underestimate her informant. "I'm interested in the transformational panels generally, especially the ones showing birds as psychopomps."

"Oh," said Mercedes, brightening further, "if birds are your thing you should plan a hike to Virgin Spring sometime. That's the biggest and best bird around. Eight miles in, though—unless the chopper pilot could drop you from a ladder?" She waited.

This was a test question. Pam shook her head. "I wouldn't approach any of these sites like that. The approach seems to be part of the experience. Got to be quiet and respectful, make a decent effort. The BCS people were more integrated with Gaia than we are, they knew what was what."

Mercedes smiled at Pam, a real smile. "Well, if there's nothing else, I'll get off and fax you those directions."

"There's nothing else. I might get back in touch afterwards if that's okay."

"Any time. Dead Mule is a bit of a scramble; wear good boots. Should I send the info on Virgin Spring?"

Pam considered. She'd read about the Virgin Spring site, the wonderful rain bird and the long hike to find it. Something to be worked up to, in every sense. "Not for today, but later in the fall I might backpack in." If I'm still around by then, she added mentally.

~

The pilot set Pam down at the steep edge of another dry wash, turned off the rotors as instructed, and climbed out with a folding chair and a paperback, to find some shade. Deep ringing silence flowed into the space vacated by the chopper's whacking. Pam shrugged into her backpack, slopped on sunblock, and clamped hat on head and sunglasses on face; the glare was dazzling. It was a beautiful day. She walked to the canyon rim and compared what she could see against the sheets of photos Mercedes had sent over with the maps.

From up here the correct alcove was actually in view—a good way off though and easily confused with similar dimples in the mounds of slickrock, which looked as if they'd been sculpted in bread dough by a race of giant bakers. Pam waved at the pilot and dropped over the rim.

As soon as she'd started down the steep, vaguely wandering trail, the alcove containing the pictographs disappeared from view. The canyon floor, when she reached it, turned out to be loose deep sand, effortful to walk in, and the walls that rose high on either side were white slickrock; these features gave Dead Mule quite a different character from the nameless canyon she'd hiked into with Liam. Vegetation here was close to nonexistent.

Almost at once the canyon veered to the left as the walls became higher and steeper and then closed in, creating a slot canyon: something Pam had read about but never seen, so narrow you had to sidle through it. A lethal place to get caught in a storm. Every year people drowned in slot canyons out of ignorance or recklessness, the victims of flash floods; but Pam, neither reckless nor ignorant, knew that no rain had been forecast for this area and was not anxious. But the tightness and twistingness gradually produced in her a sense of making a ritual entry through a passageway, into another reality.

Probably a birth-canal thing, but also it made a Bible verse come to mind and she spoke it aloud: "Strait is the gate, and narrow is the way, which leadeth unto life, and few there be that find it." The verse in turn made her think of a cowboy song, "Roll On, Little Dogies," that picked up the same thread from Matthew. "The road to that bright happy region," Pam sang as she threaded her infinitesimal way between the tall white walls of stone, "Is a dim narrow trail, so they say, But the broad road that leads to perdition, Is posted and blazed all the way." Trapped in the slot canyon, her voice was resonant. Then as the walls opened out again it became thin and lonely-sounding, and she stopped singing and consulted her sheaf of papers.

Okay, here was the picture that matched this part of the wash; but the canyon twisted too much for a person hiking along the floor of it to sight very far ahead. Pam walked on, sucking water through her canteen tube, checking what she could see against the stuff Mercedes had faxed over. Each boot, each stride, slipped back a little with each sandy push-off. It quickly became obvious that, barring a very lucky guess, she would never have been able to find the alcove she wanted without Mercedes' pictures; there were dozens of them high on the canyon wall, and the wall was steep, the footing rather treacherous. Slickrock could be smooth to the point of complete featurelessness; you had to be careful and take your time, especially when the walls angled up this sharply. You could wear yourself out hunting through all the possible caves for one particular cave, yet be in sight of it the entire time.

But she could see it plainly now, a knife slit near the top of the bread-dough wall. Mercedes had marked the picture with an arrow. Pam shucked her pack, hung her camera around her neck, retied her book laces, and started to climb.

The ascent was easy at first, but Pam's mind was too much on the target and too little on where she was putting her feet. When she had almost reached the alcove it was necessary to push and kick to haul herself up past one difficult humped-out place in the rock. Still regaining her balance atop the hump, eyes still on the prize, there came a surreal moment when her attention snapped into focus on the fact that the soles of both her boots, flat and parallel on the slick surface, were sliding sideways toward a point where there would be no more rock to slide on.

Her eyes darted around, seeking a way out of her predicament. Incredibly, there didn't seem to be one. The surface here was very smooth; she should never have tried to stand on this part of it. There was nothing to grab hold of—no shrub, no irregularity in the rock itself. It was a long way down. Pam's mind flipped into problem-solving mode, cast about efficiently—but could find no solution. It seemed she was going over the cliff.

And then she wasn't. A foot from the brink, the lugs of her lower boot fetched up against the merest bump, and she stopped sliding and teetered there in a state of extreme tension, searching the rock surface minutely for someplace to step to. She teetered for what seemed quite a while before finally being forced to accept that stepping was not an option. So she sat down, lowering her center of gravity with exquisite care, for fear of dislodging the tenuous pressure of boot on bump, and spread her palms flat on the bare surfaces at her sides. Then, holding her breath, leaning back a bit, putting all her weight on her sweaty palms, she hitched herself sideways and slightly backwards, back from the long drop, toward a place where her boots as well as her palms could get some traction. The fabric of her shorts, a rough cotton weave stretched tight across the seat by her flexed position, held her body in place just long enough for her hands to scoot a little back and a little back. It was a very tense business, the amount of traction it was possible to achieve in this way was barely adequate, she could easily have started to slide again, but finally she'd inched back to a flatter place and could sit without bracing herself on her arms.

The danger over, reaction set in; Pam started to shake, partly with fury for having been so stupid, for having understood the risk yet placed herself at risk anyway, through sheer birdbrained inattentiveness! *Bloody idiot! If you fall off a cliff, what happens to Lexi?* She did not think: *How would Humphrey manage without me?* or *What about my duty to the Gaians?*; still less did she think, *My God, I might have died!*

When the shakes wore off and her breath and heart rate had slowed, Pam saw that she'd fetched up just to one side and down a little from the mouth of the alcove. Her palms were burning; a lot of skin had been abraded. She turned them up to look, thinking that for once those big hands had come in, well, handy.

Then she stood, knees wobbling, and looked back the way she'd come, across the mounded doughy rockscape to the straight line of the canyon rim at least a mile away. There was the chopper, a gleaming dragonfly. There were Mercedes' papers, an incongruous scatter on the slope directly below. Above everything there was the sky, still of that intense dissolving blue that was actually painful to stare into. Deliberately she pulled this sky into her lungs, making each breath as deep as possible and holding it as long. Finally then she turned and covered the short distance to the rock shelter she'd come to find.

This was smaller and shallower than the Adam-zad site, less an empty eye socket than a ragged wedge cut into a tree. The floor, level along the entry, rose almost at once to meet the back of the upswept ceiling. Clearly more of a place to make a vision quest or perform a ritual than one suited to housekeeping. When it rained you would get wet in here.

Senses heightened by her brush with death, Pam thought she perceived an atmosphere about this hollow place in the rock not present at the first site, or not discernible from the ground below, or at any rate not by her (though Liam might disagree). There was a hush, a quality of waiting and abiding, not creepy at all, just the opposite in fact. As if the place were both watching and being watched over. *Hot Spot*, said Pam's Apprentice training, and her years at Hurt Hollow, touchstone for such places, said the same.

Well, she was here. The shelter had no back wall; standing in the level entry, Pam scanned visually across the roof of its open mouth, making complete methodical passes from side to side. She'd just begun to doubt whether this was the right alcove after all, when suddenly there they were, strung out in a horizontal line. She had been looking too deeply into the shelter's throat.

Remarkable how unassertive the painted figures were, how little they demanded to be looked at (and how uncomfortable it was to look at them for long—the price of staring was an aching neck), when their impact was so visceral! Nothing at all of Easter Island here, these figures were supple, even jolly in a serious way, some almost seemed to strut. In a flash of insight Pam grasped, really for the first time, how this art could get such a grip on people. Her own rock art library was pointless in one way, since to look at this panel with even the remotest idea of what you were seeing, you had to have descended by the steep trail, labored through sand, squeezed through the slot canyon, scaled the canyon wall and found for yourself the line of little figures dancing lightly, gracefully, across the living rock and the millennia. Apart from the minimal frame created by the alcove's arch, you couldn't put a frame around these figures. You couldn't send them around in a traveling exhibition, you couldn't saw a couple out (as vandals had attempted to do here; Pam saw the deep straight clefts where someone had tried and given up) to put in your house, or in a museum. You couldn't pay ten bucks to see them, you had to pay with effort, sweat, determination. If you were careless enough, you might have to pay with your life.

This panel had been studied a lot. The ram-headed serpents, the plants and "hybrid" plant people, the "hollow" armless anthropomorphs, all had been scrutinized and compared with similar figures from other sites. The conceptual (but not stylistic) resemblance of the horned or "plumed" serpents to Quetzalcoatl had been noted. Before this day Pam had focussed on the figure of the ascending bird at the far left, but now she saw that this bird could not be meaningfully separated from the rest of the panel, any more than the panel could be separated from its alcove or canyon setting. She took a few close-up shots anyway, having brought the camera so far and through such peril.

The artist had understood perspective; the bird ascended, not simply to the right, but away from the viewer. There were pointed ears? feather tufts? short straight horns? on its head. The long wavy line trailing behind the bird ended in a pair of legs, with tiny feet turned the opposite direction (left and west) from the direction of its general trajectory. Someone had written that while there were those who saw in this an emblem of shamanic transformation, others saw it as proof that in the case of rock art symbolism it's mighty hard to know what you're looking at, or words to that effect. Admiring the panel now, Pam knew in her bones that the trailing bird was about transformation, but also that the second statement was far from incorrect.

Several figures holding plant bundles had roots growing down from their feet, and therefore seemed transformational too—who was that girl in the Greek myth who was saved from rape by being turned into a tree?—as did the panel's three snakes, all with limbs and unusual heads, especially the one whose long thin body transected the line trailing below the bird. Its little arms reached toward the slender anthropomorph at the far left of the panel in a kind of antithesis of Liam's backward-leaning anthropomorph defending itself from the bear; but the most striking thing was the way the two lines formed a wavy X that balanced the composition and pulled that part of the panel together.

The artist had had a phenomenal eye and superb technical control. The composition and rhythm of the whole long, complex panel, of which the bird made up a very small part, was phenomenal. The more Pam stared, the more amazing it became. The *whole thing* pulled together! You knew with complete certainty that the panel hadn't been painted just to decorate the cave or, expressive as it was, out of mere personal self-expression, which as a concept probably didn't even exist when the artist stood where Pam was standing to dip a yucca brush into a bowl of red hematite that had been powdered and suspended in its binder of (probably) urine. Everyone who had studied the panel felt this, that the information in the panel had been tremendously important to the painter, as message and as art. Everyone felt its ethereal spirituality.

Where, then, was the fear? Or, Pam mused, mindful of being rather shaky on her pins still, where did art stop and experience begin?

Already she wanted to come back, spend time alone at the site with no deadline pressure—give herself up to the power in whose presence she felt herself to be, for as long as she liked. Hot Spots in general had that effect on people; it was why in Orrin's and Hannah's day so many visitors had kept wandering back to Hurt Hollow, without being able to explain what they got out of being there. It might be plenty scary to spend the night up here alone. Speaking of fear. The idea nevertheless took hold of Pam powerfully, a yearning to come back at dusk and unroll a sleeping bag beneath the lively figures overhead, busy with their mysterious affairs; but that wasn't going to happen today.

She gave the images a last long look, hung her camera back around her neck, and started down, detouring to pick up the scattered sheets of paper. Paying appropriate attention, she reached the wash without difficulty and turned back, toward the rim and the chopper.

Her mind, as she slogged through the sand, was filled with admiring curiosity about the artist, a member of a hunting and foraging community, who had imagined those figures or seen them in ecstatic trance, and afterwards discovered in himself as he worked the capacity to infuse them with such feeling, using paint and a brush. Despite the flaking and exfoliation, you saw immediately how sophisticated his work was. Where did they practice, these shaman painters? How did they learn the skills? Pam would have denied that it was possible for an untutored person of any era simply to pick up a brush and *ta da!* paint the Dead Mule Canyon pictograph panel in all its delicate complexity. Yet you didn't see sketches, not in BCS. Practice rocks had never been discovered. Not *everything* in that tradition was Great Art for sure. Some panels, like the bird shaman ones in Texas, were blocky, chunky, interesting for subject and theme but of marginal esthetic importance; but many were so fine! She knew this from reproductions, and knew already that to be in their physical presence would intensify the effect. A great mystery was here.

Bringing a transceiver up to that alcove, scanning back to see how the space had been used during the past eight thousand years, that would be fascinating and entirely doable. And entirely wrong. Humphrey had rejected the idea as applied to the dart-headed Hefn in Texas, on the grounds that whatever the people said would be incomprehensible. But you could learn a lot just from observation. The real objection, Pam saw, was that it was wrong to use technology to spy on people who could make such pictures. You were supposed to find out by yourself, maybe with the help of a mescal bean or two if you were the mescal-bean type. A picture floated into Pam's mind, of a boy hanging a watch and compass on a bush because they were preventing him from finding a bear he was looking for in the woods. She saw one printed sentence: "He was still tainted." That was it exactly.

Halfway back through the twists of the slot canyon, she thought: maybe it's something about Hot Spots, maybe being at the right Hot Spot empowered a spiritually attuned hunter-gatherer to create art that would be beyond his (her?) abilities elsewhere. A kind of channeling, or automatic painting. Something in any case not available to, nor desired by, a Hot-Spot-dwelling homesteader named Orrin Hubbell.

~

After the thrills and chills of Dead Mule, Pam found the Feet of Sinbad panel anticlimactic, though objectively it was just as intriguing, and the impact of seeing a human artifact in the vast unpeopled landscape just as visceral. A different artist had painted this panel on the face of an exposed cliff, but had used the same storyboard approach, with a similarly rhythmic grouping of figures. Horned snakes and large birds with weeping wings—stylistically very like those at Dead Mule—had been worked into the composition, though the anthropomorphs here were of a different type. The flight of tiny birds, leading off stage right, even caught something of the feel of Pam's first lucid dream.

What made this panel especially fascinating/maddening was that only the lower two-thirds was available for study; the top part had broken off before Europeans had penetrated into this part of Utah.

What made it intriguing to Pam, and the reason she had chosen it for this day's excursion, was that the figure on the far right, the direction in which the snakes were slithering and the little birds were flying, was the bottom half of a large, seated animal with extended clawed feet, that was generally believed to represent a bear.

One educated guess about the panel was that it showed the large human being at the far left being gradually transformed into the bear, metamorphosing through several intermediate forms in the process. Pam had come, for Liam's sake and for the sake of the second lucid dream, to see for herself.

The chopper could have landed right next to the cliff, she'd walked the last mile over a flat plain purely from respect, and maybe that was partly it, that getting there had been easy. Partly it might have been the wide-openness of the setting, its lack of intimacy and secrecy. Pam stood before the panel for quite a while, opening herself as best she could to whatever important thing it had to say in its fascinatingly unintelligible medium of communication. In the end, though, as best she could make out, it didn't seem to be telling two-thirds of a story about a shaman turning into a bear.

She appreciated again how the painting on the smooth cliff face was "framed" only by an alcove so high and broad that it was itself continuous with its surroundings, like and also unlike Wallace Stevens' jar in Tennessee that "made the slovenly wilderness / Surround that hill" where he had set it down. But if the place was a Hot Spot, she was too tired to tell.

~

"I saw another bear today," she reported to Liam. "Half of one, I should say. Not Adam-zad. This one was sitting down with his legs stuck out like a teddy bear, and he had claws and no top half. Also, he was facing away from the people in the panel. I don't think you would have had another freakout if you'd seen him."

"That's consoling."

"Incidentally, do you happen to remember a story, some classic story, about a kid who's trying to find a legendary bear in the wilderness, and he finally realizes that his watch and compass are getting in the way, and he hangs them on a bush and then he sees the bear?"

"That's in *The Bear*, by William Faulkner. We read it in school."

"That's what it's called? Just *The Bear*?"

"Yep. Great story. I thought your *speech* was great, by the way, as a tightrope-walking act. So, come clean: have you been avoiding me?"

Pam had given some thought to how she would handle a question of this kind. "Thanks. As a matter of fact, yes I have, for a good reason. There's something I know that I'm not allowed to tell you yet, and it was either avoid you, or keep it to myself and try to act natural, or tell you the truth, which is what I'm doing right now. Avoiding you was easiest."

"And deceiving me was impossible. You're the worst liar I ever met."

She had deceived him very successfully for almost a week. She looked forward keenly to rubbing that in one day, but for now— "I know, but don't bother guessing because I won't tell you till the time's right. I can't."

Liam looked gratified; he loved to ignore Pam's instructions about how he should behave. "Why can't you? Is it about me?"

"What I will do," Pam said doggedly, "is hang up. A lousy liar I may be, but I'm getting a lot better at rudely hanging up on you, as you may have noticed. I give you fair warning. Change the subject."

"Fine. When you hung up on me *three weeks ago*, I was trying to find out if you'd had any more of those dreams, and I still want to know: have you?"

This was a trick question but Pam was ready for it. "I'm actually thinking I might be going to have one tonight. The first site I went to was just awesome, plus I nearly plunged to my death before I got up to it—don't tell Lexi, whatever you do!—and I've got this hunch that it might have put me in the right mood."

She expected he would try to make her promise to tell him about the dream, if she managed to have one, but instead he looked appalled. "What do you mean, 'plunged to your death'? What happened?"

Pam described the near-disaster. "It was like when we got charged by Adam-zad—I tried and tried to solve the problem, all the time certain there had to be a solution. But there didn't have to be. I got lucky."

Liam had tensed up. "You're not exaggerating? You could really have been killed?"

"Exactly as 'really' as that time in the Poconos. It was a close call, and it was totally my own stupid fault. I kept thinking, What happens to Lexi if something happens to me?"

He looked astonished. "That's all? 'What happens to Lexi?' Hey, *What happens to me* if you go pitching headfirst over some cliff? Didn't you think about that?"

Pam was taken aback. "Well—no, actually. Would it make that much difference to you? I mean, realistically, it's not like we're in touch very much any more."

To her amazement, Liam's face worked and turned red. He made a strange noise, half angry outburst half sob, then his hand jerked up and *he* hung up on *her*.

Oh God, what now. Pam sat back, nonplussed. Evidently she'd been insensitive. Should she call him back? At the thought of having an emotional scene with Liam right now, a wave of enervation sloshed over her. This was succeeded by sharp exasperation: what *was* it about this oldest friendship of hers, that they could never get the balance right? Either she wanted more from Liam than he could give, or he wanted more from her. The pendulum never stopped swinging between extremes. As she sat there undecided the phone chimed. Liam was calling *her* back. Wanting terribly not to answer, Pam gritted her teeth and muttered "Phone on," and there he was, familiar and maddening as ever. "Hi," she said. "Why the Sam Hill are the two of us eternally out of kilter?"

"Julie could probably explain it," Liam said. "So could we, probably, if we tried—don't look so horrified, I didn't mean right now. I just called back to apologize for hanging up on you."

"Oh well. Lot of that going around."

He managed a twitch of a smile. "You really shocked me, Pam. The thought that you could be dead right now, and didn't think I would even mind very much if you were—"

"Sometimes," Pam said truthfully, "I do know better."

"Yeah?" And then, plaintively, "Well, what if it was me? How would *you* feel?"

"If you—?" She heard again his wild, ungrateful *I could have died, I could have died, why didn't you let me die?*—the ghastliness that cry had opened in the universe—and shuddered. "Come on. Need you ask? I was the one—"

"Okay, I know, don't remind me. Well look, you have to believe this, it's the same with me, even if I—don't show it the same way, or even always realize it, I guess."

The muddle was all too much. "If I just say 'All right,' can I go to bed?"

"Say you believe me."

"I believe you mean it right now. That'll have to do, Liam."

He sighed. "Go on, go to bed. See if you have a dream. Put on the Beethoven loop."

Released, she said, "You read my mind. That is my exact intention."

~

And she did dream, but not lucidly. Only fractals, more fractals, streaming snippets of nonsense—and then, toward morning, one clear memorable scene. Jesse Kellum, looking exactly like himself except that his face and hair appeared to be sculpted in copper, was sitting in the loose deep sand in the bottom of Dead Mule Canyon. The sky was heartbreakingly blue, the sand the tan-gray of Santa Barbara beach sand. He was barefoot, and sat with both legs thrust out before him, one leg so swollen below the knee that his baggy jeans fit it like a sausage casing; but he was smiling and relaxed, clearly not in pain.

It was simply wonderful to be with him again. In the dream Pam basked wordlessly in Jesse's presence, and for a while Jesse was happy and silent too. But then he said conversationally, looking right into Pam's eyes, "Upon thy belly shalt thou go, and dust shalt thou eat all the days of thy life, and I will put enmity between thee and the woman, and between thy seed and her seed, it shall bruise thy head, and thou shalt bruise his heel." Then his blue eyes in his long face— no longer copper but plain pink flesh—twinkled at Pam. "Think

about it, Punkin. You haven't been thinking about it, have you?"
And she woke up.

She lay still as she could, breathing quietly, steeped in the bliss
of her love for Jesse, who had died so many years ago. The love,
her capacity to feel it, was a wonderful surprise. It was so hard to
believe that she had once moved around inside her life brim-full
of this transfiguring emotion, not just for Jesse but for Humphrey
too, and all the time. Back then, being alive at all was to be sloshing over with love for a homesteading widower and a pelted alien.
Incredible! She had not felt loved back by Jesse exactly, never quite
dared even to wonder whether he loved her back. She knew he was
fond of her but not how far the fondness went—whether it had
reached that kindling point. And certainly she had never felt loved
by Humphrey, for all his bonding issues and "my dears." It wasn't
as the object of love that her days were invigorated then, but as the
subject. She was not the loved one. She was the one allowed to do
the loving.

The dream's emotion seemed to clarify one thing anyway. According to Pam's unconscious, Jesse had felt about her then the way she
now felt about Lexi, the chosen not the natural child, the only living
being who now reliably evoked much depth of feeling in Pam at
all—she refused to count her intense, erratic lunges and plunges of
feeling for Liam, which were as much an affliction as a source of
strength.

The blissfulness gradually faded as she came thoroughly awake.
When it could be held onto no longer she rolled over, smiling and
stretching, and saw the loop player still softly beating *pom, pom-
pom-pom, pom, pom, pom-pom-pom, pom* . . .

The lucid dream ploy. Well, it hadn't worked. There would be
nothing new to conceal from Liam.

As she reached to switch off the player, the image of Jesse reappeared in her mind. He was sitting in the Utah desert, right in the
wash. His face—his face was made of copper, like an Indian-head
penny.

This was a normal dream, subject to analysis in a way familiar
from the years of therapy leading up to the bradshaw. Interpreting dream symbolism wasn't much different from interpreting the
symbolism of good poetry. Unless you were digging up ghastly
secrets, it was fun.

So fine, what was her unconscious bringing up into consciousness this time? Jesse was sitting in the dry wash with his swollen leg
stuck out in front of him; that alluded to the time he'd been bitten by
the copperhead—

Copper head! Pam sat up in bed. She was getting rusty, to miss
such an obvious transposition, especially given the quotation from
Genesis, about the serpent who had tempted Eve in the Garden of
Eden. Pam smiled; the living Jesse would never have quoted the
Bible, he didn't *know* the Bible. What had he said? To think about
it? About getting snakebit? There were a lot of snakes in the desert,
active in warm weather; maybe her unconscious meant she should
be careful where she stepped out there. Jesse had stepped on the
snake that bit him, she had stepped on the slickrock without checking to be sure it was safe.

That seemed reasonable, but there might be something to her
first association with the Indian-head penny too. She'd been thinking during Liam's visit about the Indians that had lived in the area
around Hurt Hollow before the Europeans drove them out: village-
dwelling farmers who hunted and gathered as well—good Gaians,
like Jesse. But the ancient Barrier Canyon artists were Indians
too.

Pam started to get out of bed. Instead she dropped back and sat
on the side, having just realized that the way Jesse was sitting in the
sand, a very unnatural position for long-legged Jesse, was extremely
natural for a teddy bear. Or for a Hefn.

Or—

She saw the Feet of Sinbad panel, the clawed (*bear-foot!*) animal
seated with legs thrust forward just above a crawling snake, horns
or feathers on its head, feathers in the war bonnet of the penny
Indian. She saw the horned snakes in the cave in Dead Mule
Canyon, the snake with the little arms reaching toward the left-
most human figure, its sinuous body crossing the contrail of the
ascending bird. Snakes were ubiquitous in BCS art, in shamanistic art of every kind, as common and important as birds, often
paired with birds when she thought about it—but Pam had not
been thinking about it.

Now her unconscious had issued a useful corrective. As above,
so below: bird and serpent, blue sky and silver sand, two sides of
one equation, like yin and yang, like rage and devotion, like soaring

ecstasy and venomous dread, like Quetzalcoatl, the bird-snake, the plumed serpent.

Pam stood, drawn now a little deeper into the mystery.

CHAPTER 14

Boning Up

2 OCTOBER - 7 DECEMBER

By October it seemed so improbable that the Church would try snatching Lexi again, given the paradigm shift of the final year, that Jack the bodyguard had been relieved of duty. Jack himself was less convinced that Lexi didn't still need protecting, and he'd become fond of her. Before departing he'd made an urgent pitch for getting her a dog. He knew of some standard poodles that hadn't passed muster as guard dog trainees and were about to be put up for adoption. One of those might be just the ticket.

"A *poodle*?" Pam pictured a small yappy lapdog with pompoms on its ears.

"Standard poodle, the big ones. They got an image problem but they can be great guard dogs, I've worked with a few."

"I thought guard dogs were all, like, Rottweilers. German Shepherds."

"Nah. A lot of cops and security people, they got allergies just like everybody else, they can't work with the regular dogs, and poodles don't shed, see, they're, whaddyacallit, hypo-allergy dogs. But they ain't one of them naturally aggressive breeds, so the trainers'll work with 'em for a while and get to know 'em, and the ones that ain't cut out for it, they get put up for adoption. But just because they ain't fit for police work don't mean they don't do a great job guarding somebody's house or somebody's kid. And they're smarter'n I am. Why not just go take a look?"

So they went down to the training center, and were shown into the presence of two curly, black, medium-size dogs in a kennel run, snarling and play-fighting together, docked tails wagging like crazy. They were clipped short all over, no pompoms. "These two were littermates," the trainer explained. "BJ and Feste. Temperament-wise they're just as sweet as they can be, both of them, they'll make great pets. They sailed through training, but they just didn't have what it takes for us to keep them in the program—well, Feste came closer, but he's a little on the small side for the work. I'd better warn you, he's a barker, if that would be a problem."

He interrupted their game and brought the dogs out on leashes for Lexi and Pam to see up close. Lexi's hands sank into soft curly fur on the heads of two grinning, panting poodles with lolling pink tongues. She crouched down; Feste licked her cheek. "*Oh, Pom!*" she gasped, and then urgently, "Wouldn't it be a great idea if you had a dog with you at Hurt Hollow? Then we could take them both!"

This was the very first time Lexi had sounded anything but flatly opposed to being left in Salt Lake while Pam went off to the Hollow. The trainer, seeing Pam's eyebrows shoot up, said quickly, "We've been feeling bad about having to separate these two, that's a fact. They went from a puppy mill that got closed down, to a shelter, and when the shelter called us they were both so sick we didn't think Feste would pull through. It was January, and they'd been sleeping piled together on a little scrap of carpet on a concrete floor, there's no doubt they kept each other alive in that shelter, so . . ."

They would still have to be separated, of course, but not all the time, and only temporarily. Pam left it to Lexi to decide which poodle stayed with her and which went to Hurt Hollow. While Lexi agonized, she and Pam somehow made time for lessons in guard-dog handling, each working with both BJ and Feste—Feste with an e, not an a; he'd been named for the clown in Shakespeare's comedy *Twelfth Night*—in hopes of clarifying Lexi's choice.

The uncertainty crisis dragged on for a week. Then one morning Lexi came down to breakfast and declared. "I dreamed the solution. BJ stays, Feste goes."

Privately Pam sagged with relief, but she only said, "Good, I'm glad it's decided. What was the dream like?"

"BJ asked to stay with me." Lexi sat and dumped raisins into her bowl of oatmeal, then brown sugar. "I'm throwing the ball, and BJ gets it, and when he brings it back he sits down and lets me take it out of his mouth, and then instead of running back out, he goes, 'I want to stay with you.' And I go 'Why,' and he goes, 'Pom loves Feste.' And then he runs out for me to throw the ball again, and I wake up."

"Really?" Pom loves Feste? She was taken aback. "So how does it feel? Is that what *you* want?"

"It feels good, like it's all settled now. Please pass the milk." She started to eat. "I didn't know you loved Feste."

"Neither did I, I mean not any more than BJ." In fact Pam had consciously refrained from forming a preference, which wasn't hard; to her the two dogs still seemed as alike as two jumping beans in a pod.

The following morning Lexi announced that she had dreamed the explanation: "Feste was sicker."

If he was, Pam thought, she hadn't known it. Or thought she hadn't; but then the memory surfaced: "That's right, the trainer said they were worried he might not make it. I'd forgotten about that."

"Me too, till BJ reminded me. And guess what else! He told me what 'BJ' stands for!"

The adoption papers had given initials only. "What does it stand for?"

Her grin lit up the kitchen. "Baloo, Junior!"

~

The double adoption reconciled Lexi to Pam's absence, finally, but a few weeks more went by before she was able to leave. Learning to handle the dogs was essential if they were not to forget their training; but time for lessons was hard to come by, with Lexi tied up all day almost every day at the studio, working on the series and with the tutor she shared with her co-star, Neil. Martin had to be invited/persuaded to move into the house while Pam was away, and the guest room made ready for a semi-permanent resident. They had to assume that new abuse cases might still come in occasionally; Jaime needed somebody in the office besides just himself, and that had to be worked out. Several tricky conversations with Liam, involving his wish to visit Pam at the Hollow and Pam's determination to prevent that from happening, also took place.

Now that she was actually going, Humphrey made no effort to hide his delight. Pam reminded him again and again that there were no guarantees, she couldn't promise to deliver what he wanted (whatever that was) but could only be open to whatever came, but nothing she said made him beam less joyously each time they spoke on the phone. Unlike Liam he never wheedled to come and see her at the Hollow—though, of course, if he took the notion he would simply turn up one day. All Pam could do was plead for solitude and promise to initiate contact as often as was consistent with feeling her way into the center of the experience, if any, she was trying to have. "There's no instructional viddy, I have to make this up as I go. The fewer distractions the better, unless you can find me a teacher."

Humphrey continued to beam. "I too have been boning up on shamanism. Many shamans learn by becoming apprentices to those more experienced—apprentices! ha!—but others are taught by the spirits direct. 'Boning up,' that is also a joke, yes?"

"It's a joke all right."

"Because shamans in trance often see themselves as skeletons."

Pam groaned. "Humphrey, we've told you a million times, it wrecks the joke to explain the punch line."

But finally on a blue bare morning at the end of October she and Feste boarded a plane that took them from Salt Lake to Louisville, and later that same day they stepped off the steamer together, onto the dock at Hurt's Landing.

The season was over, the place deserted. As she'd done so many times through so many years, Pam took a key from her pocket, twisted it in the lock, and pushed the gate open as the boat reversed and turned cumbrously, headed on upriver. Feste, released, trotted a little way up the bluff toward the house, peed against a tree, then stopped and looked back; and so was the single witness to the clanging of the heavy gate behind them, the moment of Pam's coming back into possession of her Ground.

～

Pam hadn't lived in the house for years, but other people had, and she certainly hadn't forgotten how. The Place Where Time Stands

Still was exactly the same, except that the house and studio were in better repair than when Jesse had bequeathed them to her.

In late summer the volunteer staff let the tourists watch them can whatever the garden was producing, taking turns sweating merrily over the wood-burning cookstove in period costume all through August and September, in a reenactment of how Hannah Hubbell used to do it. When they closed for the season they usually gave away all the beautiful jars of berries, beans, and tomatoes to local assisted-care facilities, but this year Pam had asked them to leave the cellar well stocked, and they had complied. She also found onions, beets, carrots, and potatoes in the root cellar. There was also plenty of firewood stacked around, from the male volunteers' reenactments of how Orrin Hubbell used to do that. She found kerosene, candles, matches. She even found two ceramic dog bowls on a shelf under the sink. "Look at this, Feste! You're gonna be dining after some very distinguished dogs."

But the house needed airing and cleaning. The gutters and cistern had to be checked out, also the fittings of the outhouse, which she preferred to the rest room with septic system that had been installed for visitors; it was more convenient to the house, and she had used it since childhood. Also, they needed extra supplies. Feste required food and treats, and a backup stash of tennis balls. The bird feeders needed to be set up where the squirrels couldn't reach them, and filled. The phone line had to be reactivated (a strict condition of the deal with Lexi was that they would talk with each other every single evening), and a powerful new computer had to be purchased and installed (Lexi wanted a life-size Pam on the screen). This involved a boat trip back to Louisville. Pam's library of print books had accompanied them on the plane as far as Louisville and would arrive at Hurt's Landing in a day or so; space to shelve them had to be created.

More than a week went into organizing all this, also into tramping for miles through the November woods with Feste, to teach him how to find his way home. Already it was dazzlingly clear, as so many people on a childless Earth had long since discovered, that a dog was a wonderful idea. Loyal. Affectionate. Not given to complicated betrayals. Great company at the Hollow. Feste wasn't used to running loose, and Pam kept him close at first, but there would be no reason not to let him roam wherever he liked once he knew his way around. The whole sixty-one-acres of river bluff had been enclosed and the fence electrified. A fence that had failed to exclude athletic members of the local deer herd had kept the coyotes out completely; and if Feste should encounter a porcupine or a skunk the consequences would be only very disagreeable, not fatal. He learned in one lesson not to touch the fence and never went near it again.

But a rainy morning eventually came when Pam had finished breakfast and done the dishes, when a fire was snapping cozily under the beaten copper hood of the hearth, when Orrin's table and chairs and polished plank floor, and Pam's books and mechanical devices, all lay in mellow lamplight; and there was no more cleaning or arranging to be done. The time to start doing what she had come here to do had arrived.

Realizing this, Pam realized also, with a stab of panic, that she had no idea how to begin.

The date was November 12; she left for a brief visit back to Salt Lake on December 5, two days before Lexi's twelfth birthday. That gave her . . . twenty-three days. In which to do what, exactly?

Have a dream that would provide Humphrey with information about the future. So that what?

Not so the Baby Ban would be lifted; it wouldn't be now, regardless of what Pam learned. Yet Humphrey consistently implied that the ultimate fate of the human remnant on Earth would be impacted by this information, if he could just get hold of it in time. But he wouldn't tell her why, or what it concerned, or what it had to do with the extra year the Gafr were pretending to give them before final judgment about the Ban was pronounced upon humanity.

She had left Lexi, left Jaime in the lurch, and come to Hurt Hollow, because this, her personal Ground, a Hot Spot, lived into by her throughout her childhood, was surely the place most likely to produce a condition in herself . . . that would in turn produce the lucid dream or dreams in which she would acquire the essential information. Even though the previous dreams had both come unbidden, while she was still in Utah.

Pam looked around the beautiful fire-lit wooden room, at the rain streaming down the windows, at the black poodle snoozing under Orrin's table, and said aloud, "This is crazy!"

~

12 November 2037, Thursday 1:30 p.m., HH. What's not crazy about it is hard to hang onto, but I'm here now and I may as well do my best. Keeping in mind how in therapy my point of view would suddenly shift treacherously and I would be afraid I was making it all up, and Julie would say, "Stick with the facts: your dread of staying overnight at your grandmother's, losing your intuition when your dad died, your many dreams of penises being washed in sinks. These are effects that have a cause."

So now in like manner I have to cling to the hard nuggets of fact in a bog of weirdness. It is a fact that I learned, by non-rational means, that:

1. the Ban will never be lifted;
2. Lexi had been abducted by Mormons (or run away to escape being abducted by Mormons);
3. Lexi was/would be taken to Green River;
4. Gillian is "preggers."

Shaman schmaman, the label doesn't matter. I don't know if I even believe in shamanism—I'm far from sure I understand what it is, to tell the truth, for all my diligent study—but I can and do believe in the objective truth of the list above. And in my own experience, even if I'm not ready to say what that means either. I suppose you could quibble that (1) has yet to be confirmed by events, the deadline still being more than six months away; but Humphrey said there will be no lifting of the Ban and that's confirmation enough for me.

Tonight I'll try the Bach loop again; but I wonder this morning whether the direct approach is my best gambit. I'm at Hurt Hollow! Why not just be here, make being here its own end, and not a mere means of trying to give Humphrey what he wants. I may or may not be a Latter-day Shaman, but I am now as ever a Gaian, true and blue and through and through, and this place is my personal Ground.

14 November 2037, Saturday 9:30 a.m., HH. That little Feste is smart as a whip, and funny as the clown he was named for (by some unknown Shakespeare-literate Mormon police-dog trainer I guess). Yesterday we worked on some of his commands, which he executes so promptly and beautifully it's a joy to behold. I suppose he'll inevitably lose his edge under my handling, which is a lot less snappy than what he's used to, but for now it's a pleasure to see anything performed with such consummate grace and conviction, even Down! Heel! Come front! By me!

Having Feste here means I'm both alone and not alone. I'm more alone by far than if Lexi were here, or if Liam or Humphrey were, but when I lived at the Hollow before it was just me and the bees and goats. Both required attention, but didn't put their chins on my knee and fix their big brown eyes on my face, asking to be loved on. Do I remember right that Faust had a black poodle as a familiar? Hm.

I have been reading, of all things, Wordsworth's *Prelude*. Somehow I never got around to it before—one of those book-length Major Poems, like *In Memoriam* and *The Faerie Queene* and *Paterson,* that people only read anthologized excerpts of in these corrupt times. But there's a copy here that belonged to Orrin and Hannah, one of the books I moved onto the cot upstairs to make room for my rock art library, and yesterday after dinner my eye happened to fall on it and I picked it up and started in. I'm reading it aloud, as O and H would have done to each other. This quickly put Feste to sleep, and I have to admit that a lot of it is not exactly the most engaging stuff by WW that I've ever come across, but I'm finding it strangely relevant to my recent grapplings with art and greatness.

Something I hadn't known but learned today, from a footnote, is that the eighteenth century thought in esthetic categories of the Beautiful and the Sublime, first codified it seems by Edmund Burke, the English philosopher; at any rate I've turned up a 1757 essay by him entitled *"A Philosophical Enquiry into the Origin of our Ideas of the Sublime and the Beautiful."* In a nutshell: "Sublime" applies to a landscape (or painting, or poem) when it is overwhelming, immense, magnificent, possesses grandeur, and is disordered to the point of astonishing and, get this, terrifying the viewer! "No passion so effectually robs the mind of all its powers of acting and reasoning as terror, and whatever is terrible with regard to sight, is sublime." Examples: Stonehenge and *Paradise Lost.*

The Beautiful is small, tame, tidy, and smooth, and seems to apply in Burke's mind mostly to flowers and to "the fair sex"; at any rate its effect is to inspire not fear but affection, not tension but relaxation.

THE BIRD SHAMAN

I think that a lot of what he calls "beautiful" we might want to call "pretty"; but the point is that these terms strike me as being analogous to my categories of "great" and "not great"—and that Wordsworth exemplifies them in the child-self persona he creates in the *Prelude*. He describes himself as a little savage, running wild among the lakes and mountains, but hypersensitive to the influences of Nature in both joyous and frightening form. A nascent shaman, in fact, in another place and time. "I grew up," he declares, "Fostered alike by beauty and by fear." The *Prelude* gives lots of examples showing how the ominous side of nature was as important as the magnificent side in the formation of his character.

But then the story progresses to a point where WW becomes domesticated under the influence of his sister and his wife. In youth, he says, looking back all chastened,

> I too exclusively esteemed that love,
> And sought that beauty, which as Milton sings,
> Hath terror in it. Thou [sister Dorothy] didst soften down
> This over-sternness; but for thee, sweet friend,
> My soul, too reckless of mild grace, had been
> Far longer what by Nature it was framed—
> Longer retained a countenance severe—
> A rock with torrents roaring, with the clouds
> Familiar, and a favourite of the stars:
> But thou didst plant its crevices with flowers,
> Hang it with shrubs that twinkle in the breeze,
> And teach the little birds to build their nests
> And warble in its chambers.

Talk about saying one thing and meaning another! Has William convinced anyone in this classroom that he really believes he's better off in his new configuration as a cottage garden, than he was as a rock with torrents roaring? An artist of Wordsworth's caliber must take care; no matter what he sets out to say, the work itself will reveal what's really on his mind. But the Romantics came a whole century before the discovery of the unconscious, and so could be blissfully ignorant both of what they really felt, and of how they gave themselves away.

Judith Moffett

The passage goes on and on, repeating its point again and yet again, as if by telling the lie enough times he'll finally succeed in turning it into a truth. Tipped off by another footnote I looked up "Tintern Abbey," which I hadn't read in probably twenty years (more fool me, it's damn good), and found there an even better portrait of our nascent shaman, complete with rock and torrent:

> For nature then . . .
> To me was all in all.—I cannot paint
> What then I was. The sounding cataract
> Haunted me like a passion: the tall rock,
> The mountains, and the deep and gloomy wood,
> Their colors and their forms, were then to me
> An appetite; a feeling and a love . . .

—inanimate Nature this would be, W's sensibility doesn't seem to apprehend the biosphere. But now, alas (from his perspective when he wrote the above), "That time is past, / And all its aching joys are now no more, / And all its dizzy raptures." Thanks largely to the influence of his friendship with Coleridge, he's moved on, well into "a sense sublime [!]" having to do with "the joy / Of elevated thoughts," i.e. the large human philosophical and religious questions which I take loosely to equal the intellectual enlightenments of civilization, figured with vast possibilities and new terrors of their own (the French Revolution). But when he looks at his sister in "Tintern Abbey" he sees no hanger of twinkling shrubs, but rather can read his own "former pleasures in the shooting lights / Of thy wild eyes," and pleads, "Oh yet a little while / May I behold in thee what I was once." Then he proceeds to finish off the poem with a passage so splendid in its praise of Nature's redeeming powers as to puzzle the dullest reader: what was all that you just said about the joy of elevated thoughts being abundant recompense for what he'd lost? Sure don't sound like it to me.

That was in 1798. By 1805, Dorothy is planting flowers in his crevices and no longer appears in the guise of alter ego.

I find this pretty fascinating. You can read the *Prelude* as the desperate effort of a particular man to convince himself that his wimminfolk know best, even though unconsciously he would like to murder them both. Or you can read it, if so inclined, as a symbolic male hunter-forager's efforts to persuade himself that hanging around in one place all summer, so the wimminfolk can tend the gardens, is actually a good idea because it's safer. I mean, why have the shaman go into trance and bargain with the Keeper of the Animals, and then keep the rendezvous with the designated elk, when you can stay home and have a nice piece of roast squash for no trouble at all?

Maybe the womenfolk forced the issue then too; security was more on their minds, after all, and for good reason. Women did the planting and produced the squashes; men came to depend more and more on garden produce and got a bit softer and a bit lazier; little by little they were drawn into complicity; and what had been lost was lost so gradually that they were hardly aware it was gone.

Every time I look up from this pad I see Orrin's lovely painting of cornshocks and spring fields, that unearthly green that turns out to be the exact green of winter wheat in those exact bottom-land fields hereabouts, with the bluegray river bluff beyond, and the small suggestion of a farmer and mule team just barely brought inside the frame. It catches at my throat. It isn't magnificent, obscure, or vast; nor is it smooth and tidy. The feeling it evokes isn't fear, isn't affection, but is something more like reverence. Reverence in Burke's scheme is a subset of the sublime, but the painting's not sublime; still less is it "pretty."

It's simply beautiful. Beautiful and true.

17 November 2037, Tuesday 3 p.m., HH. I am not dreaming. Rather, I'm dreaming fractals and flotsam. Humphrey couldn't stand it any longer and called yesterday to find out why he hadn't heard from me. I told him there's nothing to tell, I even hinted that all this elaborate effort to invoke a dream might be why I'm not having any, and that pressuring me frankly wasn't helpful—especially, I said sternly, because I don't understand what it's all about.

That always takes the wind out of his sails. He managed to hang up without begging, but he is beside himself with anxiety.

So much so, in fact, that I wonder just how much is riding on this information I'm trying to extract from the timestream. Surely the Gafr aren't still considering whether to sterilize the Earth of people. After all this time? When the population will plummet in a few decades anyway? But then what's Humphrey so worried about?

Faust didn't have a black poodle familiar, I looked it up on this snazzy new computer. Faust saw a skinny black poodle following him in the street and carried it home. The poodle slipped behind the stove and emerged as Mephistopheles. Don't you do that, Feste!

I'm not dreaming, but I'm brooding long and deep over my photos of the Dead Mule Canyon pictograph panel. Burke would be at a loss as to which pile to put the panel in. It evokes, not affection, but fascination. It's small in itself, but inseparable from its landscape setting, which is rough and grand. It's intense with mysterious meaning, but not "difficult" in the sense that it was difficult to build Stonehenge or write *Paradise Lost*. I'm afraid there are more things in heaven and earth than are dreamt of in Burke's philosophy.

18 November 2037, Wednesday 8:15 a.m., HH. I thought I remembered this. In Hurt Hollow Orrin writes: "I doubt that I could for long be contented and happy alone in the absolute wilderness. I would soon begin to long for a rural countryside—say, what it was seventy-five or a hundred years ago [written in 1973 or '74]—with the habitations of men in the distance and the effects of their innocent work to be seen here and there." But then he amends this: "Even so, I yearn for the wild, I lean toward its absolute solitude, I long to ascend the river to its headwaters in forested mountains, to flow with it down to the sea, the ultimate wilderness."

And here's another one, where he pulls that punch just a bit: "In my old dreams of a wild existence on the riverbank the shelter I would build of unhewn timbers and hillside stones would be a dark, smoky cavern with an earth floor, like the habitations of the pioneers. The cabin in Hurt Hollow as it was when we first began to live in it offered only the bare essentials—shelter, windows for light, a place to build a fire, yet even then it was not the earthy hut I had dreamed of. A woman's[!] influence was already manifest. . . . I sometimes regret that my old longing to live closer to the earth can never be fulfilled, but our life together has been richer, more satisfying and productive, than my solitary one would ever have been. Of this I am sure."

I am too; but, musing on WW and Dorothy, I wonder: was Orrin? Every single minute of every single day?

19 November 2037, Thursday 9:20 p.m., HH. Here's a chart I made this morning:

Burke	[Primal] sublime: Alps	Beautiful	[Civilized] sublime: *P Lost*
WW	Rock w/ torrents: pantheism	Twinkling shrubs	"mind of man" social and moral philosophy
Gaians	Hunter/Gatherer	Homesteading (Crux)	Ecodisaster
Orrin	Primeval wilderness	Brief flowering	Urban blight
PP	Great/major	Not great/minor	Great/major

These categories are too sloppy to be useful except by loose analogy. Burke's are about esthetics and Wordsworth's allude only to his personal development as an individual, and I've taken liberties with both. Orrin and the Gaians are talking about lifeways (in similar terms, naturally, Orrin being the immediate model for everything Gaian). My categories refer to the potential for different stages of human social development to produce great art.

Still, I think I understand some things better as a result of expressing them this way.

If I could get two questions answered by shamanistic means, I'd ask whether it's humanly possible for us to do two things we've never done yet: (1) build our civilizations without losing our awareness of the living Earth; or, failing that, (2) balance at the Crux forever.

If (1) were possible somehow, what a bright world this would be. Without knowing much about them I have the impression that the Eastern religions are much closer to the spirit of Question One than Judaism/Christianity/Islam are; yet only think what India and China were like before the Takeover. Better say: without losing our awareness of the living Earth, stratifying into classes, or over-breeding.

Show of hands for yes? For no? That's what I thought.

No way we could ever have sold (2) to enough people, with the Hefn hanging about poised to wipe Directive violators. I'm remembering last spring, when we all sat in this very room and munched on that bitter truth. But the Gaian dream dies hard. I still wonder if there mightn't be some way, in different circumstances, to make time stand still not just in Hurt Hollow but everywhere, for everyone. To make Time really be One. So I'd still like to ask the powers that shamans communicate with, whoever they may be, whether it's even possible for people to do that, and still be people.

22 November 2037, Sunday 9:20 p.m., HH. Still not dreaming. Still brooding.

I've never wanted to be anything but a Gaian Elemental, even before there was a Gaian movement as such. Jesse gave me this hollow cut into the river bluff that he and the Hubbells had lived into, which is supersaturated with the spirits of all three of them. The tornado happened here, we all nearly died. Even if the place weren't also a powerful Hot Spot, no ground could possibly be more holy to me. The Missionaries would've had their first convert in me if I'd been a total math ignoramus and had never met Humphrey.

Despite all distractions the genius loci is finally starting to seep in, I'm starting to feel centered and peaceful. I'm eager to meditate twice a day, and move into trance quickly when I do. It's been crisp and dry. Feste and I take long rambles every day, part training practice and part pure pleasure, and go out on the river in the johnboat, which he's come to be crazy about after a skittish beginning. Years since I was able to soak myself—my soul, Wordsworth would say—in the soul of this place, as in pure water. I'm better for it in every way.

Yet at the same time I can feel how I'm being drawn away—no, drawn through Hurt Hollow, toward something wilder and stranger. I see a trailing bird and a standing bear, and sometimes a horned snake, inside my forehead when I close my eyes to meditate, and Orrin's landscapes when I open them; it's as though I can enter a primal reality through the portal of Orrin's sensibility where it comes to the surface, which is everywhere in this place he found and made.

26 November 2037, Thursday 11:00 a.m., HH. Thanksgiving Day. Just in from a wonderful hard walk. Doing this daily is whipping me into shape; when I climb the trail to check the upper gate I don't puff nearly as hard.

Feste and I took the steamer to the Madison market yesterday and bought a wild turkey. If I had a shotgun and knew how to use it I could have bagged one right in the Hollow; I never swore off killing wild poultry, and we've got lots. Very Pilgrimesque, I had to gut and pluck the bought bird, plus dig lots of birdshot out of his breast meat. I've concocted an amazingly real-looking dressing— eggs, onions, sage, last week's bread—for this bird, which is now roasting peacefully, making heavenly smells, as I sit and write this. To the main dish will be added canned green beans from the cellar and baked yams from the root cellar. By far the most ambitious cooking I've done since I got here. Feste can think of nothing else, and lies close to the stove where the aroma is strongest, head on folded paws, eyes fixed on me.

I've loaded three feeders to capacity with sunflower seed, thistleseed, and goat suet, all homegrown or gathered by the volunteers. Through the window, without moving, I can see a junco, a white-throated sparrow, two cardinals, several goldfinches and house finches, a downy woodpecker, a titmouse, and three chickadees. Birds feasting, bird to be feasted upon. Balance is restored.

Lexi has today off, and she and Martin are engrossed in their own version of this scene, but with a tame local turkey, a "Bourbon Red," one of the breeds that had almost disappeared before the Hefn came. She's getting excited about my trip back. When I was her age I pitied kids with birthdays close to Christmas, but when I asked Lexi if she was bummed to be born in December she said no, "I feel like December's my month! The whole month!" She looked happy and relaxed. Martin came on for a minute, wearing an apron and an oven mitt, and he looked happy and excited. It must be just wonderful for him to have Lexi to himself for Thanksgiving and Christmas both, and I must say they seem to be getting along like a house afire. I confess to a few pangs of jealousy, caused alas by the fact that Martin is Lexi's biological father, when I'm not her biological anything. The assumption is the same one that powered the whole doomed Homeland project: family trumps choice. But of course it usually does.

On the other hand, if Lexi and her dad can form a healthy relationship now, after everything that's happened, it's the best possible news for her. So let's suck it up here and be a grown-up.

Besides, it means that a good thing has come out of my leaving her, and that's the best possible news for us both.

This point is relevant because, much as I miss Lexi and much as I want to see her, I'd rather not go back right now, I don't want to interrupt what's happening here. No dreams, no no no, in fact I've stopped even thinking about dreams—but a kind of mellow merging with the place that I haven't felt so deeply or peacefully since I was a kid here. It took a while to lose the layers of ordinary life so the spirit of the Hollow could begin to soak into me, and I am loath to feel those layers start to build up again.

In a way I would love it if Lexi wanted to be here with me. The idea of playing Jesse to her Little Pam has enormous sentimental appeal; but she understood herself last summer that while this may be my Ground, it isn't hers. So what I'd like to give her for her birthday is "a bit of earth." When she's a little older we can find her a real garden, one she can get to on her own and do with as she likes. For now we can start with a practice place, the side yard between the house and the fence—not too exciting, but enclosed already on three sides; it would be a simple matter to throw a tall fence across the fourth side, with a gate she can shut and lock behind her. She'd have an apricot tree for starters, and some bamboo. She could make flower beds and maybe have a swing. Not quite the Secret Garden, bringing something old, overgrown, and neglected back to life, but if she likes the idea . . .

What I want to say, before it's time to stick the yams in with the turkey, is that all this past week, climbing up and down the hillside, working and playing with Feste, rowing on the river, tending the fire, and deeply, thoroughly appreciating where I am, I've been feeling more and more clearly what Orrin felt: a yearning for something wilder. The more so because I have no companion to temper that impulse with an attractive present alternative. The smoky hut with an earthen floor thing doesn't appeal to me—much better this actual house graced with Hannah's elegant touches. But I catch myself imagining the life of the first people to occupy that high eye-socket alcove where Liam reencountered Adam-zad: the painters of the panel.

This has turned my reading in a new direction (sorry, William, I'll be back); and everything I read makes clear how different my real upbringing and conditioning have been from that of even contemporary native peoples.

A lot is known (not by me, though, before now) about primal people—the Inuit, the aboriginal peoples of Australia, the Kalahari Bushmen, the Saami, others—who've survived into modern times; and some of the North American tribes have made an effort to keep the worldview going, even after they'd lost the lifeway that made it so natural. The story is everywhere the same. Individual identity merges with group identity; apart from the tribe, life is meaningless. The tribe is grounded in place and embedded in nature, and everything in nature is alive, sentient, and sacred, even rocks, even rivers, "yea, in the wave itself / And mighty depth of waters." The created world, which is continuous with the spirit world, is perfect just as it is and needs no improving; nor do the apparent divisions between plants and animals, and animals and people, really exist: everything merges with everything. Likewise, time is not chronological but "eternal." Every aspect of life is religious. Harmony, not justice, is the valued goal. There is a primary creator spirit, but the creator's holiness is shared with lesser spirits and spread throughout creation. You get an impression of continuous mystical flow, and of people perceiving essences within appearances by ordinary habit of mind.

The appeal is phenomenal.

But the reality is, someone like me could never be anywhere but on the outside looking in. To possess this mindset it's necessary to be acculturated within it; this is one religion you can't be converted to. I've looked into tribal adoptions during the colonial period in the United States. The Shawnees, for (local) example, raided white settlements and took prisoners, many of whom were adopted into families. People captured as adults (famously, Daniel Boone and Mary Engles) escaped if they could. The children were brought up as members of the tribe and learned to view the world as the Shawnees viewed it.

The lifeway available to me—a single woman lacking even family, let alone tribal, membership—is the Gaian way, where my upbringing and membership are beyond dispute. The most I could aspire to would be a shift from Elemental to Sacramental.

But all the time I'm thinking about that alcove.

4 December 2037, Thursday 9:45 p.m., HH. All packed. We leave in the morning. I'm wonderfully calm, not a bit concerned any more about having to disrupt the even tenor of my days here. I'll be back in a week, and will pick up the thread and continue to follow it. Meantime it'll be wonderful to see Lexi and BJ.

Something's been going on, but I couldn't say whether it's leading me any closer to Humphrey's goal. Certainly I've had no lucid dreams or mysterious answers to burning questions, nothing at all like that. Humphrey's in a terrible swivet, which he does his unsuccessful best not to let me see, but it doesn't seem to touch me. The world outside Hurt Hollow doesn't touch me. I walk upon this land, I command and commend my sweet clever Feste, I listen to the coyotes ki-yi'ing beyond the fence, and the great horned owls hoo-hooing, I stand on the dock absorbed in the steely river and sit by the fire cracking walnuts, I read with luminous comprehension, meditate, cook and eat stuff, wash dishes, wash clothes, sweep, bathe in the tin tub, patronize the outhouse, sleep in the Hubbells' bed. I do all this in a trance of calmness, somehow enabled to let whatever's happening happen.

CHAPTER 15

A Birthday Interlude

7 - 15 DECEMBER 2037

Pom was coming home for Lexi's twelfth birthday, and Lexi could hardly stand the wait.

They had talked on the phone every day, so in some ways it was like when Lexi was on location for a long time and Pom couldn't visit, only now when she came back to the house, her dad was the one in the kitchen cooking dinner. His dinners weren't that much worse than Pom's, and it was nicer than Lexi had expected to get to know him better. But he didn't read to her at bedtime, and she didn't feel right about reciting the poem of the week for him—he didn't care about poetry or Mowgli, he liked to tie flies and go trout fishing. So bedtime was when she really missed Pom.

One good thing about spending more off-the-set time with her dad, though, was that he'd started telling her stories about what it was like growing up in the house with Granpa as his stepfather. Granpa had been really mean to her dad and her Uncle Isaac, but in a sneaky way, so Granma wouldn't know. They tried to tell her but she never believed them, she was just like Lexi's mom in that way. Granpa had always put on this big pious front in the ward and with the neighbors, he was a Scout leader when his stepsons were the right ages for that, and later he sent them both on missions. Everybody always told them how lucky they were that Heavenly Father had provided them with such a great dad after their own had died in the accident, and Granma had told them the same thing when they tried to complain to her about him. Lexi was thrilled to find out that her father had always hated Granpa, but knew he wasn't supposed to let on to people, and what a huge relief it was for him in one way when Lexi's story came out, in spite of the terrible remorse he felt too. He apologized to Lexi again and again for leaving her alone with Granpa. But Granpa hadn't been interested in boys in that way, and he'd always acted loving toward Lexi. It truly hadn't occurred to her dad that the guy who had abused his stepsons emotionally might abuse his granddaughter another way when he got the chance.

"Well, and besides, Mom always thought he was so great. Even after, you know, she still stuck up for him. They kidnapped me together!"

Martin shook his head. "They were in cahoots from the start. He completely took her in, I always knew she agreed to marry me because she was so smitten with Brother Edgar Young, the Prophet's direct descendent. But that doesn't excuse me for wimping out on you, Lexi. I was completely at fault for letting RoLayne and Ed decide everything about you. I turned a blind eye, it was so much easier than struggling with your mom."

Counseling had taught Lexi not to smooth over this dereliction of duty. "I know. You should have paid more attention, and you should have stood up to them."

Counseling had taught Martin the same thing. "That's exactly right. That's what a father's supposed to do. What finally warped it for me with the Church was seeing that the leadership cared more about protecting itself than about protecting kids like you. Even if I'd realized what Ed was up to and gone to the bishop, he wouldn't have listened."

"He's nice, though, Bishop Erickson," said Lexi. "He was nice to me in the helicopter, he untied my hands. He didn't get mad at me for not cooperating about the viddy. Course, he didn't know I made the Gaian salute."

"He's an LDS bishop first and a nice guy second," her dad had said. "That's the whole size of it."

"And mom was always an LDS daughter-in-law first and a mom second." She could see this, it explained her mother's behavior.

"And a wife last," her father added grimly.

"But you know what? I might want to make up with her anyhow someday? Not right away, but someday, when I'm older." Counseling was helping Lexi figure out how she felt about this, and her first adamant refusal to have anything to do with RoLayne ever again had begun to soften.

"Well, I don't," Martin said, "but I think that would be right, for you. She's your mom, and she loves you, I know she does, in spite of what she did. It's complicated. Her own dad had those seven kids and was a lot more interested in a couple of her brothers, and Ed was such a big shot in the ward."

"She wanted a dad more than a husband," Lexi said wisely. "She married you so she'd have a cool dad—I get it. That's what you were saying, before."

Martin smiled and gave Lexi a little cuff on the chin with his closed fist. "You haven't had much of a dad either up to now, have you? But I'm hoping to make up for that. I feel like we're making some progress here, don't you?"

She nodded. "I'm glad Pom went to Hurt Hollow and you stayed here with me. Even though I really miss her."

~

That had been several weeks ago. Now Martin's packed bag was standing by the door, and Lexi had put on her coat and gloves, snapped BJ's leash onto the ring of his blue leather collar, and gone out to walk up and down the shoveled sidewalk, waiting for Pom to get off the Ninth East streetcar.

BJ paced along at heel beside her. His manners were beautiful. Though he and his brother had washed out of guard dog school, having been judged temperamentally unsuitable for the work, they'd been trained to a fare-thee-well in dozens of standard commands as well as some that were just for guard dogs. Thanks to this wonderful training, BJ at two years old would dependably hold a down-stay on the set for as long as a couple of hours at a time, if he got to chase a ball madly for fifteen minutes in between down-stays. The whole studio was nuts about him. There was talk of training him to act in films. It wouldn't be difficult, he was so smart and knew so much already.

Not that there was any shortage of dog actors nowadays, in a world where children were few and far between, and pets and pet supplies were big, big business; but there was something about BJ that made the studio people think he might have star quality.

Lexi came to the end of the block farthest from the streetcar stop and did an about-face. BJ turned with her smartly. She walked a few paces and stopped; BJ promptly sat beside her left leg and looked up for instructions. "BJ heel," Lexi said, and they started off again—and, oh my heck, there was the streetcar stopping, and there was Pom getting off! "BJ, look, it's Feste!" Lexi shrieked. She stooped quickly and unsnapped his leash.

Manners flung aside, barking frantically, BJ hurled himself toward an identical barking shape hurtling toward him from the other end of the street. The dogs collided in a whirling, leaping, yodeling tangle, so utterly overjoyed to see each other that it made Lexi's eyes sting to watch them; but she was running herself, past the heap of ecstatic poodle, and flinging herself into Pom's arms. "I feel like *them!*" she said, half crying, squeezed against Pom's big chest, and Pom said, "Me too! Hi, sweetie, I'm *so glad* to see you!"

They walked to the house with their arms around each other and stood by the gate of the newly fenced front yard, waiting to let the dogs get over their initial reunion hysteria before trying to call them in. Behind Pam the front door opened and Martin Allred came down the porch steps wearing his coat and carrying his bag. Pam unlatched the gate and went through to greet him. "Leaving already? I'd hoped you could stay for supper."

He set the bag down and shook Pam's hand. "Thanks, I appreciate that, but you and Lexi should have your first evening together alone. She's missed you a lot."

Pam glanced down at Lexi's beaming wet-eyed face and beamed back. "Come for the birthday dinner, then, if you're not doing anything else."

"Hey, if I were doing anything else I'd cancel out of it. Thanks a lot, I'd like that—if it's okay with you, hon?"

His daughter nodded hard, beaming up at Pam. The birthday was two days away; Pam could feel Lexi thinking that by then she wouldn't mind sharing her Pom with her dad.

The dogs had not stopped leaping around in the snowy middle of the street, but the leaps, though boisterous, were beginning to look less frantic. Pam held the gate open for Martin and called "Feste, come!"

"BJ, come!"

They came immediately, grinning, shoulder to shoulder, distinguishable chiefly by BJ's blue collar and Feste's red one. "Those two are something," Martin said. "I wasn't wild about the idea that Lexi was getting a dog I'd have to be in charge of on the set, but that was before I met BJ."

Both dogs had tolerated the six-week separation well, not moping or refusing to eat, but their joy at being reunited was so manifest that the next morning Lexi went off to the studio without BJ, so he could play with Feste all day long. In one morning the dogs beat the snow in the front yard dirty and flat. In the afternoon the weather warmed up. They came in for dinner happy, tired, and caked with sand. "They never quit!" Pam reported to Lexi while giving the second bath. "Hour after hour they keep it up! They'll stop to bark at somebody passing on the sidewalk and then go back to it. Feste, hup!"

Feste, dripping and unrepentant, hopped onto the towel spread out for him and stood to be dried. Lexi draped a second towel across his back and started rubbing vigorously; her wrist, now completely healed, bent normally in all directions. "D'you think they'd play like that if they were together all the time?"

"I don't know, but I'll tell you what. How about taking BJ to work with you tomorrow? I need to focus on this birthday dinner."

Specifically, to assemble the things she would need to decorate the cake: cardboard for the stone wall and gate, a tiny wire key, red and green icing to make rose bushes, a little tree and swing, three dolls dressed and fitted out to represent Mary, Dickon, and Colin, and Colin's wheel chair. No ambiguous pictographs for Lexi; the top of her cake was to be a model of the Secret Garden, standing for Pam's present to her of the "bit of earth" between the side of the house and the fence.

CHAPTER 16

Rosetta's Different Baby

15 DECEMBER 2037 - 23 JANUARY 2038

A week later Pam and Feste were back at Hurt Hollow; but not until the 23rd, Christmas Eve Eve, did Pam become clear about whether to bother celebrating the holidays there in a formal way. Having gone all out for Thanksgiving, and for Lexi's birthday, she wasn't much inclined to fuss over an occasion so emphatically Baptist in its personal associations.

As the Day approached, she found herself thinking about the Christmases of her childhood. These had always included an excursion to Hurt Hollow to see Jesse; and Jesse had always put a little cedar in a stand Orrin had made, and decorated it with live candles and strings of popcorn. When Humphrey had spent Christmas at the Hollow ten years before, Pam had scrupulously followed Jesse's example, dipping lengths of wicking in beeswax to make candles and popping the previous summer's hoarded Indian corn in the Dutch oven. She had done all this for the pleasure of pleasing Humphrey, who dearly loved that sort of simple folksy celebration. That year there had been a freak early snowfall and a soggy, but genuine, white Christmas.

These memories made her sad. How passionate her love for Jesse used to be, how simple her love for Humphrey in former years. Nothing was simple now. The peace and clarity of her retreat, not damaged at all by the week in Salt Lake, had become clouded by anticipatory holiday gloom.

A lot of people went into a slump at Christmastime, that was a well-known contemporary truth. The annual clash of expectation and reality had flattened large swaths of the population long before the Hefn came; but Christmas without children, hence without focus or distraction, was awfully hard on everybody. How could a holiday extolling the birth of a baby be anything but a sad irony nowadays? Even the sincerest Christians had a struggle keeping their spirits up. On Christmas Eve *A Ceremony of Lessons and Carols* would be broadcast from Kings College Chapel, as it had been for fifty years, but in a version recorded two decades before. The pure sweet voices of the boy trebles would only make people cry.

There was a live child in Pam's life, however, and ultimately that decided her. She would not allow sadness about the losses of the past to have the final say about the holidays. Lexi was the future. Lexi would like to see the little tree with all its candles glowing when she called on Christmas morning. Therefore let there be a tree, let tradition be revived.

As soon as she'd decided this, Pam felt better. After lunch she took the hatchet and went out with Feste to find a tree.

—And discovered that she knew exactly how to proceed. Which was not by striding around sizing up small cedars till she located one of the right height and shape, but by wandering attentively and thoughtfully over the land until she happened upon the one cedar that wanted to be Lexi's Christmas tree at Hurt Hollow. So she wandered, full of trust that when she found the right one she would know.

And so it proved. Except that Feste actually found the tree, and sat down to wait next to it till Pam caught up.

She surprised herself again by knowing exactly what to do next: express gratitude for the gift, then chop it down in a reverent spirit. She dragged the tree back to the house and filled a bucket of water to stand it in, then went inside, built up the fire, and threw her coat on the table and herself into a chair, all in a kind of exaltation: *Wow. What was that?* Right from the moment of stepping out the back door she'd felt herself moving through two realities, one where she was conscious of being in an altered state, and the state itself. To that extent it was like dissociation, though dissociation could not have felt more different.

And whatever it was, it wasn't Gaian. That was not how Orrin, a man perpetually reverent in the face of Nature, picked out a Christmas tree, or went about his life generally. He responded, responded, responded to Nature, but he chose things for himself.

~

For years Pam had done whatever she'd done about Christmas on Christmas Eve, and she stuck to that part of her own private tradition. By nine o'clock the bristly little cedar—set on the table where Feste couldn't knock it over or catch himself on fire—had been fitted with candles in holders and draped with strings of white popcorn and dark red buckberries. Pam had wrapped a sheet around the tree stand and piled her little hoard of presents on it. She'd taken a bath and put on clean clothes. The Kings College Choir in their red robes and white surplices—not the broadcast from England but Pam's own recording—was processing down her computer screen beneath the Chapel's fan vaulting, singing "Once In Royal David's City."

Now she held a long splinter in the fireplace flames, then used it, very carefully, to light the candles. When the little tree was twinkling twice, once inside the room and once in the big window, "What about it, Feste," she said, "shall we open our presents and call it a day?"

Feste's present from Pam was a pig's knuckle. It thrilled him unspeakably. She smiled upon his blissful gnawing for several minutes, wondering how she'd ever lived so long without the company of a creature so easily made joyful, before picking up her first package. This was something large and flat, sent by Liam last week from California, and turned out to be a round photo of herself in a fabric frame. She was standing high on a slope littered with rocks, looking at something through binoculars. The hatted, booted, intently concentrating figure looked little against the backdrop of the box canyon, whose red walls streaked with black thrust up into a dark blue sky. It wasn't possible to tell from the photo what the binoculars were trained on, but of course Pam knew: the Adam-zad pictograph, on the ceiling of the alcove she couldn't stop thinking about. The one that would send the sneaky photographer round the bend, only a couple of minutes after capturing this moment on film. It was a picture of someone looking at a picture.

I didn't know Liam had even brought a camera along that day. He'd only gotten that one chance to use it. She propped the photo against a bowl of apples—thinking that even a still photograph can be a kind of time window—before slitting the envelope and sliding out the homemade card. This made her smile; Liam had printed 'HAPPY HOLLOWDAYS" in big letters across the front. All it said inside was, "A souvenir of everything that was about to happen. Liam." No arguments there. She stood the card next to the photograph and briefly contemplated both, with perplexing emotions, before unwrapping the next box.

This was Humphrey's present, a pound of dark chocolate caramels. Mmm. Humphrey was a sucker for food treats. She popped one in her mouth and opened her last package, a box she'd brought back from Utah two weeks before: her present from Lexi. The box was filled with little hard somethings individually wrapped in paper, with a note on top: "Dear Pom, You gave them to me, now I'm giving them to you. Ye know the Law! Look well—look well, O Wolves! Merry Christmas and lots of love from Lexi. P.S. I miss you!"

One by one Pam unwrapped the objects and set them on the table. As each came to light her wonder grew, till she was having hard shivers every time she added another to the assembly. Lexi's present was sensational. The somethings were figurines she'd obviously made herself, out of clay, and painted: a tiger, a bear, three wolves and four wolf cubs, a black panther, a python—and a naked brown baby. There was also a real gray rock the size of Pam's fist. Lexi had used the *Jungle Book* scene at the Council Rock, where Mowgli's fate is first decided, as the model for what in Christmas context was unmistakably a crèche. She'd based her figurines on an illustration in her own copy of the book, adapting it to reduce the total number of wolves to seven—Akela, Mother and Father Wolf, and the four cubs—and to include Kaa the python, who hadn't actually been present. She'd also altered the perspective.

The aptness and inventiveness of the idea alone would have given Pam the shivers, no matter how well the little animals had been made, but she was totally blown away by Lexi's obvious, but till now completely unsuspected, talent. This was an ambitious project, eleven figurines! Lexi must have started working on it almost as soon as Pam had left Salt Lake in October, or even sooner.

The little animals were so cleverly done it crossed Pam's mind that Martin might have helped her; but if he had he was pretty talented himself.

With the book illustration in mind, Pam started to assemble the figures on the sheeted table. Mowgli the man-cub went in the center, along with the four wolf cubs, each in a different posture, sit, down, stand, on-your-side. Mowgli himself sat like a Teddy bear propped on his little hands, what finicky work! Bagheera the panther had been shaped on the bottom to fit the flattish top of the rock precisely if you slid him around. As in the book, Baloo the bear stood upright; Pam put him where he belonged and moved Liam's photograph so the binoculars were aiming straight at him. The wolves, all seated, went in their places. Shere Khan the tiger—not quite as skillfully formed as the others, but beautifully painted—lay outside the circle to enclose it on one side; and Kaa, shaped not in coils but in a long thick curve, with a raised head and a red forked tongue made of wire, enclosed it on the other.

Thus arranged, you saw that relative to one another the sizes were a little off—the panther was bigger than the tiger, Baloo as large as both cats combined—but Lexi had succeeded in making the group pull together by the simple device of having them all look at Mowgli—Look well, O Wolves!—while Mowgli looked at the ground, indifferent to the extreme danger of his situation.

No stable, no manger, no Mary and Joseph, no Wise Men, no shepherds, no Friendly Beasts, only this savage assembly focussed, for a variety of reasons, on the deceptively helpless human baby.

Baloo was speaking for Mowgli, urging the wolves to let him live. Wave after wave of shivers rippled down Pam's legs.

Feste got up, clicked across the floor and thrust his muzzle into Pam's lap. His eyes looked up into hers, and looked worried. "Ohhhh, little Feste," she said in a great sigh. "You're descended from wolves, did you know that? Is your pig's knuckle all gone?" She looked, but there it lay, considerably smaller. She massaged behind the dog's ears with both hands, then leaned over and gave him a hug, dodging his attempt to lick her on the lips. "*You're* a Friendly Beast, aren't you? so we've got one after all. Okay, I'll snap out of it, I think I was about to recommend that they go ahead and kill him." She jumped up and stretched. "Whew! Want to go down and check out the river? You do? Are you sure? No, sweetie, leave your good bone here."

THE BIRD SHAMAN

She threw on her coat and popped another caramel in her mouth. With a dozen quick gestures she snuffed the candle flames.

~

In the first week of January it finally snowed heavily enough in the Wasatch for the final footage of *A Thousand Miles* to be filmed, after which Lexi was for the time being unemployed. Instead of going to work every day, she started back to school with the couple of dozen other Salt Lake kids of middle-school age, which was fun at first. She also had BJ, but her life on balance had become less interesting and she missed Pam more. A small package arrived at Hurt Hollow containing two more figurines, a pair of cunning black poodles wearing ribbon collars, one red, one blue, to add to the Council Rock scene. There was a note: "Dear Pom, I thought they should be there too and be together. BJ is in a sit stay and Feste is in a down stay. Love, Lexi. P.S. When are you coming home?"

She'd made the poodles all by herself, like the rest of the crèche; Martin swore he'd done nothing to help but shop for the clay and paints. Pam thought Lexi should have art lessons if she was interested. She'd asked Martin to look into it; but the feeling was growing on her that she was needed at home. For one thing, Lexi was about to enter puberty. Pam had noticed certain changes during the birthday visit. Her charge was taller and not quite so slim below the waist, and bumps like acorns had appeared under her pullovers. Nothing had been said; but Pam was aware that her time at the Hollow was running out.

She felt profoundly changed, yet there was nothing tangible to show for the retreat—no dreams, no information, nothing that might be helpful to Humphrey.

Gazing at Lexi's Christmas figurines one evening, Pam was surprised to feel the special discomfort in her chest that meant a poem was trying to emerge. She grabbed the pad and settled down to it. After Christmas she'd taken up the *Prelude* again. Wordsworth's ready blank-verse cadences lay at the surface of her mind and she sought no further for a form.

A couple of hours later she had this:

Judith Moffett

CHOOSING TARZAN

I read the Burroughs tales, when I was nine,
with pure conviction: Tarzan was what I played
and also who. In the bright ten-year-old
of Tarzan of the Apes, free feral orphan,
I saw, or willed myself to see, myself—
my doughty, daily, after-school persona,
arboreal, neuter, fluent in Ape-English.
So later, when I'd found The Jungle Books,
whipped through and through them, memorizing every
poem with urgent joy, why was I never
Mowgli? Feeling back, I know I sensed
how Kipling's art soared above Burroughs' hackwork,
yet—when a wolf says *thou* in conversation
with pythons, panthers, bears, he's in a story
where language is the fiction. Tarzan seemed
simpler and safer. KOTAR YO MANGANI!
Tarzan loves Jane, a cipher; Mowgli loves
Bagheera, Baloo, Kaa, his brother wolves.
When Tarzan bids his apes farewell, I felt
what he does: nothing. Mowgli wrung my heart.
When Mowgli leaves the jungle for the world
of Men, drawn thence by forces he can't silence,
I'd cry as hard as he did—hard as when Shane,
bearing his wound, rides out of town forever,
or Mary Poppins opens the Other Door,
lifts her umbrella, soars, begins to shine . . .
Why did I suffer so, time after time?
What had I lost, by ten, to cause such anguish?

At this point the compositional trance popped like a soap bubble. Pam blinked, then double-spaced, indented, and keyed: "*That's* plain as a pikestaff, I'd lost my mother! I could never trust her again. And Lexi's lost hers; but somehow she can stand to read about Mowgli sobbing on Baloo's breast, when he has to return to the world of humans (though I bet Liam couldn't); and that, I guess, is at least partly because she's got me. But she hasn't got me with her, and she's fed up. So she makes the crèche, cleverly using

Mowgli's world to summon me back into hers, exactly the way Liam uses Kipling's poetry. A kind of sympathetic magic."

Pam clicked the pad off and laid it in her lap. The exercise had served its purpose. Even if she had to go empty-handed, it was time to go.

~

Lexi jumped up and down, ecstatic. "A week? Yippee! Have you told Humphrey yet? Is he all upset?"

"Not yet. He'll be calling tomorrow anyway, that's our regular day. I'll tell him then." Lexi knew Pam had put Humphrey on a schedule, to keep him from driving her nuts by calling whenever he started going nuts himself. "Anyway, I wanted you to be the first to know."

"So did it work, being there? Did you have a dream?"

Pam hesitated. "I didn't have a dream, but to say it didn't work wouldn't really be true either. I'll try to explain better when I get back. Bottom line, though, I haven't got much to tell Humphrey. He probably *will* be upset and want me to keep on trying, but I'll tell him I'll keep trying in Utah."

"He can't *make* you stay back there, can he?" Lexi said, suddenly alarmed.

Smiling, Pam shook her head. "He can make just about anybody do just about anything, but making a person have a lucid dream in a certain place isn't one of 'em. This was an experiment, like any other. We didn't get the results we were hoping for, but that happens a lot, he knows that."

"Well, I'm sorry, but—*yippee!*" Lexi squealed again. She called BJ over and gave him a rumpling hug. "BJ, BJ! Feste's coming home!"

The dogs always stared blankly at one another through the phone screens, it seemed a scentless image carried no information, but when Lexi said *Feste* BJ's head swiveled around so hard his ears wrapped around his head, and he started to bounce. Pam and Lexi laughed. "Don't tease him," Pam said. "Let him be surprised. Is your dad home?"

"Unh-unh, he went to Smith's."

"Would you give him a message for me? Tell him please not to feel like he needs to move out on a moment's notice, just because I'm coming back? There's no rush at all. Actually I'd like him to stay on, at least for a while, if he's comfortable with that."

"Okay, I'll tell him." She seemed pleased.

They said goodbye and got off. Pam pushed back her chair, stood and looked around the little house, made different already by the knowledge that she was about to leave it again, for who knew how long?

A week would make a kind of drawn-out transition. But to prepare to leave this watery Hurt Hollow world for transplantation into that other world of desert exile would not be a simple business, not after what had been happening here. Pam believed she had an excellent chance of thriving in the desert now—but, to ensure that the transition would go well, there were things to be seen to: ceremonial acts to be performed, you might say. Feeling her way through those, she figured, might very well use up the best part of a week.

What she needed to do would come to her, all that was required was to set about it correctly. She even felt eager to begin.

~

"You're Mowgli now," Baloo growled. "How do you like it?"

It was night, but the full moon made it easy to see. From her place at the center of the circle Pam turned her head to be sure everyone was there, and everyone was. Bagheera, a black blot, lay on his rock. A tiger-shaped shadow loomed behind the wolves. There were a lot of wolves with shining eyes, and the two grinning poodles, out in front and side by side, one sitting, one lying down. A loud, sighing *Aaa-sssssh* in the shadows told her Kaa was present to complete the circle.

"Thank God!" Pam exclaimed, with measureless relief; and then in a voice of command—lest she wake up and lose this one long-sought chance—"Show me why the Gafr need another year!"

Instantly she was alone in the glowing circle. Or seemed to be; but as she leapt up in dismay, a long mottled shape poured into the moonlight and flowed across the clearing toward Pam. It reared up several feet of its front end. Small glittering eyes looked straight into her own; its tongue flickered in and out, nearly touching her face. "Kaa is short for Copperhead," the snake hissed. "Climb aboard, Little Frog."

Pam understood that she was meant to wrap her arms and legs around this upright upper part of Kaa, as if shinnying up a thick pole. She hadn't actually climbed a pole in decades, but her body remembered exactly how to arrange itself. The snake's scales were cool and smooth against her bare skin.

Clinging expertly to the pole of Kaa, Pam became weightless. There ensued an interval of swiftness and roaring, during which she could see nothing, but the motion of the ride was unexpectedly joyful and she clasped her supple broomstick with thighs and forearms, palms and instep, as if traveling like this were something she'd been born to do.

When they broke out of that other dimension they were in water, Kaa swimming powerfully against a powerful current, Pam still weightless and still wrapped around him. She could feel his muscles working and the enormous length of him behind her, beating the water with sinuous S-strokes, so that she was swayed from side to side. Simultaneously she was watching their progress from the air, her consciousness swooping along directly above the python and the bump behind his head that was not a meal he had swallowed whole, but herself. Remote viewing this was called, she had read about it. Far below by the light of the winter moon, Kaa was churning upstream in the middle of the broad familiar river that twisted and gleamed like a gigantic, less mobile version of his own body. They whipped past Hurt Hollow and the house and goat stable, very small, very far below—Pam felt the tiny sting of the two sparks that were her sleeping self and Feste's—then past the Scofield water tower, then under and over the dark bridge linking Madison and Milton.

Moments later she sighted a smaller silver ribbon, the Kentucky River, flowing into the Ohio from the south. She felt Kaa thrash to change directions, sensed the different quality of the water, also watched him swerve to enter the mouth of the smaller river. Now the great snake lifted his head out of the water, scouting ahead; the part of Pam clinging to his neck felt the water roil in resistance and herself be lifted also; the part watching from the sky remembered the Loch Ness monster and smiled. That part scanned for stars, but the moon was too dazzling.

But now Pam's separate perspectives snapped together, for Kaa had left the water altogether and was thrashing into the sky like a wingless dragon, and they were swimming westward through the air together as they had through the water, Kaa's long body whipping, propelling them along then shooting lower over hillsides spectral in moonlight and hairy with the tangled branches of bare trees. Then he was arranging his huge coils amid the brush and cedars of an abandoned ridgetop pasture, and Pam had weight again. She released her grip and stepped away.

Briefly she took in the shaggy hillscape, so like the Hurt Hollow she remembered from earliest childhood, when you could still tell that the land had once been farmed. Then, directly in front of her, the ground became transparent and she saw that a large excavation had been made under the lintel of a fallen tree, and that she could see into this den with painful keenness through the clarified ground. A female black bear lay down there with her paws tucked up, half on her side and half on her back, deep in hibernation. Two little suckling cubs, obviously born that winter, were attached to the nipples of her chest.

The babies were of a size, but they were not alike.

White moonlight shining through the glassy ground illuminated everything inside the den—roots, clods, rocks, creatures. Understanding that she must examine the cubs, Pam flopped down and squirmed under the log. She knelt close to the huge heap of the mother bear, who opened her eyes but did not object.

One of the cubs looked like a miniature version of its mother, but the other was different. Pam lifted the different cub from the nipple, gripping it firmly in both hands. In protest the cub wriggled and waved its little limbs, wrinkled up its little face. Moonlight, and Pam's razor-sharp vision, caused each hair on its body to burn with individual actuality. And now at last—at last!—everything was clear, everything became a flood of comprehension.

"Your name is Fubsy," Pam told the cub tenderly, profoundly moved, and was bending to kiss its forehead when, through a spinning kaleidoscope vortex of den—bear—cubs—

Pam fell awake, gasping, shocked as much as anything by the quality of the light, which wasn't the light of moonlit midnight at all, but that of mid afternoon on a bright January day. Feste stood shoved up against the cot, long nose twitching on the pillow an inch from her face, eyes intently peering; training alone had kept all four of his feet on the floor. When he saw she had woken he sat down abruptly and started to pant.

Pam made a huge effort to wrench her mind into focus. "Oh, sweetie, were you scared? Did I make noises? Come on, you can get in." She scooted over and patted the mattress, and Feste hopped up at once and settled down against her, tucking his nose under her chin with a huge sigh. His whole body was trembling. Pam stroked the top of his head and scratched beneath the red collar, and he closed his eyes and sighed again. They lay together like that, Pam's hand moving automatically, calming the dog, till finally he stopped shivering and started to snore. Then her hand dropped and she lay still, staring at the ceiling boards, thinking.

She'd stretched out after lunch for a little snooze. Some snooze.

After a while she murmured, "*Histah!*" and Feste stirred and lifted his head. Amused through her distraction, Pam said soothingly, "No, no, sweetie, not *Feste*. That's how you say snake in Ape English. Go back to sleep."

~

She was heating up some leftover goat stew around six o'clock that evening when the gate phone startled her by suddenly going *Brrrrrrring!* Feste, who'd been waiting politely on the mat for his dinner, jumped up, already barking.

The phone was wired to both gates, the one at the top of the bluff and the one on the dock. She peered out the window, cupping her hands to cut the room reflection, but the dock was mantled in darkness. A caller at the upper phone wouldn't know whether anyone was in residence, but one standing on the dock would have seen the lanterns in the window and on the porch step. She cursed briefly, but crossed the room and lifted the receiver. "Yes?" And then "Feste, that'll do."

A male voice croaked, "Is this Pam Pruitt?" While she was considering how to answer that, the person cleared his throat and rushed ahead. "My name's Denny Demaree, I'm a wildlife biologist, I've been studying black bears in Anderson County, the Habitat Recovery Program? I'm a Gaian, the farm I've been working at is my family Ground. Something's happened. Could I speak with you?"

Pam's eyes closed; she leaned against the wall. "How did you know I was here?"

"The Hefn Innisfrey told me. The Observer for Habitat Recovery in this district?"

377

Innisfrey was supposed to be in Santa Barbara, or so Liam had said, but that was . . . a while ago now. When had she last spoken with Liam? "What do you mean, something's happened?"

"I, uh, I can't tell you about it like this, I need to talk to you in person. I'm on the dock."

"Look, I'm making a retreat."

"I know, I'm really sorry, but this is—this can't wait. This is huge," the man said. "Please!"

"Innisfrey told you I was on retreat?"

"Not exactly, but I guessed it might be that. I'm really sorry," he said again.

Pam still hesitated. "How long have you been a Gaian?"

"Since I was thirteen. I'm a steward in the Madison, Indiana Mission, I grew up in Milton."

"What's your specialty?"

"Elemental." His tone said, *What else would a wildlife biologist be?*

There was no foolproof way to test him, and really no way out for Pam. "Okay, I'll come down for a couple of minutes."

She hung up, dragged the pot of stew off the stove, and pulled on her coat. "Hey, little wolf cub, here's your big chance to strut your stuff. Feste—on guard!" She swung the front door open and Feste shot through it, barking hysterically. Pam caught up the lantern from the stone step and followed him down the path. Long before she reached the gate, Feste was leaping and snarling at someone through the woven wire, putting on a terrific show, so black in the moonless night that Pam could scarcely see him. From the other side of the fence all you would be able to see of him would be ravening teeth and eyeshine. It was pretty funny, and quite useful. She imagined telling Lexi about it.

At the gate she held the lantern high to get a look at her caller, a scrawny young man in dark clothing, who had indeed backed well away from the fence and Feste's faux ferocity. He'd dropped his duffel backpack on the dock. "Okay," said Pam, "I'm turning the power off. Push up close against the fence and spread your arms and legs. Feste, check 'em out. Good boy, check 'em out."

Rather to her surprise, both man and dog did exactly as she'd said. Feste stopped lunging and began to sniff the spread-eagled stranger industriously all over, a low growl rumbling in his throat. "Now, turn around and do it again," she ordered, and again they both obeyed her.

According to Feste the guy was unarmed. "All right then. What's your name again?"

"Denny Demaree."

"Denny Demaree. And I'm Pam Pruitt, of course. Better leave the bag where it is. Feste, watch!" She opened the gate.

Eyeing the dog warily, Denny stepped through. In Pam's presence at last, he seemed suddenly aware of his appearance. "Sorry I'm so grubby. I've been camping out and didn't get a chance to clean up."

Pam held the lantern up again. "Camping out where, in a coal mine?"

Denny grinned. "On the farm where my study was being done. Innisfrey terminated the project and threw me off the place, uh . . . oh, around two or three weeks ago now I think it was, I've kind of lost track."

Pam's eyebrows shot up. "He threw you out and you snuck back in? Have you got a death wish? You could get yourself wiped for that."

Denny rolled his eyes. "Like I don't know that! My study wasn't *finished*! But anyway, the reason he gave was that thanks to all our great work, blah blah blah, the east central district is good to go on recovering by itself now, so they're reassigning the biologists to where they're needed more. But the thing is, that's *not* the reason. Something really wild is going on."

Knowing what she was about to hear, Pam both wanted and didn't want him to continue. Her scalp prickled. Slowly she lowered the lantern. "What do you mean?"

"You're not going to believe me," Denny said, sounding desperate. "I can't prove it to you, but last night I went into one of my study dens to check on the cubs, I hadn't seen them since the day I got pulled out, I had a flashlight, and one of them, Rocket, the little male, he wasn't there!—he'd been switched somehow—"

It was happening now. Not in the future, now. "Oh-kay," Pam said. "You better come on up to the house then. Get your stuff and close the gate—slam it good and hard. Feste, school's out. Good job."

Denny stared at her openmouthed. Then he was backing away. "You know about this. You knew what I was going to say." He slipped through the gate and clanged it shut between them. "You're tight with Humphrey—"

"I think I do," Pam said. "If I tell you how I know, you won't believe *me*—but I didn't find out from Humphrey or Innisfrey, or any of the other Hefn."

"What other way could there be? You're lying." He snatched up his duffel, darted out of the circle of lantern light.

"Wait!" she yelled, "Hey! Wait a second!" The sounds of fleeing stopped. "You and I might be the only ones who know, and I'm gonna have to decide what to do about it. Whatever you know, I need to know too!"

His voice came out of the dark: "How do I know you won't turn me in?"

Pam paused. Why should he believe her, after all? "I guess you'll have to trust me on that, just like I'm gonna have to trust you. But Gaians *don't* lie to each other, do they? and I give you my word I'll do everything humanly possible to keep Humphrey from finding out you were ever even here. And anyway, you're in a peck of trouble right now, so unless you've got someplace else to go . . ."

Denny trudged behind her up the path to the house, dragging his duffel. Pam set the lantern down and opened the door onto the warm wooden room and the firelight. The dog slipped through ahead of them both. "I expect you've been here before if you're a local boy," Pam said, wondering what he'd say to that.

"A few times. Never at night, though." He got his first good look at Feste, now wagging his stump of a tail and trying to lick Denny's hand, and let out a snort of laughter. "A poodle? Your guard dog is a poodle? I had the bejeezus scared out of me by a *poodle*?"

"Hey, poodles can be great guard dogs, as you're now in a position to confirm. Most people don't even realize he's a poodle in that buzz cut."

"Our neighbors had a standard poodle when I was a kid. I remember that long nose." Denny rubbed the dog's head and stifled a yawn, and then his eye lit on Orrin's painting of the Kentucky bottomlands. "Oh, hey, it's great to see that again. The exact color of winter wheat in April, but who would believe it if they hadn't seen it growing?"

"I know." Pam had been sizing Denny up. He was indeed very scruffy and unkempt, and done in to judge by the look of him, but she was now 90% convinced that he was who he said he was. "I'd like to let you get some sleep before we go into things, but I'll be getting a call from Humphrey in the morning, it's our regular time, and I need to be ready. Are you up to talking for a while if I feed you first?"

"What *is* that wonderful smell?" Denny said, by way of reply. He had dropped his duffelpack in a corner and hung his filthy coat on a hook. "Wow, do I smell terrible! I'm sorry." Removing the coat had released a powerful cloud of unwashed-body odor.

The aroma of goat stew was no match for Denny. Pam filled a pail half full from the steaming kettle and added cold water from the tap. "Take this upstairs and do the best you can, there's a bar of soap on the sink up there, and a basin on a nail. Tomorrow maybe you'll get time for a real bath."

"Thanks. Oh God, hot water!"

He disappeared. Pam put the stewpot back on the stove, transferred the group of *Jungle Book* figurines to a shelf, and set two places with bowls, plates, and cutlery at the Hubbles' long heavy table of dark wood. By the time she'd finished, Denny was back, still stubbly but much improved despite being barefoot and dressed in a ratty pair of orange corduroys and a shapeless cotton sweatshirt with both elbows out. "These are my last pieces of clean laundry. I left some socks and stuff soaking in the bucket, maybe they'll dry overnight."

"We'll hang 'em over the stove. They'll dry."

Denny was famished, and Pam let him eat without making him talk. She was hungry herself, but too agitated to eat much. She was certain she was about to hear a waking-life confirmation of the brand-new lucid dream. When the stew was gone she gave Feste the bowls and pot to lick while she got his proper dinner ready, then trotted down to the cellar for a canning jar of something or other—it turned out to be peaches, the volunteers had put up quarts and quarts of those, using honey instead of sugar—all the while preparing herself to hear what she was about to hear.

Except for the three halves Pam dished up for herself, Denny ate the entire jar of fruit and syrup. "They're so good, they're so good," he kept saying. "Peaches in Mecca! The Hubbells never had peaches!"

"Not peach trees, but in season people would bring them some and Hannah would put 'em up. It's still within the tradition. The staff would die before they'd do anything inauthentic."

"I used to come down here with my class, before I joined the Gaians—school trips, you know," Denny told her. "Jesse Kellum was still here then. We got watermelon in summer and popcorn in winter. No peaches."

"So you remember Jesse." Pam regarded Denny differently; this was a person who had known Jesse himself, not just known about him, as the Utah Gaians did. "He must have been pretty old by then."

"I guess. He seemed ancient to us little kids. He used to tell us stories about *you*—the time he got snakebit, the tornado, all that. You and Liam O'Hara, you guys were part of the basic spiel. The Hefn Humphrey too, but not as much."

But finally he was finished, and ready to tell his story over a mug of steaming tea. ("Sorry, no beer at the Hollow, no coffee even." "I know, I know. Tea is fine.") Pam piled on firewood and settled down to listen.

Denny was a Milton native. He'd become a Gaian in his teens, studied field zoology at the University of Kentucky, then joined the new Habitat Recovery Program four years ago, straight out of graduate school. He was delighted when he managed to get himself assigned to a study area that included his own Ground, an ex-farm in Anderson County that had been in Denny's family a hundred or so years before.

The Hefn had started the program, which was coordinated by the different state Departments of Fish and Wildlife, to study bears, coyotes, elk, and white-tailed deer in the eastern United States. It was their initiative, they were monitoring the ecological health of the planet by monitoring its keystone predators and their prey species as these reclaimed habitat that year by year was returning to a wilder and wilder state. Pam had heard a little about this from Liam but hadn't tracked it closely. Till recently, "brief flowering" had been the focus of her work, "primeval wilderness" a mere recreational sideline. Liam had kept up with it more; there were bear studies ongoing in the New Jersey and Pennsylvania mountains and he took a personal interest in those.

Denny's decision to join this program had been deeply conflicted. He really loved the work, but he really hated the Hefn. By his own lights it was probably the worst time in the history of the world to be a human being; but, ironically, it was also one of the best to be a wildlife biologist in your own back yard. Absent the Directive and Baby Ban, there would *be* no black bear population in east central

Kentucky—or elk population, or population of coyotes approaching the size of wolves, busily subspeciating in the fascinating ways they were doing. Without the Hefn Takeover, east central Kentucky—now a recovering oak-hickory hardwood forest—would still be growing tobacco and Black Angus steers, and spindling big round bales of tall-fescue hay, and all the state's black bears would still be in the Daniel Boone National Forest on the West Virginia border, way over in the Appalachian foothills.

He ignored the contradictions most of the time, but got his nose rubbed in them quarterly when one of the Hefn—usually Innisfrey, who was Observer for Habitat Recovery—dropped by to check up on how he was getting along. Denny knew he was very damn good at his job, but he'd still had to kowtow on a regular basis to the goddamn Hefn. Funding for his field study in Anderson County partly depended on how successfully he did this. It was galling and humiliating, and every time he was forced to show up for one of these meetings the conflict would boil up inside him again.

One day a couple of weeks before, Denny had been a little late for a scheduled rendezvous. He'd needed to weigh, measure, and tag a pair of newborn cubs, and that had taken longer than expected. Innisfree could be crabby about lateness, but this time he wasn't. Instead, after praising Denny's work to the skies, he informed him that the study was being terminated.

From a scientific perspective Denny's bear study had a couple of years left to run. Denny had been shocked, then hopping mad, and had protested as much as he dared, even bringing up the fact that he was a Gaian working on his own Ground. Innisfree expressed regrets about all this, but the study was still over.

The other east-central researchers had been yanked out of the field that same day, rounded up at the regional Fish and Wildlife office in Frankfort, then heli-lifted to Louisville for reassignment, including the woman who ran the Frankfort office; they were closing it down.

Most of the others eventually accepted the realities of working for the Hefn and let themselves be reassigned. Denny hadn't. He'd understood that day for the first time why people had sometimes been driven, despite the utter pointlessness of defying the Hefn, to defy them anyway. It was the Final Year and he argued with himself about waiting till after June 6, 2038, to risk the wrath of the Hefn, but he quickly realized he just couldn't, that losing six months would wreck his study. He would pretend to go along, but at the first chance would drop out of sight, sneak back to the farm somehow, and go right on studying his bears. This was an act of scientific dedication, but also a subversive act fueled by rage and passion, in defiance of all the sucking-up other people were doing to convince the aliens to lift the Ban.

In Louisville he told them he was taking an unpaid leave to "think things over," and boarded a steam packet bound for Pittsburgh; the boat had paddled itself right past Hurt Hollow. At Carrollton he'd slipped off and taken passage on a mule-hauled flatboat headed up the Kentucky River. As dusk fell on the following day he stepped off the flatboat at the Tyrone landing, waited for full dark, then started walking. (Following the map of his journey mentally, from the air, Pam was struck with goose bumps. She could visualize the route precisely.)

Not more than a mile west of town he'd run into a line of sign-posts, brand new, marching away at right angles to the road on both sides and forward along both edges. It was too dark to read the smaller print, but the word in large type at the top was WARNING! By continuing along the road he was, in effect, entering a narrow corridor through a forbidden zone. Denny knew the penalty for disobeying a direct order from the Hefn, he knew what those signs said besides WARNING!—that persons caught willfully trespassing on posted land would have their memories erased. He'd seen the bewildered, pitiful products of Hefn mindwipe on TV and, like everyone else, been horrified. He'd never expected to risk letting that happen to him, but he'd gone too far by then to think of backing out.

He reached the farm before dawn, squirmed under the new fence, and spent all that day in an old tobacco barn on the property, in a sort of mouse-nest of hay. It was a long day. After dark he broke into the cabin and liberated a tent and sleeping bag and some cookware from a stash in the basement. He was stealthy and quiet, but felt intuitively that there were no Hefn around. After pitching the tent and camouflaging it with cedar boughs, he'd crawled inside and passed another long day dozing and waiting for night. Between snatches of sleep he worried about how he would manage if it snowed, and he couldn't stir without leaving tracks.

But it didn't snow. That night—the previous evening, in fact, the one Pam had spent fooling around with her Mowgli poem—Denny had been stumbling around in the woods. Not daring to use a flashlight, he struggled up the tree-clad, brush-choked hillside, toward the den where he'd been working on the day his study was terminated. Well as he knew the terrain by day, it had taken him quite a while. Luckily the moon was full. He'd tried not to make any noise, but couldn't help crashing around a good deal.

Finally he was standing triumphantly at the den site, fishing out the flashlight, tugging his leather gauntlets on, flopping on his belly and crawling in. He switched on the light, the first light he'd used to break the darkness for three days running.

The mother bear, Rosetta, lay on her side, head tucked down, enormous paws curled inward. She was awake, but deep in hibernation, and she was habituated to Denny. The cubs were snuggled against her, cradled in her arms. Denny hitched himself forward, frantically eager to see how the cubs were doing, how much they'd grown in more than two weeks.

His right hand had closed on the nape fur of the first cub, Rodeo, when the beam of the flashlight fell on the second cub. Which wasn't the little male, Rocket—he could see that at once. This cub was a little bigger than Rocket had been two weeks ago, but visibly smaller than Rocket's sister was right now, and more nearly black than cinnamon brown. How in the world had it gotten here? Releasing his grip on Rodeo, Denny reached for the changeling.

Just as he was about to touch it the cub had shifted its hold on the nipple, screwing up its face against the light, and Denny's hand jerked back as if snakebit. This wasn't a bear cub at all! Its shape and color were wrong, its proportions were wrong . . . what the hell *was* it? He squirmed closer and aimed the flashlight directly at the cub's head, trying to see its face. Again it screwed its eyes shut, and this time it let go of the nipple and made a thin sound of complaint. Its hairy little forelimbs, that had been rummaging in Rosetta breast fur, waved in the air, little arms ending in little forked hands.

There could be no doubt. The second "cub" was a baby Hefn—in a black bear's den, in the middle of winter!

Denny backed out of Rosetta's den a lot faster than he'd crawled in and fled downhill in a blind panic, having understood the instant he laid eyes on the baby Hefn that his situation was not one of calculated risk but of imminent suicide. It wasn't possible that the baby had been put into the den by anyone other than an adult Hefn, Innisfrey or one of the others. He understood that the field biologists had been thrown out of their study areas so the baby could be planted in the den. The Hefn would surely be back, often, to check on their little bundle of joy. He had to get out of there fast, or be the featured attraction at the next Hefn humiliation event on the telly. No disobedience of Hefn fiat could more plainly result in mindwipe than this.

"I broke camp," Denny said. "I ditched the tent and stuff in the well and hiked back to town, and caught a flatboat from Tyrone this morning. Then a steamer from Carrollton. I got off in Milton and walked in the back way. The phone at the top gate is busted, the cord's been cut, so I walked around to the dock. I couldn't think what else to do. I knew you were tight with Humphrey but you're a Gaian—*the* Gaian around here, the local Gaian celeb, the one I'd heard about my whole life. I decided I had to risk it."

"I'm glad you did," Pam said. "You have no idea how glad." She meant this. Tell me something. Is there a heavy log across the top of Rosetta's den?"

"Yeah, a big white oak that blew down in a tornado, that year they had all the tornadoes? She dug under that. How'd you know?"

"The same way I know the rest of it, God help me," Pam said. "I'll tell you tomorrow, but right now I think we'd better call it a night. I need to sleep on this. When Humphrey calls, I've got to be clear about what to say and what not to."

Telling his story had reanimated Denny, but already he was visibly sagging. "I'm not gonna twist your arm, I don't think I've ever been this beat in my life."

Twenty minutes later he was snoring heavily on the cot, and Feste was snoring gently in his bed under the table; he'd had a big day too. Pam, too perturbed to fall asleep immediately, burrowed gratefully into the bed designed by Orrin Hubbell to stand invisible against the wall all day, be lowered each night, and disappear again each morning. This bed had supported, for decades, the sleeping bodies of Orrin and Hannah Hubbell and of Jesse Kellum. It had supported her own body through many black months, eleven years before.

Not since leaving the Baptists had Pam believed in prayer, any more than she'd believed in an afterlife. But now something broke through from a place deeper than conscious belief, and she heard herself murmur aloud to the three beloved people who had sanctified this bed by sleeping in it for so long: "I need to be wise tomorrow. There's another kind of tornado bearing down on us. Everything will change . . . what I'm going to tell Humphrey is already there in the timestream, I know that, but it still has to be spoken, I still have to find the best way to confront him without exposing Denny. Please, Orrin, Hannah, Jesse, please help me do this right."

CHAPTER 17

Time Is One

24 JANUARY 2038

Right on schedule Humphrey popped onto Pam's screen. For once he looked less like he was about to burst from not saying what he was dying to say, than like the cat that swallowed the canary. "Good morning, my dear!" he chirruped, "Gillian Jacoby's infant is a little female!"

"You don't say," Pam said evenly. "The bear's infant is a little Hefn."

The effect of this statement was metamorphic. In demeanor and appearance Humphrey went from Chuckles the Clown to Fretful Porpentine in two seconds flat. His erected pelt filled the viewscreen; his facial expression sought to imitate nothing human. In that blood-freezing memorial-service voice he blatted at Pam, *"You have dreamed this?"*

"I have dreamed this."

"Tell the dream!"

"I will, but can you calm down a little? It's hard to talk to you when you're this agitated."

Humphrey appeared to struggle. His hair became less erect, but not very. In his human voice he said, "Forgive me, my dear, I cannot be flatter. Please tell the dream."

So she told the dream, all of it, just as she'd told it to an incredulous Denny over breakfast: Lexi's crèche coming to life with herself in Mowgli's role, the passage through the roaring void, clinging to

Kaa while he churned through the two rivers and took flight, the landing, the ground becoming transparent, the den and what she had seen there. As she spoke of realizing that one of the cubs was a baby Hefn, Humphrey's pelt slowly rose until it filled the screen again.

She finished. He waited expectantly, then anxiously. "This is all?"

"This is all. What does it mean? What haven't you been telling me?" Putting Humphrey on the defensive right away was a calculated move, almost the only one she'd been able to plan without knowing what he would say. He was very agitated. She waited to see if he would tell her why.

What he said was, "I cannot tell you even now, if this is all." His voice had shifted halfway back to alien but his hair had now completely deflated.

"Humphrey," Pam said, "you have to tell me *something*. Why did I see a baby Hefn in a bear's den? Is it symbolic or literal? If it's symbolic, what does it symbolize? If it's literal, what on earth is that about?"

"I cannot speak of it," Humphrey said, sounding frantic now, "until you have dreamed the whole truth!"

"When I've dreamed the whole truth, if that ever happens, I guess I won't need you to speak of it," said Pam, careful to keep her voice steady. "So this was a partial truth, but you won't tell me whether it symbolizes something or is something."

"No. Alas, my dear. I simply cannot say more."

She had maneuvered him into acknowledging tacitly that the dream was partially true in one sense or another. "You don't think knowing a partial truth is more dangerous than knowing a whole one?" He didn't reply. "In this case, Humphrey, it *is* more dangerous. It damages my ability to cooperate. I'm not like a transceiver, you know, without any feelings or values, you can't turn me on whenever you like, look through into the future—Aha! Gillian's pregnant with a girl!—and then just turn me off when you're through! You're always reminding me that I'm a shaman—well, shamans have never worked that way, like servants. I'm not playing Hefn to your Gafr here, if that's what you've been thinking." *I mean this,* she realized with a little inward start.

Humphrey seemed startled too. "Of course not, no no no!" (He clearly had been thinking it, though, driven by the extremity of his need. She had touched a nerve.) Tacitly admitting as much, he said, "But will you not play servant now for the good of your people?"

"How do I know it *is* for the good of 'my people'? You're asking me to take *too much* on faith! It hasn't mattered up to now, but this time I have to know what I'm helping you to do!"

He stared at her for a full minute, eyes fully opaqued. She stared back steadily. "Wait then," he said finally, and opaqued the screen as well.

Pam sat back, breathing hard. *Well!* The dialogue had clarified one issue anyway. Dreams about the welfare of Lexi and Liam—"my people" in a sense she could accept without irony—belonged to herself, her own life. This new dream had implications for the future of humanity. Even had it not been corroborated in the waking world by Denny, she would have needed to draw the line precisely here.

Denny himself was out somewhere in the beautiful weather, roaming through the bare woods with the now adoring Feste, waiting to be signaled that the coast was clear. No telling how quickly Humphrey would call back—he was presumably conferring with the Gafr—but until he did, she would do well to keep Denny away from the house altogether. On the other hand, she didn't intend to sit around all day waiting for the phone to ring. She stood and stretched, letting relief flow through her that she'd kept her head thus far—and there on the clothesline, in plain view of the phone camera, were four wool socks and two pairs of white cotton briefs.

Relief was replaced by a sharp thrill of panic—replaced in its turn by common sense; Pam's own socks and briefs, which would look no different from Denny's to a Hefn, had often been drying on that line when Humphrey called. The oversight, while unfortunate, could turn serious only if the Hefn were to mount a search for Denny.

Which, of course, they might. But she decided not to take his laundry down and give someone a reason to wonder why. Let this be like the case of the purloined letter. Yet her confidence in her self-control had received a jolt, and a reminder that this day was far from over.

It got to be lunchtime and Humphrey still hadn't called back. Pam had just started dithering about whether to go out and try to find Denny—he must be going crazy by now, wondering whether she'd ratted on him to the Hefn after all—when the phone finally ching'ed.

"I am not authorized to tell you this," Humphrey said. His hair was so flat against his body it looked greased down, and he was making a rotating hand movement Pam had never seen before. "By speaking of these things I play disobedient Hefn to my Gafr, I join the rebels and will pay the rebel's price." Pam realized he was terrified. Nothing could seem stranger than a terrified Hefn, a being of whom every human stood in hypothetical terror. "What is the rebel's price?"

"Exile, or worse. There is perhaps a price for you to pay also, my dear. I warn you and plead with you: continue in ignorance!"

But certainty had flooded her senses. "Humphrey," she said, very shaken, "I'm sorry, God help us both, but something tells me we can't get out of crossing this bridge together. The shaman risks great danger on behalf of her people. If you can bring yourself to tell me, then I have to know."

The rotating hand dropped to his side, limp. "Then. You shall know."

~

Denny, preceded by Feste, came trotting up the path from the goat stable as soon as he heard the bell, his face a study in wariness and worry. Pam greeted Feste effusively—he made a big fuss about being reunited after even a couple of minutes' separation—then straightened up and faced her guest. "I got the scoop. Humphrey may have put his life on the line to do this; he was defying direct instructions from his Gafr. I didn't think he would ever do that. Come on in and let's have lunch, and you can think about whether you want to know what he said."

"Nothing about me?"

"No. Either nobody's checked that den yet or you did a very good job of covering your tracks. Maybe both. Humphrey completely accepted that I knew about the baby Hefn from the dream."

Denny's whole body had slumped in relief. "I can believe you, right? You're not blandishing me with offers of lunch till a posse can come and arrest me?"

Made distraught by Humphrey's manner, as of one speaking from the tumbril en route to the guillotine, Pam said tersely, "You can believe me. Or you can take off. Actually, you'd better take off pretty soon either way, this isn't a good hidey-hole anymore. With Humphrey out of action I can't protect you, in fact I'm at risk myself. I can give you some supplies."

Taken aback, Denny said, "Okay, I hear you. Should I go now?"

"No, we've got time to eat something, we just mustn't take too long about it."

They went in. Pam looked distractedly in the press and brought out a cheese on a plate and some bread and butter. She reached back out the door for a jug of cider. Denny set the table and sat down; Feste, who'd frisked around the room sniffing at things, promptly hunkered down in front of him, looking expectant. He rubbed the dog's ears absently and scratched under his chin, sneaking covert looks at Pam.

She plunked the cider jug on the table and sat. "Help yourself to whatever. Okay, I think you've got a right to know about this if you want, but if they do come after you later the less you know the better. They'll probe you if they catch you."

"I understand," Denny said, carving cheese off the block, "but I already did something they'll probably wipe me for, so . . . if I decide I want to hear this, are you going to swear me to secrecy?"

Pam shrugged. "What would be the point? If you promised before you knew what the secret was, you wouldn't keep your promise if you thought you shouldn't." She picked up a knife and stabbed at the block of cheese.

"So . . . that's a 'No, I won't make you swear not to tell'?"

She nodded. "That's a no."

"Then I want to know. I appreciate your being so fair-minded about it, but, bottom line, I'm a biologist. The Hefn have been messing with my bears! I want to know as a biologist what they're up to, and I want to know now. More than I want to play it safe. Too late for that anyway."

"Well," Pam said, "that is one hell of a good reason." She smiled at him, her first genuine smile since he'd come back to the house. "Humphrey tried to talk me out of knowing too, but I was as bull-headed as you." The Gafr would be harder on her if she told him, but Pam didn't mention that; she herself had let Humphrey risk "exile, or worse" to get this information. The situation had developed its own momentum.

She gave up trying to eat, set her plate of crumbs on the floor for Feste, and crossed her arms on the table. "Okay, here goes. It turns out that the Hefn haven't been repairing the damage we did entirely from an altruistic wish to heal the biosphere. It also turns out that the Hefn and the Gafr aren't connected only in that master-servant sense we know about. They're also sexually symbiotic."

Denny's hand, loaded with bread and cheese, froze halfway to his mouth. "Symbiotic? Really?"

"Really. Genetically they're not even closely related, but neither can breed without the other. All the Hefn are male. All the Gafr are female. Everybody aboard that ship is, or was, part of a mated pair. The ship was looking for a place that was natural and unspoiled enough for them to breed in it, because their home world, for reasons Humphrey didn't go into, is no longer a suitable place to do that in."

"They were looking for a place to *breed* when they found Earth?"

"Right."

"Four hundred years ago?"

"That's right."

"So when they marooned the renegade Hefn here, they did it planning to come right back for them fairly soon, and settle down, and start reproducing."

"If they hadn't found a more suitable world, yes. Only the ship developed mechanical problems, and by the time they got back here, Earth was no longer natural and unspoiled enough."

"But—why?" Denny exploded. "Why can't they breed on the ship?"

"This is the real boggler," Pam said. "According to Humphrey, the postnatal development of Hefn infants depends on spending a certain amount of time, at a certain stage, being raised in the wild by a predator. *As* a predator. By 2006 we no longer had a viable supply of nursemaid predatory species, and, not incidentally, we had way too many people and way too little habitat for privacy."

"As a *predator*! A free-living predator. Oh—my—God." Denny stared at her. "That's fascinating. That's absolutely fascinating." He thought a minute. "Chimps? The big cats?"

Pam got up to clear away the dishes, including the plate on the floor, now polished clean. "The big cats are all still pretty endangered in the wild, except for lions in Africa and cougars in the western US, and anyway the Hefn don't really relate to cats that well, do they, Feste?" Feste, lying on the hearth, chin on paws, moved his eyes to look at her. She hauled a bushel basket of wrinkled-looking yellow apples over and thumped it down on the floor next to the table; she wanted to occupy her jittery hands. "Chimps might have been a possibility—there's a documented account that a group of them once adopted an abandoned Nigerian boy—but the Hefn needed to work with populations that could recover faster. Shorter gestation period, multiple births, briefer childhood, faster bounceback." She snorted. "We used to wonder why Humphrey was so interested in our myths and stories about feral children. When we were kids in DC, he used to like us to talk about that. Tarzan was a big thing of mine back then." While she was talking Pam had half-filled a bucket with water and set that down next to the basket; now she began transferring apples to the bucket, where they bobbed cheerfully. She stared into the bucket without seeing them. "Now I guess I know."

"Wolves!" Denny said. "Romulus and Remus. Mowgli. Those little girls in India. My God—of course—the coyote field studies!"

Pam fetched nested mixing bowls and paring knives, and a section of newspaper, then sat and spread paper in front of her like a place-mat. She nodded. "He said they ruled out every species that hadn't been able to adapt to some degree to massive loss of habitat. Wolves are too specialized."

"Recovering well now though." He brushed crumbs off his sweat-shirt and started wrapping up the remains of the cheese and bread.

"True, but coyotes were never in any danger of being exter-minated, no matter how intensively they were hunted, trapped, poisoned—well, you know all this better than I do. The Gafr were very interested in the eastern coyotes for a while, the ones the size of German Shepherds."

He nodded. "A guy I know, Jason Gotschalk? he was running the coyote study in my district—he got pulled out the same day I did—he said a couple of the males in his study group were as big as as a small timber wolf."

"In the end though the Gafr decided that black bears were a better answer. There are other Hefn babies out there by the way, maybe a dozen besides Rosetta's, in different parts of the country. Trials, to see where they do best."

Pam had been taking apples from the bucket, quartering and coring them on the newspaper, and tossing the pieces into one bowl and the cores and excised bad bits into another. Denny now drew a sheet of newspaper in front of himself. "Black bears aren't very efficient predators though, not like grizzlies, nowhere near as good as the felines and canids." He picked up a paring knife and reached into the bucket for an apple. "They're fast, and powerful, but not very agile—not enough to prey on elk or deer, and as for rabbits and mice and like that, forget it."

"Well, it seems that from the alien viewpoint, not being specialized has worked to their advantage, and I guess they must be predatory enough for the purpose. And also," pitching a double handful of pieces into the bowl, "there's an authenticated account of a bear in Iran that carried off a toddler and nursed him for three days. Cross-species adoption, see, like the chimps with the Nigerian kid. Besides which, bears do exhibit one excellent behavior trait, if you're a Hefn."

Denny slapped the table. "They hibernate! I was just thinking of that."

"The only large mammalian predator that does, according to Humphrey."

"Oh man. What this means is—" Denny stared at Pam for a long moment. His face changed, and his voice. "The Baby Ban. The Gaian Mission. Even the Habitat Recovery Project. Think of everything the Gaians and the other eco-freaks have put up with—supported, collaborated in!—because we thought the Hefn were trying to save Gaia for its own sake and for us, and all the time they were really saving it for themselves and the Gafr!" Abruptly he flung the knife down on the table so hard it skidded to the floor. "Drastically reduce the human population, temperate forests and rainforests come back, ecosystems recover, keystone predators return—and the aliens have a choice of breeding grounds! *Our* breeding grounds! Humans are sterilized so aliens can have children!"

Pam let him finish. "I understand why you say that, believe me I do, but Denny, it's not that black and white. I know for certain there's been a genuine desire on Humphrey's part—and some of the other Observers' too—to connect with people and help them—help them adjust—just *help* them! That's why Humphrey started the Bureau of Temporal Physics, with hardly any support from the other Hefn and despite the discouragement of the Gafr—to help us find a model for living nondestructively."

"Yeah, so they could breed here."

"Not just them! So *we* could, without wrecking the planet! Remember, the Directive came before the Ban, but people refused to comply with it!" The apple in her hands was mostly rot; she abandoned the effort to cut out the bad parts and dumped the whole thing in the compost bowl, then gripped the table edge to keep her hands from shaking. "Keep in mind that Humphrey put the noose around his own neck this morning by telling me all this."

Denny, clearly unprepared to deal with an emotional Pam Pruitt, backed right down. "Yeah okay, fine, whatever. I didn't mean to upset you."

Pam made an impatient gesture that said *Me getting upset isn't important*. "I'm right, all right, but so are you. Behind everything else, even the Bureau of Temporal Physics, there was always another agenda, even for Humphrey and Godfrey and Alfrey—because whatever they think personally, however they extend themselves towards us, in the end the Hefn serve the Gafr. We tend to forget that, because we never see the Gafr, but it's all too true. All the Hefn we've ever had any dealings with stayed loyal to the Gafr when the rebels mutinied. That's why what Humphrey did today is so extraordinary, that's how much he cares about what's going to happen to us all."

"And he told you all this—what you've been telling me—because otherwise you refused to try having any more dreams about the future?" Denny bugged his eyes, though politely.

"I know it sounds crazy." Pam absolutely did not want to discuss precognitive dreaming with Denny Demaree. She got up and dumped the bucket into the sink, picked the knife up off the floor and laid it on the counter, then went to build up the fire. "I know Humphrey has always believed that the Ban might be lifted, and did everything he could to make that happen. But the whole deal has always hinged on connections between a few Hefn and a handful of people. Except for those relationships, the Gafr would have washed their hands of us long ago."

She straightened up, a bit stiffly, to lift a Dutch oven off the hearth and hang it on an iron arm affixed to the side of the fireplace, removing the heavy lid first and setting it aside. "Those relationships have been under terrible stress, though, since this past summer and the one-year deadline. We've had this rah-rah-let's-all-be-Gaians thing going on here and in Europe and Africa, and a show of cooperation in China and the Middle East, but that's mostly been a charade. The Apprentices have wondered all along why the Gafr were okay with that. Now—"

"Now it's obvious they're just giving humanity something to focus on while they were finding out whether their young will thrive here!"

And that was the answer, that was why the Gafr needed the year. "The question now is, if they do thrive here, what happens to people?"

"No," said Danny, "the first question is, what if people find out now that the Hefn and Gafr are breeding?" Again, he looked hard at Pam. "Is that why you didn't make me promise not to tell? because *you* can't, but you're hoping I will?"

Startled, Pam turned to look at him. "I'm not hoping you will, believe me! Have you ever seen a mob in action—did you catch any of the media coverage of the riots? What good would it do to have a lot of people grabbing guns and storming out to hunt down all the bears?"

Denny recoiled. "God, they would, too, wouldn't they? That's exactly what they'd do, it would be the one way people have ever had to really hurt the aliens. They'd be too out of their minds with rage to worry about getting killed or mindwiped, they might even feel like it was worth it!" At the thought of the wholesale murder of bears, Denny had gone pale. "But—if I don't tell—see—I've never been able to stand the Hefn, I told you that. If I don't expose them, I'll feel like a collaborator, or a coward. Both!" He snorted. "The plain truth is, I *am* a collaborator, even if I didn't know I was. All the field biologists are. What have we been doing all this time but helping get the biosphere ready to be an alien nursery?" He got up abruptly and carried the heaping bowl of quartered apples to the hearth, without stating the obvious—that if he was a collaborator she was a thousand times more of one.

Not that he needed to say it. For the first time in years Pam remembered the man on the *Delta Queen*, who'd growled to her and Liam that it was the collaborators who wouldn't be forgiven.

She took the bowl. "Thanks. I need about a cup of water." When Denny brought the water she poured it into the Dutch oven, dumped in the apples, stirred them briefly with a long wooden spoon. Then she clanged on the lid and swung the iron arm so the big pot hung over the fire. "Denny, I owe Humphrey more than I owe to any human being now alive, and that's still true despite the fact that our friendship's been under tremendous strain this year. He said today that they've all been under a terrific strain, waiting for conditions to improve and fearing all the time that they might never breed again, that their people would go extinct."

"Sorry," Denny said, "but I gotta tell you, I wish to Christ they'd gone extinct before they ever got here."

Pam sat down. Her head throbbed. "I understand that. But Humphrey and Godfrey are the only reason every human on Earth didn't die after the first assault on a Hefn, on the *Delta Queen*. And then again after that Klan episode you used to hear about from Jesse."

Denny said sarcastically, "Maybe they wanted us to clean the place up first. *Then* kill us all."

She frowned. "Hard to believe they'd do that, now that the breeding trials have begun, I mean think of the mess." And yet why would Humphrey be so frantic for information about the future if he hadn't believed it could happen? Should the first generation of babies thrive, all bets were off. For that matter, should they fail to thrive, how was the outlook any brighter for humanity? She said doggedly, "I suppose that if things go well they might try again on a bigger scale for a few more seasons . . ."

"Hang on," Denny said. "This is the Final Year. People expect a decision about the Ban about six months from now, that was the deal. And anyway, if the Hefn started placing their kids in bears' dens all over the map every winter, how long could they keep it a secret? A dozen denned-up baby Hefn, maybe, this year. But many dozens? Hundreds? There's no way."

"They'd post warning signs wherever they planted a baby—"

"No, listen. Some other biologist is going to refuse to be kicked out of his study area, same as I did; maybe somebody already has. There's no way they can keep the lid on. What happens even this spring, when a dozen Hefn toddlers come out and start wandering around with the mother bears?" He moved closer to Pam, stood over her. "What if somebody steals one out of a den? Or kills one? You know it could happen."

Pam frowned up at him. "Well—only if the Hefn weren't keeping close tabs on them all—"

"But they're not! Nobody's at my farm. Nobody was protecting the baby in Rosetta's den. You'd think they'd have the whole ship watching over it." As if suddenly aware of his browbeating stance over Pam, he jerked around and sat at the table again, tense as a sprinter waiting for the gun, a posture that said *Well? Explain that!*

Pam massaged the base of her aching neck. "Maybe they have to leave it up to Nature. Humphrey said this had to happen in the wild, that captive populations wouldn't work. Otherwise I don't suppose they'd have stuck around Earth."

"Yeah, and I wouldn't be cowering here on this bench, in dread of being probed and wiped."

"And the planet would still be going to hell in a handbasket."

"But it would still be ours."

Pam's eyebrows shot up. "For how much longer?"

"Ah—God damn it to hell! We've been trapped in a lose-lose situation for twenty-seven years!" Denny struck the table again; Feste, who'd been napping underneath, bolted out and up the three stairs to the upper level with his tail clamped straight down. For that moment he was the antithesis of a guard dog. At the top he half-turned and looked to Pam for instructions.

"It's okay, it's okay," she said. "Good boy. Come on down, come by me. Come on." And to Denny, "You and I should be strategizing, not sparring." But the vision that had sprung up, of a future fraught with discoveries, more riots, mob violence on a global scale, was difficult to see past.

"Yeah, I know, you're right," Denny was saying. "Sorry. Sorry, Feste. Where were we?"

Where indeed? "It doesn't matter, we won't get it all sorted out between us today anyhow. And you should get going." Abruptly Pam's need to send Denny on his way was overwhelming. She could feel herself about to come unraveled, and got up, with the idea of putting some food together for him and easing him out the door. She shook out a paper bag and moved around the kitchen, collecting things and sticking them into it. "I think if I were the Gafr, once I knew the breeding program could probably succeed, I'd break off and go on a fifty-year junket. Couple of weeks for them, then back to an insignificantly small human population and a thriving biosphere. And plenty of bears—maybe I'd leave a small police force behind to protect the bears, so I didn't get back and find they'd all been slaughtered." She pushed a sealed jar of the peaches Denny had liked so much to the bottom of the bag and folded down the top.

Peaches, Humphrey's second-favorite cobbler ingredient. Sad all at once to the point of tears, she said, "Humphrey seemed so utterly entranced with the idea of having a baby himself, his own baby. I don't suppose he'll get to now."

Denny exploded off the bench. "Well *fine*, he can fucking join the crowd! It's his fault none of us will get to either, so excuse me if I don't break down and cry over poor Humphrey! And if you want my opinion, which I'm sure you don't, I think you've been hanging out with that mange bag so long you've totally lost perspective!"

Feste got up and stood between them, looking up worriedly into Pam's face. She stroked his head. "It's okay, sweetie, everything's fine. How about you go out for a while." She got up and held the door open, and he walked through, unwilling but obedient, looking back as it shut behind him. Pam breathed a few times before turning to face Denny. "I shouldn't have told you that. I'm not thinking straight."

Denny didn't reply, but was also making a visible effort to get hold of himself, looking down and taking huffing breaths. "Me neither," he admitted. "Blow the cover on the goddam lying Hefn, versus don't blow their cover to protect the black bears, so the bears can foster Hefn babies. What a choice."

Pam nodded tersely. "It sounds a lot like the choices some of us have been making right along."

"Yeah, I see what you mean by 'not that black and white' for sure." He shook his head. "I need to think some more, I guess."

"And you need to get the hell out of the Hollow," Pam said again. Denny was going to get the bum's rush now, before she lost it completely. She yanked a drawer open. "Here, here's some money— no, take it, you're going to need it, you'll have to disappear for a while. Change your appearance, get some different clothes, burn all your old ones, the duffel too." She set the bulky bag of food on the counter. "This ought to keep you going for a few days. Sorry you never got time for that bath."

Pam's abrupt switch from talk to action took Denny by surprise, but he met her halfway. "Thanks, thanks a lot." He shoved the bills into his pants pocket, then squatted down to open his dufflepack and tuck the food inside. He lifted his filthy parka off the hook and slid his arms into it.

"Hole up someplace nobody you've ever known would ever think to look for you—but don't tell me where," she said quickly when he opened his mouth, "if they come for me I'll be probed."

"Probed? *You?*" Plainly this hadn't crossed Denny's mind. He looked shocked. "You're not gonna try to get away?"

"No. I'll go quietly. But they won't find out where you went if you don't tell me." She managed a smile of encouragement. "It should be okay, the Hefn can't think like detectives and the real detectives won't help them. You can drop out of sight right in plain view if you go about it right. Don't try to get in touch, but watch the news. And listen, think about what's to be gained from doing nothing till after June 6. Unless word of what they're up to gets out, the Gafr might decide to let things play out till then."

"I will," he said. "Well—thanks, thanks for all this. I'm sorry things kind of got out of hand. I shouldn't have said what I said, either."

A sharp bark sounded at the door and Pam went to let Feste back in, along with a draft of cold air. "I'll walk up with you and let you out, and take a look at that cut phone wire." The idea of using her muscles, after all that sitting and hard grim thinking, was a relief.

The room had grown chilly, the fire burned down to coals. Pam banked these with a little flat tool, added a couple of split logs, gave the apples another stir, then pulled on her own jacket. "Got enough matches?"

Denny nodded. He grabbed the straps, and looked as ready as he would ever be to begin life as a fugitive.

She opened the back door. Since lunchtime the brilliant day had turned damp and gray. She let Denny step out first, then followed the dog out and pulled the door to with a little bang. "I want to stop at the outhouse. You?" And when he shook his head, "Back in a minute then. Feste, sit. Stay here."

She took three strides along the path—and directly ahead of her the view of leafless trees and steep hillside and Orrin Hubbell's studio began to spin.

Denny shouted "Hey! Hey!" and dropped his bag. Pam froze. As they watched, the spinning air began to clarify from the center outward. Full of the threat of mindwipe and ready to bolt, Denny cried out "What is it—are they coming?"

Pam said incredulously, "No. It's a time window, opening from the future—that's exactly what it is, by God! I've only ever seen this happen from the *other* side." Catching sight of Denny's face, she added, "Don't worry, they can't do anything but look through and talk." And erase the event from your memory, but no need to mention that.

Feste had broken his sit-stay without permission for the first time since she'd met him, and was barking and feinting frantically at the bizarreness in the path. Pam's sternest voice was required to rein him in. He sat shoved against her leg, one front paw on the toe of her boot; she put her hand on his head without taking her eyes off the whirling air.

The lens had now clarified almost to the rim. What they saw at the middle of the circle was indeed a Hefn, standing behind a metal contraption on legs, a time transceiver. Surrounding Hefn and transceiver, a disk of April or May—pink smears of blooming redbuds, fervent birdsong—had been superimposed on the dead of winter.

The rim stopped spinning; the window was clear across its whole circumference. Stepping back from the machine, the Hefn walked around to where they could get a good look at him.

Pam had never seen him before in her life.

This Hefn was sleeker than Humphrey or Alfrey, slimmer, less motley-looking. He grinned in a way that was orders of magnitude more human-like than even Humphrey had ever achieved. "Hi, Pam. Hi, Denny. Hey there, Feste the Wonder Dog, if you don't look exactly like your pictures! Sorry to barge in on you folks like this. I'm Terrifrey, by the way—I'm Humphrey's son."

Son! Pam blurted, "Where's Humphrey then?"

"Just waking up, he was up half the winter. He's fine, don't worry. We went ahead and did the contact without him, but he—preapproved it, so to speak." He looked around, twisting his whole upper body to turn his head. "Mighty nice time of year to be at the Hollow, on this side I mean."

Pam's brain, like the lens of the window, whirled and cleared. "'We'?"

Terrifrey glanced to the side, beyond the edge of the lens, and another sleek Hefn came and stood next to him. "We," said the second Hefn. "I'm Dennifrey. Named after you, Denny. Great to meet you."

Denny goggled and gaped. "You're—you are! You're Rosetta's baby Hefn!" The Hefn nodded and did a truly superb imitation of beaming. "So what became of *Rocket*?"

"He lived a long, happy life and begat lots of little Rockettes. And Rodeo and I were close as long as she lived. I went out to see her all the time. She had lots of babies too."

At this Denny turned suspicious. "Okay, how do I know whether that's the truth or a lot of crapola? You know it's exactly what I want to hear."

"Oh, it's the truth, all right," said a third voice, and a wiry old man, nearly bald, with a bushy gray beard, strolled into the spring landscape and stood beside the two Hefn. Denny cried out "Paw!" in a shocked voice, but even Pam could see who the old man really was, and in a moment so could Denny. "No," he said, breathless, "no, that's—my God, that's me. That's me. I look exactly like my own grandfather."

Old Denny grinned at him. "Yeah, I'm always thinking it's Paw in the mirror myself, even though I've known what to expect since I was out there where you are now. Okay, now get ready for another shock, a mighty nice one." He beckoned, and the strangest figure of all entered the frame of the lens: a handsome brown-haired little boy of five or six, in jeans and a yellow pullover. "Hi, Grampa," he said, and giggled. The bearded man put an arm around him; but he had spoken *through* the lens. "I'm Jeremy. I'm your grandson."

Denny literally lost his balance and staggered. "My *grand*son!"

Now Pam broke in, to ask what she desperately wanted to know. "Does the fact that you're all over there together mean we made it through the transition?"

The figures in the lens seemed to hesitate and the boy looked sideways up at Old Denny, who said carefully, "What you see, I'm afraid, is all you get. We can't answer any questions of that kind, not in so many words, because this—the four of us—is what you and I and Feste saw in the window. This is all that was shown to us. We had to take it from there as best we could."

"We weren't wiped then—we remembered this! *Will* remember it."

"The whole point of coming through today was so you would remember."

Erasing the memories of witnesses to a time window event was the very first rule of working with the transceivers; in a way, Pam was more startled by this than anything else she'd heard. Not really expecting a reply, she said, "Why am I not over there too? Am I dead?"

They all relaxed. "You didn't come with us to the Hollow but you're just fine," Terrifrey told her, "and that's not a lot of crapola," which made everyone grin on both sides of the lens.

Denny looked hungrily at Jeremy. "Am I really your grampa?"

He nodded vigorously. "Yeah, only you look so really young! And you've got lots of hair, and it's brown—and you haven't got any *beard*." He giggled again. His eyes, like Denny's, were very blue.

But now Humphrey's self-declared son stepped back behind the transceiver. "It's marvelous to see you all, but I'm sorry, we have to break contact now. Pam Pruitt, remember, Time is One! It'll be okay." And the disk of air spun inward while alien, man, and child waved and called "Bye!"; and in a few seconds the January landscape had been restored to itself, and Pam and Denny stood staring at the empty air.

"Whuf," Pam said quietly. "Well. I guess we're not going anywhere just yet. Except I'm still going to the outhouse; back in a second." She pulled the back door open. "Feste, in you go." Denny hoisted his bag and followed the dog. When Pam came back a few minutes later, the house was filled with the heavenly aroma of cooking apples and Feste's joyous prancing, and Denny had unzipped his coat and sat down on a bench. He turned a thin, exalted face toward her. "I'm gonna have a *grandson*!"

"Sure looks that way." She sat beside him. "But does it strike you there was a hell of a lot they didn't say?"

Denny nodded. "They didn't *say* they'd lifted the Ban. But there he was—Jeremy!"

"They didn't say Jeremy was your genetic offspring, that he hadn't been adopted, or cloned, or wasn't a donor baby. They flatly declined to say whether things had worked out peacefully between humanity and the Hefn. They didn't explain why they allowed us to remember the event, and that really blows my mind. They didn't, when you get right down to it, say a whole hell of a lot." Pam was realizing how hard it was for people on the past side of an open window to trust what people on the future side were telling them, something she'd never had occasion to consider before.

"Well, they sure *implied* all that," Denny said impatiently. "They for sure implied that Jeremy was my actual genetic grandchild."

"Yeah," said Pam, but how's that possible? Did you miss the Broadcast?"

Denny frowned. "I—don't know, actually. I don't remember watching it, I was four in 2013, but my parents never said I was like out of earshot of the TV or anything. My brother's two years younger, and we've all always assumed . . . but maybe I did miss it. But isn't it more likely they lifted the Ban?"

He didn't know that wasn't going to happen, of course. Pam saw that Denny was now deeply invested in the possibility of having a grandchild, and was fending off her skepticism. So she backed off. "I guess it is. Anyway, hey, you'll find out in the course of things, won't you? You're right, there's as much reason to take it all at face value as not to." Which was true enough.

"Exactly! Denny grinned. "What year would you say it was? In the window."

Pam considered. "You looked to be, what, about sixty or so? And you were four in 2013, so you're twenty-eight now?"

"Right. And a half."

"Well then. Thirty years, give or take. So 2068, 2070? Baby Ban plus or minus fifty-six." *The Last Generation is in its fifties. All the rising generations are minuscule; it's a minuscule global human population, an umbrella with a skinny handle. Brett O'Hara is a bitter old woman, one of millions. Lexi is cresting middle age. I'm plus or minus seventy myself.*

Denny laughed. "You know what? An hour ago I'd have said all I cared about was bears, I'd have said I hated the Baby Ban on principle, personal considerations didn't have anything to do with it. Now—"

Pam prompted herself to smile warmly. "Now you're thinking maybe someday Jeremy and his family will be living out there on that farm."

"Maybe so!" said Denny, and his ferrety face positively glowed. "What did he mean about time is one, anyway?"

"It's a saying the Hefn have: 'Time is One, and Fixed.' It means that whatever happens is the only thing that *can* have happened. If two Hefn and you and a little boy appear in a time window, then events will necessarily lead to a moment when a time window opens and those four beings speak to you and me in January of 2038."

Denny frowned. "That's like saying, it'll work out that way no matter what we do. Like, if I just go to bed for thirty years, that contact will still occur."

Pam jumped up. "Oops. Hang on." She hurried to snatch off the pot lid and stir the apples, releasing a cloud of fragrant steam, then swung the arm off the fire, away from the heat; they were just starting to stick to the bottom. She came and sat on the bench next to Denny. "The Hefn have that other saying: 'What we never know is how.' If a window opens in the future, they know of one little thing that will definitely happen, but not what else will happen between the present and that moment in the future. Maybe the 'how' is that you call a press conference and announce that the Hefn are reproducing, using bears as surrogate mothers, and worldwide riots ensue. Maybe you call the conference, but not till June 7th. Maybe you go back to work for Fish and Wildlife and never say a word to anybody. Maybe you sneak back to have another look at little Dennifrey and Innisfrey catches you with your hand in the cookie jar, or you hide out in Utah and convert to Mormonism, or you go to bed for thirty years. You can say it doesn't matter, but you still have to choose among alternatives, see? You have to do *something*, you have to collapse the wave function. And whatever you actually choose, *that* turns out to be 'how.' Your choice isn't determined by anything, but it's already there, in the timestream."

Denny looked dubious. "Well, I don't really see how that's not predestination, but I don't care. I'm making my choice. I'm choosing to believe that I'm really going to have a child and a grandson. Which means that up in the future, where Jeremy is, human babies are being born and thriving, regardless of whether the Ban's been lifted or if its just happening in a very small population. So for now, I'm deciding not to expose them. I'll go back to Fish and Wildlife and take an assignment, and wait and see."

Having declared his intentions Denny stood and zipped his coat; and all of a sudden it was like he couldn't get out of there fast enough. When Pam offered to row him over to Indiana he said "No thanks, I'll walk back to Milton and catch the Louisville packet there—no big rush, now that I know what I'm gonna do." Despite these words he snatched up his duffel's straps with one hand and reached for the door latch with the other. "Thanks again, for everything. Maybe I'll see you if they send me back this way." He sounded like he hoped they wouldn't.

Pam shook her head. "I'm heading back to Salt Lake in a few days." She'd gotten up and lifted a key ring off a hook by the door.

"Here's the gate key. Just leave it in the lock, I can pick it up later."

"Well," said Denny, pocketing the key, "thanks again."

"No problem. Good luck, Grampa." She held out her hand and Denny shook it. Feste looked pleadingly up into their faces. "Okay if he keeps you company as far as the gate?"

"Sure thing," said Denny. "Feste, let's go!"

The door snapped sharply behind them. For perhaps two minutes Pam stood still as a statue, staring at the shut door. Finally she stirred, moved slowly to the door and peered through its window at the spot where on four separate occasions now a time window had opened, and people from the future had looked and spoken through it. All of the three other times, Pam herself had been one of those people. Once, twice, and again. As the dawn was breaking the Sambhur belled. Hunting Song of the Seeonee Pack.

Sometime after that she dragged one of Orrin's heavy chairs to the fire and fell into it like a sack of potatoes. She stared at the coals. Heat drained from the room, which grew steadily colder.

A blank interval later Feste barked to be let in. Denny had threaded the key ring through his collar. He licked her hand, turned around twice and slumped to the floor, panting. Noticing her freezing feet at last, Pam laid a handful of kindling and several split logs on the bed of fading coals, automatically arranging them just so, and pumped Orrin's little homemade bellows till the kindling caught and flared.

I should put the apples through the colander, she thought, but the effort was completely beyond her. She fell back into her chair. Feste gave her a sober look, then laid his chin on his folded paws.

In that solitude, in a silence broken only by the popping and flapping of the fire, the turbulent realities of the past two days gradually began to sort themselves into a narrative. The narrative included several surprising reversals and led to a startling outcome: that thirty years in the future, at least some humans and some Hefn would be, one, on apparently excellent terms, and two, breeding successfully, both of them.

It was this exact information that Humphrey had been seeking by such extraordinary means. On that point the logic of the story was clear. If he could show the Gafr evidence of a future where aliens were happily reproducing on Earth and people were still around, then people would still be around (even if they too were reproducing).

What cruel irony that the information had been acquired, not from the precognitive dream of a Latter-day Shaman, but in the usual way, by means of Hefn technology doing what it had been designed to do! Humphrey had sacrificed himself for nothing.

Or maybe not; eventually the thought struck Pam that she should contact Santa Barbara and report the time window event. They hadn't picked up the signature yet or somebody would have called. If they were even still scanning for signatures; that approach might have been abandoned. For all she knew, they might still be trying to retrofit transceivers out there.

The window event should have been called in immediately, Humphrey's fate might hang on what the Gafr thought it meant. She shoved herself out of the chair, startling the snoozing Feste, and plodded to the workstation.

She had just activated the phone when it chimed the arrival of an incoming call. She answered, and there was Liam, beside himself with excitement. "Pam! Thank God you're in! You're not gonna believe this—a time window opened half an hour ago, right in the lounge! From like thirty years from now! I saw it, Artie saw it, Sam saw it, *Alfrey* saw it—we were having a meeting in there and a whole raft of people saw it, and guess who came through!"

"I give up." But goose bumps had flashed across the skin of her thighs.

"You, that's who—you did! It was you!"

PART THREE

Resolutions

Gaia, as I see her, is no doting mother tolerant of misdemeanors, nor is she some fragile and delicate damsel in danger from brutal mankind. She is stern and tough, always keeping the world warm and comfortable for those who obey the rules, but ruthless in her destruction of those who transgress. Her unconscious goal is a planet fit for life. If humans stand in the way of this, we shall be eliminated with as little pity as would be shown by the micro-brain of an intercontinental ballistic nuclear missile in full flight to its target.

—James Lovelock, *The Ages of Gaia*

CHAPTER 18

A Braid of Time

JANUARY - APRIL 2038; APRIL - MAY 2041

The Martin handcart company of Latter-day Saints left Iowa City at the end of July, 1856, seven or eight weeks too late to make it safely through the mountains into the Salt Lake Valley before bad weather caught them. Throughout August, September, and most of October they had struggled across Nebraska and Wyoming toward the Rockies. For all that distance the staff writers on *A Thousand Miles* had entangled their characters with one another against a background formed by the actual journey's severe, but spellbindingly dramatic, hardships.

But the final weeks had been a horror story of freezing and starvation. Of the 576 Saints who had started from Iowa, between 135 and 150 died on the road. The literal truth was more than dramatic enough. Relationships among the characters faded at the last into the pitiless winter landscape, and the writers told the story as it had happened. Kate/Lexi was carried across the Platte River at Last Crossing in the first flurries of winter, snowed in for days soon after, had two frozen fingers amputated, and finally entered the Salt Lake Valley on her own rag-wrapped feet. The same day her mother gave birth to her baby brother and name him Handcart—a final fictional touch to end the series on a symbolically hopeful note. The producers knew what a baby's birth would mean to an audience under the Ban.

Over the course of the three years since it had first been broadcast, Pam had watched the final episode probably half a dozen times.

But Liam had never seen it, and some of the production people on the movie they were shooting now had expressed interest in seeing it again. So tonight after dinner there was to be a special screening on the Scofield campus, and after that a party.

Lexi and Neil were less than thrilled with the plan. The acting skills of both had matured over the past three years, to the point where watching their younger selves at work made them groan and squirm with embarrassment. But really they were too engrossed in the new movie, and in one another, to mind very much.

Lexi at fifteen was so beautiful that, had she not wanted the part so badly, Pam would have cast a different girl to play herself. Liam's qualms about Neil, who was six feet tall, were similar; but Neil wanted passionately to work with Lexi on the film, and Lexi wanted Neil; and there actually weren't that many male actors in the right age group to choose from, so in the end he got the part.

To compensate for this out-and-out glamorizing of the two young leads, Pam, whose contract as consultant gave her this authority, had insisted on casting close physical matches for the other important roles. The actor playing Jesse Kellum did look just like Jesse. They'd signed a good Orrin and a dead-ringer Hannah, and look-alikes had also been found for Frances and Shelby. Humphrey was having a rousing good time playing both himself and the acerbic Hefn Jeffrey, who hadn't been the least bit interested in being in a movie.

The venerable *Delta Queen*, still plying the waterways of the eastern United States, would play herself as well. The movie was to open just as the beautiful old steamboat was about to cast off from the wharf at Pittsburgh. She would be taking on provisions, firewood, and last-minute passengers. From their position at the railing, where they could watch the bustle of departure, the two vacationing math prodigies would see Humphrey (as Jeffrey) come up the landing stage with his party and disappear inside. Then as the boat backed into the river amid a cheery racket of boiler, paddle wheel, calliope, and people calling goodbye, and straightened out and started downstream, an orchestral arrangement of Liam's little song "Stars" was to surge dramatically, not quite drowning out the background noise, while Lexi and Neil faced forward, happy as two larks, hair whipping in the mid-river wind, completely unaware that they were embarking on a personal journey that was to change history. Roll title across stunning footage of springtime in the valley of the Beautiful Ohio: *Hurt Hollow*. Roll credits: Pamela Pruitt, Alexis Allred. Mark William O'Hara, Neil Reeder. The Rev. Otie Bemis, The Rev. Otie Bemis, Jr. The Hefn Humphrey appears as himself and as the Hefn Jeffrey.

Junior had been signed to play his father. There was really no avoiding it, he looked exactly like Otie and he'd been acting from the pulpit most of his life. Since his role mostly called for preaching, the performance he'd been turning in was actually quite decent. Pam would have liked to veto him on the grounds that she couldn't stand him; but he was the best man for the job, so she settled for trying to keep out of his way.

They were shooting the scene where Pam and Liam disembark from the *Delta Queen* and are met by Pam's parents. This had actually occurred at Scofield Landing, a few miles further downstream, but the script called for them to get off at Madison so that photogenic footage of the historic part of town and the bridge could be included. Actors and crew had been at the Madison river front all day.

A crowd of extras had been recruited for the scene at the landing, which would run a couple of minutes in the finished film but was taking all day to shoot. Older adult extras worked for free and the fun of it, but adults under thirty and children of any age were being paid to be in the landing scene, and people had brought kids from miles around, enough kids to make things look the way they might have looked in May 2013 on a typical day. Liam had decided to be an extra too; he'd taken a notion that Jiffy should be in the scene and that meant he would have to be in it himself. Nobody else had the energy or the patience to manage her; she never held still, and unless she was singing she never stopped talking. At the last minute he had prevailed upon Pam to come along and help; so there they both were, in period costume and makeup, moving through the crowd after the perpetual motion machine that was Jiffy O'Hara at three years old.

Jeff-in-the-dream had been correct: Pam had known when the moment came to tell a bowled-over Liam that Gillian Jacoby was pregnant, "almost certainly" by him. She then sent him to Humphrey, who sent him to Oakland to see Gillian and her boyfriend Wayne Cameron. To everyone's surprise and relief these two had taken the news calmly. It happened that Wayne had watched the Broadcast with his family, and clearly remembered both it and the ensuing uproar. At first he and Gillian had tried to convince each other that they'd somehow been immune, but the calendar made the truth too obvious. They hadn't tried to find out for sure, but had already accepted the probability that Liam was the father and Humphrey the catalyst, and went along without protest for the DNA testing, done in utero, that settled this question officially.

Instead of resenting Liam, as a lot of men in his position might have done, in the end Wayne was simply grateful. He had longed for children in the obsessive way of Liam's sister Brett, and had been overjoyed, as in fact was Brett, about Gillian's pregnancy, however it had come about. He persuaded Gillian that they should get married—and invited Liam to take part in the ceremony, in the radical role of father of the bride's unborn baby. And the upshot was that little Jiffy had two functioning fathers, both present at her birth, both devoted to her welfare, both utterly besotted with her, and by a miracle neither resentful of the other. It seemed inevitable that the baby should be the spitting image of her mother and her long-dead Uncle Jeff.

The name on the birth certificate was Anne Jacoby Cameron O'Hara. It was Wayne, watching her crawl furiously across the carpet one day when she was about eight months old, who had said "You're gonna be walking in a great big jiffy now, baby girl, and then God help us all." And it was Liam who heard him say it, and started calling his daughter Jiffy. Which was Pam's cue to tell him, finally, about the lucid dream.

There was a look on Liam's face these days that Pam had never seen there before, a look of peace after great suffering. Humphrey had a way of watching Liam with his little girl and saying pointedly to Pam, "What we never know is how."

"What we never know," Pam said now to Liam, "is how. How to keep her from poking through horse droppings. How to keep her from running underneath the horses' bellies and getting herself trampled. How to keep her from affectionately assaulting every other kid in the crowd."

"How to convince her not to yell 'Pop, I wanna do it!' while the cameras are rolling," Liam said. Jiffy had shrilled this during a take an hour before. "Do it" was the term Feste and BJ had been taught for when it was time to go outside, and Jiffy, passionately interested at present in all aspects of elimination, had taken note. BJ, on lead with Pam in the crowd, had given Jiffy a look of approval, as if to say "What an excellent and thoughtful suggestion." Lexi had cracked up completely, and the director had yelled "Cut!" and given Liam a dirty look as he hustled Jiffy off towards the portapotties, while Lexi caught Pam's eye across the crowd and laughed with delight. Which, even wearing those hideous genie pants and that tent-like tee, made her look too dazzlingly beautiful to be real, let alone to be adolescent Pam.

"Places, please, everybody," the director called through his megaphone. "Let's try to get it right this time."

For various reasons—a cloud, a blooper, a stuck boom—quite a few more takes were required before Lexi/Pam and Neil/Liam finally made it successfully down the *Delta Queen's* landing stage and through their initial encounter with Frances and Shelby. Liam and Jiffy had come back long since, and were in the crowd shot when the camera panned across the landing. "That's a wrap, thank God," the director called. "Ten minutes, folks. Take your rest breaks now."

Liam swept Jiffy up in his arms. "That remark was intended for you, Munchkin."

"BJ wants a rest break," she informed him.

"Think so? You're probably right," Pam agreed. "BJ, wanna do it?"

He did. They headed for the grass.

BJ had been acting for the past two years, mostly in productions with Lexi, like now. This time he was playing Jesse's dog Curly, a part written specially for him. Jesse had never kept a dog at Hurt Hollow. Two rangy brown mutts named Curly and Snapper, litter mates, had been living with the Hubbells in the summer of 1964— Pam and Liam had seen them both in a time window—but neither bore the remotest resemblance to a black poodle.

However, the writers and producer thought a dog added a nice touch. When they approached Dan Webster, the actor playing Jesse, he made the expected remark about being upstaged by animals and children and complained that he was already being put in the shade by a herd of goats; but in fact he and BJ hit it off like gangbusters right away. So they wrote BJ in. At least he was, indeed, extremely curly.

When BJ had sniffed out a suitable tree and lifted his leg, taking his time about it while Jiffy crouched down to improve her angle of concentration, they started back. "I wanna go now," Jiffy announced.

"I'm hungry. I wanna talk to Mommy and Daddy. I wanna see Terri-frey. I wanna talk to Aunt Brett. Let's *go*."

"We can't go yet, hon, the bus won't be driving back till they're done filming," Liam told her.

Before Jiffy could get started, Pam said, "Yes we can. Jiffy, that's the best idea I've heard all day. We can take a taxi. I will person-ally pay for this taxi, my feet are killing me." She stuck BJ's leash in Liam's free hand. "Just give me a second, I want to tell Lexi we're taking off. Jiffy, you can help him look for a taxi, okay?"

"Okay! I see one! I see one, Pop! We can go in that one!" She struggled to get down, tangling her foot in BJ's leash.

Liam, looking harried, gave in. "Okay, but step on it. We'll be in that one by the tornado monument, see it? The white horse?" He was standing Jiffy on her feet as he spoke. At the instant of landfall she took off running, careening off people's legs, and Liam and BJ had no choice but to give chase.

When Pam turned around she bumped into Lexi, who said, "You guys heading back now?"

"Yeah, we are. Not a moment too soon, either, Jiffy's getting cranky and I'm fading fast. I was just coming to tell you."

"Wasn't that a steamer when she screamed out 'I wanna do it'? I thought Buster was gonna blow!" Buster was the director; Lexi respected but didn't much like him. "'Pop, I wanna *do* it!'" she repeated, this time in perfect mimicry of Jiffy's cri de coeur. "I didn't realize she'd picked that up."

"Me neither, but everybody knows now."

They chuckled. Lexi said, "Well, I'm glad I caught you. We're about to do the scene where Frances and Shelby tell us about those guys getting mindwiped? They'd seen it on the telly?" Pam nodded. "So, do you remember how you felt at the exact minute you found out?"

Pam cast her mind back—and heaved a sigh. "Upset. I was upset, and so was Liam. I remember defending the Hefn, they'd only done what they said they'd do, those guys had fair warning and so on, but the truth was that it made me feel queasy as hell."

"Was it, like, you were caught in the middle? Like, guilty for being an Apprentice?"

Pam considered. "Caught in the middle for sure. Guilty?" She shook her head slowly. "I was too devoted to Humphrey. Just very very uncomfortable. I wished like anything it hadn't happened."

"Same for Liam?"

"I expect so. You can ask him."

Lexi glanced over Pam's shoulder and said "No time, here comes your escape vehicle," and then Jiffy's shrill imperious voice was calling "Pom, come on! Come on, Pom, we're going back!"

Lexi looked startled. "Pom?"

Pam popped her eyes and shrugged. "I reckon she picked that up too, from somebody or other." She waved and called "Be there in a jiffy!" which, as always, made Jiffy chortle with glee.

Lexi said, "Hey, I'm not so sure I like that!" But then she laughed. "Pom and Pop, typical parents of the new world order!" She waved at Jiffy too. "You better go, the break'll be over in a sec."

"See you at the screening?"

"Oh," said Lexi, already heading back to start her scene, "I guess. If Neil wants to. Or we may just catch the party."

~

The taxi clopped into Scofield the back way, to avoid the steep climb up the river bluff. Pam gave their driver directions to the house. They were all staying there, Lexi, Liam and Jiffy, Humphrey and Terrifrey, and of course Pam herself, in her parents' old bedroom, since Lexi now considered Pam's her own. They were full up, there was no space for Neil, for which Pam was thankful. Think of fertility being problematic! But it was, for old reasons once again relevant, a sign of life returning to something more like normal.

The others piled out of the taxi while she paid the driver. Jiffy ran up the walk screeching "Terrifrey! Terrifrey! I'm back!" and banged into the house, with BJ, dragging his leash, right behind her.

"How old am I?" Liam asked Pam. "Am I really only forty-two? How is it that I'm so exhausted all the time?"

"Feed her something, maybe she'll get sleepy. She didn't have a nap today."

"A nap. Oh God, the sheer bliss of that concept."

They were walking toward the front door, which Jiffy had left standing open, when Humphrey appeared in it. At the sight of him they stopped and gawked. "Humphrey!" Liam said, "Why are you doing your Fretful Porpentine thing?" The entire frame of the door appeared to be filled with hair.

In his robot voice, which had been packed in mothballs for years now, Humphrey intoned, "Gafr my decides visit here afternoon this." His perfect if eccentric English had come to pieces. "Learned I of this just," he explained.

"Your *Gafr*? Coming *here*? Here, to Scofield, your *GAFR*??" Pam would have said "Are you serious?" but there could be no doubt that he was.

Liam said, "*Why*? I mean, why here, why now? Why at all, for that matter, after all this time?" Hearing his tight voice, Pam realized Liam was frightened. He didn't want any more change, there was too much at stake now.

Humphrey tried. "See Terrifrey. See. Things. All people. See you Pam Pruitt Liam O'Hara."

"When was the last time she saw Terrifrey?" Pam wondered. Humphrey's Gafr was, after all, in some mysterious symbiotic fashion, the mother of his son.

"Birth," Humphrey creaked. "Galadriel then." Galadriel was the name of the bear who'd fostered Terrifrey. Abruptly he disappeared from the doorway. They rushed into the house and found him twitching and wheezing on the living room floor, with Jiffy and Terrifrey standing over him and both poodles licking his face.

Before the adults could move, Terrifrey pushed his father's head around to make eye contact. The position was awkward but Terrifrey was quick. "It's okay. He's very scared and very excited but he's not sick," the little Hefn told them. "He wants—he wants something to eat, something, I don't know what it's called—"

During the decisive winter of 2037-38, Humphrey in crisis had become an out-and-out cobbler junkie. He believed in cobbler as antidote, and it seemed to work that way for him. Back in Salt Lake from the Hurt Hollow retreat, Pam had defrosted some of the cobblers in her freezer there and made up a batch of individual servings, like insulin injections, to refreeze against times when Humphrey might require them. In Scofield the following summer she'd baked more from fresh ingredients, so there was a stash of cobbler fixes in this freezer as well. She defrosted one of these and shoveled it into the petrified Hefn, who rallied quickly and was able to finish eating it by himself.

"I want cobbler too," Jiffy declared. Soon Pam was hotting up bowls of cobbler for everybody. Then she rounded up two pig's ears for the dogs, and the emergency morphed into a party before the party. Little Terrifrey, who'd scarfed down plenty of blackberries as a foster cub but never before encountered them in this form, proved to be a chip off the old block. Fairly soon, though, the kids piled their empty dishes on the counter and scampered off with purple faces to play in the yard, Jiffy still in her wardrobe jeans and red sweatshirt, Terrifrey, too young to walk upright very well, bounding like a spring lamb. The dogs bounded with them. Indoors the hubbub subsided.

Humphrey straddled his Hefn chair, voice and grammar restored, form almost down to normal size again. The cobbler party had had a normalizing effect on them all; but Humphrey was mortified by his collapse and had to be fussed over before they could find out anything about the impending visit from his Gafr. She would arrive by shuttle (he told them), at five sharp, piloted and accompanied by Hefn who were not Observers and so would be unfamiliar to Pam and Liam.

Pam jumped up. "That only gives us an hour to get ready!"

"This is naturally an historic occasion, a-a-an occasion of great import—" hearing himself beginning to sound metallic, Humphrey paused to make throat-clearing noises before going on. "—importance yes yes but there is nothing to be done. Done by you. To. Get ready." He paused again. "The shuttle lands on the girls' athletic field, my Gafr emerges, she observes Terrifrey, she observes people if that is her pleasure, she observes this world she has never personally visited if *that* is her pleasure, she extracts tissue from me that an infant Gafr might be initiated, and after this she returns to the shuttle which returns to the ship."

Liam broke the astounded silence. "She does *what*?"

~

Three years before, when two time windows opened on the same day in January 2038, from thirty years in the future, everything changed.

In important ways it was a change for the better for almost everyone.

For the first time since the Hefn came, those present when the time windows opened were left with intact memories of what they'd seen and heard. Immediately afterwards, a full five months before the agreed-upon date, Humphrey confirmed everyone's worst fears by proclaiming that the Baby Ban would never be lifted, but relieved another anxiety by adding that neither did humanity have anything further to fear from the HefnGafr. He admitted everything. The Gafr had decided way back in April never to revoke the Baby Ban. They had lied about the purpose of the Final Year, which was to keep people distracted while making certain they could breed successfully on Earth. The ultimate fate of humankind had continued to hang in the balance, right up until the window at Hurt Hollow had revealed a future in which aliens and humans both were reproducing, and were getting along together.

The Proclamation set off worldwide demonstrations of mourning and protest, but the expressions of outrage were strangely muted. It almost seemed as though the millions of people "being good" like kids before Christmas, in hopes that Santa would bring them what they wanted, had known deep down what the real situation was. How long this mood would last was anybody's guess, but for the time being the war had been lost, and what people wanted most was just to get back as soon as they could to something like normal life.

Pam was intrigued to learn that an underground project involving missiles and nuclear devices *had* actually been in progress near Baikonur in Kazakhstan. The aliens had known about it almost from the beginning. Concluding that the project posed no menace in the short run, they had monitored it carefully but allowed it to go forward until the time windows opened in January; after that a Hefn delegation paid the Russian scientists a visit. No one, however, was punished.

As the weeks went by it became clear that, after so much uncertainty, just knowing what to expect was also—whatever else it was—a huge relief to Earth's collective human psyche. On several TV talk shows Julie Hightower compared it to the relief of knowing that the marriage has failed, that the closely guarded secret is out, that the parent on life support has died, that the missing person's body has been identified, and, yes, that your own side had been defeated in the war: awful news that nevertheless brings a period of painful anxiety to a close. Now that people of childbearing age knew *for certain* that they would never bear children by natural means, now that their parents knew that there would be no grandchildren of their own flesh and blood, they could all finally do their grieving and get on with their lives.

Because the biosphere should now be able to recover on its own—or rather, find its own new balances, given another century during which the vast majority of humans would gradually die out of it—the aliens lifted nearly all restrictions on what people could do. (Nearly all; cloning, nuclear testing, harming a Hefn, and a handful of other activities where a small number of people could make a sizable amount of mischief were still crimes punishable by mind-wipe.) After twenty-five years of those restrictions, of course, the practical means of doing a lot of things the Hefn deemed destructive were no longer available, and sustainable means of doing them were widely in use. But humanity was no longer under pressure, at least for the time being, to prove it could occupy the planet without destroying it, and that too was a great relief. The Proclamation said in effect: You are now free to hurt the Earth as much as you like or can. A few years from now, you won't be around and you won't be replaced. In a century or two the ozone hole will close, the rain forests return, the oceans cleanse themselves, and climate change will be proceeding on its own schedule.

In a strange way this too was a relief. Some of those unwilling to make planet-saving choices in the old days, furious at the aliens for taking away their freedom to choose otherwise, and to reproduce, could still be stirred by the thought of an Earth grown healthy and beautiful again, though not having children of their own to pass it on to gave the feeling a bittersweet tang.

The Gaian Movement persisted in its mission for a year or so, but the air had been let out of the balloon. Gaia could save herself now, no matter what her Missionaries did. Many of these, dedicated since childhood to a cause that now seemed to have both failed and triumphed, discovered that they too had lives to live and decided to get on with them. As a movement the Gaians endured; as a mission they gradually faded away.

When the news that the aliens were breeding, and how, spread around the world, several bears in India and Alaska were killed; but the mass slaughter Pam and Denny Demaree had worried about did not take place. Some of the conditions that breed terrorists—rage, frustration, no hope of changing things—were still present, but others, such as poverty and oppression, had dissipated. It emerged that people generally preferred to make the most of what was left of their own lives, rather than sacrifice those lives taking revenge on the Hefn—and that in most cases there was still enough life to make the most of, enough hope of a limited sort, enough happiness to reach for.

In this context it mattered enormously that humans were not to be altogether displaced on Earth by aliens, that human babies would continue to be born into the world where humanity had evolved into itself.

It was also true that people were generally comfortable enough—in the developing countries, a good deal more comfortable than before the Hefn came. No children meant fewer laborers, but also far fewer mouths to feed and much less illness in the villages. Though the aliens had always kept out of human politics, and on the whole seemed to favor wars as a means of reducing population numbers, the alien presence had worked a stupendous change on oppressive governments and civil and international disputes. After the first post-Directive years of famine and hardship, which had been truly terrible for many, feasible ways to produce and distribute food and consumer goods had been worked out; and there were always more jobs than workers to do them. The aging population alone generated a huge demand for services of all sorts.

The crunch would come later, when the Last Generation to be conceived before the Ban—the wide hem at the bottom of the population umbrella—could no longer provide for those still older and sicker than they were, and a very small work force, the umbrella's slender, slowly lengthening and thickening handle, would somehow have to hold up all those childless elderly people while also running the world. But in 2038 that worry was still an abstract one.

Also, there was the Santa Barbara time window message from ca. 2070 to hang onto. That message had actually been recorded. The figure in the window had chosen a time and place where recording equipment was sure to be available, and had waited patiently while Apprentices and Hefn raced about feverishly to get it set up. She had wanted everyone in the world to hear what she had to say.

~

Bit by bit they got it out of him, though Humphrey was too pumped and jumpy to answer questions very clearly. Baby Gafr were nurtured by Hefn, baby Hefn were nurtured by Hefn and a suitable predator. Mature Gafr incubated both sorts of baby, but did no nurturing at all. This new little Gafr about to be "initiated," by a process none too pleasant to judge from Humphrey's demeanor, would therefore stay in the ship's artificial environment and be cared for by Hefn up there, though not very much by Humphrey himself, whose duties, except during hibernation, would continue to keep him earthside.

His Gafr had been selected to mother the very first Gafr baby of the new generation, a great honor for them both. They had had to produce a successful Hefn offspring first, in order to trigger the hormonal changes necessary for his Gafr to "ovulate." Evidently little Terrifrey was held in high regard. Dennifrey and five other bear-reared Hefn children were older; but, in addition to having produced Terrifrey, Humphrey's Gafr seemed a force to be reckoned with. So, despite Humphrey's bizarre views and behavior, he was to be allowed to initiate the first baby Gafr.

"What's your Gafr's name?" Liam wondered. "We can't just keep calling her 'Humphrey's Gafr.'"

"Name. Her name. Is G-G-Gavnl." He made throat-clearing noises. "Gavnl. But you will have no occasion to address her. She will not speak with you."

"Sounds like she's going to look down her nose at us miserable puny humans," Pam said.

"Nose. No. No nose. But look down, oh yes, far far down. 'Look' being in this case a figure of speech, however. No eyes."

No eyes, no nose. "Humphrey, what does your—Gavnl, what does Gavnl look like?" As soon as she asked, Pam remembered something she hadn't thought of in a long time. "Wait, those shield figures you showed me in Moab—you said those were pictures of the Gafr!"

"Yes. An impression only," Humphrey said. His jitters got the best of him and he dismounted from his chair and started to pace, pelt going up and down as if breathing on its own. From the back yard, woofs and shrieks came faintly through the windows.

"So what do they look like? Come on, Humphrey, it's better if we have some idea of what to expect." Liam turned to Pam. "What do the shield figures look like?"

She started to answer, but Humphrey decided to be a bit more forthcoming. "She is round," he said. "And white. Round, white. Like a full moon, so beautiful."

Round and white. "Spherical, like the moon? A shield, or a sphere?"

"Sphere."

They waited for him to expand, but he was jumping out of his furry skin. Regardless of how flattered he might be to have been judged worthy of fathering the first Gafr baby of the immigrant generation, whatever lay in wait for him this evening clearly had the character of an ordeal. Pam went to the computer. "Come on, Liam, I'll show you the shields. One was late Basketmaker if I remember and one was . . . ?"

"Fremont," Humphrey croaked feebly.

"Fremont. Here we go." She tapped for a bit. "Hm, not Basketmaker, Pueblo III. A lot later. I wonder if that's right." She pushed back to let Liam look.

He peered over her shoulder, frowning. "The Gafr have horns?"

Pam snorted. "Well—maybe, but horns like these are a Fremont stylistic feature. There's another figure almost exactly like this little guy, only he's not inside of an eggshell. Hang on." She tapped again, to show him the figure, then went back to the previous screen. "*And* he's got eyes as well as horns, they've both got eyes."

Humphrey had come and stood behind them. "It is, as I have said, an impression. They are both impressions, you will understand this when you see my lord, I cannot explain further. Pam Pruitt, now I am going to please microwave one more cobbler."

"Okay. Try not to let the kids see you, we're running kind of low." To Liam she said, "Horns are associated with shamanistic power in rock art everywhere, but these Fremonters are using 'em for decoration. Some Fremont petroglyphs are beautifully composed and executed, but not powerful in that way at all—more *cute* I always think, even when the figures are holding stylized severed heads! They were farmers, they harkened to the serpent and ate of the apple, and it shows." She nodded at the screen. "This is exceptional."

~

On April 22, two weeks before the filming of *Hurt Hollow* was scheduled to begin, Pam and Lexi had flown out to Louisville with BJ and Feste to get ready for a houseful of company. Around 7:30

the next morning a deeply disturbing event had occurred. Pam had been jolted from a sound sleep by a *blam!* on the window pane not six feet from her head. She rolled out, pulled up the blind, peered down—and, oh God, there was a big hawk rolling and flopping on the ground directly below. Pam raised the window and screen, heart thumping, but as she leaned out the hawk stopped rolling and lay flat on its back, wings open, one feathered leg extended, the other drawn up. Its underwings and breast, all buff, and its hooked yellow beak and yellow talons, filled her eyes. The hawk's beak was agape, it was panting hard. It tried several times to turn over.

Pam yearned above the desperate bird in a passion of hope that it was only stunned and would recover. Even from the second floor the hawk looked enormous. All its body feathers had fluffed out, the way Humphrey's hair did, in the extremity of its situation. It lay perpendicular to the house, head toward the wall; and a moment came when the hawk's gaze locked with Pam's in that upside-down position and stayed locked as it continued to pant and struggle. When finally it did succeed in rolling over, showing the slate-colored feathers of its back, it died almost instantly.

All this Pam witnessed with a vision sharpened by shock and horror. When it was over she snatched her robe and ran downstairs and outside, shutting in the dogs, to gather up the dead hawk, broken neck lolling, bleeding from the beak, and bring it inside. She laid it on the kitchen table and went to get the field guide and a tape measure; she knew, but wanted confirmation. And yes: this was a Cooper's hawk, a species long endangered in Kentucky, only now beginning to recover well, a female, seventeen inches long. An intensely beautiful large bird with a rounded tail, still warm and soft. Its closed eyelids were covered in tiny feathers. Pam put the book aside, sat down with the hawk in her lap and stroked the beautiful sleek body so perfectly formed for predation: buff below, slate above, the long flight feathers on wings and tail barred with white and black. She pulled up on the topmost bones of one wing and the wing unfolded smoothly like a fan, then smoothly folded closed. She opened the hawk's armored feet, curled and lifeless now. Her hands shook. She was utterly sick with regret.

And badly shaken also. A bird shaman could not fail to realize that a message had been delivered that morning to the window behind which she had been sleeping.

She was still sitting there when Lexi came downstairs, yawning and tying the sash of her robe. She stopped when she saw what Pam was holding. "What's that—*oh!*"

"She flew into my bedroom window." Pam stood and tenderly placed the dead hawk into Lexi's hands. "A Cooper's hawk. Attacking her reflection in the window, I suppose." Pam didn't believe that, but what she believed wasn't Lexi's problem.

"Ohhhh. Oh, what a shame. Oh, she's—*so*—*beautiful.*" She stared at the hawk, then tentatively began to stroke her breast feathers with one finger. "Oh, Pom."

"I know. I hoped she'd only been stunned, but her neck's broken."

"You watched her die?"

"Mm-hm." Pam felt again the long moment when those amber eyes had glared into her own, and shivered. "Honey, I'm going to hit the shower. Can you manage breakfast on your own? Or if you want to wait half an hour I'll make French toast."

"Go ahead, I'm fine," Lexi said absently. She stroked the hawk's breast feathers with her finger.

Pam stood with closed eyes and let hot water pour over her head and stream down her body. If only the hawk hadn't died, if only she had recovered and flown away. The meaning of the message was unreadable, but delivering it had killed the messenger. There was no way to see that as good news, and no question that a response would be required of Pam (but what response was suitable?). And coming just as they were about to start filming the story of how Otie and his mob had nearly killed Humphrey . . .

Pam turned off the water and reached for a towel. *I'll find an hour to meditate on this today,* she thought, *but for now the thing will be to get through the morning without throwing Lexi off her game. I'll put the hawk on ice till I can get clear about what to do with her body.* She dried herself vigorously, pulled on sweats, combed her wet hair, and trotted downstairs with a smile on her face and a clenched fist in her stomach.

Lexi was sitting at the dining-room table in a posture of intense concentration. A large square sheet of brown paper lay in front of her. Art pens in forty colors were scattered over the table. She had propped the open field guide against a stack of other books, and the dead hawk lay on its back on a dish towel, both wings spread wide; she had pinned or weighted them somehow to hold them open.

When Pam came in she started and looked around. Pam paused in the doorway. "Can I see?"

Lexi glanced back at the picture, then nodded, and Pam came and stood behind her.

She had used her pens to draw the Cooper's hawk—but the hawk as she must have looked an instant before smashing into the glass. She stood firmly on the brown paper, legs spread, talons spread, beak open, eyes glaring, wings arched and spread, as if in fierce response to some unseen threat, filled with her living life to the tips of her feathers. Pam gripped Lexi's shoulders; her scalp rippled with goose bumps; her eyes watered; she had never in her life seen anything so absolutely alive as the bird in that picture.

Lexi looked up, her own eyes swimming. "I didn't even make a sketch! I just sat down and did it, and it came out like this." She looked at the picture in wonderment. "Like I just knew how. Like she was showing me."

~

They listened to the lander approaching for a few minutes before it appeared above the trees, described a slow graceful curve, and settled with a roar onto the fresh spring grass of what everybody still called the girls' athletic field. Even Pam and Liam had seen landers on recordings only. Till now, landers had been used exclusively to transport Hefn between the moon and bases outside Santa Barbara and Washington, DC. This one, a featureless rounded metallic enigma, sat on turf where muscular college jocks had once kicked soccer balls, and geriatric conferees now jogged or practiced Chi Gong.

The ship's arrival coincided with the arrival of the bus convoy returning from Madison. The buses pulled over; cast and crew poured out and pressed against the tall chain-link fence surrounding the field, though nobody was stupid enough to try to go inside, and the crowd was hushed. Camera people grabbed cameras and started filming.

Humphrey and Terrifrey, looking like an owl-eyed Yeti and his shaggy pet something, had been waiting on the track when the ship landed. As soon as the roaring stopped they moved directly toward it across the grass, Humphrey holding himself upright, Terrifrey scampering alongside. "He looks like he's walking to his execution," Pam murmured to Liam. They stood outside the fence with the others. Jiffy, out like a light after her napless day, was dead weight in Liam's arms.

Lexi and Neil had spotted them through the fence and now rushed up panting. "What's going on?" said Lexi, and Neil said "Is that a lander?"

"Humphrey's Gafr's in there," Pam told them, "she's come to pay Humphrey a little visit."

"A *Gafr*? No shit!" said Neil. "What's it doing here, is Humphrey in some kind of trouble?"

Pam hid a smile; good Mormon boys never said 'No shit,' they said 'My heck' or 'Oh, for hell's sake.' "According to him, she's here to be impregnated with a baby Gafr."

"*What?!*" Lexi and Neil exclaimed together.

"Just watch," Liam told them. The two Hefn had nearly reached the lander. As they approached, cracks appeared in the metal and a section of the hull slid down to become a low ramp. "Now either Humphrey and Terrifrey will go in, or the Gafr will come out. Ten blackberry cobblers says they go in."

"You'll make 'em? I'm in for twenty," Pam said. "I can't keep up with the demand."

"Done. That's a lot of blackberries. "

Lexi giggled. "Did you dream this, Pom? Liam, better think twice before you bet against a shaman."

They were fooling around, trying to control their nervous excitement. Pam said, "I'm as much in the dark as anybody, but I do want to see a Gafr before I die. And I don't want to bake any more cobblers for a couple of years at least."

"Those aren't good reasons to bet on something," Neil objected. "That's just wishful thinking."

"Well, plus that ramp's a lot flatter than it needs to be for Humphrey and Terrifrey to go up it."

The two Hefn hadn't moved, but now there was movement in the wide opening in the side of the lander and a collective gasp and murmur from the crowd. Pam had won her wager. Humphrey's Gafr was coming out.

She emerged on some kind of mechanized flatbed that crawled slowly down the ramp and onto the grass. Locomotion would otherwise hardly be possible for such a creature. The meaning of everything Humphrey had said about his Gafr now snapped into focus: Gavnl was, yes, white and round as a full moon, a large round organic blob that in Earth's gravity easily held its spherical shape. Her body's diameter looked to be about two meters, more than six feet. Pam and Liam muttered to each other their instant calculations of the volume of this living sphere, a number many times greater than the volume of Humphrey or any other Hefn or human, more like the volume of an elephant, but with no visible appendages, not even vestigial ones.

The massive creature appeared to be covered smoothly in fine-grained leather, a huge unstitched softball wrapped in bleached deerskin, but much softer, perhaps very soft; perhaps the Gafr's flesh filled up her leathery integument the way air fills up a balloon or a basketball liner, while the integument, like the rind of a ripe orange, protected the softness inside.

The Gafr would be soft to the touch, and warm, Pam thought. She imagined stroking her warm, smooth, yielding skin, so completely unlike that pelted hide of Humphrey's that Otie Bemis had once gone after with a knife, what a pleasant sensation that would be, or nuzzling her cheek against it—or even lying naked face down with the whole frontal surface of her torso and inner thighs in contact with it, like lying on an overfilled white kidskin waterbed—

"That thing," Neil said flatly, "is a great big humongous tit. A breast."

~

They had pinned Lexi's drawing of the Cooper's hawk to the living-room wall, and Pam had made the French toast and fed the dogs. Lexi got dressed. Feste and BJ had their training session.

When they got back to the house, Pam meditated for half an hour and then sat down with Lexi and explained what a sky burial was, and why she thought the hawk should have one. "Her life was in the sky. It seems wrong to put her in the ground. There were Indian cultures that used to build platforms in trees and place their dead on them, wrapped in a blanket—well, I don't know exactly how they did it, but the idea was that scavengers would find them and they'd go back into Gaia. Of course the dead go back anyway, no matter how the body's disposed of, even if they burn it, but instead of feeding worms and bacteria, or returning chemicals directly to the soil, the Indians would feed crows and ravens, and maybe vultures, but not wolves, and the dead person's flesh would fly away."

Lexi listened soberly. "I like that. At least I like it better than burying her in the dirt."

They discussed the best way to return the hawk to the sky. "How about putting her up in one of the trees where you played Tarzan when you were a kid?"

Pam considered that, but something was wrong. She waited for the picture to form in her mind. When it formed, what she saw was the small runestone marking the Hubbells' grave: *Orrin* and *Hannah* engraved inside a graven heart. She said, "Would it be better to take her over to the Hollow?"

Lexi's face lit up. "Yes! There's already a little cemetery started over there. I like it a lot, it's just right."

So they'd caught the afternoon packet, and two hours later were standing on the sloping ground of Hurt Hollow, soon to be the location of a major motion picture but not for a couple more weeks—long enough. Several trees stood near the Hubbells' grave and Jesse's, but only one, a shagbark hickory, had a low, semi-horizontal branch, so that choice was made for them. Pam knelt on one knee and Lexi, holding the hawk, stepped up on the other. She laid the body on its back lengthwise, then bound it loosely to the branch with binder's twine.

Then they both stepped back. Above their heads, looking noble and calm, a warrior dignified in death, the hawk lay on the branch, her head turned slightly toward them. The wind wouldn't blow her down, but a scavenging crow shouldn't have much trouble pulling her free of the twine.

For reasons past telling, this was as solemn a moment as Pam had ever lived through. Lexi felt it too and was crying a little, and Pam's own throat ached; but the terrible regret of the morning had been transformed by Lexi's drawing, as if Gaia herself had spoken a gentle rebuke: *My ways are beyond your understanding. Accept them nevertheless, and be content.*

Pam accepted them. She took Lexi's hand and spoke the first four lines of Vladimir Nabokov's strange, beautiful poem "Pale Fire":

THE BIRD SHAMAN

"I was the shadow of the waxwing slain
By the false azure in the windowpane;
I was the smudge of ashen fluff—and I
Lived on, flew on, in the reflected sky."

Mostly for Lexi's benefit she talked a little about Nabokov's through-the-looking-glass image: the waxwing flying not just into but *through* the glass, dropping its body as it passed the unbroken barrier yet no less alive in the reflected world beyond. "A cedar waxwing is just the sort of small songbird this Cooper's hawk would have hunted and killed. Hawks like this are among the top predators that keep the whole ecosystem healthy. She was young and strong, her life might have served that cause for many years, and not ended till she got too old to serve it any longer. This Cooper's hawk died a death with a different meaning. We'll do our best to submit to what we don't understand. We now give back to Gaia what was never ours to give or keep."

"We give her back to Gaia," Lexi said, and then took a deep breath and blew Pam completely away by reciting Gerard Manley Hopkins's difficult sonnet "The Windhover" from start to finish:

"I caught this morning morning's minion, king-
   dom of daylight's dauphin, dapple-dawn-drawn Falcon, in his
      riding,
   Of the rolling level underneath him steady air, and striding
High there, how he rung upon the rein of a wimpling wing
In his ecstasy! then off, off forth on swing,
   As a skate's heel sweeps smooth on a bow-bend: the hurl and
      gliding
   Rebuffed the big wind. My heart in hiding
Stirred for a bird,—the achieve of, the mastery of the thing!

Brute beauty and valour and act, oh, air, pride, plume, here
   Buckle! AND the fire that breaks from thee then, a billion
Times told lovelier, more dangerous, O my chevalier!

   No wonder of it: shéer plód makes plough down sillion
Shine, and blue-bleak embers, ah my dear,
   Fall, gall themselves, and gash gold-vermillion."

She spoke the entire poem with flawless breath control—a tall order—and maintained her clear simplicity of expression and emphasis through all its twists and convolutions. This would be impossible for anybody to do without practice. Till that moment Pam had had no idea that Lexi had ever even heard of Hopkins. The place, the hawk, the perfection of the poem, and of Lexi's performance, undid Pam almost from the first line; by the end tears were dripping steadily onto her sweatshirt and she was flushed and almost sobbing. This wasn't grief. It was an outgush of raw pure generalized emotion, unstoppable and probably long overdue.

In four years Lexi had never seen Pam in anything like such a state, but she seemed unfazed. "I came across it in an anthology a month or so ago, and I don't know, it was hard, but for some reason I liked it, and I thought it would be fun to learn it and surprise you."

"You surprised me all right." Pam blew her nose juicily.

"But I didn't really know why I'd picked that one." She turned and gazed for a long moment at the Cooper's hawk, buried in the sky. "And now I do."

A few days later Pam, with both dogs but without Lexi, was back in Hurt Hollow to take stock of the house before the crew arrived to turn it temporarily into a movie set. On the climb up from the dock she began to see feathers, small fluffy buff ones, scattered about. Someone had found the hawk. The offering had been accepted. And now Feste found her also, spread on the ground at the base of the burial tree. Her head was missing, her insides scooped out; nothing left but wings, bones, skin, feet, talons, most of her feathers, and a little blood. One wing showed bite or abrasion marks, the other was perfect. The joints of both worked smoothly; when Pam held the body up by the wings it fell into the graceful symmetrical shape of a thunderbird. The hawk was flexible and soft as the day she died. On the ground, thick white blots of bird droppings: a sky burial indeed.

Sighing, thankful that Lexi hadn't come, Pam folded her up again. The branch with the twine was out of reach; instead she chose a little cedar growing near the burial tree, reached as high as she could and tucked the body into a tight, clingy crotch formed by several small branches and twigs.

When she returned with the crew the following week, the hawk had disappeared.

THE BIRD SHAMAN

~

The first time Pam watched the recording of the time window that had opened in the lounge at the BTP, her attention had instantly been riveted on her own chest. What was left of it. Sometime in the next thirty years, Little Pam was going to make good on her avowal: Big Pam was going to get a breast reduction. She barely noticed her own iron-gray hair or the blue bags under her eyes, in the happy shock of seeing herself with breasts of exactly the size she'd always wanted them to be. She had ceased to obsess about these objects long ago; she liked them no better than ever but had learned to tolerate them with a far better grace. But the breastless look on that old lady on the screen awoke such a yearning that Pam had had to ask Sam to start the recording again. She hadn't heard one word she had said.

So when Neil interrupted Pam's sensuous fugue by calling the Gafr a giant breast, she knew instantly that he had nailed it, and felt angry and invaded; she'd been lured into re-experiencing her infantile love for her mother's breast, after so many years of loathing her own. "The Gafr must be able to project or evoke emotional states," she said, "maybe that's the source of their control over the Hefn. Something's having a weird effect on me. Anybody else feel it?"

"Me," Lexi said. "All of a sudden I'm missing my mom really bad."

Liam and Neil looked at each other. "Not me." "Not me." But Jiffy half-woke and stirred in Liam's arms. "I want Mom-my," she whined, and started to whimper.

Lexi poked Neil with her elbow. "*You're* the one that saw what it looked like!"

He fended her off, grinning sheepishly. "I *was* thinking about you, actually, but I do that all the time anyway."

"*Me?*" Lexi looked again at the monstrous sphere on the flatbed device. "In your dreams!"

"Well—exactly!"

"Cut it out, you two," Liam said sharply. "Something's happening."

They clutched the fence again. Humphrey still stood stiffly in place, but Terrifrey was going right up to the Gafr now. A long vertical slit had opened in the white sphere, and now a pale proboscis-like structure had begun to protrude from it. Terrifrey stood up on his back legs, balancing himself against the white hide, while the Gafr—his mother, after all, in some weird sense—ran this structure, a sensory organ evidently, over his face and body. The organ seemed less pliant than an elephant's trunk, but certainly more pliant than the elephant-sized erect penis which it otherwise resembled, so obviously so that people had started snickering nervously all around the fence, and Liam had a big smirk plastered on his face. He was still swinging gently from side to side, but Jiffy had gone back to sleep; the feelings that went with this inspection and its visual counterpart were not at present within her frame of reference.

"How d'you suppose our little Terrifrey hatched himself out of that dinosaur's egg?" Liam wondered. "I don't see any other orifices."

"You didn't see that one till she was good and ready to show it to you." Pam expression was strained, and so was Lexi's, but 'dinosaur's egg' had reminded her of the shield figures and she told him so.

"Aha. A being, potentially dangerous, enclosed in a white sphere."

"You can't see through the shell, but so what, you don't paint what you see. You paint what you sense."

Apparently Terrifrey had passed inspection, for now he dropped onto all fours and went a little way off, and it was Humphrey's turn to approach Gavnl. His fur lay fairly flat, but Pam thought he seemed extremely apprehensive, and she was uneasy; for the first time it occurred to her that he might really be in danger. "'The female of the species is more deadly than the male,'" Liam muttered out of the side of his mouth.

"They're *not* the same species, you know," she muttered back.

"A mere technicality."

Humphrey stopped directly in front of his Gafr, leaned forward slightly, placed his hands on either side of the gaping slit and pressed himself against her. The Gafr had retracted her probe so that Humphrey could make full body contact, but suddenly they saw him lurch as if from a blow. At the same instant a discomfiting jolt of lust shot through the entire assembly at the fence line. Lexi cried out. They couldn't see, but sensed, that Gavnl's probe, as if spring-loaded, had been thrust straight into Humphrey's midsection, where Pam was very sure she had never noticed the hint of an orifice in all her years of knowing him. Gavnl then seemed to flow forward on both sides of Humphrey, till she had formed a kind of body cast out of her own body, within which she held Humphrey in a powerful clasp.

From the pained looks on the faces along the fence, being assaulted by intense sexual arousal without warning in the wrong context was as disagreeable to them as it was to Pam. Conversation stopped. Even walking-libido types like Junior Bemis looked discomfited, and the jolt had sent Lexi reeling. Pam quickly put an arm around her, Neil gripped her shoulder. Jiffy woke up screaming and was hustled away, back toward the house. "Want to go?" Pam asked, but Lexi shook her head. "I have to be sure he's okay." She smiled tensely. "They're consenting adults, I guess."

"*They* might be, but the Gafr's making you feel *your* feelings." That seemed to be how it worked, for no sooner had she concluded this than the girls' athletic field, and everyone on and around it, including Lexi, turned plastic—proof to Pam that beneath Humphrey's "consent" lurked some genuine threat. Not since the day Liam went over the moon about Gillian had Pam had a dissociative episode. As always it felt ghastly; but she too had to stay put, to be sure that Humphrey was okay.

The tension was protracted miserably. Then followed a collective reflex of relief. Humphrey backed away from Gavnl. Neither proboscis nor slit could now be seen to break the smoothness of her skin. The flatbed began to reverse up the ramp. When the Gafr had disappeared inside, the ramp itself rolled up and sealed the door opening. Humphrey and Terrifrey, who'd waited together until then, turned and started back across the field, while the lander lifted off, making up in noise for its lack of fumes or flames.

Humphrey was wobbling a bit, oozing also, the hair of his belly matted and wet with some dark substance. Whether or not he normally had an orifice more or less where a human's navel would be, he now definitely had a bleeding wound, or perhaps was leaking fluid from the tissue Gavnl had collected to start the baby Gafr. Pam wondered with a thrill of alarm where his internal organs were and whether any damage had been done to them, but common sense said not. And, strangely enough, he seemed to be all right—beat up, but moving with more of the air of a marathoner who'd finished the race than that of a soldier dragging himself off the field.

As he wobbled toward her, Pam realized the world he was moving through was no longer plastic, and turned to reassure herself that Lexi too had thrown off the grip of remembered trauma.

Judith Moffett

~

Once she'd gotten accustomed to the novelty of someday not having a big chest anymore, Pam had settled back and watched herself deliver a goodwill jeremiad from the future to all the people of Earth.

"I know exactly what I'm going to say today," she began, "because I've heard myself say it before. Many times before. Nothing could be weirder. It's good that people who are present when a time window opens aren't normally allowed to remember, let alone record, what they saw. I hope this is the only exception ever." (That a window had opened in Hurt Hollow on the same day this one did in Santa Barbara had never been made public.)

"By the time you catch up to where Humphrey and I are now, the Last Generation will be in late middle age and humanity will be well launched on the only fresh start it's ever likely to get. We're hoping to help you make the most of a unique opportunity. You guys at the BTP know this message is authentic, but others who see the recording may think I've been made up to look old, in order to perpetrate a hoax. A very understandable suspicion. But please listen anyway, because what I have to say is what matters, not when."

Then Elderly Pam delivered what amounted to a sermon. The Pam of 2038 could have written a lot of it, but certain parts made her sit up.

"For hundreds of thousands of years, humans lived pretty much like bears and raccoons. We were omnivorous predators. We had a few tools but our world was almost entirely natural and we didn't wish or try to change that. We typically didn't live very long, because ours was a dangerous lifeway full of uncertainties, but those of us who made it past early childhood were healthy and strong, and everything we did was determined by what's been called 'the ancient lost reverence and passion for the earth and its web of life.' 'The earth and its web of life' pretty much equal what science calls the biosphere, and what Gaians call Gaia, but neither science nor even the Gaian Movement has fully addressed the 'reverence and passion' part of that description, and that's what I want to do now.

"The millennia rolled by, and finally something momentous occurred in different places around the world. Certain grasses mutated into early forms of rice, wheat, and corn, and people discovered them growing wild and started cultivating them on purpose. Domesticate a few goats and you have, in an oversimplified nutshell, the beginning of agriculture.

"Now, many of you already know the Genesis myth from the Bible, and if you don't it's easy to look it up, but I'm going to tell you an alternate version. In my version the Garden of Eden is a big wild place, and Adam and Eve are part of a twenty-to-thirty-member kinship group. They hunt game, they scavenge, they dig for roots and collect nuts and everybody shares. But the serpent tempts them too, with the promise not of immediate Godlike knowledge but of a more dependable food source that's easier to come by, and they yield to temptation in my version too, and leave the Garden voluntarily. At this point my version links up with the original. Cain cultivates the soil, Abel is a shepherd.

"Now, from my perspective, what matters isn't which one killed the other. What matters is that neither one of them ever spent one minute thinking about how to prevent their different ways of controlling the food supply from damaging the Earth. Cain's descendants did of course eventually acquire Godlike knowledge, but by then they had completely lost that ancient knowledge they'd started out with, of passionate reverence for the Earth and its web of life. They dismissed all that as primitive superstition. They'd forgotten they were part of the web. And that's why things were in such a desperate state when the Hefn came.

"Most of you are familiar with the Gaian message, if only indirectly, from all the things the Gafr wouldn't let us do. And long before James Lovelock formulated the concept of Gaia, some people did think about the damage to the ecosystem caused by agriculture, and tried to raise food and make things in ways that respected the web of life. But even those people had forgotten what their pre-agricultural ancestors had known in their bones: that every rock and leaf, every creature, every river and lake, every pigweed and squash vine borer, all of nature animate and inanimate, is filled with spirit. The Gaian lifeway is an honorable way, but even we Gaians, who reverence the Earth, didn't remember far enough back. We forgot that there are primal forces that should be respected—propitiated, some would say—when soil is stripped for cultivation.

"I forgot it too, for a long time. But—events—have made me remember.

"Let me be clear. This is not superstition. This is truth supported by quantum field theory—look carefully at the range of radical
experiments that were being done in quantum physics, just before
the Hefn came. Religious mystics will relate to this but don't let that
put the rest of you off; this goes way out to the limits of the universe,
and way back to long before there were Catholics or Sufis or Hare
Krishnas. It goes back to when people knew they were part of the
web of Nature, and that everything in Nature was filled with spirit.
And that's still true. Everything in Nature truly is filled with spirit,
including you, little Liam."

She paused to let this sink in. In 2038 her counterpart sat and
marveled: *Thirty years from now I've come to have total faith in this. I
haven't been disabused, "events" have confirmed me in it. What events?*
She thought also, *I make a pretty cool old lady, but a really ugly one.*

"I consider the source," Liam said drily.

"So now we come to it," the ugly cool old lady said. "My charge
from the future to the past. I know most of you aren't buying what I've
said. So I beseech you, not to believe me, but to ask yourselves, What
if it were true, what would that be like? And then to ask, Suppose we
were to live *as if* this were true, what would *that* be like? And finally, to
go ahead and live that way—and let life take you out of *as if* into *is*.

"Because you can. You can raise crops and livestock, and make
consumer goods, and get it all distributed, *and* remember all the
way back to what we knew before we learned to farm, *and* bring
that ancient awareness all the way forward into high civilization. I'm
telling you that the greatness of the Lascaux cave paintings and of the
most modern high art can be held within the same conceptual frame,
when that frame is imbued with spiritual awareness.

"'Imbued with spiritual awareness,' you're thinking, 'what is this
crapola?' I can only promise that if you live as if everything I've said
were true, if you reimagine and remake society to take it all into
account, you'll find out.

"It won't be easy, working out how to bring a nature-based spirituality into the farms and cities, and to hold yourselves open to
what's valuable in all three simultaneously. By their own nature
people don't operate this way. Not many people. I don't say it'll be
easy, only that it's possible. And that it's worth it, whatever it takes."

She stopped, and it seemed she was finished. "Pam," Liam's voice
said, "I'm afraid I think a lot of that *is* crapola, sorry, even though

you're so old and wise up there and I'm so happy to see you still haven't fallen off any cliffs, but speaking theoretically, what makes you imagine that this has any chance of working, when all of human history proves it never has and never will?"

"Well, speaking theoretically," Elderly Pam said serenely, "why shouldn't this turn out to be the next stage of human enlightenment? And when will you ever get a better chance to find out?"

She was moving behind the hood to close the window when Will spoke up too. "Wait a sec, if this is a sort of Second Broadcast we're supposed to put out to the public, I don't see how Time Is One applies, I mean why tell us how we're supposed to proceed, if future events are going to lead up to the moment you're speaking from anyway?"

Samantha's voice said, "Yeah, Pam, by thirty years from now, either we've gone for it or we haven't."

Elder Pam *tsk*ed and shook her head at them, smiling a fond smile. "You youngsters don't need me to tell you the answer to that one." And the lens spun shut.

~

Leaders of most world religions had denounced Pam's message as unapologetic paganism. No surprises there; that was pretty much what it was. Buddhism, a nontheistic religion, took a more benign and open-minded view; but in the three years since the Second Broadcast, Pam had heard of no intention to integrate wilderness experience into education in the Buddhist countries either. The Gaians liked it—all they had to do was add an interesting dimension to what they were doing already—but there weren't that many Gaians. Native peoples were gratified, but there were even fewer of them.

The stunner for Pam personally was what had happened among the Mormons. About a month after the release of the Second Broadcast, rumors had begun to circulate busily around Salt Lake that the Mormon Prophet, President Heber K. Wells, had received a new revelation. By the time Jaime heard about it and alerted Pam, the revelation had already been approved by the Prophet's counselors and was being considered by the Quorum of the Twelve Apostles, including Pam's old nemesis, Brigham Parker. If the Apostles' vote

was unanimously in favor—pretty much a foregone conclusion—
it would be recommended to the whole church membership at the
April 2038 Semiannual General Conference.

In the early years of church organization, Joseph Smith had had
more than a hundred revelations, all duly recorded and published
in a book of Mormon Scripture called *Doctrine and Covenants*. But
once the Church had been well established in Utah, direct revelations of scriptural status became extremely unusual. So this was
widely viewed as a remarkable and amazing development.

The content of the new revelation was general knowledge, and
was even more remarkable. Apparently the Earth herself had spoken
to President Wells. According to another Mormon scriptural text,
The Pearl of Great Price, she had spoken to a prophet once before—
the Prophet Enoch, father of Methuselah. Pam looked the passage
up on her computer. "And it came to pass," she read, "that Enoch
looked upon the earth; and he heard a voice from the bowels thereof,
saying: Wo, wo is me, the mother of men; I am pained, I am weary,
because of the wickedness of my children. When shall I rest, and be
cleansed from the filthiness which is gone forth out of me? When
will my Creator sanctify me, that I may rest, and righteousness for a
season abide upon my face?"

Enoch, moved to tears by this lament, pleads with God to have
compassion on the Earth. Will she be allowed to rest when Messiah
comes? No. First must come "days of wickedness and vengeance,"
when God's hot displeasure will send misery and affliction upon
men; but a Holy City will be founded to preserve the righteous, who
will make their way to it from every corner of the Earth; and after
many tribulations the Earth will rest for a thousand years. A version
of this general story line was familiar to Pam from her Baptist under-
pinnings. "Wicked" and "righteous" in this text had always been
understood by the Mormon faithful in the Old Testament terms it
so obviously imitated.

But according to rumor, Earth had revealed to the Church
Prophet that this passage from the Book of Moses was now to be
given a different interpretation.

It took some doing but Pam managed to get hold of a text of
the new revelation, which she read with mounting incredulity. "The
wickedness of men is wickedness unto me," the Earth had said to
President Wells, "and great is the suffering that hath been visited

upon men and the sons of men, for that they have not considered me in their sin and in the wickedness of their hearts. My waters have they poisoned with their filth, yea, even my forests have they slain in their iniquity; deep in my bowels have they delved, and brought forth that which is unclean for burning, and all my skies are blackened with the smoke thereof. Now wherefore should not the heavens groan and weep at my exceeding distress? But out of Zion, my Holy City, shall come my redemption. For worlds without number hath the Lord our God created, and inasmuch as Enoch of old was forbidden the knowledge of all, save only me, unto the prophet Heber K. Wells is now given that knowledge forbidden to Enoch; for behold, out from among the worlds which the Lord hath created with His hand hath He sent forth an army to my aid, hairy even as my son Esau was hairy; and they have come from afar in power and glory, to be as an helpmeet unto thee and unto thy people in the Lord. And ye shall be as an helpmeet also unto them, and shall give them your blessing, and counsel with them in all things. And yet a little while, and I, the mother of all living creatures, of the great whales and fishes of the sea, and the winged fowl, and the beasts and creeping things, and the lily of the field, and the plane tree by the water, and the mother of men, will rest and rejoice."

To reverse a previous revelation was not without precedent. Plural marriage, which had been revealed to Joseph Smith as a sacrament, had been renounced by the authority of a revelation to President Wilford Woodruff in 1890 (thereby allowing Utah to petition for statehood). According to the *Book of Mormon*, only white males were eligible for induction into the all-important Aaronic and Melchizedek Priesthoods, but in 1978 it was revealed to President Spencer W. Kimball that males of other races were now to be admitted too.

Both those reversals had been much desired, as they brought LDS practice into conformity with the positions of the United States on marriage and race. The same could hardly be said of this one. The fledgling Mormon environmental movement of the last decade or two before the Hefn came had flapped and floundered within the constraints of Church doctrine—the part that expected the world to end any day now, so why be careful with it, and the part that insisted the Earth had been made to be used by "man," so the only legitimate conservation measures were ones that benefitted people. While the new revelation didn't speak to any of that directly, it did give the Hefn authority in such matters, and the Hefn had always put endangered species ahead of human convenience. So it was an extraordinary day when the general membership of the Church of Jesus Christ of Latter-day-Saints voted to accept President Wells's revelation. Nobody seemed a bit happy about it, but God has spoken to His Prophet, and that was that. A lot of the early Saints had hated plural marriage too, including the men.

Within the Church the Hefn were soon being referred to as the Sons of Esau, which didn't make a lot of sense but had the virtue of bringing them within a familiar frame of reference. Pam's Sunday School had flogged the Old Testament much less vigorously than the New; all she could remember about Esau was that he had been born with that rare condition when the fetus retains its hair, and that he had sold his birthright for a mess of pottage. Like her Mormon neighbors, who were now reexamining the story of Esau for all they were worth, she dug out her Bible and read up on him.

That night Pam dreamed she was out in the Utah desert somewhere near a campground. Tents were set up, but the campground seemed deserted except for a woman in a Bedouin robe and burnoose, who was bending over to stir a big pot on the fire. When Pam walked over to the fire circle to see what was in the pot, the woman stood up straight, big metal spoon in hand, and turned to face her.

"Mom!" said Pam. It was Frances. She looked about 35, but otherwise entirely like herself, except for the hostile expression. Pam was overjoyed to see her mother but immediately felt embarrassed, almost guilty, on account of this joy. She tried to conceal it by asking a ho-hum question: "What are you dressed up like that for?"

Frances said wearily, "Wo, wo is me." Like those of the bowels of the earth, her woes had no *e*'s. She sat down on the ground. Behind her the flap of a tent was pushed aside and two little boys, smaller than Jiffy, came out and crawled into her lap. One of them was a nondescript little kid with dark hair and light brown skin, wearing overalls and sandals, but the other looked just like Terrifrey dyed orangutan orange. As soon as they got into Frances's lap they started shoving and poking at each other. Frances ignored them.

Pam, still trying to pretend things were normal and pleasant, said "Why do you say that? You always wanted a boy."

"All they do is fight. It's killing me." She looked at Pam resentfully.

Moved by a humiliating hope of making her mother like her better, Pam picked the squabbling boys up one at a time, the smooth tan one in her left arm, the hairy red one in her right. Trying to conceal her lack of confidence in dealing with small children, she said to them with false heartiness, "You're not identical, are you? You're biological twins!" In the dream, "biological" was the correct term for "fraternal."

As if they hadn't heard, the boys went on tormenting each other. They were heavy and awkward to hold, and Pam realized she wasn't going to be able to keep it up; already they were slipping down out of her arms. And then the dream turned lucid.

The instant she realized she was dreaming, Pam's feelings of inadequacy vanished. She willed herself to be powerful. She willed the boys to stop fighting. In a huge and furious voice she thundered, *"I'm sick of this! Why can't you kids learn to work together?"*

~

While people gathered in the auditorium on the evening of Humphrey's impalement, or whatever it was—they were going ahead with the screening and the party—Pam found herself thinking about all this. She'd had only one lucid dream since that layered, obvious, non-shamanic one about Jacob and Esau. The very last had been deliberately induced, later that same spring, in an overnight trip back to Dead Mule Canyon—a living out of the fantasy of sleeping alone beneath the Trailing Bird panel where she'd nearly slid off the slickrock. And that was all. Pam could still invoke the altered-consciousness state of the Hurt Hollow retreat, but seldom did so; the death of the Cooper's hawk had broken a long abstinence. Her certainty that every leaf and stone was filled with spirit lay in the future, if anywhere.

Humphrey, wearing a bandage like a cummerbund, was folded uncomfortably into the seat beside her. He had lain in a darkened room for an hour, isolating and containing the painful aftermath of his experience. That would be enough to get him through the evening, but he'd already declared his unavailability for the entire next day. The schedule called for Pam's living room and kitchen to be turned into locations for interior scenes, but they wouldn't need the bedrooms so that was okay. Pam had already moved Lexi's drawing of the Cooper's hawk into her old bedroom.

Humphrey could have been in his room now, but even in pain he couldn't bear to miss a party. He did, however, complain at intervals that the screening was supposed to have started a good while ago.

"It's late because everybody's all in an uproar for some reason."

"This is irony, yes?" Humphrey said faintly after thinking about it for a minute.

"Yes. Listen, why did your—Gavnl come down here, to the planet surface, to get impregnated? She didn't do that for Terrifrey, did she?"

"A new Gafr requires the electromagnetic field of a planet that has been lived into by Hefn."

"And a new Hefn doesn't?"

"No, but—" he winced and shifted his position. Pam had forgotten to bring him a pillow. "I will explain this more completely another time," Humphrey said. "Why do they not *begin*?"

Pam craned around. "I think they will in a minute, see, they're fussing around with the player now, and the place is filling up." She spotted Lexi and Neil hurrying down the aisle and waved, and they carefully squeezed past Humphrey to sit on the other side of Pam, who said, "So you decided to grace us with your presence."

"We decided a show of solidarity would be good, but you may have to put up with some moans and cries of anguish." Lexi leaned across Pam to pat Humphrey's hand. "Speaking of anguish, how are you feeling?"

"I am feeling that this screening should have begun one half-hour ago."

"*I'm* feeling they should have canceled it and just had the party," said Neil, "but I guess we're in the minority here."

Lexi said sympathetically to Humphrey, "I would have thought you'd just skip all this tonight, and focus on healing up your wound."

"Not this party animal," Pam told her. "He wouldn't miss a social function unless he couldn't move at all. Anyway, he says it's not a wound, just normal trauma." She glanced toward the back of the auditorium and stuck her arm in the air. "Here comes Liam."

When he reached them, Liam took in the number of knees he would have to push past and started to go around and enter the row from the other end, but Lexi called, "It's okay, we'll move over, you can sit by Pom."

When Liam had climbed over from the row behind and flopped into the vacated seat beside her, Pam said, "Did you get the kids settled?"

"Yep. All four of 'em." He spoke with the air of a harried housewife, but this was pure bluff. "Jiffy was still a little upset so we called Gillian and Wayne and she told them all about it, then out she went like a light, poof!" He leaned across Pam. "Humphrey, Terrifrey wanted to come but he was so tired I talked him out of it. I told him I *had* to be here, and so somebody responsible had to be left in charge of Jiffy and the dogs." Pam smiled, picturing this, and Humphrey emitted vibes of fondness. Terrifrey was a very capable little fellow and strong as a horse; and, young as he was, that powerful Hefn need to serve and be loyal was already well developed in him. As soon as there were young Gafr on the ship, he would be paired with one of them; till then, like the stranded Yorkshire hobs, he served Pam, Liam, and Lexi, his father's bonded humans. If his namesake Terry Carpenter had been part of his life, Terrifrey would have served him with particular zeal; but Terry was still in Washington, still heading up the Senate Committee on Alien Affairs.

He did not serve Humphrey. Hefn were hardwired to serve, not other Hefn, but The Other.

While Liam was asking Humphrey about his wound, and Humphrey was explaining again that "wound" was the wrong word, the lights dimmed and there was scattered clapping and people saying "Finally!" and then a sound of people settling into their seats as the blank screen came alive.

The final episode of *A Thousand Miles* began, like all those before it, with music—the Tabernacle Orchestra playing "Come, Come Ye Saints"—and a pastiche of the Henry McPherson family on their long journey from Scotland to Zion. There were glimpses of McPhersons—shawls, sunbonnets, broad black hats, suspenders—at the railing of their ship the *Thornton*; on the train; encamped in Iowa; and finally hauling their loaded handcart out of Iowa City in the company of hundreds of other people in period dress. The handcart haulers were all happy, excited, and charged with purpose, and they laughed and called to one another as they strung out over the flat countryside.

Cut in quick succession to river crossings, rough camps, mounted Indians, the first injuries, the first graves, the first mountains, the first snows. The trailer showed how jubilation gave way to sobriety and then to suffering as the difficulties increased and the death toll mounted. It was the whole story compressed into a few moving images, but it didn't include the most harrowing parts or the end of the journey; those had been reserved so the final episodes would get the full dramatic benefit. Every Mormon in the world knew the story of the Martin company, but knowing wouldn't lessen the suspense, even for them, maybe especially not for them.

There were close-up shots of Lexi and Neil, looking very young and fresh-faced, in most of the intro scenes. The audience whooped and stamped whenever their gigantic faces flashed onscreen. Lexi slid low in her seat, but Neil leaned forward, ignoring the commotion, to study Marcee's work.

The final episode opened on a view of the Martin company's tattered, crippled survivors, including of course Kate and Jason with their parents, floundering through a blizzard.

They had been camped and snowbound for days without food, still nearly four hundred miles from the Salt Lake Valley. Rescuers had found them, fed them, and managed to get them moving again. One of these, a young man named Joseph A. Jones, wrote in his journal that "A condition of distress here met my eyes that I never saw before or since. There were old men pulling and tugging their carts, sometimes loaded with a sick wife or children—women pulling along sick husbands—little children six to eight years old struggling through the mud and snow. As night came on, the mud would freeze on their clothes and feet. There were two of us and hundreds needing help. What could we do? We gathered on to some of the most helpless with our riatas tied to the carts, and helped as many as we could into camp."

That was how the episode began, with a voiceover, an actor reading from Jones's diary while the cast acted out what he described. They took their time about it. There were no small children in the regular cast, but a few had been brought in to labor through the snow of South Pass so the sentence about them needn't be cut. Kate and Jason labored with the rest, Kate wrapped in tatters, Jason with a rag tied like a pirate's kerchief around his head and ears. Jason pushed the family cart with his pregnant mother aboard while Henry hauled from in front. Kate, trudging behind, helped push too in the steepest places. The snow flew all around, and flew, and flew. The wind howled. Directors and producers had done a brilliant job of evoking both extreme physical misery and grit.

Liam quickly became absorbed in the story. Pam, feeling the tense concentration he radiated, knew he was imagining himself hauling Jiffy in a handcart up that pitiless trackway through the drifts. She knew something else: that he actually *yearned* to do something of the sort—to push past the uttermost limits in acting out his devotion to her, and through her agency to that other child, Jeff, whose three-year-old face now danced before his eyes whenever his daughter's was there. Pam sometimes worried that Liam might unconsciously put Jiffy in danger, simply in order to snatch her out of danger's jaws; but she trusted Julie to help him toe the line there, to recognize the impulse when it came, and to resist.

Jiffy O'Hara, Liam's daughter, Jeff's half-niece. There was a kinship link between Jeff and Liam now, if you wanted to look at it that way, and Liam certainly did want to look at it that way. Pam envied it, just as she envied Lexi's genetic connection to her father, Martin. Patiently she reminded herself that her own link with Lexi, as revealed through the episode of the Cooper's hawk, transcended genetics.

Lexi was sitting up straight, her attention, like Neil's, now riveted on the screen. Despite their grownup protests about "just another acting job," this was their own story too and they couldn't help getting caught up in it again.

Though a few lines had been written for the cast, voiceovers had been used throughout—actors reading from the journals and memoirs of survivors—so this final episode had more of the quality of a documentary reenactment than a drama—except that these terrible things were happening to characters the viewers had become involved with over the whole long run of the show. As Kate sat on an overturned bucket, biting on a twist of rawhide while her fingers were being amputated, an actor read from the journal of Ephraim Hanks, who had performed the necessary surgery on frozen feet and hands: "Many such I washed with water and castile soap, until the frozen parts would fall off, after which I would sever the shreds of flesh from the remaining portions of the limbs with my scissors."

The company was still east of South Pass at that point, still had to fight their way through the worst weather, but relief was nearly at hand. Wagonloads of supplies began to arrive over the mountains from Salt Lake, first four, then ten more, then more after that. The weakest and sickest, like Margaret, were loaded into the wagons. Some kept walking, with three hundred miles still to cover.

Kate and Jason kept walking. With their help, Henry, stubborn Scotsman that he was, hauled his lightened cart over the pass. The relief was real, but a wagon was as cold inside as out, and the ride bone-rattlingly rough, so there was still serious concern about Margaret and the baby. This baby of Margaret's, like Margaret herself and the rest of the family, were fictional; but a Martin company baby actually had been born in a wagon on the last leg of the journey, so it wasn't as much of a stretch as it might seem.

It took the whole month of November 1856 for Kate and Jason to walk from the snowbound camp near the North Platte into Salt Lake City. Marcee had brought her emigrants into the valley through Emigration Canyon itself, the road packed with snow to conceal the concrete beneath the wagon tracks and hoofprints. All the footage that showed any sign of modern development had been cut or tweaked. The canyon was too narrow for a major highway ever to have been built there, and didn't go anywhere much, not in modern times; and anyway the emotional impact of this touch of authenticity was worth any amount of trouble. Not just for the Mormon sector of the viewing public either, since almost without exception the cast and crew of the show were LDS.

Pam watched Lexi covertly as the caravan of wagons and handcarts wound down through the tight curves of the canyon. "Margaret Dalgliesh, a gaunt image of Scottish fortitude, dragged her handful of belongings to the very rim of the valley," said the voiceover. "But when she looked down and saw the end of it she did something extraordinary. She tugged the cart to the edge of the road and gave it a push and watched it roll and crash and burst apart, scattering into Emigration Canyon the last things she owned on earth. Then she went on into Salt Lake to start the new life with nothing but her gaunt bones, her empty hands, her stout heart." A line of text at the bottom of the screen attributed this anecdote to Wallace Stegner, the Western writer, like Pam a non-Mormon captivated by Mormon history.

Watching this footage for at least the half-dozenth time, Pam now thought for the very first time: *Here's where Homeland fell short.*

I talked about Mormon family ties and the Mormon pioneer heritage, but I didn't go back far enough, I never gave them a sense of why the feelings that drive it all are so powerful. But it's right here. When people have suffered and sacrificed like this for an idea, the experience will own them forever, it'll even own their descendants forever at some level, even if they come to view the idea itself as nonsense.

She studied Lexi and Neil, brought up within a community united by stories like this one, which had all the power of myth, but had really happened to real people, their own forebears in many cases. Lexi, a birthright member of that community, had revolted when it failed her; yet the story of what Stegner had called "Ordeal By Handcart" owned her in a way she could never reject or escape, just as, in a much less complicated way, it owned Neil. Neil would be going on his mission as soon as *Hurt Hollow* was in the can. He sat now holding Lexi's hand, his look exalted.

Had there been a way to make more people feel that passionately about Gaia, that the Apprentices and Missionaries, and Pam herself, had simply failed to imagine? If they'd done better, might the Baby Ban be lifted now? To think so was a knife in the gut; but that other lucid dream, the one nobody knew about, the one she still didn't fully understand, said otherwise.

~

One April evening three springs back, Pam had been dropped off at the rim of Dead Mule Canyon, with pickup arrangements fixed for the following day. The hike through the slot canyon and up the slickrock slope was easier this time, backpack and all. There were no close calls. An hour after starting she stood puffing beneath the pictograph panel that had so haunted her imagination since she'd seen it for the first time, eight months before. By then the sun had slipped behind the canyon wall. She ate a sandwich and an apple, drank some water, unrolled the pad and sleeping bag right where she'd imagined unrolling them, removed her boots, and crawled in.

Absolute darkness fell, stars in astonishing multitudes became visible. The moon rose, just past full. Pam lay on her back and began the meditation she usually did while sitting in a chair. Time passed. After a while she got the trance, but it was light and fitful. Her intention of clearing away the mental debris, being entirely mindful in this extraordinary moment, was proving hard to realize; there was too much agitation, too much interference, she wasn't doing a good job here. Also the flat area at the base of the alcove was not very wide and Pam was a little too conscious of the long drop to her immediate left.

Finally in exasperation she unzipped the sleeping bag and climbed out, and stood up. Surprisingly, morning had come. Light filled the alcove, but the pictographs had vanished, the sloping wall was blank. There was a bowl of red paint in her left hand and a brush in her right, and she understood that she had climbed up here to paint the panel in her mind onto the living rock.

As she filled the brush with color, there came a shift and she also understood that she was dreaming. *I know how to paint this panel!* Pam thought in triumph, and she did. *I know what it means*, and she did know. The meaning was crystal clear, impossible to imagine what the mystery had been. She tapped the brush, moved to the left, and began. The images flowed onto the wall with consummate delicacy and precision: tall anthropomorph, trailing bird and snake, plant cluster, large striped anthropomorph, small lively figures with drooling serpent above them, more figures and more. Again and again she dipped the brush into the bowl, working her way across the rock ceiling as authoritatively as if writing out one of her own poems in cursive script.

When she'd finished Pam stepped back and read the entire message aloud in a clear, expressive voice. "For humans to live wisely. Upon the Earth that made you. Is not natural. Because it is unnatural. The Hefn. Who do not dream. Must help you. This is well. This is why they have come. You two must learn. To help each other. You can! You can! You'll see! A window in time. That opens. Bright on the future."

~

Whatever the source of that message, whatever had used the materials at hand to get it delivered, Pam accepted her experience; how could she not? It left her doubtful that the Gaians could have swung it by their own efforts, no matter how clever and inspired they'd been. Maybe humanity needed the Hefn's help as much as the Hefn needed humanity's planet. They'd gotten off on the wrong foot with each other, but things might go better now. Maybe in its own wacko way the new Mormon revelation expressed the same idea as the message in the dream. Who knew how many different ways there might be of tuning into that frequency? Not Pam.

Here Humphrey sat in the padded seat next to her, forked feet pointing at the ceiling, bandage gleaming whitely around his middle. He'd seen the final episode before, but seemed to be as intent on the unfolding drama as Liam and the kids. The sight of physical suffering was repellant to him, always had been; Pam wondered why he'd insisted on attending the viewing when he might have just come to the party, as the kids had planned to do. Something about the way the sufferers were pulling together might appeal to him, she thought, though group solidarity wasn't really his thing either. What he'd loved from the outset, what had evoked his commitment to humanity, was the intimacy and intensity of one-on-one bondedness, first with Terry, then Liam, then Carrie, then with herself, and now with Lexi.

Well, he'd found out that human bonds were usually more complicated and less merely joyful than he'd thought at first. Yet here he was anyway, back at Scofield to relive the early tough times he and she and Liam had been through together, by making the Hurt Hollow movie. And not just going along with it either, but throwing himself into the project with characteristic gusto. One way and another, she and Liam and Humphrey had taken a lot off each other and survived to sit lined up in adjacent seats in this auditorium like three peas in a pod. With another thirty years or so of ups and downs ahead of them, it appeared.

Humphrey twisted his body suddenly and caught her eye. "You are looking at me, my dear, instead of at the film," he said in his rumbly whisper.

"I was wondering what you were getting out of it," she whispered back.

"Ah. Shall I tell you? I was feeling how my bond with Lexi makes the story of these pioneers important to me. Kate is very hungry, she is very cold, two fingers are cut off with scissors, she is walking through the snow. Kate is Lexi, therefore for me also this is painful and disagreeable, but also meaningful."

Judith Moffett

Of course. Pam patted his arm, turned back to the screen.

Now the tatterdemalions of the Martin company, most riding, some still pulling their carts, were nearing the bottom of Emigration Canyon. A stir was moving through them, they knew they had nearly reached the goal for which they had paid so dear a price. The camera pulled back; viewers could see how the range of mountains stopped abruptly at the edge of an open plain, see the Great Salt Lake shining blue in the distance. They could see the mouth of the canyon where it spilled into the broad valley, and the ant-train of carts and wagons about to emerge from between its twisting narrow walls into the open. At that moment the Mormon Tabernacle Choir, accompanied by the orchestra, burst into "Come, Come Ye Saints"; and now the camera homed in again on the emigrants, who would enter the valley as individual humans on a human scale.

On they tottered, hundreds of them, tears streaming down their haggard faces which were nevertheless glowing with joy. They had buried husbands and children and wives in snowdrifts, they had thrown away their most cherished keepsakes to lighten the carts, they had been through a hellish experience, were emaciated and tired almost to death, but this was Zion, this was their New Jerusalem, the Holy City of God on Earth, and they had finally arrived.

Now the camera found the McPhersons. Henry stopped for a moment, hands clenched tight on the bar of his handcart, face working, when he saw the opening out of the valley floor at the mouth of the canyon. Margaret, already in labor, raised herself awkwardly to gaze over the side of the wagon in wonder. Jason and Kate stopped too, for a breathtaking instant—but then they plunged ahead together hand in hand as the canyon walls fell back, raced down, down, past halting walkers, past mules and wagon wheels, then suddenly out into open spreading space where a great crowd of Saints was waiting to welcome them. Faces wet, eyes shining, they entered Zion running and caught their breath on holy ground.

THE BIRD SHAMAN

The story really ends here, and readers who resent an author's pulling everything together too tidily at the end should stop here. But if you're that other sort of reader who, like me, would rather know what happens later, here's a little more information.

OPTIONAL EPILOG: *COR MEUM DABO*
1 SEPTEMBER 2069

The time window spun shut and vanished. As Pam ducked out from under the transceiver hood there was a spatter of applause in the BTP lounge, which was filled with people. Apprentices who'd been meeting in the room when the time window opened, thirty-one years before—Rhagu, Sam, Will, Artie, and of course Liam—were sitting in the same chairs their younger selves had occupied that day. Present also were a mix of Apprentices, prominent Gaians, and specially invited guests: Lexi and Neil, Jiffy with Gillian, Jaime Rivera and his wife, Denny Demaree's daughter Anna, Julie Hightower in a wheelchair. Alfrey and Godfrey were present too, astride two Hefn chairs.

And Humphrey was there, fresh and sleek from his long sleep, leaning in the doorway and beaming like a strobe lamp, each forked hand clapping individually, like two pairs of tongs. Pam acknowledged their applause with a grin and a bow, then went straight up to the Hefn and hugged him hard against her flat chest.

People started to get up and mingle. Humphrey and Pam moved away from the door so the heaped carts of refreshments could get through: Carrie Sharpless's party favorites of first dessert, cheese-and-crackers and crudites, little sandwiches, second dessert. There was also a cart of drinks.

Liam joined them. "Good show," he said. "If a time window ever opens from *our* future, who'll be in it, I wonder?" He snagged a couple of petit-fours as a tray of them rolled by.

"If that happens it won't be our problem, thank God," said Pam, and hugged him too.

Rhagu Kanal, a Nehru lookalike nowadays with his shock of thick white hair, ambled over. "Hi, 'little Liam.' Pam, you did great, even if we've seen it all before. Hi, Humphrey, good sleep? Wish I felt as fit as you look."

"Very good sleep, yes. Very good show, worth getting up seventeen days early to see."

"You know," Rhagu went on, "I found myself thinking just now about the Hurt Hollow conference back in '37, when Pam here first spoke of you as a religious leader. Remember, Pam?" She nodded, and he turned toward her. "The very first time anybody had expressed that idea, far as I know. You said Humphrey made a pretty credible founder for us Gaians in lots of ways, except for a few little problems created by the Ban and the threat of mindwipe."

"*I* remember that," Liam said. "The carrot and the stick. Artie and Will threw a couple of fits apiece."

Rhagu shook his shaggy head. "Back then, who could have dreamed what thirty years would do to the way people thought about the Hefn?"

"Well, not 'people,'" Pam said. "Young people, with no stake in the past. In a healed-up, cleaned-up world they could thank the aliens for providing them with. Able to have kids whenever they wanted. Horrified by images of the mess we'd made of things."

"Smugly sure," said Liam, "that *they* would never have let things get that bad. Thinking privately that really the polluters and over-breeders had it coming."

They all smiled, sardonically or sadly. Still, it was the rising generation that collectively had created the transforming myth Pam had failed to imagine for their parents. *Conjured by intentionality out of the quantum universe, the HefnGafr appeared on Earth to save themselves by saving us. The Hefn Humphrey struggled heroically, in the face of Gafr disapproval, to teach correct behavior to a benighted humankind. But we didn't learn, and in the end the aliens were forced to save both us and themselves in the only way they could. The process produced martyrs on both sides, and great suffering. But now a new age has dawned. Hefn and humans have joined hands and vowed to help each other live harmoniously, together and with Gaia.*

There was plenty of recorded data to qualify this version of events pretty strenuously, but the young humans (hardly the first ones to do so in such a situation) had invented the version they required, then chosen to believe in it.

Will, hearing his name, had wandered over holding a plate and munching a little crustless sandwich. "We were still trying to get the Ban lifted then, remember. I don't suppose it was psychologically possible to think beyond that, about there being any kind of bright side to failing."

"Probably not," Liam said. "We all felt we had to try everything, out of compassion for people like—well, like my sister."

"Thank God for Jiffy," Pam added. Jiffy, and later her little boy, Jeffrey, had been the lights of Brett's life until her death three years before. As of course they were of Liam's. But for many millions of people there had been no Jiffy.

Now in 2069 Earth's population was small and mostly young, well marinated in Gaian values and in the extraordinary spiritual implications of quantum theory. (Pam's advice on that latter had been taken to heart; experiments were running within a month of her appearance in the time window.) Apprentices and missionaries trained by Humphrey had provided the marinade through their worldwide network of local missions. Others had labored to set up the institutional means whereby aliens and humans could run the world together. Teams of humans and Hefn worked to integrate transceiver technology and the quantum studies. Partly in consequence of all this exploration, members of the world's few remaining hunter-gatherer and Crux-stage cultures had become widely regarded as gurus, living repositories of Gaian wisdom. Lexi had trained with a real Inuit shaman.

And now the former child prodigies were old and becoming infirm, and the course of the future, as always, had been handed off to others. Today's event had an air of closure to it for everyone past the age of sixty or so, which included all the Apprentices and most of the others in the lounge.

Liam nudged Humphrey. "You're not saying much."

"I am thinking." He sounded sad; Pam guessed shrewdly that he was anticipating a time when all the humans closest to him would have followed Carrie Sharpless and Terry Carpenter out of the world, and he would be working instead with a lot of young whippersnappers who would reverence and kowtow to him, but who had never beaten him at Monopoly as children, or harmonized in a rousing chorus of "Peace! Be still!" for his entertainment. Pam's breast cancer, though entirely cured, had shocked him dreadfully as a harbinger of what must happen. Soon now, she felt him thinking, very soon.

She took in the circle of faces gathered around Humphrey, the wrinkles and gray hair, Rhagu's white head and Liam's bald one, then spun to face the roomful of chattering people. "Gillian! Time for a song! Jiffy, how about starting a round?"

Gillian said something to her daughter and Jiffy, who had perfect pitch, set down her plate and launched into "Ego sum pauper." People stopped what they were doing and joined in, dividing into parts in a practiced way. The Apprentices and missionaries had been singing together for half a century; others, like Lexi and Anna, had learned this song and many more through long association with Pam and Liam.

She had started the round to cheer Humphrey up, and he did look brighter at once. Beneath the three-part harmony, however, Pam heard him rumble, "I am poor, I have nothing. I will give my heart. But this has not proved to be easy."

Oh dear. Singing lustily, Pam felt for his hand and squeezed it. How old was the first generation of Hefn? How much longer could Humphrey himself expect to live, before his part in the drama too was over? His people lived a long, long time—several times longer than the Gafr did, far longer than the longest-lived human. Inevitably, one day Humphrey would pay the price that all must pay who give their hearts to beings with shorter life spans than their own. Pam thought of Feste and BJ, of losing them and having to live on into a reality they were no longer part of. The poodles had died in ripe old age, within months of one another, nearly twenty years ago; but to this day neither Pam nor Lexi could talk about them without getting teary.

She became aware of Humphrey's gaze upon her. The Tallis Canon was making the room ring, and everyone but her was singing it. Shaking off these melancholy thoughts, she cleared her throat and joined in.

The world spins on. Lexi was a far more gifted shaman than Pam had ever been, traveling out of her body from a waking trance state as easily as from a dream, but Pam had done her best. They had all done their imperfect best, and soon now must prepare to discover what, if anything, lay beyond those wavy lines that separated Jeff from Liam in the pictograph she had copied onto Liam's birthday cake, half a lifetime ago. Maybe Jeff himself, who knew. Lexi thought so. Maybe an experience impossible for human consciousness to conceive. Maybe nothing, which would also be okay. *We give her back to Gaia.*

Wryly she thought, *I've gone from melancholy to maudlin: great.* She had also lost her place in the round again.

THE BIRD SHAMAN

It was just ending. As Jiffy cut off the final chord, Pam felt her other hand be taken by Liam, who gripped it, kissed her cheek, and murmured "Hey, Happy Birthday. You didn't go to Carrie's seventieth birthday party, so you don't realize how weirdly like it this one is, but you can bet old Godfrey's thinking about that. He was there."

Pam's mental response, she couldn't stop herself, was: *Godfrey, and Humphrey, and you. Everybody else who was at that party is dead.* But she bit her tongue and said only, "Wish I'd been there too."

"So whaddya say, shall we grab Humphrey by the scruff of the neck and split?"

After the first surprise the thought seemed heavenly. Still— "I haven't circulated much yet, like not at all. I should talk to Julie, she came all this way."

"You don't need to do one single more thing, not today. They've all been told of my plan to whisk you out of here early, including Julie. You can see each other tomorrow."

Pam glanced toward the wheelchair. Julie was chatting with Lexi; she smiled, waved, mouthed, "Go home!"

Liam gave her hand a squeeze. "Lexi and I baked you a cake. You will be shocked and astounded by our creativity. So let's go home and eat it. We made Humphrey a cobbler too." At the word "cobbler" Humphrey's upper body turned in their direction, and Liam said, "You're coming home with Pam and me, okay?"

"That is *most* okay."

He nodded to Jiffy, who waved the room quiet. Then everyone was clapping and cheering. Somebody—not Jiffy herself, who knew Pam thought the song too treacly, nor Lexi, who had never cared for it—struck up "Gaia Is Our Ground."

They were all singing it and waving their arms in the air, hands making the salute, even Lexi, even Julie, who wasn't even a Gaian, as Pam let herself be led from the lounge between her most loved Hefn and her most loved living person, past the deactivated transceiver pushed into the corridor, toward the tall front doors of the BTP.

Judith Moffett

About the Author

Judith Moffett was born in 1942 in Louisville. She is the author of ten previous books in five genres, four of them works of science fiction. Her first published story, "Surviving," won the first Theodore Sturgeon Memorial Award for best science-fiction story of 1986, and she received the John W. Campbell Award for Best New Writer in 1988. Three of her stories have appeared on the final ballot for the Nebula and one of these, "Tiny Tango," was also on the Hugo ballot. The first two volumes of her Holy Ground trilogy, of which this novel is the third, were New York Times Notable Books for their years of publication; the second, *Time, Like an Ever-Rolling Stream*, was short-listed for the James Tiptree, Jr. Award. Widowed in 1998, Moffett lives with her standard poodles, Fleece and Feste, in Lawrenceburg Ky. and Swarthmore Pa.